STORMING INTREPID

"A compelling, accurate, convincing high-tech thriller."
—*Denver Post*

"Plenty of techno-toys and a breakneck pace."
—*Kirkus Reviews*

"*Storming Intrepid* cost me a night's sleep."
—Stephen Coonts

"First rate . . . Harrison manages to blaze combat action across space and sky while keeping his characters sharply delineated and in focus."
—Walter J. Boyne

"A masterpiece."

—*Milwaukee Journal*

THUNDER OF EREBUS

"A page turner . . . the action is non-stop."
—*San Diego Union*

"Compelling."

—United Press International

"Harrison's depiction of clandestine operations and his narrations of the U.S. air attack . . . are masterpieces of combat fiction. No fan of the genre can afford to over look this bombshell."
—*Publishers Weekly*

"The action race[s] along like a hypersonic missile."
—*Dallas Morning News*

"A rollicking good read . . . striking . . . remarkable . . . compelling fiction."

—*Mostly Murder*

Books by Payne Harrison

STORMING INTREPID
THUNDER OF EREBUS
BLACK CIPHER
FORBIDDEN SUMMIT

FORBIDDEN SUMMIT

PAYNE HARRISON

BERKLEY BOOKS, NEW YORK

FORBIDDEN SUMMIT

A Berkley Book / published by arrangement with
the author

PRINTING HISTORY
Berkley edition / December 1997

The Putnam Berkley World Wide Web site address is
http://www.berkley.com

ISBN: 0-425-16214-1

BERKLEY®
Berkley Books are published by The Berkley Publishing Group,
a member of Penguin Putnam Inc.,
200 Madison Avenue, New York, New York 10016.
BERKLEY and the "B" design
are trademarks belonging to Berkley Publishing Corporation.

PRINTED IN THE UNITED STATES OF AMERICA

10 9 8 7 6 5 4 3 2 1

THIS BOOK IS FOR MY DAUGHTER,
ANDREA MARTINE HARRISON
(TOO CLEVER BY HALF)

FORBIDDEN
SUMMIT

PROLOGUE

— ∞∞∞ —

"Sault Saint Marie, Great Lakes with handoff Cessna three-seven-Victor, angels seven-five on IFR India-seven-three-Juliet south, copy?"

The American air traffic controller rolled his cursor onto the new blip that had just crossed the electronic threshold of his screen and clicked it into his database. Then he keyed his microphone to speak to his Canadian counterpart on the other side of Lake Superior. *"Roger, Great Lakes, Sault Saint Marie copies. Cessna three-seven-Victor, handoff execute to Sault Saint Marie, do you read, over?"*

The pilot of the Cessna responded with words from a lexicon that only pilots and controllers could decipher as they executed the intricate dance of guiding an aircraft through the night sky on Instrument Flight Rules (IFR). *"Roger, Sault Saint Marie Center, I copy handoff from Great Lakes. Am flying IFR flight path India-seven-three-Juliet on course one-one-eight at angels seven-five, over."* The aviator's voice was soft with a French *accent, and the American controller assumed (incorrectly) that the pilot was French-Canadian.*

"Roger, Cessna three-seven-Victor, you are cleared for IFR flight path India-seven-three-Juliet south. You have no traffic in your area tonight."

"Roger, Sault Saint Marie, it does look as though I have the sky to myself this evening. I will . . . wait . . . what's happening!?"

The controller leaned forward, not liking the pilot's change in tone. "Cessna three-seven-Victor, are you experiencing trouble?"

The soft French voice, laced with fear, cried, "Sault Saint Marie, I have a . . . I have complete engine failure! Losing air speed rapidly . . . trying to restart!"

The controller raised a hand and flicked on the radio speaker as a supervisor of the air traffic center appeared at his shoulder, asking, "What's up?"

The controller pointed at the blip. "A Cessna on IFR over Superior just had engine failure."

"Engine failure over Superior at night? Christ, that's as bad as it gets."

"It won't start!" *cried the pilot.*

A small crowd of neighboring radar operators started to assemble behind the controller as he keyed his mike. "Try it again, Cessna!"

"I am, I am, but it won't fire! Losing air speed! Must put it in a dive or I will stall!" *There was authentic fear in the pilot's voice as he cried,* "Mon Dieu, I'm over water! No lights anywhere! Mayday! Mayday! I am going down!"

The controller felt utterly impotent as the blip reversed course back toward Canadian airspace and the altitude numbers scrolled backward. Then his Canadian counterpart came on with: "Sault Saint Marie, the Cessna is coming back at us . . . do you still have it?"

"Yes, I have it, but . . ."

The speaker box squawked, "I'm in a-a shallow dive. Air speed dropping. I have to increase angle!"

Lamely, the Canadian controller said, "Cessna three-seven-Victor. Try to restart again."

"I'm trying!" cried the pilot. Then there was confusion in his voice. "There's something wrong with the fuel flow, oh, I don't know! I've lost the horizon! It's all dark out there! My altimeter's running backwards! I can't . . . wait . . . I see the water! No! It's too soon! Help me, please! Noooo!"

As the little square disappeared off the screen, a silent pall fell over the chamber as everyone bore witness to a life being snuffed out, and it was with a sense of resignation rather than hope that the supervisor grabbed a nearby phone and punched in a number. Almost immediately a voice responded with, "Coast Guard quarterdeck."

"This is Sault Saint Marie air traffic control station. We need a scramble for an air-sea rescue."

ONE

The snow had arrived like a windy whiplash, covering the switchbacks with an epidermis of white that made the drive both beautiful and treacherous. Frank Hannon spied the clock—about the only thing that still worked on the dashboard of his '87 Mustang convertible—and saw that he was going to be late, and that meant the guy he was to relieve would piss all over his leg when he got there. But the storm had welled up so suddenly that snow-plow crews were still snug in their beds and would not be out to clear the Mountain road for hours yet. The rear wheels of the Mustang fishtailed around one of the steep hairpin turns despite the snow tires, causing Hannon to curse as he whipped the steering wheel around to turn into the skid. He took solace in the knowledge that he had to put up with this ice and slush for only forty-seven more days; then it was off to a golden retirement on the white sandy beach of a Bahamian cay. But until then he was stuck with this daily pilgrimage to a high-tech altar hidden away in the Rockies outside

Colorado Springs. It was then that he looked up and noticed that the clouds were now parted, revealing the white neon disk of a winter moon that illuminated the haunting silhouette of Cheyenne Mountain.

Chosen for its location and geological complexion, Cheyenne Mountain had been transformed into a unique engineering marvel, nearly on par with the Golden Gate Bridge or Hoover Dam. Cheyenne was a literal mountain of granite on the Front Range of the Rocky Mountains. It had taken three years of blasting to hollow out its insides, and another two years to build its four-and-a-half-acre latticework of fifteen underground buildings and assorted passageways. This hard-rock inner sanctum housed what could best be described as the central nervous system of America's defense capability, in that it was the command post of the joint U.S. and Canadian North American Aerospace Defense Command (NORAD).

In a heavily guarded compound on the exterior of the Mountain, a forest of antennae pulled in a kaleidoscope of signals from sensors all around and above the globe. On the Arctic tundra, the Ballistic Missile Early Warning System aimed its over-the-horizon radar toward the Russian Republic, where a nest of dormant but still deadly intercontinental ballistic missiles slept in their silos. Twenty-three thousand miles above the earth, a launch-detection satellite called Teal Sapphire kept watch over those silos should an errant missile lift off. In the west Texas desert, a pyramid structure called a Pave Paws radar scanned the southern skies for a missile launch from a ballistic submarine. All of these signals were relayed to the Mountain by satellite, landline or microwave link, where they were sifted, sorted and analyzed by a small army of analysts and technicians who were led by a cadre of career officers, one of which was Frank Hannon.

Hannon parked his car in the lot, grateful the steep switchback road was behind him. Then he absently followed the perimeter of the hurricane fence to the floodlit entry point at the security building. Pushing through the turnstile, he entered the security reception area and was greeted by a couple of bored Air Force Security Police sergeants and a lieutenant. The lieutenant had a few zits on an otherwise virginal complexion, and his pale blue eyes and sandy hair made him look as though he'd stepped off the pages of a high school yearbook. Hannon eyed the young man in appraisal, noting that the junior officers got younger every year. The way the trend was going, he knew that if he did not retire soon they would eventually turn into sperm with epaulets. He went through the liturgy of showing his ID card and signing in. Then he looked at his watch and asked the lieutenant, "Where's the shuttle bus?"

"Just left, Colonel."

"Damn it. I'm late already. Guess I better hoof it on in."

"At least it's stopped snowing, sir."

"Lucky me," replied Hannon as he headed for the door. His path took him through the foyer of the Mountain's visitors' center, which had large, blown-up photographs mounted on the wall. The photographs depicted scenes of steely young men and women talking earnestly on the phone or gazing intently into their computer screens. Hannon mused to himself that he felt neither steely nor intense as he pushed open the door to the lash of the cold wind, causing him to groan with the sound a whale must make as it bleeds ambergris into the sea. He bent forward and headed toward the tunnel entrance.

Foreboding and lit by garish klieg lights, the craggy tunnel entrance loomed out of the snow like the menacing jaws of a shark, but Hannon marched forward like some unsuspecting prey, wanting to cover the third-of-a-mile distance to the entry point as quickly as possible.

The massive tunnel actually cut through the entire Mountain like a wormhole through an apple, and the entryway into the NORAD command center complex was cut into a sidewall of the tunnel—this was designed to vent the blast of a nuclear bomb away from the entry proper should one fall outside the Mountain. At least, that was how it was supposed to work. The Almighty be praised, it had never been subjected to an actual test.

Hannon walked past the twin twenty-five-ton blast doors that were three times taller and thicker than anything you'd ever find at Fort Knox, showed his ID to another sentry stationed just inside, then headed for his duty station. Hannon remembered his first impression of the NORAD complex, in that it had been something of an anticlimax. The exterior of the Mountain and the tunnel with its rocky walls were so ominous and so awesome, but the innards of the NORAD facility were not much to look at. The structures inside the hollowed-out chamber resembled a bunch of mobile homes braided together, all of them windowless and painted a uniform cream color. What went on inside the mobile homes, however, was something else again.

Hannon weaved his way along the elevated passageway, and under the grillwork he could see the large coiled springs that supported the mobile homes. All the structures rested on these springs to absorb the impact of a nuclear blast—a constant reminder of why Cheyenne Mountain had been hollowed out in the first place. He nodded to a couple of comrades who were on their way out, then came to a door in the side of a large mobile home that had a cipher lock. He punched in the number, then turned the knob and stepped inside the Space Control Center of Cheyenne Mountain.

The low-ceilinged chamber imparted a claustrophobic feeling which Hannon never got used to, and with its pale fluorescent lighting it resembled the viewing room of a funeral home. A double-sided bank of consoles ran the length of the chamber, with large cathode ray tubes staring back at their technicians—but now, on a December graveyard shift, technicians were in short supply. In the room there was only Hannon and two others.

"There you are, Colonel. I was starting to worry. I hear we caught a blizzard out there."

Hannon sighed with relief as he took off his gloves and the Air Force parka with the fur-lined hood. The person he was replacing was a Marine major named Larry Drake, a good guy who wouldn't bear a grudge over his tardiness. "Sorry, Larry. The plows aren't out yet and the snow slowed me down."

The ramrod Marine smiled. "Not a problem, Colonel. Although we almost did have a problem. Henderson was our duty tracker tonight but he came down with intestinal flu. His ass is glued to the latrine with a fever and he can't move. I was able to get ahold of Airman Wick; he'll be here in a little while."

Hannon chuckled. "Wick the Prick? Okay, he's a good man, if a little opinionated."

"More than a little."

"I'll survive. C'mon. Give me the handoff briefing so you and your tracker can sign off and get out of here."

"Roger that, Colonel."

They walked past a large tote board that listed the more problematic bogeys in the galaxy of space hardware that encircled the globe, while along another wall were a series of teleprinters that linked the room with "all source" intelligence providers like CIA, NSA and NRO. The Space Control Center, or SCC, was the nexus point where over seven thousand objects in outer space were tracked and monitored—everything from satellites to spent rocket engines, from objects as big as the Mir space station to as small as a spacesuit glove left in orbit by one of the Gemini astronauts.

Drake led Hannon to the duty officer's station—a small alcove that had a metal desk with a battery of phones, a computer terminal, and stacks of paper. "All the decayed orbits have been updated, but just be advised that the de Gama satellite looks like it's in its death throes. No more than a week to go before it burns up, I'd say."

Hannon nodded. "The press is having a field day on that one."

"As well they might," replied Drake. "And it looks like a couple of launches are in the offing this evening."

"Oh, is that Raduga satellite finally coming off this time?"

"Right. Launching via Proton booster out of the Baikonur Cosmodrome sometime this morning. Guess they got the kinks ironed out."

Hannon scanned the run sheet. "And the other?"

PAYNE HARRISON

"An Ariane launch, scheduled to lift off from Khorou anytime."

Luc Grassé ambled slowly along the narrow rocky beach on his evening vigil, a slight limp betraying his arthritic hip. It was a warm tropical night, with only the sound of the waves and a gentle breeze whistling through the palm trees to keep him company. The tide had retreated, leaving bits and pieces of driftwood lying along the sandy shoreline like so much broken furniture fallen off a moving van. He found a twisted piece of dead and waterlogged mangrove, which he bent down to pick up and place in his sack, but the effort caused him to wince in pain from the inflamed ball joint in his pelvis. *"Merde,"* he cursed to himself, then spat a stream of tobacco juice onto the beach. A few more genuflections later his bag was full of driftwood and he made his way back toward his hutch alongside the beach where he eked out a living fishing in the tidal basins of the French Guianan coast.

The result of a lusty night between his mother and a Moroccan sailor, Luc had lived out his life along the docks of Cayenne, doing stevedore work in his prime, then odd jobs as age overtook his strength and vitality. He was a wiry sort, with a bronze complexion that laughed at the sun and a beard as coarse as steel wool— but as the years sailed by, Luc had retreated from the rough life of the docks to homestead on a deserted strip of sand. Life here was austere and lonely, but the ocean provided him the means to fill his belly, and his thoughts were on that very subject now, for a few matches and some old newspaper would soon turn the driftwood into a flame that would roast the grouper he'd pulled in that morning. Then he'd top off his dinner with a pull from the rum bottle of his private reserve, then drift off to sleep at the sound of the incoming tide. His mind was so preoccupied with the dinner and the rum that awaited him that he heard it before he saw it—a dull rumble that caressed his tympanic membrane and caused him to turn and look upward toward the heavens. It was like a Roman candle arcing across an inky black sky—a manmade comet that possessed the power to frighten even a leathery old soul like Luc Grasse, and caused the old man to cross himself.

The spent outrigger boosters of the Ariane rocket fired their explosive bolts and broke away from the main fuselage, then began their tumble toward a watery grave in the Atlantic. The rocket, however, continued its ascent, belching out a conflagration of smoke and flame as though it were an airborne Vesuvius turned on its head. In its wake it left the expended outriggers, a gaping Luc Grassé and a gantry at the Kourou French launch facility on the Guianan coast.

At fifty-three miles altitude, a series of explosive bolts fired around the ring seal of the main Ariane booster, cleaving it from the second stage; then, at ninety-four miles altitude, the second stage's solid fuel was expended and it, too, separated from the payload.

The Ariane rocket, the workhorse of the French commercial space industry, was lifting a heavy and expensive payload into orbit—a communications satellite built by Hughes Aircraft for the Sultanate of Abu Dhabi—and now that payload had reached escape velocity. The flight controllers at the Khorou launch center would insure the vessel was in alignment with mission specifications, then fire the payload rocket, boosting the satellite to a geosynchronous orbit that was 22,300 miles above the horn of Africa. There it would be in a position to handle the burgeoning fax, data and voice traffic into and out of the oil-rich sultanate.

And once the payload was on its way, the spent second stage would be left alone, like a bride at the altar, sailing along on a lonely orbit that would slowly decay until it succumbed to the overwhelming force of the earth's gravity. Then it would fall into the upper reaches of the atmosphere where its 18,000 mph speed would sear the aluminum alloy skin like an acetylene torch, reducing it to an incinerated piece of space debris-like so many meteors that met the same fate every day. But that wouldn't happen for several weeks, and until it did, the spent vessel would continue to orbit the globe, like a lonely sentry walking his post, as the earth slowly rotated underneath its groundtrack.

The arrows looked like a handful of compass needles tossed on a thread strung against a green background—a dozen arrows in all, dangling on the thread at random angles with an alphanumeric citation at the tip of each point. Two of the arrows were blinking, the rest were not, as the image remained unchanged—until finally a third blinking arrow appeared, which evoked a response of . . .

''Ah, there it is, sir. I been lookin' for that sucker. Bet that's the one out of Khorou. Just caught it on sector one of the picket.''

''Okay,'' replied Hannon, ''the launch alert bulletin says an inclination of eighteen degrees. Is that what we've got here?''

"Roger that, sir. And the trip time on the picket conforms with launch parameters."

Hannon stood up and stretched, his back cramped from leaning over the airman's shoulder to read the data on the screen. "Okay, then, let's finish the update."

The airman picked up his light pen and replied, "You betcha, sir. No problem. Already got the inputs inputted." Then he pressed the glowing tip of the light pen against the first blinking arrow. "Okay, sir, I make the first one to be item Foxtrot-niner-seven four six, the second stage of an SS-18 test shot out of the Baikonur Cosmodrome. Not long for this world with a perigee of fifty-eight miles on an orbit that is rapidly decaying."

Hannon made a tick mark on the printout of his clipboard and said, "I confirm."

The airman hit a keystroke, causing the arrow to stop blinking as some new alphanumeric figures appeared at the point of the arrowhead. Then he moved his light pen to the next blinking arrow. "This one is item Sierra-six-eight-four-four, the de Gama Saturn probe, perigee fifty-four miles."

Hannon shook his head. "Five hundred million dollars lost in space. Ouch."

The de Gama Saturn probe was supposed to follow on the success of the Magellan probe to Jupiter, but after being placed in orbit by a Delta booster, its payload rocket failed to ignite, leaving it to circle the globe in a rapidly decaying orbit. There was too little time and too little money left in NASA's budget to execute a shuttle rescue, putting some more expensive tarnish on the space agency's long-forgotten luster.

The airman grunted. "Why doesn't NASA just launch

payloads of greenbacks into space? Save money in the long run, I bet.''

Hannon nodded. "No doubt. Or better yet, just give it to us. I confirm.''

The penlight moved. "And last on our hit parade, the second stage of our Ariane booster out of Khorou. I don't track the payload, though.''

Hannon ran through his printout. "Payload booster was fired twenty-eight minutes ago, so you won't catch it on a low-altitude scan. I confirm the Ariane second stage. Okay, that should update us for the moment. Now get on with the follow-up checks on the previous shift's entries.''

There was a disgruntled sigh, then the airman said, "Yes, sir.''

A wry smile creased Hannon's face. "C'mon, Airman Wick. Just fourteen short years to go and you can retire, too.''

Chester Wick was a puckish sort, with a face of freckles, a slightly bucktoothed smile, and crisp red hair with a defiant cowlick that matched his "in your face" persona. His ego was only slightly smaller than the galaxy he scanned for space debris, and he was never short of opinions on any subject you'd care to mention, particularly the fairer sex, which had garnered him the handle of "Wick the Prick" among the female airmen on post.

As he tapped his keyboard Wick looked up and inquired, "So you're really punching out, Colonel?''

Hannon nodded. "With vigor, Airman Wick. With vigor. Twenty-three years of anything is enough. Forty-seven days to go, then I'm on a one-way ticket to the Bahamas. By the way, thanks for coming in on such short notice. I understand Henderson came down with some kind of intestinal flu.''

Wick's bucktoothed mouth brayed—not unlike a donkey's refrain. "Henderson? Sick? How would you know?''

"Okay, so he's a quiet sort. But he does a good job. I daresay almost as good as you, Airman Wick.''

"The Sphinx? As good as me? Gimme that proverbial break, Colonel. The guy is dysfunctional. He can't talk. I'm the best you've got in this mausoleum. I was just telling this sweet young thang the other night that when it comes to scanning the skies I'm the—''

"Yes, yes, Chester, I'm sure you did. Now if you'll excuse me, I've got to work on my in-box. With the Sphinx—I mean, Henderson—ill and people already peeling off for Christmas leave, it's you and me against the world tonight.''

"Piece of cake, Colonel. I got everything under control.''

"Umm.''

And with that, Frank Hannon returned to the solitude of his alcove.

The Space Control Center was the nexus point where over seven thousand objects in outer space were tracked and monitored by NORAD. The primary means of tracking so many objects was an electronic "picket fence," which was a series of overlapping radars that ran the length of the continental United States. The radars were fixed and pointed straight up, creating an electronic "curtain," and as a satellite or other object passed overhead it tripped this electronic picket fence, providing the analysts in the control center with the bogey's altitude, orbital inclination, speed, apogee, perigee, flight path and such. Once the "trip" data were analyzed, the information was saved in a massive database that could produce the track of virtually any satellite. And with over seven thousand existing objects and new ones being launched all the time, NORAD employed a number of analysts like Chester Wick to constantly monitor and update the data, and a number of officers like Lieutenant Colonel Frank Hannon to monitor the monitors.

Hannon plopped into the swivel chair in the alcove and dropped his clipboard onto the cluttered top of the metal desk. Leaning back in the creaky government-issue chair, he pulled on the dregs of a cup of coffee as he caught his reflection in the glassy face of the computer monitor. Lately, Hannon had become something of a fixture in the Bison Bar off post, contemplating the conclusion of his military career. His reflected countenance in the computer monitor showed a creased face that was worn out by a steady diet of officer club food, two ex-wives, Air Force paper, and a growing reliance on demon gin. Hannon's ruddy features were a little on the sunny side of swarthy, with dark hair that had begun an advance to the rear—and there was a huskiness to his form that came with the embrace of middle age. Cheyenne Mountain was his final duty station, where he was one of a dozen shift officers-in-charge assigned to the Space Control Center—a place where a vigilant eye was kept on the heavens twenty-four hours a day, 365 days a year. And on this graveyard shift near the onset of the Yuletide season, the Mountain was winding down toward a skeleton crew.

Hannon looked at the paperwork before him with a sigh, then started to dive in when one of the teleprinters on the far wall clattered to life. He rose to the summons and went to the printer that was linked to the Air Force Intelligence Center in the Pentagon. He leaned over and read:

```
TO: HQ, NORAD/SPACECOM
FROM: HQ, AFI, PENTAGON
SUBJECT: LAUNCH ADVISORY

BREAK BREAK

TREATY NOTICE INDICATES PROBABLE
LAUNCH OF RADUGA COMMUNICATIONS
SATELLITE FROM BAIKONUR COSMO-
DROME AT 0830Z THIS DATE. RUSSIAN AU-
THORITIES HAVE PROVIDED VERBAL
CONFIRMATION TO DEPARTMENT OF
STATE OBSERVER. NSA CONFIRMS TELEM-
ETRY CONFORMS TO PRE-LAUNCH CHAR-
ACTERISTICS OF PROTON BOOSTER.

END MESSAGE
```

Hannon ripped the routine communiqué from the printer. So this was the one Drake had advised him about on the shift change. The Russians didn't have the *dinero* to launch many rockets these days, and the ones that did get off the ground had become routine with ample fore-warning through diplomatic channels, as stipulated by international treaties. Still, Hannon knew he'd best let his "crew" know it was on the way. "Looks like we've got a new one coming our way from Mother Russia, Airman Wick. Be launching in about ten minutes, so we should see it before our shift is up. Be on the lookout, okay? . . . Airman Wick? . . . Airman Wick? . . . Chester?"

Silence from Chester Wick was sort of like finding an iceberg in the Caribbean. It didn't happen, so Hannon leaned over the bank of computer terminals to see what the problem was. The young airman was there, to be sure, but something about him had changed, transformed. His eyes were transfixed on the screen and his bucktoothed mouth was half open in an expression that betrayed—what? Shock? Fear? Anxiety? Or perhaps a little of each? What made it so indelible was that Wick's "in your face" puckishness had somehow been siphoned out of him—that he was, for lack of a better word, scared.

"Chester? . . . Chester, are you all right?"

Wick's gaze did not waver from the screen, and his voice was barely audible as he said, "Colonel . . . I . . . I think you'd better come look at this."

Befuddled by the change in the young man's demeanor, Hannon stepped up behind him and leaned over. "So what have you got?"

In reply, Wick pointed at the monitor. Again, there was a green background with a jagged horizontal yellow line running from left to right in the middle of the screen, depicting the electronic picket fence. Hannon glanced at the symbology in the corner of the screen and saw this image represented the section of the picket line from the east coast of Virginia to western Tennessee. There were several stationary compass needles representing old "trips," but over central Virginia there were four blinking arrows indicating a quartet of new bogeys. The four arrows were tightly spaced together, and Hannon glanced at the notation on their points, which indicated they were on a bearing that was west-southwest.

"Hmm. So what do we have here?" asked Hannon.

"Some satellite that broke up into four pieces?"

Wick slowly shook his head and softly replied, "No, sir."

"No? So what is it? White Cloud?"

White Cloud was the U.S. Navy's ocean surveillance system that tracked Russian surface ships with a millimeter-wave radar system that used several satellites flying in formation—but again Chester Wick shook his head, leaving Hannon more perplexed than before. Then the airman pointed at the screen. "These four bogeys initially showed up on the right of the screen, over central Virginia. They were at a hundred forty-two nautical miles altitude and traveling at a very shallow inclination from the equator only fourteen degrees. The time was eight-twenty-eight Zulu."

"So?"

Wick scrolled into the next image. "Here they are again, about midway in sector one, just over eastern Tennessee—about three hundred miles distance."

Hannon blinked. "Huh?"

"Exactly, sir. And look at the time elapsed."

Hannon stared. "Eight-twenty-nine Zulu. That's one minute elapsed. How's that possible? It takes ninety minutes for an orbit."

Silently, Chester nodded; then he pointed at the screen and softly whispered, "Yes, sir, ordinarily it does take ninety minutes . . . but these bogeys are, uh, well, they're not on an orbital track."

Hannon looked closely at the cluster of arrows; then it dawned on him, plain as day. "What the . . . ? They're . . . they're pointed in the *other* direction."

Again, Chester nodded; then he scrolled backward and forward between the two images. There was no mistaking it. The four blips first crossed the electronic curtain headed west-*south*west; then three hundred miles later they crossed the picket fence going west-*north*west.

Hannon felt his pulse ratchet up as he stared at the arrows that were, by all rights, defying the laws of physics. "I . . . I don't get this. It looks like these satellites are, well, changing direction."

Chester nodded again, his face a ghostly white.

"What could do that?" asked Hannon, somehow knowing in his gut what the answer could be. "What could change direction at eighteen thousand miles an hour?"

Chester's voice was barely a flutter on the wind. "Nothing that I've ever seen, Colonel."

Hannon felt his palms turn moist as the hairs on his neck came to attention. "How old is this data?"

"Six minutes now, sir."

"Have they crossed the picket anywhere else?"

Wick keystroked his computer. "No, sir. All the other sectors are clear. Nothing but routine . . . *whoa,* what's this?"

The four arrows appeared on a new screen, crossing the jagged yellow line.

"What's that location?" demanded Hannon.

"Sector two, over eastern Missouri. Altitude one hundred eleven miles. A lower altitude. Damn! They've changed direction again! West-southwest this time."

"How old is this?"

"It's realtime, sir."

Hannon pulled up a neighboring chair as Wick read off the data. "Uh-oh . . . here they are again. Another trip over Kansas . . . shit, west-*north*west again, speed slowed to sixteen thousand knots, altitude ninety-one miles . . . switching to sector three . . . over eastern Colorado now . . . new trip.'' Wick's voice was barely a whimper now. "Sir it, it's almost like . . . like they're riding the picket.''

"Using it as a beacon of some kind?''

Chester shrugged, his face ashen. "Damned if I know, sir. Shit, oh, shit. Okay, okay. New trip just west of the Front Range.'' In a reflex action, Hannon looked up at the ceiling, wondering what had just passed overhead as Wick continued his recitation. "Altitude seventy-four miles. Speed slowed again—maybe twelve thousand knots now. West-southwest . . . Nothing. . . . Still nothing. . . . Wait. There. Huh? Look at that.''

"The arrows . . .''

"Yeah. They've crossed the curtain again, but this time they're headed due south. Straight south. Altitude forty-two miles. Speed more than halved at fifty-two hundred knots.''

"Where is this exactly?''

Chester perspired, despite the cool chamber. "It's in northern Utah, near the Hill Air Force Base picket station.''

Hannon tried to pull his mind out of the manacles of shock. "Did they trip the West Coast sector of the picket?''

Chester played his keyboard as though it were a Steinway, then scanned the screen. "Nothing, sir. And they woulda been there by now the way they were travelling.''

"Pull up the last trip.''

Chester did so.

Hannon pointed. "Altitude forty-two miles, headed due south?''

"Yes, sir.''

"Pull up the FAA air traffic data for that region."

"That would be the Salt Lake Air Route Control Center."

"Do it."

Again, Chester tapped on his keyboard and the screen changed again. Once more the background was green, but the long horizontal line and the four vertical arrows had vanished, replaced by random little squares, perhaps two dozen of them, with little numbers beside each one and a small spike of a line sticking out of each square. At the bottom of the screen was nomenclature that read, "SLARCC," along with the date time group. It was the radar imagery of the Salt Lake Air Route Control Center, a radar facility that covered a huge chunk of air space over the Great American Desert. The blips represented civilian aircraft with the readouts providing their altitude, speed and bearing.

"See our bogeys anywhere?"

Chester continued scrolling through the FAA radar sectors as though they were the pages of a book. "I don't see anything . . . wait . . . there."

"Where is this?"

Chester shrugged. "Not certain. Central or southern Utah, I think. Again, they're in formation. Headed due south. Speed thirty-four hundred knots. Altitude sixty-three thousand feet, descending rapidly. God, look at 'em zip past those others. Now they're slowing. Whoa! Really slowing. Altitude thirty-eight thousand. *Damn!* They've stopped! Midair . . . thirty-three thousand feet now. Look . . . they're descending."

Hannon watched the altitude notation of the blips scroll backward with an even-paced rapidity, which meant they were not falling, but in a controlled descent, and as they went down Hannon felt his pucker factor increase by an order of magnitude.

"Nine thousand . . . eight thousand . . . seven thousand . . . six . . . five . . . four . . . three . . . two . . . one thousand . . . five hundred . . . off the scope."

An oppressive silence descended over the chamber, broken only by the electronic hum of the equipment, neither man wanting to acknowledge to the other the images they'd just seen. Hannon could hear the sound of his own breathing as he felt a dampness in his arm pits. "You ever see anything like this?"

"No, sir," replied Wick.

"Could it be a problem with the equipment?"

Wick snorted. "Don't kid yourself, Colonel."

The admonition shook Hannon out of his reverie, and despite the extraordinary nature of the imagery, he knew what he must do. A bogey was a bogey and there were procedures to follow, whatever they might be. He jumped up from his chair and returned to his alcove, where he ripped the red telephone out of its cradle and said, "This is the officer-in-charge, Space Control Center. I have a flash message for CinC NORAD."

Morgan Raines closed the door of his convenience store-diner and locked it. In the little crossroads hamlet of Bluff, Utah, he remembered a time when he could leave a door unlocked without fear of the consequences. But now—well, the doors stayed locked and a loaded Colt .45 was hung under the counter to deal with the nastier miscreants who drifted along the back roads these days.

It was late—too late for a man seventy years old to be burning the midnight oil over bookkeeping just to keep the IRS happy. He threw the hood of his parka over his head and looked at his watch, then groaned. It was 1:38 A.M. Not much time before he'd have to heft his large-framed body out of bed to face another day with all the tribulations associated with a wife stricken with Alzheimer's. He shook his head and shuffled up the path to his A-frame house perched on the slope above the Quonset hut of a store-diner. The night was clear, crisp and cold, with the moon having gone down, leaving the stars to shimmer with their icy clarity. He paused to look out across the vast expanse of darkened desert whose history had been his life and calling. That his life had reached its final chapter in such a state of tribulation was a source of great lamentation for the old professor, but the desert—even in darkness—still held its sense of mystery and wonder for him. He drank in the view for a few more minutes, communing with the scene, then was about to turn away to resume his journey when he saw them.

The lights.

At first they were mere pinpoints, lost against the backdrop of stars, but then they slowly became larger and more distinct. Initially, he thought they might be a conventional aircraft of some kind, but as they descended there was something indefinable about their nature that held Morgan Raines in a hypnotic trance. The luster of the lights possessed a milky luminescence that changed from silvery to gold, then back again as they came down towards the horizon. Their pace was deliberate and constant, and as they approached the horizon Raines feared it—whatever *it* was—was going to crash. But just above a distant mesa they halted and hovered; then the four lights—which he had thought were a single

24

craft of some kind—split apart into four distinct lights and circumnavigated the airspace above the mesa like a pinwheel spinning in the wind. Then they rejoined into their original formation and slowly dropped out of sight behind the ridgeline of the escarpment that ringed the top of the mesa. Raines knew there was an escarpment at the summit because he'd climbed that mesa as a youth—a mesa that rose out of the desert floor with a form that was almost perfectly cylindrical.

A mesa known as the Kiva Tower.

"The CinC's out of town," came the response from the duty officer in the NORAD Command Center. "He's on a goodwill tour to visit his counterpart in the Russian Rocket Forces. What have you got?"

Hannon stammered. "I, uh, I'm not sure. If he's out of pocket let me talk with the deputy CinC."

"He's in the base hospital with a bad case of intestinal flu. The Chief is top gun tonight."

"Then patch me through. I need to speak with him direct."

"No problem. He's in the conference room."

"The conference room? At this time of night?"

"I'm looking at him right through the glass. You wanna talk to him?"

Hannon thought it over, then realized this wasn't something easily explainable over the phone. "Tell him to stay put. I'm on my way."

"Roger that."

Hannon hung up and shot past Wick, saying, "Keep your eyes glued to that FAA screen, Chester. If the bogeys reappear call me in the Command Center conference room. I'm going to talk to the brass about this."

After Cheyenne Mountain opened for business in 1965, Hollywood had a field day portraying the NORAD Command Center as a cavernous amphitheater with rows upon rows of consoles and massive screens displaying airplanes flying around in Soviet airspace. This was pure fiction, for in reality the command center was simply two of the mobile-home structures stacked on top of each other. In other words, it was very unimpressive. In 1991, however, the NORAD Command Center received an expensive facelift that resulted in a chamber that would do justice to any Hollywood production designer. The room itself had large elevated screens on the forewall, and below them were two banks of consoles staffed by intense-looking young officers, and in the center chair on the back row was the ''cockpit'' where a flag-rank officer could always be found on duty. Behind and above this working chamber was a large glassed-in conference room, and in the event of a ''hot'' situation the Commander-in-Chief (CinC) of NORAD would likely follow the action from this venue.

Hannon entered the room to the sound of a speaker blaring, ''Launch detection!'' so loud it made him wince. In the command center below, four men grabbed phones at the same moment, causing Hannon to hesitate before continuing.

At the center of the conference table was a silver-haired patrician named Owen Shrake, who was wearing an Air Force pullover sweater with shoulder boards denoting his two-star rank. Absent the uniform, he might have been mistaken for a bank president or a hospital administrator, but with the uniform there was no mistaking that he was the NORAD Chief-of-Staff, responsible for keeping the operations within the Mountain humming smoothly. Hannon was surprised that the Chief would be here at this time of night, but he was even more shocked to see the person seated at Shrake's elbow. He was wearing the new Air Force uniform with the stripes on the sleeve that made him look like a pilot for the friendly skies of United—but he was no pilot. Like Hannon, he'd come up the career path of Air Force intelligence, and he was Frank Hannon's superior officer, nemesis and Macbeth all rolled into one. He was a full colonel by the name of Lawton Tyndale, known to those who knew him intimately as the Tin Man. Hannon's reaction to seeing his superior officer at the table wasn't exactly like a cat arching his back—but it was close. Tyndale was the officer in charge of the Space Control Center, and Hannon was surprised, if not stunned, to find him here at this time of night with his face shaved, trousers creased and hair coiffed.

Hannon was about to speak when the speaker blared again with, "General Shrake?"

"Yes?"

"BMEWS confirms launch detection is a Proton booster out of Baikonur Cosmodrome on a trajectory in conformance with the preannounced launching of a Raduga communications satellite. No threat."

"Very well," replied Shrake as he graced Hannon with a welcoming smile. "Come in, Colonel. I understand you wished to see me?"

Swallowing the bile that always welled up whenever Tin Man was present, Hannon said, "Yes, sir. We just caught something in Space Control that—well, sir, it . . . it's unlike anything I've ever seen."

"Indeed?" said the general. "What precisely was it?"

"Hard to explain, sir. I can show you better than I can tell you."

Shrake motioned him to a chair. "Take a seat and use the panel."

Hannon slid into one of the chairs at the long table and pulled out a kind of drawer that held a phone, a CRT and keyboard. He keystroked in a few instructions, then hit the SCN button and the picket fence imagery came up on a large flat-panel screen on the wall. He scrolled back the taped imagery until he came to the first bogey sighting. "A few minutes ago four bogeys, apparently in formation, tripped the picket line over central Virginia. As you can see they are tightly spaced, altitude one hundred forty-two miles with a velocity of eighteen thousand two hundred miles per hour. . . . Here they trip the picket again over eastern Tennessee."

There was a silence, then Shrake said, "But their direction has changed."

"Yes, sir."

"My word. Continue, Colonel."

Hannon walked them through the slalomlike descent of the bogeys as they traveled across the continental U.S.; then he switched to the FAA data that tracked them on a southern trajectory across the length of Utah.

"Here they go from thirty-four hundred knots to a dead stop over southern Utah somewhere at thirty thousand feet. Then they descend straight down . . . ten thousand . . . five . . . four . . . three . . . two . . . one . . . five hundred feet . . . off the scope."

There was a silence until Hannon broke in, saying, "Sir, I've got my man back in Space Control monitoring the FAA data. I think we should scramble the alert F-16s in Arizona and get them over Utah as soon as possible. Our air threats people can vector them to the point where they went off the scope and . . ."

Shrake raised a hand. "Just hold on a minute, Colonel. I must agree that all this is very intriguing, but let's not go off the deep end, shall we."

Tyndale chimed in. "Yes, Frank. Let's not rattle the pots and pans too loudly here. As the Chief said, this is intriguing, but I don't know that it constitutes a threat of any kind."

"Nor do I," echoed Shrake. "Could be some type of natural phenomena. Some type of atmospheric or cosmic distortion that's playing havoc with our radar."

"Or sunspots," said Tin Man.

"Sunspots?"

"Of course," replied Tyndale. "They can play havoc with the electromagnetic spectrum."

Hannon was incredulous. "Are you out of your gourd? These are four craft, flying in formation, executing a controlled descent over the sovereign airspace of the United States. They may still be on the ground in Utah as we speak. We have a duty to— "

"That's enough, Colonel." Shrake's voice came across the table like a headmaster's cane, and Hannon felt the sting. "I appreciate your sense of duty, Colonel Hannon. But in my judgment this does not constitute a threat for the moment. I can assure you, however, that I will look into the matter personally."

"I think the CinC should be informed."

"The CinC is in the Russian Republic," continued Shrake, "making a courtesy visit to his counterparts in the Russian Strategic Rocket Forces, and the deputy

CinC is currently incapacitated with a very bad case of intestinal flu.''

Tyndale leaned forward. ''So it falls to General Shrake to make the call on this, and he has given you his assurance that he will look into the matter. You and your analyst may return to your regular duties.''

Hannon found he couldn't give up so easily. ''But what if Airman Wick sees them again?''

There was a noticeable shift in Tin Man's demeanor. ''Wick? I thought Henderson was on duty tonight.''

Hannon was equally surprised that Tin Man would carry the details of the duty roster around in his brain. ''Henderson got sick at the last minute. Intestinal flu like the deputy CinC. Wick came in to pinch-hit.''

Tyndale rubbed his temples. ''Wick . . . he's something of a loudmouth, isn't he? A braggart?''

Hannon shrugged. ''Well, yes. But technically he's one of the best.''

Shrake cleared his throat. ''Well, Colonel, I think it best you remind Airman Wick that all operations within the Space Control Center are classified. And until you hear differently from me, I'm putting this under a Top Secret Umbra heading. Neither you nor Airman Wick is to speak of this to anyone without my personal authorization. I will take it up with the CinC when he returns next week, but until then—as far as you and Airman Wick are concerned—this, ah, 'situation,' shall we say, never happened.''

Hannon protested, ''But I still think we should investigate the—''

''That will be all, Frank,'' replied Tin Man.

And he smiled with the warmth of a cobra.

•   •   •

When Hannon walked through the door of Space Control, Chester Wick was on him like an energetic puppy greeting its master. "So what's going down, Colonel? A scramble? Are we on alert? DEFCON One?"

Hannon sighed as he looked into the face of youthful innocence, then replied, "It never happened, Chester. It never happened."

Morgan Raines had tried to sleep, but sleep would not come, despite the fatigue in his weary old bones. Instead, he rocked on his front porch, wrapped in a parka and blankets, staring out into the dark void towards the Kiva Tower. The hour was nearing 4:30 A.M. and the temperature was subfreezing, yet he rocked on, still trying to absorb that which he'd seen only hours before. What were they, those lights? His old but supple mind wrestled with the question, trying to fathom their nature. Were they some kind of extraordinary helicopters? If that were the case, then why had they come here, to the middle of the desert, in the dead of night? The questions would not go away as fatigue began to overtake him. . . . Then—

Lights again.

But these were not the lights that had hovered over the kiva. No, not at all. These were vehicle lights—yes, definitely vehicles—a number of them, making their way down the old mining road that wound its way around the column of the Kiva Tower like a spiral. Quite a few of them, in some kind of convoy. Raines was dumbfounded, not sure what to do. Should he call the sheriff's office? And tell them what? He was grappling with what to do when the first lights reappeared. Slowly they rose above the escarpment of the kiva alternately pulsating lights of silver and gold as though they were alive. They hovered for a time, and Raines was again entertaining the possibility they were helicopters when— in the time it took to crack an egg—they whisked straight up and out of sight, lost in the galaxy of stars.

Hannon walked into his leased condominium and flicked on the light. It was an unremarkable affair, with the living-dining area downstairs and the master bedroom in a loft above. He peeled off his parka and hung it in the closet, then sat down, jettisoned his shoes and propped his feet up on the large, heavy wooden coffee table. He began to doze, caught in the grips of fatigue and an anxious mind as he tried to perceive what it was he'd seen on those radar screens. And what were Shrake and Tin Man doing in the command center at that time of night? His mind was enshrouded by a stinging mist as it began to cross the threshold from consciousness to slumber—but then a part of him held back, and he pulled his feet down to reach for one of those large picture books on the coffee table, the kind that weighed only slightly less than an Olympic shotput. This one had a close-up picture of a luminescent blue-green parrot fish swimming over a bed of pink coral and white sand, and in red letters above the fish were the words *The Bahamas*.

Like a child unwrapping a candy bar, Hannon opened the book and thumbed through the pages, mentally transporting himself into a mask and snorkel cruising above the coral bed. It was a ritual he performed every night, almost like evening vespers, and he found it to be a tonic for the soul. He'd visited the Caribbean for the first time a decade ago and had become enraptured with its blue water, white sand and life under the sea that possessed a color unlike anything in nature—colors that were like a drug on the optic nerve. Having made the wrong choices in marriage (twice), and locked in a career that was nineteen parts paper to one part action, Hannon had vowed not to screw up his retirement. Therefore, he'd planned it with meticulous care, choosing the right island, the right beach, and locking up the right property with the dollars that weren't sucked away by the legal vacuum cleaner of divorce settlements. But now the exes were behind him and Hannon had his ticket signed off by the court, and in forty-seven days he'd have Uncle Sugar's retirement checks coming in. That bizarre business in the Mountain was forgotten for the moment, and he could almost feel the Caribbean sands caressing his toes as sleep enveloped him like a whirlpool.

TWO

The limousines rolled up to a curbside swept clean of snow as the paparazzi pressed themselves against the red-velvet restraining ropes with their flashing strobe lights. In rapid succession the elegant chariots disgorged the reigning scientific and cultural elite of Europe, all of them wearing their evening finery as they deigned to pause in the Scandinavian cold before the television cameras and the great unwashed. Once that was done, they hustled inside to the warmth of the Stockholm City Hall for the ceremony that returned them to this venue every year, like the call of the Pribiloffs.

It was an annual pilgrimage that had its genesis back in 1867, when an obscure chemist named Alfred Nobel was issued a patent for a substance called dynamite, and with the fortune it earned him he endowed a foundation with the mission of improving the human condition by awarding medals for achievements in chemistry, medicine, physics, literature and—ironically, from the inventor of dynamite—for peace. (A sixth prize category was added in 1968, when the field of economics was elevated from flimflam to science.) Since then, on the December 10th anniversary of Alfred Nobel's death, a glittering banquet had been held in the Stockholm City Hall at which new laureates were anointed with their medals and formal certificates called diplomas. Under the protocols established by the Nobel Foundation, all prizes were awarded in Stockholm, except the peace prize, which was conferred in a separate simultaneous ceremony in Oslo.

On this night the crowd of onlookers and paparazzi jostled each other under the klieg lights as the celebrity Richter scale increased with each new arrival. Princess Stephanie of Monaco arrived unescorted; then came the Prime Minister of Sweden, followed by King Carl XVI Gustaf and the Swedish Royal Family, with Britain's Prince Edward in tow as their guest. The men who exited the limos were stuffily attired in white tie and tails, in contrast to the women, who were adorned in dazzling gowns by Givenchy, Yves St. Laurent and Iva Braovac.

Then the amperage of the onlookers ratcheted up even higher as a detail of tuxedo-attired men filed out of the city hall doors and took positions along the interior of the restraining ropes. They were young men for the most part, and athletic, with their eyes constantly searching the gawking crowd for any suspicious movement.

At the curb two Stockholm police cars rolled past, followed by a security sedan. Then came an enormous Cadillac Fleetwood limousine, with diplomatic flags unfurled atop the fenders and a seal with an eagle stamped on the door. As the crowd realized who was borne by the shiny chariot, a spontaneous cheer went up, followed by applause as the door of the armor-plated limousine opened, allowing the American Presidential contender to emerge.

The effect Treavor Dane had on a crowd was always electric, causing them to respond with outstretched hands in front and "leapers" in the rear—those who struggled against gravity to get a glimpse of the young and magnetic Secretary of Defense of the United States. While every politician of Presidential timber projected his own distinct persona—John Kennedy the handsome rake, Eisenhower the avuncular grandpa or Nixon the bitter loser—Treavor Dane was unmistakably the boyish anchorman type who could charm, disarm and turn hearts aflutter with a glance. Once free of the limousine, Treavor Dane waved to the crowd, then paused for the photographers before slowly moving along the barrier, shaking hands and bringing a bit of a rush to the stoic Swedes. Once he was inside the city hall chamber, an aide took the Secretary's coat and ushered him to the head table, where he was seated between King Carl Gustaf and Queen Silvia, and across from the rather dour Prime Minister and his wife.

The mood of the bejeweled crowd was festive as they reveled in the illusion of their own self-importance on this, the premier night of the civilized world when meritocracy gained supremacy over aristocracy or celebrity. As the guests worked through an epicurean dinner of Swedish delicacies, the American Secretary of Defense and the King warmed to each other as they shared anecdotes about the overlapping orbits of their political and royal lives, before the King disengaged himself to mount the podium and begin the ceremony. The crowd hushed as the Swedish monarch made a smooth opening gambit—honed by years of giving the same speech. Then came the conferring of medals and diplomas.

First came the award for chemistry, given to a German who had discovered something nobody could understand about organic compounds. But it must have been important because the Swedish Royal Academy of Sciences had chosen him for the medal.

Next came the award for medicine, which was given to a Japanese doctor for his work on antiviral pharmaceuticals. He was shorter than the podium and had to stand on a footstool to deliver his speech in an indecipherable English. Once that was done, the good doctor sat down and King Carl Gustaf announced, "For the prize in physics, Michel Bertrand of the United States."

As the King spoke the name, a somber mood fell over the crowd in a kind of collective condolence, but that was quickly dispelled as Treavor Dane rose to accept the medal and diploma on behalf of his late teacher, mentor and friend. The bejeweled crowd looked on expectantly as he paused for a private moment to open the velvet case and inspect the medal with Alfred Nobel's profile struck on its face. Then he softly closed it and took out his notes to begin his remarks.

It was a tender speech, with Dane recalling his days as a student at Princeton where he came under the guiding hand of a brilliant physics professor named Michel Bertrand—a naturalized Frenchman who became his surrogate father. And when he recounted how his friend's private plane went down over Lake Superior after a Canadian fishing trip—only hours after the official Nobel announcement was made—it was a moment of great poignancy.

•　　•　　•

Chester Wick stood at the Delta boarding gate of the new Denver airport, utterly dumbstruck and fuming with anger. He hadn't been asleep for more than four hours following his Mountain shift when the squadron clerk had pounded on his door, waking him with a set of new orders. The young airman had sleepily read the orders, but when his eyes hit his new posting as Ballistic Missile Early Warning Station, Thule, Greenland, he came wide awake.

"*Greenland!?*"

"Yep," replied the clerk. "And it's immediate. You've got ninety minutes to pack your gear. A van will take you to the airport. Looks like you'll have a white Christmas for sure."

"But I was going home for Christmas! Got my leave signed and everything!"

"Canceled," said the clerk. "Sorry, but that's the military. I guess they're really shorthanded up there."

"But-but . . ."

"Ninety minutes," said the clerk.

Now he was shuffling in line, waiting to get his boarding pass so the Delta flight could take him to Atlanta. From there he'd catch a commuter to Charleston Air Force Base and board a C-130 Hercules transport for Thule. As he shoved his ticket at the prim Delta clerk he remembered from his high school history class that the Viking Erik the Red had named Greenland "Greenland" to try and con some other Vikings into moving there from Iceland—when in fact there was a lot more ice in Greenland than there was in Iceland. Wick was wrestling with the illogic of it all when the clerk ripped his ticket apart and said, "You'll be boarding first, Mr.

Wick. Looks like you'll have time for a cocktail before we take off if you want.''

"Huh?"

"We board out first-class passengers first, sir."

"First-class?"

"Yes, sir. You have a first-class seat."

Chester Wick had never flown first-class before, so he took the ticket back and inspected it. Sure enough, it had the first-class notation on it. Well, how about that. Somebody had screwed the pooch on this one. If Uncle Sugar was robbing him of his Christmas leave, then Uncle Sugar could damn well eat the first-class fare.

"You may board now, Mr. Wick."

Chester nodded. "Damn straight I'll board now, lady." And he strutted down the jetway.

On the 757 he found his window seat, then eased into the leather seat and shoved his grip under the chair in front of him. He scanned the first-class cabin and saw that he was alone except for a crabby-looking septuagenarian across the aisle and two rows back, wearing a seersucker suit and a pair of hearing aids.

The comfort of the leather seat was a small salve to his angry soul. Then a voice of Southern comfort said, "Oh, I do believe this is my seat." Chester turned and just about slid off his chair. She was wearing those black lycra stretch pants that après-skiers seem to favor, along with a Sami sweater and a red ski parka that amplified the impact of her long golden hair. She doffed the jacket and stretched to place it in the overhead bin, giving Wick a superb view of her hourglass figure. Then she lithely slid in beside him and smiled. "I declare, I was afraid I was gonna miss my plane, the snow up towards

Vail was holding up traffic so. I guess you're going to
Atlanta, too. Is that home for you?''

Chester was apoplectic, unable to respond, thinking
this only happened in the movies.

"I said, is Atlanta home for you?"

"Uh, uh, no. Just passing through Atlanta."

"Oh, passing through to where?"

"Greenland."

"Greenland? You mean way up north?"

"Way, way up north."

"My goodness, I didn't even know Delta flew there."

He found himself laughing, disarmed by her Southern
charm as he shook his head. "You're right, they don't.
I'm in the Air Force."

The flight attendant leaned over. "Care for a cocktail?''

The blonde smiled at him. "Join me in a champagne
cocktail. I just love champagne, don't you?"

"I do now."

Once the cocktails came, they clinked their glasses
and she lightly touched his arm, saying, "Now you must
tell me all about this Greenland business. It sounds so
exciting.''

Beguiled by her charms, Chester would have told her
anything.

Frank Hannon punched in the number on the cipher-lock
door and entered the Space Control Center, his mind still
clouded by the events of his previous shift. As he pulled
off his parka he saw the Marine major, Larry Drake,
ready to make the handoff. But instead of a junior enlisted man there was a tall, ramrod-straight chief master
sergeant with more stripes on his arm than a zebra. Han-

non nodded. "Evening, Larry. Hullo, Chief. What brings you up here at this time of night?"

Chief Master Sergeant Lucian Wintersgill was obviously one of those athletic types who lived on a diet of legumes and Evian water between running marathon races. His body and features were angular, but he often had a wry smile and a knack for putting senior officers and junior enlisted men at ease. He nodded to Hannon and said, "Shorthanded, sir. It was me or start putting people on double shift."

Hannon turned to Drake. "Henderson still have the flu?"

Drake nodded. "Still laid up, sir."

"And I guess Wick the Prick took off on leave?"

Wintersgill shook his head. "No, sir. He got orders this morning for the BMEWS station at Thule. Already on his way."

"Thule? *Greenland?* But he still had some time before he rotated, didn't he?"

Wintersgill shrugged. "Yes, sir. But I guess they were hurting for people up there."

Absently, Hannon hung up his parka, saying, "Well, that is strange."

There was a brief silence, with Hannon seemingly detached, until Drake said, "Colonel, if you don't mind, could we go ahead and execute the handoff?"

"Sure, Larry, sure."

"I'll just go over the previous shift's run sheets and see where we stand on the status board," said Wintersgill.

Hannon said, "Thanks, Chief," and escorted the Marine major to the alcove. After a quick debriefing, Drake was on his way, leaving Hannon to ponder Chester

Wick's abrupt departure from Cheyenne Mountain. What was behind it? Coincidence? A genuine manpower requirement in the frozen wastes of Greenland? . . . Or something else? Lost in thought, Hannon went to the coffee maker and poured himself a cup, then retired to the alcove, turning over in his mind all that had happened during the previous shift. Had he really seen those bogeys as they executed their incredible movements? Or had he imagined it? His spirit cried out for some sort of verification, that he had in fact seen what he had seen, so he keystroked his computer terminal to bring up the imagery from the computer bank. He scrolled through the picket fence data, and when he saw by the date/time group that he'd passed the critical juncture he scrolled backward . . . but it wasn't there. The routine satellite and space junk "trips" on the picket fence were present, but the unearthly bogeys had vanished. He scrolled back and forth a dozen times to make sure he was in the right time frame, but the bogeys had simply disappeared—erased.

For Frank Hannon, it was like that little bump in the night aboard the *Titanic*—something that seemed so inconsequential when it happened, yet the more intuitive passengers on board knew their lives had changed forever . . . or were coming to a close. In a voice that was dry, he called out, "Chief, could you come over here a minute?"

In a moment, Wintersgill was at his side. He and Hannon were about the same age, and after working in each other's orbit for three years they'd grown close, and when they were alone the fabric of rank all but disappeared between them and they let their hair down. On the surface they were different as could be—Hannon the disheveled one with a growing weight problem, Wintersgill the abstemious athlete—but despite the appearances they were kindred spirits, and although it always remained unspoken between them and below the surface, each one knew the other shared a contempt for their superior officer, one Colonel Lawton Tyndale.

"What is it, sir?"

Where would Hannon begin? How, exactly, could he explain what he was looking for? Something he himself had difficulty believing. "Chief . . . there were some, ah, unusual bogeys last night. I talked with Shrake about them and he put a heavy lid on it, but I wanted to go over the data again. I've called up the same time group on the picket, but the trips from these strange bogeys are, well, gone."

"Gone?"

"Erased."

"Erased? That's not possible. Sure you're looking at the right pages?"

"I'm sure.

"Show me."

Hannon ran through the electronic pages, explaining where the trips should have been, but weren't—leaving Wintersgill scratching his head.

"How could that have happened?"

Wintersgill shook his head. "That's just it. It couldn't. Once the data are laid down on the recording tapes there's no way to manipulate the historical data. It's like exposed film, you might say. It's impossible to do that."

"Impossible?"

"Well, by that I mean impossible through normal procedures. Technically someone could take the old tape, go through it and erase a section of the historical recording, then fabricate the new data and lay it down on top of the erasure. But you would physically have to have access to the computer center to do that. Remove the tape and doctor it.''

Quietly, Hannon said, ''I see.''

Wintersgill sensed there was something amiss, so he asked, ''What kind of bogeys were they, sir?''

Hannon shook his head. ''Unlike anything I've ever seen. You'd have to see it to believe it. Otherwise you'd say I was a lunatic.''

''Hmm. Well, maybe we could check the buffer file.''

''Buffer file? What's a buffer file?''

''Don't you remember? Couple of years ago there was an electric fire in the recording machine. The tape got scorched and we lost a chunk of data. Had to pull the old tapes out of storage and run double shifts for a week to reconfigure the data.''

''Oh, yeah. I remember now. I hadn't been here that long.''

''Right, sir. So a buffer tape recorder was created in the computer center as a realtime backup. It's on a twenty-four-hour continuous-loop recording. When did these bogeys appear?''

''About zero-one-thirty yesterday.''

Wintersgill checked his watch. ''That still gives us time. I can run down to the computer center and load the buffer tape onto a drive and bring it up here.''

Hannon thought for a minute, then said, ''Okay, Chief, do it. But verily, verily, I say unto you, this is hush-hush. If the brass got wind of this it could be our collective arses. *Comprende?*''

''Roger that, sir.''

And in a moment he was out the door.

• • •

Her long legs, bronzed by the sun, were wrapped around his ass like a vise, coaxing his manhood with each successive stroke like some kind of frenzied milkmaid working a churn. Chester Wick was transported to a sexual nirvana unlike anything he'd ever dreamt of, as though all his boasting about women had finally come true. Finally he could hold back no longer, and released himself into her with a sexual spasm that was a hybrid of pleasure and dynamite. Then he collapsed on top of her like a soppy rag doll. She caressed his neck, then licked his ear, saying, "Could you roll off me, sugah. A girl needs to catch her breath." With difficulty, Chester complied, his own lungs heaving for air as he looked at her through the dim light filtering through the drapes of the Atlanta Airport Sheraton. She was a vision, a lissome body with breasts that jutted upwards like two fleshy Matterhorns. And what was so amazing was that she had come on to him, telling him all about her vacations at Vail and Cozumel, and her Daddy in the oil bidness.

She smiled, and he was overwhelmed. "I declare, sugah, you men in uniform are quite the studleys, I must say."

Chester brayed. "Well, I guess you could say we're America's finest."

"That you are, darlin'. That you are. Whatever are you gonna do up in Greenland? It must be nothing but snow and ice up there."

Chester grimaced. "It's a big radar station. Not much else there, really."

"But why are they making you miss Christmas?

Seems an awful shame, you being away from your family and all.''

"Yeah, and the Air Force is gonna learn they made a big mistake on that score.''

She turned on her side and stroked his chest. "Oh? So how's that?''

Chester felt the tingle of her touch. He didn't want to lose her, and the need to boast was like a siren's call. "I think I got transferred because I saw something. Something the Air Force wants to keep quiet. So they're sticking me in a place where I'm cut off from the outside world. But they're gonna learn they screwed up on that score. Big time.''

"Oh, how's that?''

Without a word he rose off the bed and went to his grip where he extracted a small floppy disk from a zippered pocket; then he lay back down beside her and held it up, saying, "See this?''

She shrugged. "What about it?''

"This is gonna make those Air Force pricks who are sending me to Greenland sweat like the pigs they are. Because I got a buddy who works for a TV news department in Indianapolis, and he's gonna have kittens when he sees this.''

"But what is it?''

Smugness oozed from his every pore as he said, "Hold onto your Magnolia, honey. You ain't gonna believe this.''

In the adjoining room, two hearing aids lay on the bedside table and a seersucker jacket rested on a chair as the septuagenarian sat on the bed with a pair of headphones clamped to his ears, the volume tweaked almost to the max. Listening to the breathy young bodies gyrate together had brought beads of sweat to his forehead and an awakening in his crotch he no longer thought possible since his prostate operation. But the prurient images that danced in his head were soon put to rest when he heard Chester Wick explain the intricacies of the electronic picket fence to his newfound Southern belle, then boast about the unearthly radar blips he'd seen.

With a sigh, he ground out his cigar on the room service ashtray and picked up the phone.

Chief Master Sergeant Lucian Wintersgill walked through the door and said, "I got the buffer tape loaded onto a drive and we can pull it up here."

"All on the Q-T?" asked Hannon, having second thoughts. To cross the NORAD Chief-of-Staff on the cusp of his retirement was maybe not so smart after all, but Wintersgill was reassuring.

"No sweat, Colonel. I play golf with the deputy NCO of the computer center. He loaded up the tape for me—and told me something . . . under wraps."

"What was that?"

"Seems that last night General Shrake and Colonel Tyndale walked into the computer center and impounded the Space Control tape. No reason given. Then he went off shift. When he came on duty the same time as us, the tape was back on the drive."

Hannon felt validated, but uneasy. "What about the buffer tape?"

Wintersgill sat down at a console, saying, "Shrake and Tyndale didn't touch it," as he brought up the imagery. "Now then, Colonel. Show me exactly what it was that compelled our esteemed superior officers to make a midnight raid on the computer center of Cheyenne Mountain.''

The Southern belle stepped out of the shower, trying without success to wash away the slimy feeling that came with something like this. That gawky, donkey-faced jerk had had all the sexual finesse of an adolescent as he pawed her body and brought forth a revulsion which was grindingly difficult to stomach. But she forced it out of her mind, knowing it was the price one paid. Indeed, she was already starting to feel strung out, and needed to get on with the deal.

There was a tap at the adjoining door, causing her to wrap her extraordinary body in a towel and unlock the dead bolt. She pulled it open and the septuagenarian was standing there, his eyes running down the length of her in appraisal.

''I kept my part of the deal,'' she said, in a voice whose Southern luster had been replaced with a hard Chicago edge.

''That you did, my dear, and I am here to keep mine.'' He reached into the pocket of his seersucker jacket and removed a Ziploc bag filled with a white powdery substance. ''Given your appetites, I thought you'd like to take it out in trade.''

She'd agreed to the deal for five thousand in cash, but a glance at the bag told her it held ten thousand in coke easy, so she snapped, ''Deal.''

He handed it over, saying, ''Very well, my dear. I believe this concludes our business. You may leave at your convenience. I must say that your Southern accent was very convincing. You should be an actress.''

She spat more than said, "I *am* an actress," then slammed the door and headed for the bathroom.

"Grenville, Air Force Safety Office. I'm here on a spot-check inspection. You the duty NCO?"

Master Sergeant Arthur Marsten looked at the proffered ID card and winced. His crew had to finish out the refits and maintenance sweeps on a half-dozen birds before sunup, and some safety-office geek had to show up in the dead of night. The new arrival definitely was a geek, too, with short orange hair and coke-bottle glasses, and a fatigue uniform that looked two sizes too big. But Marsten played things by the book, and came to attention to deliver a salute. "That's correct, Captain Grenville. What can I do for you?"

Grenville pocketed his ID card. "First of all, where is your officer-in-charge?"

"Not feeling well. He took off early. His replacement should be here about zero-six-hundred. I'm in charge for the moment."

"Hmm. Well, tell me what aircraft you are presently servicing."

Marsten waved at the interior of the massive hangar. "Well, at Charleston here we service incoming and outgoing transport aircraft, mainly for Europe and the Mideast. Those three Starlifter transports have just come in from the Gulf. That C-5A will be headed for Frankfurt after daybreak, the C-117 is on a shakedown flight, and that C-130 will be heading for Greenland this morning."

Grenville nodded. "I see. Well, Greenland is a hostile flying environment so I think we'll start with that one. Pull your records on all the work you've done. I'm going to have a look at the aircraft."

Marsten grumbled, "Yessir, but if we could hustle this along I'd appreciate it. The Herc is slated for pre-flight at zero-seven-hundred and takeoff an hour later."

"I'm afraid safety has no timetable, Sergeant, but I'll try to have it out of here on schedule." And with that, Grenville executed an about-face and strode toward the C-130 Hercules. It looked like a bloated guppy with wings, but the turboprop aircraft had been a mainstay of air transport for decades, having seen action from Vietnam to the Gulf. Grenville climbed up the deployed ramp under the tail section and scanned the interior of the cargo bay. It was empty except for the uncomfortable canvas seats that were strung along the bulkheads and back-to-back along the centerline of the cargo bay. Grenville knew what he was doing, and knew he didn't have much time. He went to a floor panel and extracted a socket wrench from his pocket as he knelt down. Swiftly he unscrewed the four bolts that kept the panel in place, then pulled it off and reached down to finger the taut cables that were strung beneath. Finding the cable that controlled the elevator in the tail, he reached into his other pocket and extracted a tubular vial with a small dial on the side. He set the dial for seven hours, then used a puttylike substance to secure the vial to the cable—a putty that would harden in minutes. Quickly, he closed the panel, screwed the bolts back into place and stood up just as he heard the sound of approaching footsteps.

"Captain Grenville?"

"Yes, Sergeant Marsten."

"I've got the records ready if you want to see them."

"Yes, I would. But I'll look at them after I inspect

the flight deck. Rest assured I won't be too long. We certainly want this bird to get airborne on time.''

Lucian Wintersgill ran through the picket fence imagery for the seventh time, still unable to fathom what he was seeing. Finally he shook his head and said, ''A lot of meteorites show up on the picket. You know that. But I've never seen anything like this.''

''Me neither,'' replied Hannon.

''And Colonel Tyndale and General Shrake were in the conference room at zero-one-thirty yesterday when this happened?''

''Yep,'' replied Hannon. ''Now that I look back on it . . . it's almost as if they were, well, expecting me.''

Wintersgill scratched his head. ''And then they show up in the computer center, confiscate the tape, have it doctored and replace it on the drive. And if they were expecting you, it must mean that they . . .'' And he pointed at the screen.

''Were a part of *this*?'' Hannon was incredulous.

Wintersgill shrugged. ''Stands to reason. It fits a logic pattern.''

Hannon rubbed his brow. ''But if that's the case, then maybe this is some sort of black program the Air Force has got going. Some sort of follow-on to the SR-71 Blackbird that has been rumored for years. Maybe Shrake and Tin Man were operating under orders.''

Again, Wintersgill shrugged. ''Maybe so, but I've never heard of anything like this, and I think I'm wired into the grapevine as well as anyone. I never heard squat about an aircraft that can go from eighteen thousand miles an hour to a dead stop.'' There was a prolonged silence, then the chief asked, "What are you going to do? Take it up with the CinC?"

Hannon paced for a couple of moments, then said, "I don't know. Something tells me that if they—whoever 'they' are—can manipulate the system downstream, then they must be able to manipulate it upstream as well. So if I take it up with the CinC and he's in the loop, then I've put my nuts on the block . . . and I can kiss the Bahamas good-bye." He paced some more, then said, "Pull up that FAA data. Where they dropped off the scope."

Wintersgill complied and Hannon leaned over his shoulder, saying, "Make me a printout of this page, Chief."

Wintersgill turned. "You'd be violating the regs if you take a printout of this out of the Mountain, sir. It's classified material. And I'd be an accessory."

"Then leave the room and unaccessorize yourself."

Wintersgill shot him a look of disdain, then key-stroked the instructions to send the image to the dot matrix printer along the wall. The two men were standing beside the printer, waiting for it to finish, when the telephone rang, causing both of them to jump. The chief went to the alcove and ripped the receiver off the cradle, saying, "Space Control Center." He listened for a few seconds, then turned to Hannon with a troubled look in his eyes. "Yes, sir. I'll tell him. Right away." He hung up the phone and said, "Colonel Tyndale is in the conference room. He wants to see you right away."

Hannon entered the Star Trekkian conference room of the Mountain and found Colonel Lawton Tyndale sitting alone, reading an open file in front of him. Swallowing his disgust, Hannon stepped up to the other side of the table and took a posture that resembled parade rest. During business hours, Hannon always conducted himself with rigid formality whenever Tin Man was concerned, and recent events had only crystallized that attitude. He wondered if this summons could possibly be about his lifting the buffer tape from the computer center.

But Tyndale only smiled as he looked up from the open file and shoved a twix across to him, saying, "Sorry to pull this on you at such short notice, Frank, but you know how the Air Force is. This just came down the pipe. Seems there's a pressing need for someone like you in an intel billet."

Hannon picked up the twix and scanned it, unable to suppress his shock. "A posting to the staff of the 35th Fighter Wing of Pacific Air Force, in Misawa, *Japan*?"

"As I said, it's a pressing need. Big exercise coming up, Thor's Anvil, and the 35th will be deploying to South Korea. They have a hole in their staff they need filled right away."

"But I've got forty-six days to retirement! There's gotta be five hundred intel guys who could handle this!" And he waved the paper.

Tyndale raised his hand. "You think I didn't tell them that? But would Personnel listen to me? They make their own rules, you know that."

Hannon knew this had nothing to do with a "pressing staff need" in Japan. That he was being sequestered just like Airman Wick, who was shipped off to Greenland. "Look, this is crazy. I'll take it up with General Braddock if I have to."

Braddock was the deputy chief of Air Force Intelligence who looked after NORAD's intel staffing needs.

But to Hannon's rebuttal, Tin Man held his hand up again. "Relax, Frank. Relax. No need to do that. I think I've found a solution that will keep everybody happy."

Hannon was wary. "What's that?"

Tyndale extracted a form from the file and slid it across the table.

Hannon grabbed it and read. "A request for terminal leave?"

Tyndale nodded. "I checked your records. You're maxed out at sixty days leave with forty-six days to retirement. If you put in for terminal leave I'll approve it, then you're out of the picture as far as Personnel is concerned. They'll have to find someone else. Head down to your cay in the Bahamas for Christmas, then come back here for your retirement ceremony."

Hannon felt deflated. Putting him on terminal leave was a master stroke to get him out of the picture, and there was nothing he could do but swallow it from the smiling Tin Man. He took the form, scribbled his signature and shoved it back across the table. Tyndale took it and put his own signature in the approval block, saying, "Yes, a jaunt to the Bahamas before mustering out. Not a bad way to pack it in. You can sign out at the end of your duty tour this morning. By the way, I understand General Braddock plans to come down for your retirement ceremony."

Hannon was genuinely surprised. "I wasn't aware of that."

The Tin Man leaned back in his leather chair and clasped his hands behind his head. Flanking either side of the wall behind him were the American and NORAD flags, symbolizing values like duty, honor, country and a dozen others that had no business in Tin Man's presence as far as Hannon was concerned. "Did you know, Frank, that it looks like I may be General Braddock's successor?"

Hannon was stunned by the news, saying only, "No. I wasn't aware of that either."

Tyndale smiled—the smile that Hannon remembered from the dark recesses of their past. Frank used to brag that his buddy the Tin Man could lift any skirt or pay any bar tab with that crooked smile of his, never dreaming it was an evil mask. As he ripped out Hannon's copy of the triplicate leave form and pushed it across the table, Tyndale said, almost apologetically, "Look, Frank, I know we've had our differences. I guess you could say we share a different 'outlook' on the world and our place in it. That situation back when we were lieutenants— God, we were young, weren't we? Well, that was a long time ago. Your being here at Peterson when I arrived was as much a surprise to me as it was to you. It's been difficult for both of us, I know. But we've managed, haven't we? I would like to put the past behind us and just say what's done is done. And if you'll allow me, I'd like to raise a toast to our old friendship at your retirement ceremony."

Hannon fought back an urge to vomit, and only said, "Sure, Lawton. To old times."

As Hannon walked back through the door of the Space Control Center, it hit him. Hard. Twenty three years in the Air Force and in a few hours his career would be over, ended ignominiously by a man for whom he had nothing but contempt, for reasons that remained unfathomable to him.

Lucian Wintersgill saw the dazed look on Hannon's

face, and wondered if the proverbial jig was up. "So, uh, what happened, Colonel?"

Hannon looked up at him, as if he didn't hear.

"I said, how'd it go, Colonel?"

With a distant look, Hannon raised up the leave form and mumbled, "I just retired from the Air Force."

THREE

∞∞∞

The man steps out of the sedan at Huntington Park where a light fog drapes over the hills of San Francisco, dropping the temperatures and causing him to shove his hands deeply into his pockets. He blends in with the noon hour lunch crowd of tourists and office workers coursing over Nob Hill in search of their midday meal, and he easily looks the part of a businessman, a banker or a lawyer, but there is something about him that is certainly none of these.

From her table at the coffeehouse window along California Street she watches him buy a newspaper from the machine outside the Fairmount Hotel, then take a position leaning against the stone perimeter wall across the street from her, as if waiting for the next cable car.

Across the street a car pulls out from the curb, allowing the red Honda Civic to grab one of the cherished parking spaces. The driver emerges slowly, looking awkward as a child in the grips of stage fright before his first school pageant. He closes the door and takes a

57

moment to admire his new automobile, oblivious to the cars almost grazing him as he turns the rearview mirror up to take a final self-appraisal before going to his appointment. Yet despite the wheels and his physical aging, he is still the same old Joey. So awkward it is painful.

The scene takes on a slow-motion quality. He turns and sees her in the window. . . . She raises her hand in a reluctant salutation. . . . He strides across the road to the sound of a blaring horn and a near-miss, while the man behind the newspaper pulls out a cellular phone and punches in a number, his black eyes fixated on Joey. . . . Her conflicting feelings of exasperation and pity well up as Joey approaches. . . . Then, as he steps onto the sidewalk, his windbreaker erupts in a burst of blood, bone and gristle as though he's carried a small hand grenade under his armpit. A red mash splatters on the window of the quaint coffeehouse, bringing Miranda to her feet as she opens her mouth in a silent scream.

Miranda Park shot up in the bed like a sprung mousetrap, sweat glistening off her naked torso as her pulse pounded with a sprinter's pace. Hands trembling, she wiped her brow with the sheet, then reached for the pack of Camels on the bedside table. She fumbled one from the pack, but could barely line up the tip with the lighter's flame because her hand was vibrating like a flag in a force-eight gale. At last she connected, took three nervous puffs, then stubbed it out on the bedside ashtray, trying to cope with the aftershocks of a nightmare that was getting worse, not better. If anything, it was becoming a more frightening experience than when it first happened in reality.

In revolt at the thought, she spun herself off the bed,

naked except for the black silk panties she slept in, and went to the bathroom for the therapy of a shower. She shed her panties and turned the stream of water to stinging hot; then she stepped in to let the water rinse out the tension from her soul and the sweat from her auburn hair. The steamy water coursed down her body, which was athletic and wiry as a lanyard—the result of aerobics and a passion for rock climbing where surplus body fat served as an anchor that could drag a climber down. Her height was five-foot-seven and her legs were shapely but with a muscular definition—as were her back, buttocks and arms. Her breasts were small and high, with nipples the color of dark coffee beans that stood out like islands on the white patches of her skin that were untanned by the sun.

After five minutes of hot and five minutes of icy cold, she emerged and dried off, then wrapped a towel around herself and opened the curtains. The first rays of sunlight were turning the distant towers of the Bay Bridge from a rusty color to a blood red as the City slowly came awake. The bedroom window in her run-down leased townhouse on Halloran Street afforded her this distant view of the bridge, which was why she'd rented it in the first place. Firing up another cigarette, she sat down at the computer on her work desk and powered it up; then after the screen came alive she guided her mouse into her electronic secretary, where she called up her calendar for the day, although she knew what was on the agenda.

A.M.—office
LUNCH— SF Supervisor Brainard—background
2:30 P.M.—new hire interview

4:00 P.M.—Drinks, Saint Francis, Hewlett-Packard
PR guy

She felt as if her life and her career at the Associated Press were stagnating, as though she were stuck in autopilot and couldn't disengage, and afraid to sleep because of the maddening nightmare that might revisit her. It was at that moment—exhausted yet fearful of sleep—that Miranda Park knew she had to get to the bottom of Joey Dreason's death. It was the longest of long shots, but she was willing to try anything to purge that maddening image from her slumbers. She sorted through her dictaphone tapes and extracted the correct one, then stared at it as though it were a vial containing snake venom. Then she clenched it in her fist and closed her eyes, saying in a voice that was part whimper, part curse, "Damn you, Joey. Damn you to hell." Then, from a drawer, she pulled out a U.S. Geological Survey map of Utah. She moved her finger across the contour lines until it came to rest at a steep uplift in the terrain located near the Four Corners.

It was a mesa called the Kiva Tower.

The Beechcraft King Air cruised low above the frigid shores of Lake Superior, executing a methodical grid search over the snow-covered landscape. In the passenger cabin sat two very bored and surly men playing gin rummy with headphones strapped to their ears, while up in the cockpit the flight crew grew apprehensive about the icing conditions.

The junior man, who was something of a dreebenheimer, slapped his cards down on the folding tray and said, "Gin."

The bigger and more surly of the two had wide Slavic features and a widow's peak of dark hair that was a counterpoint to his thick mustache. If you'd found him atop a horse on the Russian steppes, you would've sworn he was a Cossack, and indeed, that was what his colleagues called him. But in the cabin of the King Air he was a disgruntled cardplayer, throwing down his cards in disgust as the dreebenheimer counted the points and penciled in the total. "Looks like you owe me forty-eight bucks," the junior man observed. "Want another hand?"

With disdain, the Cossack said, "Deal."

As the cards were shuffled, the Cossack looked out the window. They'd been canvassing the Lake Superior region for the better part of two months, listening for the signal from that transponder he'd planted on the small Cessna before it left New Jersey. He felt the odds of it showing up were nil, especially now, because the battery had to be depleted by this time. But Number One had decreed that the search continue, and so it continued—just in case the little Cessna had not actually met its fate in the cold dark waters of the great lake.

The Cossack had just picked up his cards and was sorting them with an appraising eye when a dull tone came through his headphones. He jumped as though his seat were electrified, and went to the bank of electronic equipment in the rear of the King Air, shouting to the flight crew, "We've got a contact!" He fiddled with the radio direction finder, but the signal was puny and quickly faded from his headphones. "We lost it!" he shouted through his intercom. "Come back around!"

"Listen!" retorted the pilot. "The icing is becoming

intense. We can't stay up much longer. Even with the deicers it's dangerous.''

''Shut up and bring us around!''

The pilot sighed with the weariness of a man who knew he had no choice. He replied, ''Yes, sir,'' then banked the plane around.

The two men in the rear pressed their headphones to their ears, and slowly the weak tone returned. It peaked quickly and then began to fade. The Cossack keyed his intercom switch, saying, ''We've got something! What's our location?''

''On the Canadian side,'' said the pilot. ''Over the Bruce Peninsula, near the little town of Wiarton.''

''Bring us around again!'' ordered the Cossack.

Once more the pilot complied as the Cossack stuck his head into the cockpit and searched the ground as the tone returned to his earphones. There was nothing but snow-covered forest below, and the Cossack was beginning to wonder if he was getting a false signal when he spied something that looked like a slash through the trees. He pointed and demanded, ''What's that?''

The pilot banked the King Air so he could see better, and as he flew over the slash the tone in the Cossack's earphones peaked. ''Looks like an airstrip,'' observed the pilot. ''A deserted one. There's nothing about it on the chart, but looks like a couple of old hangars down there.''

''Put us down,'' ordered the Cossack.

The pilot examined his chart. ''Let's see, the nearest strip would be at Owen Sound. That's about fifteen miles away. . . .''

''No,'' said the Cossack as he pointed. ''Put us down *there—now*!''

That inflamed the pilot. "You're out of your mind, mister! There's no telling how deep the snow is on the strip. Our nose gear could snap and we could tumble over!"

"Very well," replied the Cossack. "I'll simply inform Number One you've refused to carry out your orders."

The objections quickly melted away as the pilot replied in a dry voice, "Then get back in your seat and strap yourself in—tight."

As the Cossack buckled up, the junior man looked apprehensive, having heard the exchange with the pilot. "Like he said, it could be our ass if he tries to put it down here."

The Cossack grunted. "It would be our ass if he didn't try. Now just shut up and hold onto that precious ass of yours."

The King Air came onto final approach as the pilot lowered the gear and extended the flaps. Despite what the Cossack said, he was going in for a power-on landing. He would graze the snow with the gear, and if he didn't hit pavement immediately, then it was wheels up—the bastard in the rear and Number One be damned. He pulled up level in the landing flare, adding power just as the rear wheels gently probed the snow. The wheels hit something firm and the pilot felt a rush of relief as he lowered the nose gear onto the tarmac, easily cutting through the thin veneer of snow. But the relief was cut short as the plane lurched suddenly when its left gear bounced through a pothole. The pilot recovered, barely, then reversed the prop pitch harshly, sending up a cloud of white around the King Air. It was then that the aviator realized this must be an abandoned World

War II airstrip—hard-surfaced but in bad disrepair. The north shore snow had been light thus far this winter, which made this landing madness doable. As the ground speed bled off he applied the brakes, and finally the King Air came to a halt.

The Cossack pulled on his parka and wasted no time in dropping the door-stairstep. He and his sidekick double-timed to the first hangar, which was nothing but an open, rusting hulk. Then they mushed through the snow to the neighboring structure and saw that although it, too, was a rusting hulk, there was a new stainless-steel combination lock on the hasp of the sliding door. The Cossack looked around, then pulled out his .44 magnum and put a round through the locking spar, ignoring the gunshot that echoed over the deserted countryside. He barked, "Come on! Put your shoulder to it!" And the dreebenheimer helped him shove the frozen and rusty sliding door open. A shaft of harsh light stabbed into the chamber, illuminating the cowling of the parked Cessna that seemed to smile back at him—a mocking pose not unlike that Cheshire Cat Alice encountered in Wonderland.

To the silently laughing Cessna, the Cossack could only stare back with a growing sense of dread as he choked out the words, "The little bastard. . . . That fucking little frog bastard."

The acid had burned through the control cable for over fifteen minutes, putting more and more pressure on each surviving metallic strand.

Chester Wick was bundled up in his winter gear, trying unsuccessfully to get comfortable in the web seats of the C-130's cargo bay. He knew he ought to be angry, having his Christmas destroyed en route to Greenland, but he was still in the afterglow of his tryst in the Atlanta Sheraton. God, what a woman! Every fantasy he'd ever dreamed of had been fulfilled. And when he'd told her about those bogeys he'd seen in the Mountain, she'd been definitely impressed. Impressed enough to rally his body for one final surge before he'd collapsed in sleep.

As the Hercules cruised over the high latitudes of the massive Greenland ice cap, the daytime winter sky was pitch black except for the stars and the ethereal ribbons of the aurora borealis dancing through the heavens. Chester began to doze, a faint smile on his lips as he recounted her Grecian legs. Two other airmen were dozing as well, equally disgruntled about the Christmas duty they would be pulling in Thule. And on the flight deck the crew also dozed as the autopilot kept the aircraft straight and true on its programmed vector. All seemed stable and secure when the cable finally snapped in the belly.

The absence of tension on the cable caused the elevator control surface in the tail to spring up almost vertically. This pushed the tail down and the nose up, as if the Hercules had taken an invisible uppercut on its chin. Having dispensed with their seat belts, Chester and his two companions were thrown towards the retracted loading ramp in the rear of the plane as the pilot disengaged the autopilot and frantically worked the control column— but the aviator's efforts were to no avail. For a brief time the momentum of the Hercules kept it going almost straight up in a vertical climb. But then the aircraft's overwhelming weight began to overtake the thrust provided by the turboprops and the massive vessel began to fall, tail first, toward the ice cap, until the tail came up and the transport turned turtle, falling towards the earth with its belly toward the sky. Inside the cargo bay, Wick and his companions were tossed around like wet laundry in a dryer, and Chester screamed until his head struck a bulkhead that rendered him unconscious. Then as the Hercules continued its freefall from 28,000 feet, the nose started to pitch down until the left wing—not built for such aerodynamic maneuvers—sheared off near the fuselage, causing the remains of the aircraft to cartwheel down towards the dark, unforgiving ice cap of a Greenland winter.

The ringing of the phone felt like the business end of an ice pick shoved between the eyes, sending an arc weld of pain dancing over his synapses like a clumsy dentist's drill. His hammy hand fumbled for the receiver, only to knock it to the floor with a sonic whiplash that brought him awake like a de-hibernated grizzly.

Hannon had come off his final tour of duty at 8 A.M.—a time of day when it was hard to find a decent tavern. So to purge the recent events from his mind and soften the abruptness of the termination of his Air Force career, he'd made straight for his liquor cabinet, pouring up some sour-mash delights as other people were embracing their morning coffee. He'd siphoned off the last of the whiskey as the noon hour approached; then fatigue, frustration and alcohol overtook his consciousness and he fell asleep on the living room sofa—his head only inches away from the phone that now rang like Quasimodo's refrain. He ripped the receiver off the cradle and moaned, "Who . . . the . . . fuck . . . *is this?*"

The voice that came through the line was flat, businesslike. "Colonel, this is Chief Wintersgill. Are you all right?"

Hannon fumbled for a kernel of equilibrium as he groggily responded with, "Uh . . . sorry, Chief. Sorry. . . . got a little plowed last night. I mean, this morning. Celebrating civilian life, you know. Wha-what's happening?"

Despite his pickled brain, Hannon detected a trace of anxiety in the voice coming through the phone. Like someone negotiating with a kidnapper who has his child. "Sir, I'm in the headquarters squadron day room."

"Yeah?"

"We just got word. Airman Chester Wick's transport aircraft, a C-130 that was flying him to Thule—well, sir, we just received a twix that the aircraft went down over the Greenland ice cap."

Hannon never remembered sobering up so fast.

Yolanda Martinez was grateful to have a job. While some fools might think that being a maid was barely a cut above a serf, she'd grown up under the deprivation of Castro's Cuba. After making landfall in America seven years ago, she never tired of the thrill of a paycheck—and more importantly, the thrill of having something to spend it on. So every day she attacked her housekeeping chores with a vigor that impressed her supervisors and earned her the enmity of a few slackers on the hotel's housekeeping staff. She was nearing the end of her shift, going back to the rooms where the guests had checked out late or were staying over. The supervisor had parceled out the work, sending her down the hall to 517. The "Do Not Disturb" sign was still there, yet it was 3:20 P.M. She didn't like to do this, but policy required it, so she pulled out her passkey and knocked loudly on the door, saying, "Housekeeping!" No response, so she inserted the key and slowly opened the door, knocking loudly again and repeating her "Housekeeping!" call. Sometimes guests went to bed drunk and could sleep through an artillery barrage, or were in the shower. But there was no shower, or TV, or sound of sheets rustling with someone coming awake. Yolanda entered slowly and saw the bed had been tousled but was empty, so she figured the guest had left the sign on the doorknob and forgot about it when departing. She went back to her cart and pulled on her rubber gloves, then grabbed the bucket of cleaning supplies and headed for the bathroom. She opened the door, then froze for a moment before emptying her lungs in a scream.

The blond woman lay on the floor, her eyes fixed on the ceiling in a glazed death stare. The towel half covered her naked body, leaving one of her magnificent breasts exposed, and on her upper lip was a white smudge. The floor around her was covered in a white powder, as if someone had dropped a small bag of sugar.

"Attention ... Attention ... The library will close in one hour. The checkout desk will close in forty-five minutes and applications for new cards will not be accepted after that time."

Hannon and Wintersgill were sitting in civilian clothes at a table in the map room of the Colorado Springs Public Library. Hannon was wearing slacks and a turtleneck, while Wintersgill was in jeans and a wool lumberjack shirt as a testament to his outdoor religion. On the table were a dozen U.S. Geological Survey maps

of southern Utah and the printout of the Salt Lake Air
Route Control Center radar imagery that had come out
of the dot matrix printer in Cheyenne Mountain. Both
men were dealing with levels of shock and disbelief that
were beyond them, like a sledgehammer blow to a delicate inertial-guidance system, and they had cloistered
themselves in the map room as if they were a pair of
monks breaking their vows of silence. Neither could absorb the reality of what had happened on the Greenland
Ice Cap, but Hannon knew he must absorb it because
there was a haunting feeling that he was now woven
into the fabric of a sinister web—the size and dimension
of which he could not fathom. That the forces which
had brought down an aircraft on a frozen wasteland
could also come down on him.

The better part of Wintersgill's career had been in
mission planning and target selection, so Hannon gave
him a free hand as he pored over the U.S.G.S. maps and
the air traffic printout while working with a protractor,
ruler and pencil.

"All right, sir," said Wintersgill. "I think this is as
close as we can get. Here are the GPS coordinates for
the two aircraft in the vicinity where the, ah, bogeys
went down." He tapped some real estate in southern
Utah near the Four Corners area—where the borders of
Colorado, Utah, New Mexico and Arizona come together in a crosshair. "We were lucky that these two
aircraft had GPS transponders," observed Wintersgill.

"You mean, like our fighters and such?"

"Yes, sir. Some private aircraft now carry transponders that take their location data from the Global Positioning Satellites and transmit their position on their
transponder channel. Should a plane go down, the radar

center would have its GPS location for search and rescue. I marked the GPS location of the airplanes pegged by radar control on this U.S.G.S. map. These should be accurate to within a hundred meters. Then with this protractor I took an azimuth to the bogeys' location on the FAA printout. From true north it was one-zero-three degrees from this aircraft, and two-six-two degrees from the second aircraft.''

"Keep going, Chief," replied Hannon. "You're doing great."

"Then I drew those azimuths from the known GPS coordinates to an intersect point on the U.S.G.S. map. Where these lines cross is where the bogeys fell off the radarscope, and we take our coordinates from the border of the U.S.G.S. grid."

Hannon nodded, truly impressed. "All right, Chief. You've sold me. Maybe this will lead to something that will let me put Tin Man on ice once and for all."

Wintersgill pursed his lips, figuring it was time to get it out in the open. "I'm no fan of Colonel Tyndale, sir. I've never said as much, but we both know it's true. He's an ass-kisser extraordinaire. But I always sensed there was something deeper between you two. Something that went beyond office politics."

"Was it that obvious?"

"You could cut it with a knife," replied Wintersgill.

Hannon sighed, then shook his head as the memory welled up. "I was a newly minted lieutenant when I went through the Air Force intel school at Goodfellow," he recounted, "learning all about the charms of eavesdropping on the airwaves. Right out of school I got collared for a posting that was really out of my league. I don't know why, but I got the nod."

"For what?"

"Nicaragua was bleeding big time by then. The Sandinistas were kicking Somoza's butt and the fighting had escalated into a full-scale shooting war. I was pulled into a small group called the Intelligence Support Activity, or ISA, and it was there that I linked up with another lieutenant named Lawton Tyndale."

Wintersgill cocked an eyebrow.

Hannon continued. "Surprisingly, it was an Army program, but they drew on interservice assets. We had about half-a-dozen Beechcraft King Airs—twin turboprops—that were crammed with electronic listening gear. We were so hush-hush that we were stationed in the Panama Canal Zone and would take long flights up to execute our missions, doing midair refuelings over water. We'd penetrate the Nicaraguan border, mainly at night, listening and trying to draw a bead on the Sandinistas' base camps—and we were damned effective. More than once, Somoza's planes and his henchmen tore those camps up based on data we passed to them. I'd say we probably extended the war by a year or two, until finally the Sandinistas caught the drift and put the hammer down on their communications security. But before that happened, Tin Man and I snagged an intercept we weren't supposed to catch."

Wintersgill leaned forward. "And what was that?"

Hannon sighed, the bitterness of the memory still eating at him like an acid. "We picked up an air-to-ground communication—more than likely some higher-up in the Somoza military or government. He was all excited, could hardly contain himself as he talked to his partner or whomever on the ground. Seems this Nicaraguan mucky-muck was en route from Panama City to Managua on his Learjet. He says he's got a surefire way to get some cocaine into the U.S. No problem. Says he lined up a *compadre* in the U.S. military to take the coke back with him when he leaves the Canal Zone on his Sabreliner.''

''Sabreliner?''

''Our reaction exactly. An executive jet. The kind used for our own mucky-mucks. Well, Tin Man and I complete our mission, and when we get back to the Canal Zone—which is U.S. soil, right?—we go hunting down the flight line for a Sabreliner, and sure enough we find one in a hangar. Tin Man and I look at each other and say, 'What the fuck, over?' The plane is deserted, so we climb on board and look around. This was pretty brazen for a couple of lieutenants to do, but we were ISA and cocky as hell. We find a manifest in the cockpit for some three-star who was flying around on an inspection tour, and his last stop was in the Canal Zone. We open the baggage compartment and what do we find? Nothing less than a footlocker filled with packets of cocaine—had to be at least forty pounds of the stuff.''

Wintersgill whistled.

Hannon looked at the ceiling. ''So tell me—who's gonna search a three-star's private aircraft? The answer is nobody. Nobody with any brains, that is. Well, Tin Man and I quickly see we've fallen into a very deep tub of shit. We're nervous. Tin Man says we need backup. He tells me to run and find the top-gun MP on post while he stays behind to watch the evidence and phone the duty officer. I take off and run like hell, but on account of it's Saturday, it takes some time to run down the head honcho of the Canal Zone MPs. I finally collar him on the back nine of the golf course and say drop everything and come with me. He's pissed, but he follows me and we run into the hangar, with him still wearing his golf cleats. I expected to find a half-a-dozen sentries with fixed bayonets, but instead we find Tin Man and the three-star, whose name I have purged from my memory.''

"So what happened?"

"This three-star is smooth, I mean a real snake. He looks at us innocently and asks, 'What's the problem?' I make my accusations, expecting Tin Man to back me up, but he's dead silent.''

"You're not serious?"

Hannon nodded. "As serious as it gets. I started to throw a fit, and demanded we play the tapes from our eavesdropping mission. We reel in the ISA CO into our growing entourage and pull the tapes from the plane, but when we put them on the machine they'd been erased. Then I had to accept the obvious. Tin Man—my *compadre,* my brother-in-arms—had sold out. He'd cut a deal with the general and they'd made the evidence disappear. Without evidence I had no bullets. All I could do was stand there and look like a fool while my CO and the MP unload on me. Then the three-star intercedes and magnanimously says some overzealousness in lieutenants is a good thing. That perhaps I did overhear something that I misinterpreted. And that's when Tin Man did it.''

"Did what?"

Hannon looked down. "Tin Man smiled. Just like he did when he bounced me out on terminal leave.''

Wintersgill shook his head.

"Then the next day Tin Man gets orders cut for the Pentagon and he's gone. I hear he gets an early promote to captain, no doubt due to the influence of his three-star patron—then he goes on to a series of career-enhancing plumb assignments. Whereas I go on to Korea and two failed marriages. I don't lay eyes on Tin Man for another twenty-one years until I get assigned to Cheyenne Mountain.''

''With Colonel Lawton Tyndale as your boss. Jesus, sir, I had no idea.''

Hannon sucked in several cubic feet of air. ''So now Colonel Tyndale is in the pipeline for brigadier and I'm headed for pasture, but before I pack it in I'd like to wipe that fucking smile off Tin Man's face.'' Hannon remained silent for some moments, then said, ''Okay, Chief. Enough of my jaded past. Now let me have your keys.''

''Keys, sir?''

''You got one of those Jeeps, don't you?''

''Yes, sir. A new Wrangler.''

Hannon pulled a key off his own key ring and handed it over. ''I'm putting you behind the wheel of a 1987 Mustang convertible, Chief. It will be a new winter driving experience for you, believe me.''

''But, sir. I thought, well, I want to get to the bottom of this thing as much as you do. That kid Wick worked for me, too, and they won't find his remains until spring, if then. What I'm trying to say is, well, I thought I was going with you.''

Hannon leaned back in his chair. ''How many years you got in, Chief?''

''Twenty-eight, sir.''

''Got one daughter married and another in college, as I recall.''

''Yes, sir.''

"And you've got a retirement spot all picked out, I'll bet."

"In Idaho, yes, sir. In the Bitterroot Mountains."

Hannon nodded. "Then this is where you get off, Lucian. You and the missus hang 'em up in that mountain cabin of yours and forget you ever saw any of this. You've done your bit for king and country and you've got more scars than me for taking flak in the line of duty. Don't be a hero, just get off here. That is my final order."

Hannon saw the man's shoulders sag. Then Wintersgill turned and looked at him. "But what about you? You had a retirement planned. . . ."

"All I had planned was to destroy my liver under the light of a Bahamian moon. Now get your ass outta here and forget about this. If I don't come back, the Mustang is yours."

Without further argument, Wintersgill sighed, then plunked down his Wrangler key and walked toward the door, saying, "You've got more guts than brains, Frank."

And then he was gone.

With a sardonic smile, Hannon picked up the key and rolled it between his fingers, whispering, "You always spoke the truth, my friend." Then he leaned over and inspected the map of southern Utah where Wintersgill had drawn the intersecting lines. They came together at the point near the Four Corners, almost midway between Bryce Canyon and Lake Powell, at a desolate place in the Great American Desert called the Kiva Tower.

FOUR

———⊗⊗⊗———

Colonel Lawton Tyndale, Chief of the Space Control Division of NORAD, opened an armoire in his office at Peterson Air Force Base and stood before the full-length mirror mounted inside the door. He pulled on his uniform jacket and admired the way it fit his six-foot frame like a second skin. Proper diet, moderate social drinking, and a wringer game of racquetball with one of the younger officers four times a week kept the pounds off and the stomach flat. With his blue eyes, his narrow, angular face and the unbalding dark hair—well, he could've been a candidate for an Air Force recruiting poster. Most of the officers didn't care for the new Air Force uniform with the rank denoted by stripes on the sleeve, but Tyndale liked it. He felt it made him look more like an executive than a warrior, which was more on-point with his style. He had the four stripes of a full colonel now, and in a short time they would be replaced with the single broad stripe of a brigadier's star. And then? Well, who could say? He straightened his jacket, closed the amoire door and picked up his leather port-folio on the way out.

He exited through his private doorway and went down the hall to another suite of offices, where he stepped up to a male secretary-airman, saying, "Colonel Tyndale to see the Chief-of-Staff."

The startled airman looked up from his word processor and murmured into the intercom, then said, "You may go in, Colonel."

He smiled that crooked smile and said, "Thanks, son." Tin Man was never arrogant. Those little people could be such backbiters if you gave them the chance.

Tyndale entered the office of Major General Owen Shrake, Chief-of-Staff of the North American Aerospace Defense Command, and closed the door. Shrake looked tired, but relieved, his aristocratic bank-president features having lost their luster during the last few days. There was no repartee between them. Shrake simply looked up and asked, "Any problems?"

Tin Man disarmed him with his crooked smile, which worked its magic on airmen and generals alike. "No problems. Everything neat, clean and tied up with a pink ribbon. Our bigmouth is lost on the ice cap and won't be found until spring, if then, and Lieutenant Colonel Frank Hannon has been mustered out of the Air Force."

Shrake nodded. "Good. I got off the phone an hour ago with Number One. I told him everything was taken care of." Then he pointed at the leather portfolio under Tyndale's arm. "Is that for the CinC's briefing?"

"Of course. He'll want to know about Airman Wick's unfortunate demise."

Shrake turned away, feeling the blood weigh heavy on his hands. But what choice did he have now?

• • •

It was mid-afternoon when he crossed the border into Utah about thirty miles north of the Four Corners—where Colorado, Utah, Arizona and New Mexico meet at a single cartographic point on the map. As the Wrangler descended the Western Slope of the Rockies, the snow-draped forests with their ski resorts gave way to a barren landscape that seemed uninviting and unforgiving. Brown and red dust covered a parched terrain that had been sculpted over eons by ice ages, raging rivers and howling winds. Whatever stature you thought you had achieved in this life quickly evaporated when you entered the Great American Desert, and the feeling of utter loneliness did nothing to raise Hannon's confidence. He arrived at a T-intersection in the road where Highway 160 came to an end and he could only proceed north or south on Highway 191. He studied the Rand-McNally road map, then compared it to the 1-to-50,000-scale U.S.G.S. map he had purloined from the Colorado Springs Public Library. He ascertained that the Kiva Tower was located in a parcel of desert east of Lake Powell, south of the Manti-La Sal National Forest, west of the T-intersection where he was now and north of a speck of a town on the San Juan River called Bluff. He turned south toward Bluff and cruised on autopilot, feeling uncomfortably small in the vast landscape. It was like that astronaut had said—not Neil Armstrong, but the other one. What was his name? Oh, yeah. Aldrin. Buzz Aldrin. The second guy on the moon. He'd said the lunar landscape was "magnificent desolation." Same thing here.

Hannon was tired and feeling hunger pangs, having pushed through the mountain roads without lunch. He went through the tiny hamlet of Bluff in about twenty seconds, then passed the turnoff to Highway 163 toward Mexican Hat. A short distance past the turnoff he cruised by a filling station-diner-convenience store as he searched the terrain for an unmapped road that might take him the eight miles north to the Kiva Tower. Otherwise he would have to hike overland—something his paunchy and unaerobic body would protest. After several miles he gave into his hunger pangs and wheeled back around toward the village of Bluff to pull into the filling station-diner-convenience store. The structure was little more than several pieces of sheet metal slapped together in a kind of squared-off Quonset hut. He stopped, got out and stretched, then filled up the Wrangler with unleaded and entered the diner. The inside was more inviting than the exterior appeared, with tile floors and good lighting—sort of like finding a 7-Eleven on Mars. He paid $22 in cash to the bored teenage girl at the register who had her nose buried in an *Entertainment Weekly* magazine; then he visited the men's room before taking a seat at the diner counter. With reluctance, the teenager closed the magazine and slid off her stool to take his order. Hannon inspected the plastic sheet of a menu and found a Winnebago cuisine that could drop a rhino with its cholesterol count. He figured what the hell, and went for broke, saying, "Chicken fried steak with fries and cream gravy. Oh, and coffee, black."

The teenager replied, " 'Kay," and scribbled on her order pad, then slapped it on the pass-through window to the kitchen as she rang one of those desk bells, saying, "Order up, Grandpa." Then she returned to her magazine as Hannon returned to his map. The geological formation noted as the Kiva Tower was a good eight miles

PAYNE HARRISON

from the road as the crow flies, and while the cartography on the map was most precise, it showed neither a road nor a trail leading to the point of intersect drawn by Chief Wintersgill. As the cardiac blue plate special was placed before him, Hannon inquired, "Excuse me, young lady, but are you familiar with these parts?"

She gave him a blank stare in reply, like a deer caught in the headlights.

"I was wondering if you knew of a road leading to a geologic formation called the Kiva Tower. It's about eight miles due north of here."

Another blank stare, then a shrug. "Maybe my grandfather would know."

"Could I speak with him?"

She pushed open the swinging door behind her and called, "Grandpa—somebody out here has a question."

Once more her attention returned to the magazine as Grandpa emerged from the kitchen. He was a big man— might have been a lineman or thrown the shotput in his youth—and he wore one of those chest-high, grease-spattered aprons over a Pendleton shirt that had the sleeves rolled up. Hannon put him at seventy, if not the north side of seventy, for he had a shock of white hair over a broad forehead that was punctuated with the occasional liver spot. Snowy eyebrows set off a pair of black eyes that could see through to your soul in a glance, exposing every secret you hoped to keep; and as he wiped his hands with a towel, Hannon thought he looked a man who'd lived too long on a diet of disappointment and bitterness. He asked, "Can I help you?" in a bass voice that reverberated the walls of the Quonset hut.

"Yes, perhaps you could. I wondered if you could

direct me to a place on the map here called the Kiva Tower."

At the words "Kiva Tower," Hannon sensed a change in Grandpa's posture. Not exactly like a wrestler going into a crouch, but close. After a few moments, the older man inquired, "Why would you be interested in the Kiva Tower? It must be near freezing out there."

Hannon was caught flat-footed. He hadn't thought about a cover story. There had been so much else to think about. He took a sip of coffee, then volleyed back with; "I'm an amateur prospector. Had some time on my hands over the holidays. Thought I'd try my luck in that area."

Grandpa nodded. "I suppose you're here to look for those silver tailings along the Precambrian basalt fissures near the tower?"

"Exactly."

Grandpa's black eyes drilled him, and suddenly Hannon knew what a stripper must feel like when she drops her G-string in the spotlight for the first time. The stare remained in place as he said, "That will be all for today, Sheila."

Sheila looked up from her magazine like a periscope breaking the surface. "Huh?"

"I said you can go. Rest of the day off. Make sure the register is locked, then go on your way. I'll close things up and see you in the morning."

"Gee, thanks, Grandpa."

Sheila disappeared with the speed of gazelle jumping a fence, and when the door closed, Grandpa said, "There are no silver tailings. Nor are there any basalt fissures near the Kiva Tower. And if you don't mind my saying so, your lily-white hands don't look like they've spent much time in the earth like a prospector—amateur or otherwise.''

''Am I really that transparent?''

''I'm afraid so.''

With a forced chuckle, Hannon reached into his hip pocket for his military ID card, rapidly conjuring up a fallback story as he pulled it out and dropped it on the counter. Grandpa picked it up and examined it carefully, then with a look that betrayed his authentically perplexed reaction, he said, ''Air Force? . . . But I thought you already . . .''

''Already what?''

Grandpa didn't answer as he eyed Hannon warily. ''Why would you be interested in the Kiva Tower?''

Hannon lowered his voice. ''I work in Air Force intelligence, assigned to the DEA. We think some of our people were involved in a large drug deal in that area. Using Air Force planes they brought a drug load up from Colombia and had a nighttime rendezvous with their buyer somewhere near the Kiva Tower. I'm here chasing down a lead, you might say. Thought I might uncover something at the landing zone.'' Not a bad recovery, thought Hannon.

But Grandpa just handed back the ID and impaled him with the black-eyed lasers once again, saying, ''If you were to honestly tell me what brings you to the Kiva Tower, then perhaps I could help you. If not, then there's the door.''

Hannon was genuinely in a quandary as to how to play this man. He didn't expect to find someone of his stripe on the other side of a diner counter wearing a grease-spattered apron. This fellow was not what he seemed, so Hannon said, ''Okay, let's say this. It has come to my attention that something very, ah, unusual happened near the Kiva Tower during the early morning hours of December tenth. Suffice to say it's very sensitive, and I'm here trying to get to the bottom of it. I would tell you more, but quite frankly it would probably be best that you don't know, because in this case what you do know can hurt you. Will you accept that?''

Grandpa shrugged. "Very well, Colonel Hannon. What can I do for you?''

"I take it you're familiar with the Kiva Tower area?''

Grandpa nodded. "I was born down the road in Mexican Hat. I grew up around here.''

Hannon's antennae gauged his response, his body language, what he said without speaking. In a silent way that perhaps only cops, reporters, psychotherapists and intel interrogators can read, Grandpa was raising his veil just a bit, so Hannon queried, "Did you see anything— say, out of the ordinary on the morning of the tenth?''

Grandpa pursed his lips, then jerked his head, saying, "Let's step outside.''

They exited into the brisk air and surveyed the northern vista that stretched out before them. It seemed to follow a long depression before rising up in the distance where a pedestal was silhouetted on the far horizon. Grandpa pointed, saying, "The Kiva Tower is a rock formation on the summit of that column you see there. The column is a mesa that is almost a perfect circle with a ridge along its perimeter, making it reminiscent of an Anasazi kiva. I guess it so impressed the original surveyor that he named it Kiva Tower. About three years ago the Anaconda mining company discovered a copper deposit inside the kiva. They built roads and made preparations for an open-pit mine like the one near Salt Lake City.''

''So is the mine running now?''

Grandpa chuckled. ''The joke was on them. The ore was extraordinarily rich, but it was just a pocket. It quickly ran dry. You might say God salted the mine and laughed.''

Hannon nodded. ''So it's abandoned now?''

''Totally. Some of the most godforsaken country you can imagine.''

Hannon sensed where he was going. ''But you saw something on the morning of the tenth, didn't you?''

Grandpa shifted his weight, as if the ground was transmitting some form of discomfort, and more than a few awkward seconds ticked off before he said, ''On December tenth I was closing up at around one-thirty A.M. It was late on account I was catching up on my bookkeeping. I walked outside and happened to look back toward the Kiva Tower.''

''And?''

Grandpa sighed. ''I saw four lights, with a silvery-gold color. At first I thought they were a conventional aircraft of some kind, but their maneuver was, well, they came straight down towards the mesa. Then just above the tower they split apart into four separate lights and circled above the summit a few times like a carousel. Then they rejoined into a formation and dropped out of sight.'' Grandpa looked distraught as he shifted his weight in the cold, but Hannon didn't interrupt or prompt him. He sensed the story would come if he just got out of the way. ''I was tired,'' he continued. ''But after that I couldn't sleep, so I wrapped myself up in some blankets and sat out on the porch of my house up there.'' He pointed to an A-frame house up the slope.

"And?"

Grandpa scuffed the gravel with his boot. "To move the ore out of that mine, Anaconda used those huge earth movers with tires bigger than this shack here. Since a circular mesa did not lend itself to the construction of wide switchbacks to accommodate those ore haulers, the engineers made a long road that wound around the mesa, like a spiral. I saw a procession of vehicle lights coming down from the kiva on that mining road, a convoy if you will. I was curious and watched them for maybe ten minutes. I thought it strange that anyone would be up there, in numbers, at that time of night—or any time for that matter—and I figured they must be related in some way to the lights I'd seen earlier. So I watched them for a while. Thought about phoning the sheriff's office to ask if they knew what was going on up there.''

It was here that Grandpa paused, causing Hannon to prompt him. "But you didn't phone.''

Grandpa shook his head. "No.''

"Because of something else you saw?"

A nod.

"What was it?"

He sighed. "The lights again.''

"Where were they?''

Grandpa looked off in the distance. "There were four of them again. They rose straight up above the kiva, slowly, for perhaps thirty seconds. I was starting to think they were some kind of advanced helicopters, or something like that, but then . . .''

"Then?"

The black-eyed lasers drilled him as he said softly,

"In the time it would take you to strike a match, they shot straight up and out of sight."

The silence that fell between them was deafening as Hannon received his confirmation—that what he'd seen on the picket fence radar screen was real, endorsed by an all-too-credible eyewitness. Something had come down from the sky . . . to do what?

"So how do I get up to this kiva?" asked Hannon.

Grandpa motioned with his head. "Go back up 195, almost to Blanding. Take Highway 95 west. The highway makes a dogleg south. It's at that dogleg you'll pick up the Anaconda road. Can't miss it. It approaches the kiva from the north."

Hannon nodded, and as he threw up the hood on his parka his curiosity got the better of him. "So what's a kiva anyway?"

Grandpa shrugged again. "We can only speculate as to their meaning. All we can say is they must have played some vital role in Anasazi culture. They were circular structures for the most part, some small and simple, some up to sixty feet in diameter and rather ornate. Entrance was usually through a hole in a flat roof. Best guess is they had some religious meaning, and if that is the case, then religion was the centerpiece of Anasazi culture, as evidenced by the great Pueblo Bonito in New Mexico's Chaco Canyon. It has six hundred sixty rooms and thirty-two kivas."

"So they were a church maybe? A temple of some kind?"

"Possibly. Probably. But no one knows for sure."

Hannon eyed him carefully. "So how come you know so much?"

He sighed wearily. "I'm Doctor Morgan Raines, retired Professor of Southwestern History at Cedar Mountain College. And, I might add, author of *History of the Four Corners*."

Hannon was more than a little stunned. "You're a professor?"

His smile was laced with irony. "So what is a professor doing as a short-order cook, you're asking yourself? Forty years of scholarship and what do I have? A pension that's a step removed from the poverty level, a wife with Alzheimer's, and a granddaughter who dreams of being Madonna—and I don't mean the Sainted Virgin. I run a diner on this moonscape crossroads because I still have extended family in the area, I need the money, and I wanted to stay near the land and history to which I devoted my life."

"The Anasazi, you mean?"

"Yes, the Anasazi."

"So what happened to them? The Anasazi, I mean. I never heard of them."

The professor looked out to the desert. "No one knows what happened to them. They simply vanished."

Hannon absorbed what the brilliant short-order cook had told him, then mused, "Anasazi. Hard to pronounce."

"Yes. It's a Navajo word, actually. We don't know what the Anasazi called themselves, so in white scientific literature we have adopted the Navajo term for them."

"So what does 'Anasazi' mean?"

The grandpa professor shifted his weight as vapor escaped from his nose, as though he were a tired dragon. "It doesn't translate precisely, but two iterations of the word are generally accepted in the scientific community. One is 'enemy ancestors.' "

"And the other?"

The black-eyed lasers burned deep into Hannon's soul as Grandpa intoned, " 'Ancestors of the far away people.' "

The shadows were growing long as the sun dipped to the horizon, but even in the fading light Hannon found the mining road where it peeled off at the elbow of the highway dogleg. It was a dirt road and obviously in disrepair, but it was still discernible and easily passable in the Wrangler. He left the Jeep in high-gear four-wheel drive as he headed due south, and upon cresting a rise in the terrain he could see the columnar mesa rising above the neighboring landscape.

An inner voice asked: Why was he doing this? Why was he here, literally in the middle of nowhere, headed for a rendezvous with—what?

Perhaps the answers were ahead, for the mesa approached.

The road started up the columnar formation in a long, slow spiral and Hannon was amazed at how the mesa was almost perfectly cylindrical in shape. As he wound around the western side, he was treated to a glorious desert sunset with the sun painting the clouds and landscape with a dazzling palette of reds, purples and oranges. It was a natural kaleidoscope that could humble even the most arrogant of onlookers, but Hannon already felt humble enough. The road was just what Grandpa had said, in that it was a wide road, solidly engineered, but unused by the mining company after the flameout of their copper deposit, as evidenced by small washouts in the surface. As he approached the flat summit of the mesa, a high spire of red sandstone greeted him at the entry. It seemed rather out of place when compared to the elegant symmetry of the kiva, like a jagged knife blade pointing towards heaven, and Hannon figured this must be the Kiva Tower proper. He pulled onto the deck of the summit, killed the engine and got out. The sun had fallen now, and the sky was quickly changing from azure blue to a dusky indigo. Hannon was not an outdoorsman, and was new to the feelings of loneliness that the desert could impart. In the same moment he found it awe-inspiring and spooky, and the cold didn't help matters much. At least there wasn't any wind, and he realized the lack of wind might be due to the shielding ridge that encircled the column. Unlike a generic mesa, this one did not have a squared-off top. Instead, it was surrounded by a ridge escarpment about two stories high that made the top of the column resemble a crater floor rather than the flat plateau of a mesa. Hannon wasn't too good at estimating distances, but he figured the diameter was maybe a mile and a half to two miles, and off to the left he spied the yawning pit that had been excavated during the abortive mining venture.

He grabbed a powerful flashlight from the back of the Wrangler, then pulled up the hood of his parka. The convoy of vehicles the professor had seen had to have come through this entrance, so Hannon shone his light on the ground and started a search pattern, looking for tracks, and it didn't take him long to pick up the trail. The tracks were faded, but due to the wind break provided by the ridge, they had not been erased by the desert air currents. He followed the trail on foot as the stars began peppering the sky, and the loneliness of his situation honed his senses.

The tracks indicated a convoy because they overlaid each other, indicating the convoy had remained intact until it had traveled about a half mile into the kiva. At that point, individual tracks flared out into a semicircle and ended, indicating they'd parked. Hannon hunched down and inspected the tire tracks where they dispersed from the convoy, and found that some were smaller vehicles and some larger—not as big as semitrailers, but perhaps on the order of deuce-and-a-half trucks.

Anyone with half a brain would have waited for daylight to do what he was doing, but Hannon pressed on, having become a prisoner of his own curious fascination. He walked along and carefully inspected each parking site, finding a total of thirteen vehicle tracks with faded footprints around each of them. Three of the bigger vehicles had circular tracks at their parking sites, indicating they had turned around to park with their tailgates facing inward to the semicircle.

Hannon flicked off his flashlight and absorbed the elements around him. Night had fallen now, and the stars shone with a crystalline clarity, while a half-moon provided a milky illumination. The air seemed absolutely still as Hannon listened to his own breathing. There were no insects on this subfreezing night, no coyote's wail—nothing. He turned and saw the jagged tower of rock reaching skyward toward the canopy of stars, and for a moment he felt himself more in a cathedral than on a desert mesa. The timbre of the air had a tension to it, as if laced with static electricity. Something had happened here, he was sure of it. Something extraordinary. He could feel it even now, after the fact. But what was it?

What was the nature of the event that had transpired here? In search of an answer, Hannon turned on his flashlight and pressed deeper into the heart of the mesa, executing a shaky but methodical search pattern with the light. He picked up a collective trail of faded but distinct footprints and followed them to the locus point of the semicircle. All of his senses and instincts were focused on his beam of light as it probed the dust, yet in spite of that focus another feeling began to arouse his primal instincts.

A feeling that he was being watched.

It was 278 nautical miles above the earth, on the perigee of an elliptical orbit that took it over the northern and southern ice caps every 117 minutes. It was roughly the size of a semitrailer you'd pass on the interstate, and crammed inside was state-of-the-art hardware in optics, image processing, spectral sensors and avionics. This was the Rolls Royce of reconnaissance satellites known as the KH-12, or Keyhole. The objects of its attention used to be things like missile silos and mobile launchers in the old Soviet Union, and while it still examined targets within that Stalinist relic, its contemporary focus had shifted to places like Iran, Iraq and even China as it probed secret structures for things like underground nuclear reactors, chemical and biological weapons facilities and other tools of mass destruction. The Keyhole had long been just that, a keyhole through which the U.S. government could spy upon the outside world. But now it was doing something at cross purposes to its intended use as it obeyed a set of telemetry commands and pointed its optical and infrared sensors to a remote spot in the Great American Desert.

• • •

Hannon methodically worked the flashlight back and forth over the floor of the mesa, and picked up the confluence of footprints going from the vehicles to the locus point of the semicircle—again, finding them faded but discernible. Where the footprints congregated, Hannon noticed there had been a great deal of walking back and forth, and many of the toe prints were pointing at a spot deeper into the mesa, like an assembled gallery looking toward—what? He swallowed, pulled his parka tighter around him and pressed on in the direction of the toe prints, moving the light slowly back and forth. When the beam crossed the first one he didn't know what it was, so he brought the light back and focused on it, then squatted down to inspect the ground more closely. It was about a three-foot-by-three-foot-square depression in the sandy topsoil of the mesa and about two inches deep. For a few moments he didn't move as he absorbed the image illuminated by the beam; then with his heart hammering on the anvil of his chest, he reached out for the depression and touched it. His hand sprang back as though it were afire, even though the ground was cold as the rest of the desert floor. Hannon rose and splayed the light around him and found a second depression, then a third, and they were laid out in the tripod arrangement of an equilateral triangle. He paced off the distance between each one and found that they were, indeed, evenly spaced, about thirty feet apart.

Hannon stood in the center of the triangle, under the canopy of stars, and for the first time realized those stars—those pinpoints of light—were now eerily close, as proven by the stupefying evidence he'd found on this godforsaken slice of the desert. The effect on Hannon—

a tougher and more calloused individual than your average homo sapien—was beyond words. The world, and his place in it, was turned inside out and upside down. Here was the evidence that the universe did not revolve around this pale blue dot called Earth, but went beyond it on a scale that was impossible to fathom. He wasn't a scientist, a theologian or a philosopher—he was a common man; and here, on this desert night, his internal compass had experienced a meltdown that was as frightening as it was fascinating. He took several deep breaths and whispered, "Jesus, Mary and Joseph." Then he pulled out a small 35mm pocket camera and began snapping flash pictures of the depressions in the sand. That done, he began moving the light beam over the sand again, and found two more sets of tripod depressions that also had the thirty-foot spacing, then a fourth that had a spacing of sixty-five feet. He snapped pictures until his film ran out; then, with his emotions and film spent, he decided it was time to get the hell out of there.

He started back for the jeep, but as he turned, his flashlight caught the metallic glint of something on the ground. It lay beneath an outcropping of sagebrush. He pegged it with the light beam and stepped forward, thinking it was a beer can. But as he knelt down and picked it up, it quickly became apparent it wasn't a beverage container. It was approximately the size and shape of a beer can but heavier, for Hannon guessed it was made of stainless steel instead of aluminum, and there was no label on its polished surface. What struck Hannon as strange was that the lid of the vessel was secured with one of those mason-jar levers that hooked onto a metal thumb on top of the lid; then the lever snapped against the side to form an airtight seal. He debated about whether or not to open it because that lever looked uncomfortably like the safety spoon on a hand grenade. But curiosity gained supremacy over his fear so he slowly pulled the lever up. The lid made that same *pssssssst* sound a can of vacuum-sealed potato chips makes when you pull back the ring tab, and he flipped it back to shine his light inside. It was a reddish sort of material, and not wanting to touch it, he used a key on his key ring to probe it and found that it possessed the consistency of rice pudding. Again, he was totally lost as to what it might be, so he snapped the lid shut and pocketed the can as he turned to head back through the sagebrush to the Wrangler.

He'd only taken about three steps when he tripped over her and tumbled into the dust.

Outside the Beltway that encircled Washington, D.C., in the treed greenery of northern Virginia, a giant edifice of glass and steel had emerged from the forest floor as a kind of temple to the practitioners of a secret art. The gleaming structure was the new headquarters building of the National Reconnaissance Office (NRO), where U.S. spy satellites downloaded their photo imagery for analysis and storage. It was an institution that had been cloaked from the public for decades, populated by a priesthood who embraced secrecy like sacred vestments. They rarely spoke about their work outside the security fence, and even inside they were guarded about what they said to each other.

At the very moment Hannon was finding the tripod depressions, a man walked down the corridor on the fifth floor of the NRO towards his private office. It was nearing 9 P.M. and although most of the worker bees had gone home for the evening, he'd remained behind. He wasn't the cardinal of NRO, but he was certainly one of the archbishops, in that he was privy to an astonishing array of equipment and data that could do things you just wouldn't believe. His name? Well, his name really didn't matter, because he was indistinguishable from that mass of mid-level bureaucrats who bloated the federal payroll inside and outside the Beltway. He was perhaps five-foot-nine with dark hair, a mustache and a narrow face with a poxy-looking complexion that was a legacy from his bouts with teenage acne. He wore a pale blue shirt with a worsted tie, and the ever-present I.D. tag hung on his breast pocket like a plastic scab waiting to be peeled away. Physically, the only remarkable thing about him was the crescent-shaped scar under his left armpit, and that was something only his wife had seen— and she believed it to be some type of advanced heart pacemaker.

He punched in the cipher-lock combination on the door and entered an office that was not particularly remarkable, with appointments similar to your friendly insurance man's business address. On the credenza, however, were two Sparc workstation computer terminals, and what they provided access to was positively mind bending. He was known within the NRO as a "controller"—not the accounting kind, mind you, but one of the few who physically controlled the operation of the KH-12 satellites that orbited the globe. In shorthand, he was the linchpin who exercised authority over a stable of technicians and analysts who sent uplink instructions to the birds, telling them where to point their very expensive lenses. And once the instructions were sent and the imagery was captured, another set of instructions—his instructions—downlinked the imagery to a set of electronic files for retrieval by the appropriate analyst. This could be imagery of an underground nuclear reactor being constructed in Iran, or a chemical weapons facility in Iraq, or a Russian nuclear missile submarine putting to sea.

Those who worked at the NRO considered themselves to be the chosen of the chosen in the priesthood of intelligence, but in reality the controller knew them to be insufferable bureaucrats for the most part. Only he and a few others at the NRO—the ones branded with the crescent-shaped scar—could be considered the genuine elite. He'd been selected over a decade ago, and inserted into the NRO some nine years ago. The number of times his talents had been tapped by Sirius had been few but, oh, so important.

Such a time was now.

He sat down at his credenza and powered up the Sparc workstation. Entering his personal access code, he called up the imagery on the latest pass of the Keyhole-12 satellite over southeastern Utah, which had been downloaded—per his instructions—into his personal electronic memory files. He'd been told to "keep an eye" on the mesa of the Kiva Tower in the event any uninvited guests showed up after the exchange. What better way to keep an eye on things than from 268 miles up? Who would know it was there? He called up the optical imagery first, and was gratified to see it was a clear night. Because of the darkness he didn't expect to see anything with the optical sensor and he didn't, so he switched to infrared—and what stared back at him gave him a start. On the cold background of the desert floor was the outline of a vehicle with its hot engine blooming on the screen.

Why would someone be on that mesa at that time of night? In freezing weather? He looked at the date/time group of the imagery and saw it was only eleven minutes old. Per instructions, he unlocked his desk and extracted what looked like an earpiece and mouthpiece to a telephone, except bulkier. From the phone on his desk he unscrewed the conventional mouthpiece and earpiece and screwed in the others, then set the voice-encryption settings. He got an outside line and punched in the number to the private line of his study at home, where the signal was call-forwarded to an anonymous number in the 702 area code. It rang once, then was answered by a detached voice that said, "Security."

"This is bird's eye," replied the controller.

"State your business."

"Unidentified vehicle on the LZ, eleven minutes ago."

"Understood."

In the cloud of dust, Hannon fumbled for his flashlight as he felt a steely hand push against his midriff, shouting, "Get offa me!"

"Who—!? What the—!?" His hand closed on the flashlight as he rolled over and shone the beam on a face that was covered by a ski mask.

"Get that thing outta my face, dammit!"

Hannon squirmed backward a couple of feet, saying, "Wha—!? Who—!?"

The parka-clad figure came to a sitting position. "Who am I!? Who the hell are you!? You tripped over me, remember!?"

It was at that moment Frank realized the voice was a feminine one, so he got to his feet and held out his hand. Warily, she eyed his offered paw, then took it and allowed him to pull her up. As she brushed the dust off her down pants, Frank scanned the mesa, then asked, "How did you get up here? I don't see another vehicle anywhere. Did you climb up?"

She kept brushing the sand off as she cryptically replied, "Gee, you must be one of those rocket scientists. I parked my car ten miles away and walked cross-country. I wanted to be alone up here, but in the most desolate place on earth somebody trips over me. I guess I just draw men like a magnet. When I heard you drive up I hid behind some sagebrush, waiting for you to go away."

Despite her chip-on-the-shoulder defiance, Hannon sensed a trace of fear lurking behind the facade. "So, I guess you're here for the same reason I'm here."

"I don't have to tell you anything, mister! This is public land and I'm a private citizen. Now you just get in your jeep and go your way and I'll go . . ."

They both heard it at the same time.

A helicopter.

A distant sound but unmistakable. That whirring, dragonfly undertone that carried a long distance in the still desert night.

"Okay, lady, I don't know who you are and you don't know who I am, but I got a feeling if we don't get out of here pronto we're toast!"

Her defiance crumbled at that moment, and she responded, "Okay."

Without hesitation he grabbed her wrist and yelled, "Come on!" pulling her into a sprint for the Wrangler.

They jumped in and Hannon fired up the engine, but then he quickly realized that although it was dark, the pilot would be navigating with those night-vision goggles, making them and the Wrangler the mother of all sitting ducks. He scanned the kiva and quickly conceded that the jeep would not fit under a sagebrush, and he was starting to think that escape was futile when he saw the jagged finger of the sandstone tower pointing toward the night sky. At the base of the tower was a chunk of sandstone that had succumbed to the forces of wind and erosion and had broken off from the ridge of the escarpment and rolled down into the caldera. It was about three times the size of the Jeep and rested close to the tower.

Hannon popped the clutch and executed a wheely to spin the Wrangler around, then sandwiched it between the boulder and the sandstone tower. The space was so narrow they couldn't open the doors to exit, but that was probably just as well. He turned off the engine and reached into the backseat for his suitcase to pull out his Browning .45 caliber High-Power, just as the helicopter popped over the ridgeline. He chambered a round from the clip and snapped the safety off, feeling rather impotent in the process. Against the forces bearing down on him, the gun was simply a psychological teddy bear to hold on to.

Miranda Park didn't know what to think.

The pilot of the McDonnell-Douglas MD-500 helicopter pushed the cyclic forward to drop down into the bowl of the mesa while he scanned the terrain with his night-vision goggles. As he traversed the ground through his helmet visor, the 7.62mm minigun slung under the chopper's nose rotated in tandem with the movements of his head. It was a state-of-the-art weapons system, as was everything that Sirius touched, and that was why he'd been so pissed when the control cable on his collective came loose when he was running up the engine for take-off. The ground crew had it fixed in fifteen minutes, and better that it happened on the ground than in the air, but even so, Sirius did not countenance slipshod performance. He would have to answer to Number One for the delay, and that made him nervous—much more nervous than skimming the kiva floor on a night flight. He'd flown for the "Nightstalkers" of the 160th Special Operations Task Force for seven years, and nap-of-the-earth flying with night-vision goggles was as normal to him as lacing his shoes.

He would scour the top of the kiva, then drop off the mesa and follow the mining road until it joined up with the highway; then he would work his way back in a spiral search pattern around the column formation.

Hannon saw the rotary wing aircraft's silhouette as it hovered above the escarpment ridge a few seconds, backlit by a milky moon hanging in the black velvet sky. It was one of those small, egg-shaped whirlybirds, hovering in the air like a sinister black wasp with an impatient stinger. Then it dropped over the edge and they were left in darkness with only the sound of a distant whirring as it faded into the night. Hannon put the .45's safety back on, taking several long slow breaths to get his heart rate below two hundred beats per minute. When he felt he was reasonably coherent again he whispered, more to himself than his passenger, "Who could marshal an armed helicopter response to a nighttime intrusion out in the middle of nowhere? The same people who could waste a C-130 over Greenland.''

She turned and stared at him uncomprehendingly. ''What are you talking about?''

All of a sudden he wondered if this was a chance encounter, and he leveled the High-Power at her, causing her eyes to flare. ''All right, lady. Just who the hell are you and why are you here in this particular wasteland at this particular time?''

She pulled off her ski mask, then held her parka tight around her, and in the darkness he could barely make out her features and pageboy haircut. ''My name is Miranda Park,'' she replied evenly.

''And . . . ?''

Even in the darkness she could sense two things about this man—that his anxiety matched her own, and that he was not the sort to trifle with. There was a presence about him, an edge that told her he would pull that trigger if he had to—even on a woman if she was standing between him and what he wanted. ''I'm deputy bureau chief of the Associated Press in San Francisco.''

That took Hannon down a couple of notches. ''Associated Press? You mean, you're a reporter? Oh, great. That's all I need right now.''

''That's your hard luck. Now who the hell are you? And would you mind putting that thing away?''

He shoved the pistol back in his grip, her response having put him a little off balance. The last thing he expected to encounter in the desert night was press. ''My name is Frank Hannon, Lieutenant Colonel, United States Air Force . . . retired.''

''And what are you doing here?''

''You tell me first.''

She turned away from him. "None of your damn business. Just pull this thing forward and let me out. Then I'll be on my way."

He made no attempt to move, sitting silently when the faint whirring returned, and she gasped.

"I would sit tight for a while if I were you," opined Frank. "He's probably executing some kind of search pattern. Eventually he'll run out of fuel and have to return to his base, and we'll leave when he leaves. I'll take you wherever you want to go, Miss Park, but I have a feeling I may be the only friend you've got right now. So you come clean with me and I'll come clean with you—then we'll go from there. Deal?"

She eyed him warily, like a cornered bobcat. "You get us out of here first. Then we'll talk."

Frank said, "Fair enough," then reached back for the thermos of coffee he'd picked up at the grandpa professor's diner. He unscrewed the top, saying, "I hope you take yours black."

FIVE

⟨⟨⟨⟩⟩⟩

He was a frail man, and old, yet he was consumed by an energy like a distance runner making his final kick for the finish line. He'd decided to commit it all to paper—a final treatise as it were—more to purge it from his soul than to convey it to another. How long he'd been stooped over the small writing table in the cramped room he couldn't say, but it came out of him in a torrent, through his fingers to the pen and onto the paper. When at last he'd finished, it reminded him of the afterglow that came from making love, or as he remembered it from so long ago.

The weakness came over him now. How long had he been in this tiny chamber without food or drink? Hours certainly. Perhaps days. He really didn't know. The clock said 3:37, but he hadn't a clue if it was A.M. or P.M., so he went to the drapes to pull them open and a shaft of sunlight greeted him, along with the most fearsome shock of his life.

•   •   •

Had the Cossack been looking up at that moment instead of at the little meter on the homing device, the events that were to follow might never have happened. But he was head-down in the passenger seat of the sedan as it cruised by the window of Michel Bertrand's room.

The needle on the meter was dancing an irregular pattern, causing the Cossack to curse and growl into his cellular phone, "Are you sure we're in the right place? The needle is acting squirrelly. I can't get a lock-on. Might be nothing but some signal leakage from a cable TV line."

"The satellite is getting a garbled feed on the designated freq and now your transponder is starting to break up."

The Cossack's mind pondered that, and suddenly he realized what could be happening. "A jammer? Could a jammer be fouling the signal?"

"Possibly."

With difficulty, Michel Bertrand had slid the frozen window up and exited out the back of his room at the Green Mountain Inn. His leg came down into two feet of New Hampshire snow and he held his treatise tight under his coat as though it were his only child. He felt he only had minutes, if not seconds, to do something. The odds were long, he knew, and time so short. In his other hand he clutched the little device that was no bigger than a transistor radio, but it had kept him safe longer than he'd ever dared hope, and he cursed the scar under his left armpit that hid the high-tech cattle brand.

Through the snow he sloshed to the office, his eyes darting in a search for the sedan. He came through the kitchen entrance and into the lobby, where he found the proprietor stoking the big fireplace for the cross-country skiers lounging about. He approached and made a request that was imploring yet discreet.

"There now," said the voice through the cellular phone, "your signal is becoming clear again."

They had driven back and forth a dozen times now, the needle teasing them each time they cruised by the inn. "It's got to be a jammer!" barked the Cossack. "He's got to be here! Hook a U! I'm gonna find that little sonovabitch!"

The dreebenheimer wheeled the car around and drove back toward the inn as the Cossack watched the needle dance.

"He's in this inn somewhere! Got to be . . ."

At that moment the Nobel laureate stepped out the kitchen entrance, and when he laid eyes on the Cossack—a security man he'd seen many times before—he panicked and began a pathetic run in the opposite direction. The dreebenheimer wheeled around again, and in a single motion the Cossack opened the door and yanked the old man inside before he could even utter a protest.

The sedan hurtled down the country road and out of sight in a moment, leaving behind the sheets of the treatise burning in the fireplace.

The morning sunlight illuminated the dirty film that covered the truck stop window as Hannon stared at the now-empty plate which had held a rubber steak and eggs ten minutes earlier. Now that the roadside cuisine was in his stomach, he had a pretty good idea what the mechanic's shop did with their old spare tires.

He and the woman had sat in silence on top of the

kiva for almost three hours to insure the helicopter had retreated for good, then using only moonlight for illumination, they'd made their way down the spiral road. Hannon had wanted to take the mountain road back to the highway, but the woman named Miranda had insisted they go overland. Hannon didn't know much about four-wheel driving, so he'd turned the Wrangler over to her. It had taken them two hours of sand, sagebrush and cactus before they'd picked up a highway, and when they'd finally hit asphalt she'd feared returning to her rental car, so they'd pushed on across southern Utah, finally reining in at the truckstop outside the town of St. George in the corner pocket of the state. They'd driven mostly in silence, and Hannon hadn't pressed her to come clean with her story as she'd promised, sensing that she was taking stock of him as they drove through the desert night. Now he was bone tired and only wanted to lie down on some cheap motel's spongy bed, but he forced the fatigue back in order to harvest the story he'd been promised—a harvest he wanted to bring in sooner rather than later.

She came out of the ladies' room with a face that betrayed fatigue despite the recent washing. She came to the booth and slid in across from him wearing her down jacket, black lycra stretch pants, and hiking boots and carrying a backpack slung over her arm.

''Sure you don't want something to eat?'' he asked.

Miranda shook her head and replied, ''Just coffee.'' Then she looked out at the eighteen-wheelers on the concrete apron.

''We had a deal, Miranda,'' he reminded her. ''You said once we reached safe harbor you'd come clean. Well, we're safe now, so come clean.''

She sighed, then met his gaze and said, "I'll go first, then you. Okay?"

Hannon nodded. "Awright. Shoot."

Miranda took a hit of her coffee, then inhaled deeply and began. "It all started, I guess you could say, when I was a kid. I had a neighborhood friend named Dreason. Joey Dreason."

The air brakes of a semi pulling in for fuel pierced the air, causing her to wince before she continued.

"Joey and I, well, I guess you could say we had a kind of Forrest Gump and Jenny relationship in that we grew up on the same street in Oakland and were pretty much inseparable during our early years. His father was a TV repairman and my dad was night wire editor for the late, great United Press International. When we were young—like five, six, seven—we had an instinctive 'connect' that only small children have, you know?" Miranda took a heavy pull on the brackish coffee. "At about the third grade, though, things began to change. Joey just couldn't seem to keep up in an academic sense, and socially we began to grow apart. His parents had him repeat the third grade, but still he didn't do well. Everybody thought he was retarded or something, and I'm ashamed to say that's when I started to pull away from him. After school he'd wait outside my house, wanting me to come out and play with him, but I had developed other friends and he was becoming a glaring liability to my budding social life. Like, who needs a major geek waiting for her every day after school? Certainly not I, so I started ducking him whenever I could, but he always found me."

"So what happened?"

"A couple more years go by. Joey's been pulled out

of regular school and put in special ed. No question in anyone's mind now that he's retarded. But then when he's about eleven, Joey is in his dad's repair shop. He pulls open a tech manual on some TV and his dad notices he's looking intently at some intricate circuit diagrams in the manual's appendix. The next day at his special ed class it's time for all the kids to play with crayons and paper, right? Well, instead of making blue and purple smudges with his Crayolas, Joey starts to replicate those circuit diagrams he saw the day before. His teacher says, what in heaven's name is this? Daddy is called. The crux of the story is that this eleven-year-old retard has replicated those circuit diagrams exactly, and I mean *exactly,* as they were in the manual.''

''You're kidding.''

''You ain't heard nothin' yet. It turns out Joey isn't retarded at all, but is something of a rare breed called an idiot savant. He's tested by a series of shrinks and a bunch of eggheads at UC-Davis. Seems little Joey's gift goes off the chart. He can't master his multiplication tables, but he can recall from memory a semiconductor circuit diagram that's more complex than a road map of North America, farm-to-market routes and all.''

Miranda shook her head in remembrance, then looked back at Hannon, and he noticed for the first time that her eyes were that crème de menthe green, with the kind of satiny luster usually poured from a bottle. ''I mean to tell you it was spooky. The complexity of what he could recall was beyond belief. Then it got better.''

''Better?''

''Yeah, better. He was shown some incredibly complex diagram of a semiconductor and Joey pointed to a junction point—one of maybe a thousand, right?—and said, 'This won't work.' And damned if he wasn't on the money. Then one of the eggheads thought he'd try and let Joey play with a computer. Not much luck at first, because he couldn't manipulate the keyboard very well, but when the egghead started explaining the programming to him, Joey took off like a rocket. He mastered BASIC in a day, then COBOL, then Assembler language. Then the eggheads found out he could scan a thousand lines of source code in seconds and pick out the bugs like *that*.'' Miranda snapped her fingers. ''Then ten thousand lines. Eventually he could take a hundred thousand lines of, say, COBOL, condense it down by a third and convert it to Assembler language and reconfigure the computer architecture so the process would move more swiftly.''

''All that and he couldn't do simple multiplication?''

''Off the weird meter, isn't it? As it was explained to me, the best theory on Joey's situation was that his brain focused all of its power on these incredible skills of his, but there was precious little left over to handle normal behavior. And emotionally''—Miranda sighed—''he was a basket case.''

''I take it he had a crush on you?''

She looked away. ''It went beyond a crush. He always wanted to recapture the time we had as children, and never understood we'd grown into adults. He could do all these incredible things, yet he couldn't pass junior high— and all the while those coming-of-age hormones were raging inside him. His parents worked out a deal with some research group at Cal Tech, in that the group could test Joey if they provided him with special ed on how to develop the skills to live a quasi-normal life—

things like shopping at the grocery store, getting a haircut, balancing a checkbook.

"Throughout my high school years, Joey would be away for testing during the week; then on the weekend he would show up at my house. Just sit on the curb for hours on end, waiting for me to come out. I had to set up a rendezvous with my dates and sneak out the back of my house. When I went off to college Joey went into depression. The doctors thought my visiting him would help, and it did for the time I was there, but when I left it only got worse."

"So what then?"

"He was in a hospital for a year, but then he got in with a good therapist and slowly started to come out of it. Since his parents were getting on in years he had to find a livelihood, and that's when Joey pulled a kind of coup. The kid who couldn't pass junior high got a job with Bell Laboratories." Miranda sighed. "He had this gift and was able to help them structure some kind of new operating system for their Long Lines Division that leapfrogged the state of the art by a generation. To put it in shorthand, every time you make a long distance call you're going through Joey's computer."

Hannon was undone, muttering, "This is crazy."

"Bell Labs had some kind of minder who looked after him. Drove him to work, made sure he got fed and all that."

"Then?"

"Apparently word got out in the technical community that Joey Dreason went beyond being a computer whiz. He was something on the order of a national resource. He left—or perhaps I should say was 'kidnapped'—from Bell Labs and went to work at Lawrence Livermore Laboratory.'' Miranda sighed again. "By then I was working in San Francisco. I was science editor for the bureau office, and about every three months I could count on getting a call from Joey, or he would just appear unannounced at work or my apartment. One day he shows up just as I'm going out for the evening and makes a big scene with my date. God, it was embarrassing. I really lost it then and screamed at him. Told him to get out of my life forever or I was going to have him thrown in jail.''

"And then?''

Miranda shrugged. "Joey disappears. I don't hear from him for over a year. I call his parents just to make sure he's okay, and they say he's still working at Livermore. I think maybe he's over me, right? Well, two more years go by and nothing. Then out of the blue he starts calling me again. Wants to see me because he's all excited. He's finally passed his driver's test and has a new car. Would I see him? I give him the brush off a dozen times, then finally . . .''

Hannon leaned forward. "Then finally what?''

In answer, Miranda reached into her backpack and took out a small dictaphone recorder and snapped in a micro-cassette. She said, "Then finally this,'' and hit the play button.

MESSAGE BEEP

JOEY (adolescentlike voice): Uh, hi, Miranda, it's Joey. You haven't called me. I called you nine times and you didn't call me back. Why won't you . . .

(Sound of receiver picking up.)

MIRANDA PARK (irritated sigh): Joey . . . Joey, why won't you understand? We're not kids any-

more. We grew up. I grew up. We went separate ways and—

JOEY: I have a car now, Miranda. A red one. And I have a driver's license, too.

MIRANDA: That's very good, Joey. I'm proud of you, but—

JOEY: Will you go driving with me? You can drive it if you want.

MIRANDA (angry now): No, Joey, I do not want to drive it! I don't want to drive your car, I don't want to see you, and I don't want to talk to you ever again. I'm not going to restart this constant business of your calling me all the time. Do you understand? I have a life, I have a job, I have a—

JOEY: I'm going to meet them, Miranda.

Pause.

MIRANDA: What do you mean, you're going to meet "them"?

JOEY (giggle): It's a secret, Miranda. You know those people I work for? The government people? They say I'm not supposed to tell. That it's important not to tell.

MIRANDA: I don't want you to get into trouble, Joey.

JOEY: I won't get into trouble. They say I'm really smart.

MIRANDA (sigh): With computers, Joey. You're smart with computers.

JOEY: They say I'm so smart they need me to be there.

MIRANDA: They? They who? You mean, those people at Livermore?

JOEY (a childlike snicker): I don't work there anymore, Miranda. Not for a long time. I'm at the lake now. In Nevada.

MIRANDA: The lake?

JOEY: Uh-huh. They call it a lake. But there's no water there. Why do they call it a lake when there's no water? It gets hot in the summer.

Long pause.

MIRANDA: Joey—this lake where you work—where there is no water. Are there airplanes there?

JOEY (surprised): Yeah. How did you know? Were you there and didn't come see me?

MIRANDA: No, no, I've never been there. Just read about it ... I think. Joey, do you work at a place called Groom Dry Lake in Nevada?

Pause.

JOEY: No.

MIRANDA (disappointed sigh): Hmm. So, what do they call this lake where there is no water?

JOEY: It's a baby lake.

MIRANDA: A baby lake?

JOEY: It's a secret.

MIRANDA (frustration growing in her voice): Yes, Joey, I'm sure it is. You said you were going to meet "them." What did you mean by that?

JOEY: I'm going to meet them. At a kiva.

MIRANDA: A kiva? That's some kind of circle or something, isn't it?

JOEY: They say it's near the Four Corners place. They say I have to be there to see the light circuits they're bringing. To make sure they work right. They say I'm really smart.

MIRANDA: Yes, Joey. You are very smart. Now who is "they," Joey? Who are these people you're going to meet?

Pause.

JOEY: They're from a different place.

MIRANDA: What do you mean, "a different place," Joey? Where do these people come from?

Pause.

JOEY: They're not people.

Miranda snapped off the recorder and stared at Hannon as he absorbed the taped conversation, and when she spoke her voice was barely audible over the jukebox. "I agreed to meet him the next day for lunch at the Viennese Coffee House in the Mark Hopkins. I was sitting by the window reading a magazine. I looked up and Joey was crossing the street. I waved and he came toward me. Then he . . . he . . ." Her face came down in her hands and she began sobbing.

"He what, Miranda?"

She moaned, then choked in a whimper, "He-he exploded."

Hannon waited for something further—an amplification or an explanation—but there was only silence. "What do you mean, 'he exploded'?"

114

Between tears, Miranda replied, "Just that. He exploded."

Hannon was more than a little confused. "Miranda—people don't just up and explode."

She looked up with a face of naked rage, shouting, *"Well Joey did!"* in a retort that was so loud more than a few trucker heads turned her way. "There was blood and bits of him splashed against the window! It was like he had a stick of dynamite inside him and it went off!"

Hannon was stunned by her intensity, and could only ask numbly, "What did the police say?"

Miranda covered her face again. "Their bomb squad people said he must have been carrying some kind of plastique explosive in his breast pocket because the residue tests indicated that's what it was. It was deliberately planted on him and detonated to keep him from talking to me. Since then I've gone half crazy trying to figure out what his death was all about. I found the place called the Kiva Tower on a map of the Four Corners area, and decided to travel there on the chance I might find something that could shed some light on Joey's death. I hadn't been there long when you drove up, so I laid low in the sagebrush until you tripped over me. Thought I was a dead woman."

"Did you see the tripod depressions in the sand?"

She nodded. "Just before you arrived. Now then, Colonel Hannon, I've kept my part of the bargain. What brought you to the Kiva Tower?"

Hannon tossed down some coffee, then asked, "You say you used to be science editor for the AP?"

"Yes, that's right. For the West Coast."

"You know anything about Cheyenne Mountain outside Colorado Springs?"

"You mean NORAD? Radars? That sort of thing?"

Hannon nodded. "I worked until a couple of days ago, in a division called the Space Control Center. That's where we tracked satellites and space debris with radar and optical systems." He recounted in precise detail what had happened with the appearance of the four bogeys, and showed her the printout of the FAA air traffic data, then told her about the untimely demise of Airman Chester Wick on the Greenland ice cap.

Miranda mulled it over, then pointed at the printout. "This imagery and the depressions I saw you take pictures of are significant, but it's still circumstantial. Those could be faked."

"So we need a witness," he said flatly.

She nodded. "Wick was a witness who could verify the material from Cheyenne Mountain, but like you said, he's dead."

"There was another witness, but he was at a distance."

"Who was that?"

"I ran into him in Bluff, Utah. Runs a roadside convenience store. He saw the lights from a distance as they arrived at the kiva; then again when they took off about four A.M. At first he thought they were helicopters; then in the time you could strike a match—his words—they shot straight up and disappeared from sight."

Miranda shuddered. "Spooky, but still not enough evidence."

"Evidence for what?"

She lit up a Camel. "Evidence to convince an editor to go out on a very long limb and run the story of the millennium. But without hard and fast evidence we'd be treated like a couple of lunatics. Do you have anything else?''

Hannon mulled it over. ''There's another guy in Cheyenne Mountain who saw the data on the bogeys, an NCO, but I don't want to involve him. Other than that, all we have is this.'' He reached into his pocket and retrieved the mason jar/beer can.

She took it and flipped open the lid, recoiling at the spoiled smell. ''What's this?''

''I don't know. I found it on the moon just before I tripped over you. I think we should get it analyzed.''

Frank didn't realize it, but when he said ''we'' he'd subconsciously joined forces with the woman.

Miranda pondered all that had happened, then said with a hard intensity, ''We need something more. A lot more, really. Something of this magnitude doesn't need a smoking gun. It needs a smoking howitzer.''

''Like maybe one of those craft landing on the White House lawn and little green men coming out and saying, 'Take me to your leader.' ''

''That would be a good start.''

Hannon shook his head. ''I wouldn't know where to begin. This is something—forgive the parody—but this whole mess is something that's on a different planet from my experience.''

She looked at him with a trace of disdain. ''I thought you said you were in intelligence.''

''I said I worked in intelligence. I didn't say I was intelligent.''

She fired up another Camel and said, ''Okay, let's back up here.'' She took out her cassette recorder again and cued it up to the spot where she asked Dreason:

Joey, do you work at a place called Groom Dry Lake in Nevada?

Pause.

No.

Hmm. So, what do they call this lake where there is no water?

It's a baby lake.

A baby lake?

It's a secret.

She clicked it off. "That dry lake has got to be Groom Dry Lake in Nevada."

"You mean that place at Nellis Air Force Base? Where all the black Skunk Works stuff is flight-tested?"

Miranda nodded. "It's on the Nellis test range at a place called Area 51."

Hannon shook his head. "But he said it's a baby lake."

She shrugged. "You don't know Joey. That could mean anything, like he thought it was a small lake or something. The operative words are a lake with 'no water,' 'Nevada' and 'people with the government.' Like I said, I used to be a science editor. The stealth fighter, the SR-71, the reputed Aurora spy plane that officially doesn't exist—they were all flight-tested at Groom Dry Lake. That has to be the place where Joey was working on this, this, whatever the hell *this* is. I'll bet you dollars to doughnuts the people who were at the Kiva Tower came from that base at Groom Lake. Maybe we can find one of them and scare them into talking. Show them the stuff on Joey and Wick."

Too tired to argue, Frank said, "Okay. So we head for Nevada."

She took out her Utah map and flipped it over to the map of Nevada. "Since I left my luggage behind, I guess we'd better hook it down to Las Vegas to refit. Then we'll head up north to Groom Dry Lake and see what we can find."

"Las Vegas? That sounds like a gamble."

SIX

The day had come and gone, and the grandpa professor had just finished his evening dose of agony in getting his Alzheimer's-stricken wife bathed, fed and into her bed restraints. It was Hell on Earth to watch the vibrant woman he'd known and loved for forty-three years descend slowly into a vegetative state, and more than once he wondered what he'd done to receive such a Providential judgment from on High. He'd had her on an experimental gene therapy that seemed to help a little, but Medicare didn't cover it and the treatment had soon turned into a black hole that sucked down their savings, cars, home equity and credit lines secured by his pension. When the money ran dry she'd resumed her downward slide as if nothing had happened. Trying to purge it from his mind, he wiped his leathery face with a towel and trudged back to the convenience store-diner to eke out the niggardly revenue that might trickle in from sundown until he closed the place up at 9 P.M.

But tonight, despite all the onerous tasks that were

wearing him down a peg at a time, his mind was elsewhere. He paused under the twilight sky and looked out on the silhouette of the Kiva Tower in the distance. What on earth had happened there? Those lights were like nothing he'd ever seen, and he knew he wasn't hallucinating. He'd lived all of his life in this country, and he knew what was real and what wasn't. That man from the Air Force—the man named Hannon, or who called himself Hannon—what was he after, and what did he find up there? Raines recalled the last time he'd been up on that mesa. He'd been—what?—a lad of sixteen? Seventeen? Eons ago. Could it be that right here, in his own backyard, in his own territory, something extraordinary had occurred? A meeting between *worlds*? The very thought of it was something to energize his intellectually rich but scrabble poor life, and he was drawn to it like a moth to a flame. He had to find out for himself—to venture forth and see if anything was there. Now. Tonight. He simply could not wait.

Raines entered his modified Quonset hut and found his granddaughter perched on the stool behind the counter, her nose buried in a *Premiere* magazine. He recoiled at the thought that after forty years of scholarship, this was to be his intellectual legacy. Upon his entry the adolescent perked up and slid off the stool, then grabbed her purse and headed for the door.

"G'night, Grandpa. See you tomorrow."

"Wait, Sheila."

The impatient face turned. "What?"

"Something's come up. I have to go out tonight and I need you to stay and lock up. Schools are letting out for the holidays and we may get some student traffic through here tonight. We need the revenue, so I'll need you to stay.''

Sheila looked as if her grandfather had cut her heart out with a dull spoon. "But Grandpa, I *can't*! I just *can't*! Martha is picking me up in two minutes and we're going to Belle Star's in Blanding. Teddy is going to be there tonight!''

"I'm sorry, Sheila. It can't be helped. We need the money, what little there is of it. You can lock up at nine, but no earlier.''

"But, Grandpa . . .''

"That's it, Sheila. Now I have to go.''

Raines didn't wait for a further rebuttal and exited the Quonset hut. He climbed into his 1968 Chevy pickup with the shaky heater and started up the engine. He checked and made sure the beam on his flashlight had a good battery, then dropped the pickup in gear and took off.

Number One was sitting in the saddle of a U-shaped console where a host of computer monitors glared back at him, and it was rather queer how the machines seemed to exude greater warmth than he. Number One had a soul that was all but enslaved by the dark forces of its own id—a soul that had long ago bade farewell to its humanity. Even so, this hardened soul could still feel fear, and it was fear that oozed from every pore as he keystroked some instructions into the computer to call up the imagery from the Kiva Tower, taken clandestinely by his mole in the National Reconnaissance Office. On the screen appeared the greenish infrared image of a sport utility vehicle as Number One explained, "We couldn't get a tag number on the vehicle because it was night and because of the angle of the shot, but it's definitely a late-model Jeep Wrangler. Once we received word from our man inside the NRO, I scrambled the security chopper we had on standby. It was under cover in the barn of a ranch we leased nearby.''

Number One kept on talking, but his eyes never left the screen, even though he was talking to the person standing directly behind him. In a way it was as though he were playing ostrich, and the screen in front of him was the sand covering his head. ''From the time we received the intruder alert it was thirty-seven minutes until the chopper arrived on the scene—a delay of seventeen minutes caused by a broken cable on the helicopter's controls. Upon its arrival it scoured the top of the mesa and executed a spiral search pattern around it for ten miles out, but it could not find the vehicle. I have issued a bulletin throughout the Network for any data on a late-model Wrangler that fits this description. Of course, if we had a plate number it would be no problem to—''

There was a *whack!* that sounded like the report of a rifle shot, and a tiny geyser of blood erupted from the side of Number One's cranium. The bolt of pain that ran down his spine like a scald should have elicited a scream of agony, but Number One willed himself not to cry out or move to staunch the flow of blood, for the man behind him might have interpreted it as a sign of weakness.

''You have been Number One of Sirius security for seven years, and in that time you have never given me cause to question your judgment.'' The voice behind him was even and flat, as if he were giving a waiter his order for lunch. ''I chose the Kiva Tower for the rendezvous based on your recommendation. I did not want

123

them to get too close to our facility here, and based on my desires I felt your selection made sense.'' The man standing behind him gently placed the handle of a hickory cane on Number One's shoulder—a handle that was a figurine cast in the shape of a cobra's head with its hood flaring. And although it was made of silver, it seemed no less sinister than a genuine serpent preparing to sink a pair of fangs into his neck.

The voice continued. ''I also accepted your recommendation that no clandestine guards or intruder sensors be left behind on the mesa because you said the venue of the Kiva Tower was so remote that no one will ever go there, and we can monitor the site through our man at the NRO just as a precaution. Now it appears we have had an intruder where you said no intruder would appear, and we have no idea who this person may be or what they may have stumbled upon.'' A long and deliberate sigh followed, like an exasperated parent with a recalcitrant child. ''And then this business of Bertrand reappearing from the grave. My dear boy, what am I to do with you?'' A mournful pause. ''What can I say? I'm disappointed. It appears I can no longer rely on your judgment.'' On Number One's other shoulder the man rested his wrist, placing in Number One's peripheral vision an upturned hand holding a radio detonator—the same kind of device he himself had used to blow up Joey Dreason—causing his eyes to flare as the man's thumb caressed the keypad. ''Now, perhaps I should not do this, but I'm going to give you another chance. I expect you to find that vehicle on the mesa, for it's a glaring breach in our security, wouldn't you say? A hole in the dike, as it were. You plug that hole and wipe up all the water that has spilled, and I do mean all of it, and we'll forget about your little shortcomings. But if you fail, then I'm afraid your number will come up here.'' He tapped the radio detonator with a scaly finger. ''Do we understand each other, my dear boy?''

As blood trickled onto his collar, Number One remained motionless and replied with a whisper, saying, ''Yes, Mr. Krieger.''

''Very well. Now then, my boy, I shall leave you alone. You have a hard task ahead of you. By the way, you might call the dispensary. You seem to have a nasty cut on your scalp.''

Morgan Raines cursed the pickup that was almost thirty years old as it struggled up the Anaconda mining road. He figured only four of the six cylinders were hitting on the ancient engine, if that, but despite its shortcomings it brought him to the summit where the Kiva Tower rose like a sentinel toward the stars. Although it had been more than half a century since he'd been here, and the sky was dark, the memory of that youthful visit rushed over him like a wave and he remembered it vividly. He took a few moments to absorb the remembrance, then decided it was time to undertake the task that had brought him here.

Using the headlights of the truck as a searchlight, Raines began a serpentine course over the top of the mesa, and like Hannon he soon picked up the trail of tire tracks. He followed them to where they dispersed, and at that point he stopped the pickup, killed the lights and engine and got out with flashlight in hand.

Holding his parka close around him, he allowed the magic of the desert night to work its curative powers, and for a moment he was one with the mesa, drawing strength from it and forgetting his onerous problems. He'd devoted a lifetime to this land and its history, trying to keep its legacy alive when so few cared. He was one of a handful of white men who had mastered the Navajo language, and had written professional papers extrapolating how the Anasazi language might have been constructed—but what had all that scholarship gained him? He sighed at the injustice of it all, and to salve his wounded soul he communed with his surroundings a bit longer—then shook himself free of his moodiness and flicked on the flashlight to begin canvassing the kiva.

Like Hannon, he examined the spots where the vehicles had parked, then he went deeper into the mesa and found the first tripod depression. He knelt down and touched it, gingerly, as if it were a precious gem. Then, with the beam shaking, he rose and looked further, finding another, and another, and another. "God Almighty," he whispered. "What has happened here?" He was lost in his own thoughts when a sound intruded. It was faint at first, then it grew in intensity—a whirring sound, like a mosquito buzzing around his ear. Then suddenly it popped into view above the ridgeline that encircled the kiva.

It was a helicopter, black as coal and backlit by the white disc of the moon. It held Morgan Raines in a hypnotic trance, for somehow he knew that here, at this moment on a desolate desert mesa, he was beholding Death on a pale horse.

Las Vegas.

The stark contrast of the neon oasis against the desert sands was such a jolt to the senses that a chorus line of leggy showgirls high-kicking on the moon would seem less bizarre.

Hannon peered out his hotel window and watched the pirate battle in the Treasure Island Hotel lagoon for the third time. They had it every ninety minutes or so like an entertainment Old Faithful, with full-scale galleons, shooting cannons and Errol Flynn wannabes swashbuckling their way into the tourists' hearts. Gad, what a way to make a living. He turned away from the show performed under Christmas lights, and went to the desk in the room that held a half-eaten tray of room service food and the mason jar/beer can. He had to have the contents analyzed and had been thinking about the best and fastest way to do that, then decided to take a long shot. He opened his little address book and ran down the numbers under P, then dialed the number he was looking for.

After two rings it was answered with a matronly voice saying, "Special Agent Pinkston's office."

"I'd like to talk with Pinky, please. Frank Hannon calling. He knows me."

"A moment, sir."

Thomas Pinkston was the FBI's Special Agent in charge of the Colorado Springs office. Hannon had gotten to know him on a contractor fraud case the agent had been investigating at Peterson Air Force Base. Hannon's involvement had been peripheral, but he and Pinkston had hit it off, having occasional dinners or golf games ever since.

A welcoming voice came on the line, saying, "Frank! What a surprise. I called your office yesterday to invite you to our Christmas party but they said you'd left on leave."

Hannon endeavored to keep it light and breezy.

"Well, let's just say I heard the siren's call of the Bahamas. Since I had the leave accrued, I thought I'd bug out and take early retirement."

Laughter. "Can't say I blame you."

"Don't worry, though. You'll see me at my retirement ceremony."

"Wouldn't miss it," replied Pinkston.

"Great. Say, listen, Pinky. After I left the office something cropped up that's hard to explain over the phone. Suffice to say it's an intel matter that needs a swift resolution if I'm going to punch out on time. The long and the short of it is that I need a substance analyzed."

"A substance? You mean drugs?"

"It could be that, but I don't think that's what it is. To tell the truth, it looks like rice pudding, but I wondered if I could lean on you for an off-the-books favor. I'd like to run this through the FBI Crime Lab on a personal-favor basis. I'll explain it all when I get back to the Springs."

"Ummm. Okay. Cost you three strokes on the next game."

"Make it four. So who can I send this to who will put a rocket under it and give me a quick turnaround?"

"Send it to Dr. Garson Flesher. He's associate director of the lab. I'll call him straightaway and tell him it's on the way."

"Going out FedEx today."

"So where can I reach you?"

Hannon sidestepped. "Well, I'm in transit at the moment. Hope to catch a flight down to the cay and get a contractor working on the house sooner rather than later. If you need to reach me, just leave word on my answering machine at home."

"Right, Frank. Enjoy the sun. It's snowing here this morning."

"Guess it'll be a white Christmas."

Hannon rang off, then dialed D.C. information. One call later he had the Crime Lab address. He was scribbling it down when the phone rang. He answered it with a cautious, "Hello?"

Miranda asked, "Get your beauty sleep?"

"Feel like a new man."

"I got refitted. You ready to go?"

"Got to get some dry ice from the hotel kitchen and make a stop at the FedEx office."

"Dry ice?"

"To keep the sample iced during shipment. The canister I found on the kiva was vacuum sealed, and since it's been opened the top layer of this rice pudding seems to have spoiled or something. I dug out some of the fresh stuff from the bottom and will ship that off."

"Off where?"

"I'll explain later. Meet you at the front desk in an hour."

Frank couldn't get over the sea of humanity that surged through the casino like a never-ending current, offering their tithes to the slot machines as though they were some sort of god that could give them a metaphysical redemption. Frank just shook his head at the spectacle. He would stick with poker, where skill could be brought to bear.

She came around the elevator bank looking refreshed, wearing a sweater and slacks and carrying a new suitcase. "I got us some overnight reservations at the Star Voyager Inn up in the little town of Rachel," she said.

"That's about a three-hour drive north of here near the border of Nellis Air Force Base. I understand their rooms are only converted mobile homes, but it's as close as we can get to Groom Dry Lake for an overnight. Maybe we'll run into somebody up there who can help us."

Frank nodded. "I sent the sample of that rice pudding, or whatever the hell it is, to the FBI Crime Lab for analysis."

"FBI?" She sounded anxious.

"Relax. I have a friend who's doing it for me off the books."

She looked unconvinced. "Okay. Let's check out and get going."

They joined the checkout queue, and twenty minutes later had their receipts. As they started toward their car they failed to notice two men—one blond and muscular and obviously a weightlifter, and the other short, stubby and middle-aged like most men in the lobby. The only difference was that he wore a checkered, narrow-brimmed fedora like Bear Bryant always wore on the sidelines. Frank, Miranda and the two men tailing them traveled up a massive escalator, went past the theater advertising *Mysteré*—a big Vegas extravaganza—then entered the garage. As they got into the Wrangler, Frank glanced in the rearview mirror and saw the man with the checkered hat get into a blue Crown Victoria across the parking aisle. He thought nothing of it as he asked Miranda, "Okay, what's the best route to this town of Rachel?"

Miranda slapped her knee. "Dammit! I left the map in my room."

"Hmm. Well, why don't you run back and get it. I

might as well hit the men's room before we take off on a long drive anyway.''

They jumped out and returned to the lobby. Miranda went to the front desk while Frank made a trip to deflate his bladder. Ten minutes later they'd joined up again and were back in the Wrangler. Frank fired up the engine, then backed out and began driving the loop-de-loop down the multitiered parking garage. The next level down he halted to allow an elderly couple to back out with their land barge of a Coup de Ville. The car seemed to move in slow motion, and during the pause Frank glanced up in the rearview mirror again . . . once more laying eyes upon the faceless middle-aged man with the checkered hat.

As the Coup de Ville pulled out, Miranda said, "I've been thinking about what we saw at the Kiva Tower. Those footprints must belong to people from that Groom Lake base. If we can just find somebody who works there and scare them into talking—show them the stuff on Joey and Wick. Tell them if they don't talk they could be next, then maybe . . ." She cut herself off in midsentence as Hannon came to attention in the driver's seat, the whites of his eyes growing ever wider as he stared in the rearview mirror. "Hey, what's the matter with you? You look as though somebody just walked over your grave."

Hannon sucked in air like a man going down for a long, deep dive into the abyss, his color turning ashen before he slowly exhaled with an "Ohhhhh, shhhiiiittt.'' Then he abruptly wheeled into the vacated parking space left by the Coup de Ville as the Crown Victoria shot past in the rearview mirror.

"What is it!?" she demanded with a shrillness in her voice that wasn't there before.

He looked upon her as though she were a pariah of some kind, a plague-bearing banshee from whom he should flee for his life. "Dreason," he said in a whisper, for a whisper was all he could muster. "He was killed because he was coming to you, a reporter, with the story. He was a security risk. They couldn't let him follow through in contacting you, so they iced him right before your eyes. But I missed something. How did they know Dreason was about to spill his guts?"

Siphoning from his pool of fear, she shook her head nervously.

"The answer is obvious. The guy was brilliant, but he wasn't nailed down too tight. He couldn't be trusted. So . . ."

She caught her breath. "He'd be under surveillance."

Hannon nodded. "Soup to nuts they'd have the guy locked up, including phone taps. He calls your number. You're a reporter. Then after Dreason is whacked they'd want to know how much you knew, to make sure nothing had leaked out."

Now it was her turn to look ashen-faced. "They would tap my phone."

Hannon's mind raced. "Not only phone taps, but mail intercept and . . . credit cards. How did you pay for your room?"

Miranda swallowed. "Diner's Club."

"And you said you flew to Albuquerque and rented a car to get to the Kiva Tower. Somewhere along the way, they lose you." Suddenly it all came together for Hannon with a horrific logic. "So when you check in at

Treasure Island with your Diner's Club, they pick up the trail.''

"Oh, no."

"Oh, yes. They have people in the lobby ready to ID you when you show your pretty face—in the company of a recently retired Air Force officer."

Miranda drew herself up into a fetal position on the seat, but Hannon pressed on. "Their surveillance team picks us up and Frankie leads them right to his car!"

"How do you know this?"

He jerked his thumb. "I saw the same guy twice. In a checkered hat. When we came out the first time, then again just a minute ago. Couldn't be a coincidence."

"But they don't know who you are."

Hannon shook his head. "The car. This Wrangler. They'll trace it back to my NCO in Colorado Springs, and then to me. Since I was the one who saw the bogeys on the Cheyenne Mountain radar, that will make me damaged goods in their eyes, and now that they know we've made contact . . ."

Now it was Miranda who came to attention in her seat. "I'm damaged goods as well."

There was that moment of silence that comes when two people realize they share a common mortal danger. Then Hannon snapped, "We've got to ditch the car. Fast. Get your gear."

Without a word, Miranda reached back for her suitcase and Hannon reached for his. As they jumped out, Hannon said, "Back into the hotel."

They joined a trickle of people entering the elevated walkway back into the hotel. They hustled along at a quick pace and jumped on the crowded giant escalator going down. There was a large video screen pitching a commercial for the *Mysteré* show and the Ziegfried & Roy magic show in the neighboring Mirage Hotel. On either side of the screen were mirrored panels.

"Maybe we're being paranoid," whispered Miranda. "Maybe it was a coincidence."

"Just look in the mirror."

Miranda gasped, for stepping onto the escalator was the stubby man with the checkered hat, and behind him came the weightlifter.

"Any ideas on how to lose them?" whispered Frank.

Miranda looked around. "Maybe. I saw something when I was out shopping." As they reached the bottom of the escalator she took him by the hand and said, "Follow me." She peeled down a walkway to the right where a small crowd had gathered in front of some large, sliding glass doors. Above the doors was the notation *Shuttle to Mirage*. An electric trolley came up, disgorging its payload of passengers. Then the doors slid open on the entryway and the crowd surged forward. Miranda pulled Frank's hand toward the open threshold, then stopped. He understood what she was doing, and both of them kept their eyes to the front, not venturing to turn around. They waited until the door started to close, then at the last millisecond jumped on board and turned around to face Checkered Hat and Musclehead glaring at them through the glass partition. As the trolley pulled out they saw the two men turn around and double-time back the way they'd come.

The trolley traveled about 150 yards, then stopped to let the passengers off. Frank started to move forward, but Miranda held him back, saying, "Don't get off." Frank nodded in understanding, and on the return journey he could see from the elevated trolley as Checkered

Hat and his gorilla sidekick sprinted toward the Mirage termination point.

Back at Treasure Island, they blasted out of the trolley and made their way out the back entrance. Then they circled around to join the sea of humanity on the Strip. Frank veered them off towards Caesar's Palace until he could hail a cab.

Getting in, Miranda said, "Where are we going?"

"To Groom Lake, one way or another. . . . Driver, I need a hotel that can accommodate a small travel budget."

The cabbie cranked the meter, saying, "I hear ya. Bad luck, huh?"

"The worst."

Ten minutes later they were deposited at an establishment called the Galaxy Hotel, a collection point for people who were down on their luck, or had come to Vegas on a minimum wage with maximum expectations. The bell captain wore a stained uniform jacket three sizes too large, and from his breath Frank could tell he'd gotten an early start on his daily alcohol ration.

"Checking in?" the bell captain inquired.

"Actually, no," replied Hannon. "I need to rent a car."

The captain shrugged. "They got Hertz at the airport."

"No, you don't understand. I need to rent a car privately. No forms, no credit cards. Nothing. I'll pay cash."

"Cash?"

Hannon reached into his pocket and peeled off $1,500 from a roll. "I'll need it for three days. No questions asked. Think you can help me?"

The captain took the money, then pocketed it and pulled out a set of keys. "The gray Mustang parked in back."

"A man after my own heart. Back in three days."

The captain nodded. "Three days it is."

As the couple disappeared around the corner, the captain shrugged. If they didn't show up he'd report it stolen and get the insurance money. That plus the $1,500 would be a sweet deal.

SEVEN

———◦◦◦◦———

Lucian Wintersgill was prowling through the boxes of
Christmas decorations with the feeling of clumsiness that
revisited him every year. Seemed like whatever he hung
on the tree, his wife and daughters had to go back and
retrofit his efforts to make it good enough to pass muster
with Santa. He didn't know why he went through this
Yuletide exercise of trimming the tree. Perhaps it was
just a habit from when his offspring were kids. His
youngest was home from college and the eldest was in
town with her new husband. Despite what had happened
in the Mountain, he'd tried to keep things normal at
home, but everyone had picked up on his somber mood
and guessed correctly that something was amiss with his
job.

The doorbell rang and Wintersgill looked at his watch.
Who would be ringing the doorbell at 9:15 P.M.? It was
a little late for carolers.

"Want me to get it, Dad?" asked his youngest.

Wintersgill lifted himself up off the floor, wearing

blue jeans and a work shirt, then brushed the spruce needles off himself. "No. I'll see to it." He went to the door to open it, feeling both surprise and more than a little fear at the person who greeted him. "Why, Colonel Tyndale. What brings you here? I mean, come in, come in. It's freezing out there."

"Thank you, Chief." Tyndale stepped inside wearing his uniform topcoat, even though it was long after duty hours.

"Well, this is something of a surprise, sir. Can I offer you some hot cocoa or something?"

"No, no, thank you, Chief. Is there somewhere we can talk? Privately?"

Wintersgill felt an owl in his stomach sinking its talons into his gut, and he struggled to keep his voice casual. "Sure, sir. Right this way." He led Tyndale into his workshop, which was a converted corner of the garage, and they sat down on opposing work stools.

Tin Man smiled. "I won't take up much of your time, Chief. I understand you have a Jeep Wrangler. Is that correct?"

The owl was flapping like crazy now. "Why, yes, sir, but it's not here right now. Colonel Hannon has it."

"Frank has it? Whatever for?"

Wintersgill shrugged. "He took off on terminal leave. Asked if I could trade it for his Mustang for a couple of weeks. Is there some kind of problem, sir?"

"Trade it? What could he possibly want a Jeep for?"

Another shrug. "He just said he wanted to get away into the woods for a while, sir."

"Frank? In the woods?" Tin Man was incredulous. "You must be joking. He wouldn't know the difference between a pine cone and a porcupine."

"Is there a problem, sir?"

Tin Man studied Wintersgill, then focused on the silver braid of his hat. "As you know, Chief, all privately owned vehicles of our security staff have a coding in the Department of Motor Vehicles computer. Seems your Jeep Wrangler was abandoned at the Treasure Island Hotel in Las Vegas earlier today."

"Las Vegas?"

"Yes. Frank was registered there, but checked out and left the vehicle behind. Strange, isn't it?"

"Yes, sir. Very. I hope Colonel Hannon is all right."

Tin Man was the picture of familial concern. "Yes, I do hope nothing untoward has happened. If you hear from him you'll let me know right away, won't you, Chief?"

"Certainly, sir."

Wintersgill escorted Tyndale out the front door and softly closed it behind him, whispering under his breath, "You're really on your own now, Frank."

Outside, Tyndale got into his Cadillac El Dorado and drove to his townhouse, where he pulled into the garage and entered through the kitchen. He walked through the living room and into his study, which was a sacrosanct place that he considered his retreat within a retreat. Unmarried, he'd had his townhouse appointed to his personal tastes, and it had a mannish feel to it. He hung up his topcoat and uniform jacket and went to the phone, where he unscrewed the mouth- and earpieces, then screwed in the voice-encryption devices. He punched in the number with the 702 area code, and almost instantly the phone was answered.

"Security."

"This is Number Forty-three. I need to speak with Number One immediately."

"Hold the line."

There were a few clicks before a hard voice came on the line. "This is Number One."

"I talked with Hannon's NCO named Wintersgill. Hannon traded his car for Wintersgill's Jeep, so it was definitely him with the Park woman in Las Vegas."

There was a stone silence at the end of the line, then, "How much does Hannon know?"

"He knows about the radar contacts for sure. Beyond that I can't say."

"You can't *say*? Yesterday you said everything was iced and put to bed. Now this guy Hannon shows up at the landing zone, and then he shows up holding hands with that reporter. Is that your idea of something on *ice*?"

Tin Man was the quintessential bureaucrat, and he knew that when he couldn't confront an issue he should deflect it. "Do you have a trail on him or the woman?"

The sound on the other end of the phone crossed the spectrum from a growl to a moan. "The trail went stone dead after they gave my men the slip in Vegas. I've got Network people working the credit cards and NCIC computer on both of them, but except for the Wrangler we've got nothing in hand. They could be anywhere by now."

"They'll surface," Tin Man assured him. "Eventually they'll have to—sometime, somewhere—and when they do we'll have them."

"That's not good enough. Wait. I've got another call."

Impatiently, Tyndale held the line. He didn't like dealing with this Number One. He was too shrill all the time—the mark of someone who was in over his head. And he had no class. Tin Man preferred dealing with people of his own caliber.

Number One returned and the tone of his voice had changed from nervous to domineering. "All right, this is a disaster on your part. I just talked to Krieger. He wants you and Shrake on-site at S-4 tomorrow."

Now it was Tin Man's turn to sound a little shrill. "Now wait a minute! That's not possible. Our CinC just returned from a trip to Russia and—"

"Tomorrow."

And the line went dead.

Tin Man gripped the phone tightly, as if trying to choke it, for he knew it was moments like this when his consuming ambition came home to roost. With a sense of fear and anger he replaced the receiver in its cradle— and in so doing felt a bead of perspiration trickle past the scar that was cut into the flesh under his left armpit.

Hannon traversed his 12x power binoculars across the valley floor of Groom Dry Lake and took in a vista that was perhaps even more desolate than the one he'd left behind in Utah. Scrub brush dotted the sandy ground of a valley that was bordered by arid brown mountains, and along the shoreline of the dry lake was a cluster of utilitarian buildings that possessed all the aesthetic appeal of a federal correctional facility—aircraft hangars, radar dishes, a water tower and glorified pillbox structures punctuated the desert landscape under the noonday sun. Hannon was lying in a prone position on the crest of a 6,300-foot mountain called White Sides, which was on public land just outside the boundary of the Nellis test range, which was only a small part of the U.S. government's enormous real estate holdings in Nevada. Before him, on the bed of Groom Dry Lake, was the parcel of land known as Area 51.

"I've seen a few Russian MiGs flight-tested around here. They were captured during the Cold War and are kept in that large hangar over there."

Lying between Hannon and Miranda was a man named Carl Lacey who was the unofficial "King of the Gadflies"—gadflies being a group of activists who had tried over the years to pry open the secrecy lid that covered Area 51—without much success. Still, Lacey and his minions had made themselves a thorn in the side of the government by discovering this crow's nest on public land; and keeping a lonely vigil night after cold desert night with their video cameras, night-vision goggles and frequency scanners trained on the mysterious facility known as Area 51.

"After the sun goes down I use a pair of night-vision binoculars," Lacey said. "Ironically, I have a pair manufactured in Russia. Reputedly, the Aurora spy plane is supposed to be stationed here, but I've never seen it, and it wouldn't surprise me if the thing is a myth."

Intrigued, Hannon asked, "How fast is it supposed to go?"

"About Mach five," replied Miranda. "The rumor is that it's powered by a pulse-wave-detonation engine, if I recall correctly. Spits out a contrail that looks like doughnuts on a rope."

Lacey nodded with admiration. "Correct."

After Hannon and Miranda had left Las Vegas they'd taken a long drive through a desolate landscape until they'd reached the tiny hamlet of Rachel—a spot in the road that boasted a few mobile homes and precious little else except the Star Voyager Bar & Grill, which looked like a bunker with curtains. After a few questions were put to the bartender, they quickly learned that the man polishing off a space burger in the corner was Carl Lacey, the Gadfly King. With a muscular forearm he waved them over and invited them to sit down, and Miranda showed him her AP press card. Hannon liked Lacey immediately, and thought he bore a striking resemblance to Fernando Llamas. After they'd had a late lunch, Lacey offered to take them up the mountain the following morning.

"Who are those guys?" asked Hannon, looking at a pair of men about two miles distant who were wearing desert fatigues and standing next to a white Jeep Grand Cherokee. They were staring back at him with binoculars of their own.

Lacey grunted with distaste. "Those are the Cammo Dudes."

"Cammo Dudes?" asked Miranda. "What are Cammo Dudes?"

"Security," replied Lacey, "and bad-asses, the lot of them. Words like 'Constitution,' 'public land,' and 'rule of law' mean nothing to those snakes. They've detained people on public turf and—well, I can show you better than I can tell you." He whipped out a cellular phone from the pocket of his desert fatigues and punched in a number. "I'm calling Harry Winters, another Gadfly. We sort of have a code between us . . . Hi, Harry. Top of the morning. Tell Jesse and Walt we got the Cammo Dudes' attention over on White Sides and they can probably make it up the Chaparral Road to the Eagle's Nest undetected if they hurry. . . . Right. Bye.''

"What was that all about?'' asked Miranda.

"Just watch,'' replied Lacey with a mischievous smile.

About three minutes later Hannon saw a helicopter lift off from behind one of the buildings and take a vector to the north.

"So what's the deal?'' asked Hannon.

Lacey held up the phone. "It's against the law to monitor cellular traffic without a court order. The Cammo Dudes do it all the time. They just listened to my conversation and dispatched their security helicopter to the Chaparral Road to intercept some friends of mine who aren't there.''

"Umm,'' mumbled Hannon. "So security for this place is tight as a drum.''

"Tighter,'' conceded Lacey.

"If you two will excuse me, I'm going to run up to the summit for a minute.'' Miranda rose and walked to the sixty-foot cliff escarpment that separated them from the true summit of the 6,300-foot mountain. At the base she dropped her backpack and tightened her Gortex parka around her. She was wearing stretch lycra climbing pants and a pair of shoes that looked like ultra-thin Nikes. From her backpack she retrieved a pair of skintight gloves, and started going up the cliff facing like a fly.

"Well, damn. Would you look at that?'' observed an impressed Hannon.

Lacey shrugged. "I don't know why she's doing that. She can walk up the other side, no problem.''

"I guess because it's there.''

The two men watched in silence as Miranda executed a free-hand climb up the face, then disappeared over the top.

"Known her long?" asked Lacey.

"Just a few weeks, since I transferred in from the Kansas City AP office." Hannon hated to lie to such a nice guy, but he knew it was better this way. "She's the science whiz. Thought a piece on Area 51 would be a good feature. I'm just along for the ride."

"Umm. She's rather attractive. But then, stay out in the desert long enough and a female Gila monster starts to look pretty good, if you know what I mean."

They shared a laugh, and Hannon thought it would be a good moment to probe. "Say, Carl, you've been here a long time. Ever seen any—what I mean to say is—any of those, ah, UFOs in the sky?" He tried to keep it light.

Lacey replied with a wry smile and a shrug that comes from answering the same question too many times. "You can often see spectacular lights in the night sky around here, but this is the Nellis test range—the place where the Air Force runs its Red Flag training exercises, which are realistic as hell. The lights in the sky are magnesium flares dropped by the fighter planes to sucker away infrared missiles. For some people those lights have become a kind of religious experience. They see what they want to see, and in their own mind they truly become UFOs." He shrugged again. "But until the government opens up this place to public view, I guess we'll never know what goes on out there."

Hannon nodded, then asked, "Ever talk to any people who actually work at Groom Lake?"

Lacey shivered, and it wasn't from the cold. "That

friend of mine, Harry. The one I just called on the phone.''

"Yeah?"

"He tried once. And I would emphasize *once*."

"How so?"

Lacey pointed. "See any houses out there? Apartment buildings? No, you don't, because there aren't any. The people who work at this base fly in from Vegas every morning on private 737s called JANET flights. Then they fly back to Vegas in the evening. One night Harry parks at the McCarran airport in Vegas and watches a JANET flight land at the private Area 51 terminal. He picks out one of the deplaning passengers at random and follows him home, then knocks on the guy's door and says, 'Hi, I'm Harry Winters, one of the public-activist gadflies who watches you from White Sides. I wondered if you'd talk to me about what you do at Area 51.' ''

"So what happened?''

"To Harry's surprise, he was invited in. The guy pours him a drink and then excuses himself. Comes back and they chat about the weather. Five minutes later— and I mean five minutes—comes a knock on the door. In walk two plainclothes Cammo Dudes with a Vegas cop. The JANET flight guy says he wants to press charges on Harry for forcible entry, trespassing, et cetera. Harry spends the night in the slammer, and our lawyer has to get him out with a habeas corpus. He's released with a stern warning from the judge about invasion of privacy, national security and such. So, no, in answer to your question, I haven't talked to people who work there.''

Hannon grunted, feeling that his strategy on how to

extricate themselves from the gallows had just gone up in smoke.

"Well, here comes your rock climber," said Lacey. "I guess we've walked off breakfast. Let's head down and have lunch."

Lacey washed down his pastrami on rye with a Budweiser, then began his primer class for Miranda and Hannon on Area 51. "The base was first built in 1954 as an out-of-the-way spot for the CIA to flight-test the U-2 spy plane—you know, the one that Francis Gary Powers was shot down in back in 1960. Nobody was around here then except for the odd sheepherder, rancher or miner, and that's pretty much the way things are now. Since 1954, however, the base has grown and become a test facility for about every Cold War black project you can name—the SR-71 Blackbird, the F-117A stealth fighter, the TR-3A Black Manta, the new A-17 swing-wing stealth fighter-bomber and so forth. Anyway, the secrecy that covers this place is severe, which during the Cold War may have been justified, but today I think it's just a bunch of bureaucrats trying to keep their budgets away from public scrutiny. All us gadflies are aviation buffs and have an insatiable curiosity about things that fly. Sitting on those mountaintops can be hot or cold work, depending on the season, and boring out the kazoo, but at least they know we're there.

"The government appropriated the land of our White Sides observation post a couple of years ago, but we filed suit to challenge that action and finally got a temporary restraining order a couple of months ago to open it back up. I'm not optimistic, though. I think we'll even-

tually lose in court and White Sides will be closed down
for good.''

Hannon rose and said, ''I gotta make a phone call.
The lunch is on us, Carl, but I'd like you to fill in Miranda on what happened when your friend tailed one of
the Area 51 workers at the Vegas airport.''

Carl said, ''Sure thing,'' flashing his Fernando Llamas
smile as he welcomed the time alone with Miranda.

Hannon went to the cash register and cleaned out the
manager's supply of quarters, then stepped outside to the
pay phone, where he pulled out his black notebook. He
flipped through it to the main number for the FBI headquarters in Washington, then got the operator on the line,
gave her the number and started paying for the call the
old-fashioned way by chugging quarter after quarter into
the machine. He figured seven dollars worth would give
him enough time.

The line began ringing, then a metallic voice said,
''FBI.''

''Crime Lab, please.''

''One moment.''

Click-click. Ring.

''Crime Lab,'' came a bored voice.

''Calling in reference to a request from Special Agent
Pinkston in the Colorado Springs office. I'd like to speak
with Dr. Garson Flesher.''

''Hold the line.''

A few seconds went by, then the silence was broken
by an exasperated, ''All right, Pinky, all right! Can't you
give a man a moment's peace? You call twice, then the
assistant director calls three times wanting to know if
I've heard from your mysterious Colonel Hannon. Well,
I haven't, and my desk was cluttered enough without all

this tracing paraphernalia they brought in here. But anyway, this time you're in luck. I've got the results on that material sample your man Hannon sent to me.''

Frank felt as if he'd just stepped into a tub of ice water as he grunted, ''Uh-huh,'' trying to match the resonance of Pinky's larynx.

There was the sound of papers rustling, then Flesher said, ''Ah, yes, here we are. The sample sent to us by your fugitive Hannon was found to be human bone marrow.''

''*Human bone marrow!?*'' Hannon winced, but the words were out of his mouth before he could catch them—the results so shocking he couldn't stop himself in time.

''Yes, that's what . . .'' There was one of those weighty pauses, then Flesher enquired tentatively, ''Pinky, is—is that you I'm talking to?''

Hannon slammed down the receiver to break the connection as he held onto the wall for support. His mind was in a tumult, trying to fathom what the hell could have happened up on that mesa that would have involved *human bone marrow*. And beyond that, the FBI white coat had called him a ''fugitive,'' and some assistant director of the bureau was giving the hunt high priority. Christ, whoever or whatever was in charge of the conspiracy had wasted no time in connecting him with the Wrangler.

Frank went back inside, and Miranda only had to glance at him to know something was very rotten indeed. ''Oh, no. What now?''

''Where's Carl?''

''Went to the head. What was that call about?''

Hannon swallowed. ''You're the test-tube genius.

What do you know about human bone marrow?''

She looked at him quizzically, not sure she'd heard right. ''Human bone marrow?''

''Precisely.''

Miranda fingered her auburn bangs, intuitively not liking the question. ''Well, marrow is where white and red blood cells are manufactured. Treatment for some bone marrow cancers are made by using donor marrow, or by taking the patient's marrow out, treating it with radiation to kill the cancer cells, then reintroducing it back into the body. Less chance of rejection that way. Why?''

Hannon swallowed, then whispered, ''The material in that can, the one I found at the landing zone before I tripped over you—it contained human bone marrow.''

The impact was sobering, causing Miranda to wilt in her chair.

''And it gets better,'' said Hannon bitterly. ''I was on the phone with an FBI white coat who works in their lab. It seems I'm now an official fugitive.''

''Fugitive? From the FBI?''

Frank nodded.

Miranda's breathing became labored. ''And Carl told me what happened when his friend tried to tail the Area Fifty-one worker from the Vegas airport.'' They looked at each other for a painful interlude. Then Miranda shuddered and said, ''I think we're out of options. All we can do is run.''

Frank did nothing to dissuade her. ''This is too big for a couple of little pissants like us. We should've stayed at home and—''

''*Sarah!?*''

The voice sounded like some rusty gears meshing

against their will, and it caused Frank and Miranda to turn in surprise.

"Sarah?" came the question again.

He was maybe five-foot-six and rather stout, wearing stone-washed bib overalls that had been washed with genuine stones, and his black work boots had endured rock scrapings until they were whiter than white. A top-soil of gray stubble clung to his fleshy face, and an abrasive pungency suggested his last encounter with a shower had occurred about the time Nixon had resigned. His white hair, what there was of it, had a cuisinart styling that amplified the wildness of his eyes as he focused on Miranda with a glazed intensity. He looked like a prospector who'd fallen down a mine shaft in 1849 and had just emerged.

"Sarah?" he asked urgently.

"Now, now, Herky, just take it easy. This lady isn't Sarah." Carl Lacey came up behind the old-timer and patted his shoulder. "This lady's name is Miranda. Now why don't you just come over here and let me buy you a beer to take home, okay?" Gently, Lacey turned the old-timer around and steered him toward the bar where he paid for a Budweiser and stuck it in the pocket of the miner's bib overalls. Then he guided the elderly man out the door with an admonition not to drink it until he got home.

"Who was that?" asked Miranda.

Lacey sat down and smiled. "That's old Herky Hartsell. Been here since before God, digging up the ground and hoping to strike it rich. There's something like ten thousand abandoned mine shafts in Nevada—real death traps—and I think Herky dug half of them." Lacey chuckled as he shook his head. "He's harmless, but a few bricks shy of a full load, if you follow me. Lives on Social Security and comes in here for his beer ration. We always get him to go home with it because one brew will put him away and he'll drive that old pickup of his into a ditch—or worse."

"So who is Sarah?" asked Hannon.

Lacey pursed his lips and shook his head. "That I don't know. I guess Miranda reminded him of her, whoever she is."

Miranda stared through the door at the old man's ancient pickup as it drove off, having felt her reporting instincts energized. "So where does he live?"

Lacey jerked a thumb. "In a trailer up the road a ways."

"I don't understand this," said Frank irritably as he drove along the dusty road. "We've got everybody in the country with a badge after us and you want to go talk to the oldest Section Eight in the entire state so you can follow a hunch?"

Miranda turned in the seat. "Carl said this man Herky had been here a long time."

"Since before God."

"Okay, before God. Young people think they're so smart, that old people don't know anything. But old people see things over time. Things that younger people miss." She looked out the window, debating whether to tell him more. "When my grandmother was on her deathbed—eighty-two years old—she'd been in a nursing home for six years. We all thought her mind had been on hold for a long time, but when I was alone with her she looked at me and told me, out of the blue, that my father had been having an affair with my aunt for the last three years. I was unhinged—how could she possibly have known something like that, having been in the home for the last six years? After she died I asked my father about it, thinking my grandmother was delusional, but to my utter shock he confessed. I won't go into what followed—it got pretty sordid—but it taught me that old people have powers of observation that can be unreal sometimes. Maybe Herky has seen something, or knows someone from way back who has worked at the base and is retired. Someone who will talk to us. It can't hurt to try."

Frank shrugged. "I guess you're right. I just hope he's sober when we get there."

"That's his pickup there ahead."

Frank parked their Mustang and stepped outside into the chilly breeze. The house trailer in front of them was encrusted with rust and dust, and Hannon felt the only thing missing was a "condemned" sign. On the stoop a bored, one-eared cat licked its paw and eyed them with suspicion as Miranda stepped up to the door. Frank said cryptically, "Don't knock too hard. You might knock it over."

Miranda gave him a scowl, then tapped on the screen door. Almost a minute passed before the old prospector opened the door and his face came alive. "Sarah? You came back!"

Miranda stepped back and shook her head. "No, Mister Hartsell. I am not Sarah. My name is Miranda Park. I'm a newspaper reporter. This is my friend Frank Hannon. We'd like to talk to you for a few minutes if you don't mind."

He stared at her for half a minute, his face betraying

some private lamentation. "Sarah?" he repeated with a wistful timbre.

Miranda sighed, figuring the old boy was too far round the bend to be of any help. But then the prospector turned and said, "Come on."

Gingerly, Miranda opened the creaky door and entered, while Frank rolled his eyes and followed. They stepped into a confined living area that was a bit of a shock, for while the exterior of the trailer looked a half step removed from condemnation, the interior bordered on the immaculate. The wood floor was swept and polished, the single bed was made and covered with a colorful bedspread and fluffy pillows, the kitchen was neat as a pin and on the bureau was an old black and white photograph in a gleaming silver frame. The trailer had a definite feminine touch, and the only item that seemed tied to the occupant was an old leather bag of prospecting tools in the corner. Herky motioned for them to sit on two rickety chairs in the dining area while he went to the bureau and picked up the framed photograph. He passed it to Miranda and said, "Sarah."

Miranda looked at the picture, and was struck by the resemblance between herself and the image. Then she passed it to Frank, asking, "Who was she, Herky?"

Herky sat down in a worn wicker rocker in the middle of the chamber and began moving back and forth like a rusty metronome—the Budweiser on a small table at his elbow. He seemed to be talking to someone else when he said, "Jesse and me come out heah in thirty-seven." His voice did a good imitation of the creaky screen door. "We from Oklahoma. Stillwatuh. We was seventeen and the Depression still on. 'Tweren't no war yet, so we headed west. Come out heah and started prospectin'."

He continued to rock, his mind absorbing the memory. "Struck a good claim. Not silver, mind yuh, but coppuh. Sold our stake tuh a big minin' outfit. Had a little money and I sent back to Stillwatuh for Sarah. We goin' get hitched." The chair punctuated the air with a squeaky refrain. "Sarah come out. Met the train at Carson City. Jesse come along, too, and we stayed in Carson City for three days. Promenade Hotel. I find a preacher, and Jesse goin' be my best man. Next mornin' Jesse and Sarah gone. Never saw her agin."

He covered his face with a hand, trying to hide the wound that had gutted his dreams almost sixty years before. Miranda got up and went over to the chair and knelt down beside him, placing her hands on his forearm as he looked up. "I'm sorry about Sarah, Herky. I really am. But I'm not Sarah. My name is Miranda. Do you understand?"

In mourning for himself, Herky nodded.

"Herky, I'm looking for something and maybe you can help me. It's very important, it really is, so will you listen to me?"

He looked upon her as though she possessed a halo and wings, and nodded.

"Herky, have you ever seen those lights in the sky? Those lights that are like a different kind of airplane? That come from up in the sky, from the stars?"

Herky leaned his head back and silently closed his eyes for at least a half minute. Then finally he said, "Flyin' saucers."

"Yes, Herky. That's right. Flying saucers. Have you ever seen them?"

Herky's eyes remained closed, and Miranda thought

he'd drifted off until he murmured, absently, "Oh, yeah . . . I seen 'em."

Gently, Miranda probed. "Where have you seen them, Herky?"

Slowly, the chair rocked. "Up in the sky."

"Yes, up in the sky. But have you ever seen them on the ground?"

The rocker creaked. "Yep," he said casually.

Miranda shot a glance at Hannon.

"Where, Herky? Where did you see the flying saucers on the ground? At Groom Dry Lake?"

His eyes remained closed as he slowly shook his head. "Naw. T'ain't there. The ones I seen anyway."

Miranda leaned closer. "Then where, Herky? Where did you see them? Tell me."

Herky sighed, as if he were explaining the obvious. "They be over at Papoose Lake."

"Papoose Lake?"

Herky nodded, his eyes still closed. "Yeah. That's whar they be."

Suddenly, Frank felt a sensation as if a mouse with cleats was running up and down his spine. "Papoose Lake? Papoose is a baby."

"Baby lake," whispered Miranda. "Joey said he worked at a baby lake."

Hannon pulled out the geological survey map from his coat pocket and unfolded it. Then he scoured Nellis Air Force Base and found Papoose Lake—another dry bed some seven miles from Groom Lake, at the grid coordinates of S-4. He shook his head in frustration and went to the floor beside Miranda. "There is a Papoose Lake, but it's about seven miles west of Groom Lake—which means it's seven miles deeper inside the boundary. There's no way he could get there. He must be making it up."

Herky's eyes shot open, and Frank felt as though he'd been drilled with a prospector's spike hammer. Then the eyes closed again and he said softly, yet with authority, "I seen 'em."

Miranda looked at Frank, then increased the pressure on the old man's forearm. "Can you take us there, Herky? Can you take us to this Papoose Lake?"

Herky shook his head. "I cain't right now. I gots tuh go prospectin'."

With a feeling of frustration and a certainty the old man was full of locoweed, Frank said, "There's a couple of kegs of Budweiser in it for you if you take us there."

Herky's eyes shot open again and he stared at Hannon for a long moment. Then he replied, "I wunt three."

Hannon shrugged. "Okay. Three it is."

Herky grabbed his buttered leather cap and stood, saying "let's go."

They were crammed into the cab of Herky's ancient conveyance, *sans* functional heater, and after thirty-some miles of winding dirt strips that barely resembled roads, Hannon began to grumble. Slapping the map, he said, "I can't even follow where we are. If he's taken us inside the base boundary and we get stopped by those Cammo Dudes and ID'd, then we are dead meat, lady. Did you think of that?"

Herky drove on, oblivious to the conversation.

"We may be dead anyway," she said. "So let's just play out the hand and see what he wants to show us."

Frank looked out at the rolling arid landscape. "I could've been on the beach in the Bahamas right now.

This very minute. But, oh, no. Frankie has to play detective. Sometimes I think I must take a stupid pill every morning.''

''Just put a lid on it, okay? Let's play out the hand and—''

''It up ahead theah.''

Frank and Miranda looked down the road, and off to the side was a hill that rose a few hundred feet from the valley floor. Down at the skirt of the hill was an apron of tailings from a mining excavation, and this was where Herky pulled off and stopped. They exited the cab, and Herky waddled towards the boarded-up opening of the tunnel.

''What the hell is that?'' muttered Frank, but Herky didn't reply. He casually pulled a claw hammer out of his pocket and pried the nails out, then yanked off a couple of boards, making an opening large enough for them to enter. Herky crouched over and went inside, and Miranda was about to follow when Hannon said, ''If you think for one minute I'm going in there you are out of your mind, woman. The roof could fall in or something.''

Miranda hitched her backpack up on her shoulder as she disappeared into the opening, saying, ''See ya, pussy.''

Frank's manhood could not withstand such a frontal assault, so with a groan he crouched over and followed them into the mine. At first it seemed pitch black because his eyes had not adjusted to the dark, but slowly the narrow rocky walls and rotting timbers came into view, and in a voice that was two octaves above his normal timbre, he quavered, ''Oh, terrific.''

Herky flicked on his flashlight, saying, ''This-a-way.''

They tramped down the tunnel, kicking up dust that got into their nostrils and made Hannon cough. As he hacked and wheezed, he forced out the words "This is really a *bad* idea."

Miranda ignored him. They were about 120 feet inside and almost at the terminus of the tunnel when she asked, "Did you dig this out, Herky?"

"Yep."

"When was that?"

"Fifty three, fifty four. Thereabouts."

At the terminus point there was another boarded-up entrance, but this one had a door made of slats, resting on hinges with a rusty padlock closed on a hasp. Herky fumbled with keys and sprang the lock, then pulled the door open and shone the light inside. It was a vertical shaft going straight down into an abyss, with a rickety ladder affixed to the far side. Without a word the old-timer and then the lissome lady reached out and started descending the ladder, and faced with being left in the darkness, Hannon moaned, "Wait up, damnit. I'm coming."

Frank reached across and grabbed a spar of the ladder, then stepped across and started going down, hand over hand, foot over foot, on spongy wooden slats that he realized were only a little younger than himself. As he grunted and groaned, descending deeper and deeper into the black void, Frank was dumfounded, totally perplexed as to where they were going. What could possibly be at the bottom of this pit? And how did one man excavate something like this? He called out, "Herky! How on earth did you dig out this mine shaft?"

"I dint," came the casual reply. "Not this part anyways."

"You didn't? Then how—*yeeoww!*" Hannon's foot broke through a rotten spar, sending a cascade of dust, cobwebs and splinters raining down on his fellow spelunkers below.

"Hey, watch it!" yelled Miranda.

Hannon was getting pissed. "Listen, Miss El Capitan, I have a little more body mass than you, okay? This ladder has been here since the Korean War or something. It wouldn't feed a starving termite—"

Miranda snapped, "Everybody stop!"

"What is it?" demanded Hannon, looking down between his legs to see the bobbing flashlight beam playing off the dust.

"Quiet!" yelled Miranda.

"Now what?"

"Shut up, Frank. Listen!"

Hannon did as he was told, putting his ear to the air like a reluctant eavesdropper. Then he heard it. It was incredibly faint at first, and barely discernible as it caressed the tympanic membrane, but it was definitely there. "Water," he said softly. "I hear water. Like a stream, or a brook."

"Me, too. Let's follow Herky down to the—hold it! Wait a minute! Shine the light up here, Herky," ordered Miranda. "On this side of the wall."

Hannon saw the beam splay around the shaft, then freeze.

"Son of a bitch!"

"Miranda, what is it!?"

"It's . . . it's a painting."

"A painting? What? Somebody hang the Mona Lisa in here?"

"*No.* Not that sort of painting. This looks like antelope of some kind. Sort of like those caves in France, you know?''

Frank's mind sprinted forward. "So that's what Herky meant when he said he didn't dig this. Maybe it's been here hundreds, maybe thousands of years.''

The light resumed its descent, and as Hannon followed his spelunking comrades down he tried to discern the brush strokes on the wall, but they had faded into the heart of darkness.

"Whoa!" yelled Miranda

"Miranda, are you all right?"

"Hoooeee! Yeah. Yeah, I'm all right. Just hang on to the ladder. This shaft gets wider. A lot wider.''

Hannon continued down, curiosity overtaking his fear and loathing as he descended another fifteen feet—until, as Miranda had promised, the wall of the shaft fell away into nothingness, leaving him suspended on a flimsy ladder in a dark abyss. The fear and loathing returned, and with the utter blackness and loss of reference point he started to panic—then he heard Herky's feet crunch gravel as the flashlight bobbed away.

"Ya'll just wait here a bit." His voice was casual, as though a bus was expected.

Hannon fervently hoped that Herky's cranial arteries had not ossified too severely.

Miranda touched down beneath him. "C'mon, Frank. Just a little farther.''

A little farther to what? He continued down until his foot stepped on terra firma, or rather gravel, and Miranda gave him a congratulatory embrace. Then they heard the strike of a match, followed by a sudden illumination. At first they had to squint because they'd been in darkness for so long, but as the light from the Coleman lantern filled the cavern, a sense of wonder weighed upon them like a heavy rucksack. Hannon whispered, as if he were in a cathedral—and in a sense he was. "God in heaven, I've never seen anything like this before."

Miranda giggled nervously. "Wow, this is cool."

There were in a gothiclike grotto of an underground river, hollowed out over eons by the belt of water that lay before them. The pristine canal was about ten feet in width and its surface was mirror calm, except for a little waterfall from a dammed-up pool near the head-water of the chamber. The walls were a rippled yellow limestone that reflected the light of the lantern with an eerie incandescence, and the smell was moist and musky on the nose. The ladder they'd just descended rose up to a hole in the vaulted arch of the grotto, where it disappeared.

"Look!" Miranda pointed with a child's astonishment at the wall near the ceiling. "There are more paintings— I mean, petroglyphs."

"Petroglyphs?"

"Etchings cut into the stone. Look—another antelope. A bear."

"And some kinda ram."

Miranda nodded. "Desert mountain sheep maybe? And look—Indians under the sun." She drank in the faded images, then inspected the forty-foot gap from the beach to where the petroglyphs began, which caused her to emit a low whistle.

"What is it?"

She pointed. "You see where the ripples on the wall begin—just below the point where those etchings leave off?"

Frank nodded. "Yeah."

"I think the level of the water must have been up there a long time ago, near those glyphs. Then, over time, the water cut through the rock to the point where we are now. That means those etchings are incredibly old, and I suppose this river must have been a water source for the people who made them."

There was the crunch of gravel as Herky approached them with the lantern held high, Hannon thinking he might have been Diogenes in search of his honest man. The ancient prospector jerked his thumb and said, "Git in and let's go."

Frank looked behind him. On the gravel beach rested a rubber raft with an electric trolling motor on the stern, and it was at that moment he had an inkling of what was to come. "Why, Herky," he said softly, with genuine astonishment, "I'm afraid I misjudged you."

Hannon's contrition was received with no apparent reaction as Herky reached into the raft and pulled out a second lantern. This one he lit and hung on a makeshift sprit on the raft's bow; then he turned down the illumination on the other lantern and left it on the gravel beach. "This'll be a little lighthouse, showin' where we left off," said the octogenarian prospector. "Now you get up front there and sit yerself down, Sarah, and you push us off, Jesse."

Hannon's confidence took a giant leap backward at Herky's comment, but once Miranda was on board he girded his loins and pushed the raft gently into the water, then stepped in with the grace of a middle-aged hippo. Without comment, Herky started the electric motor and guided them downstream toward the point where the cathedral narrowed into a small passage. "Motor's on the low settin'," said Herky to no one in particular. "Current does most of the work goin' down. Need the motor comin' back.''

Frank was grateful he'd heard the words ''Comin' back.''

As they neared the tunnel, Hannon couldn't help but feel he was in some kind of amusement park ride—but his sense of fantasy was in conflict with the reality before him. The walls narrowed, and they entered the passage in awed silence, save for the gentle hum of the electric motor and the lapping sound of the water against the raft. Frank looked around him, his senses stupefied, for this went beyond anything he'd ever dreamt about. Using a subterranean river as a means of navigation? The very idea gear-stripped his mind as he reached out to touch the limestone walls of the tunnel, smoothed over millennia by the ribbon of water. And what awaited them at the end of this passage? Their salvation—or something else? Whatever the case, Hannon knew that their concept of ''normal'' would no longer apply.

Miranda, too, was overcome by the subterranean canal, causing her to forget, however fleetingly, that her life was in jeopardy as she beheld the awesome yet gentle beauty of nature's power. She felt privileged to be able to experience this, and was curious as to who these ancient peoples were who'd practiced their artistry on a stone canvas. But as inspiring as the dimly lit passage was, she couldn't ignore the presence of the man beside her. For all his sissy protestations, she instinctively felt Frank Hannon was someone she could rely on when things got nasty, and she felt things were going to get very nasty before all this was over. Yet through the sense of fear and the unknown, he imparted to her a feeling of safety. With a bemused smile she leaned over and whispered into his ear, "So how you doin', Jesse?"

Hannon smiled wryly. "Okay, Sarah. I just hope Herky doesn't bear a grudge. If I was going to off someone, this would be the perfect place to do it. Lord, I didn't know these sort of things existed. I'm here, but I don't believe I'm here. Where does this water come from? Where does it go? And who made those paintings?"

"Pre-Columbian certainly. Probably prehistoric. Thousands of years, maybe tens of thousands of years old when you consider the erosion caused by the river. If we didn't have people gunning for us, this would be a fantastic story. This waterway must take us to that Papoose Lake he was talking about."

"Right underfoot of the Cammo Dudes, and they don't even know we're here. Talk about stealth—yo, look at that, another grotto."

Michel Bertrand paced back and forth in the tiny room like a sentry on duty, his mind filled with thoughts of the cosmos, the laws of physics, and the future of humankind and his own life. Few could match the Nobel laureate's technical brilliance or his intensity when pursuing a scientific truth, but despite his intellectual powers, even he knew when he'd reached the end of the trail.

The scientist halted the march and sat down on the metal bed, wondering if his incredible gamble had paid off. In any case, he knew there were only a few grains of sand left in the hourglass before there was a reckoning for him.

That was when the door opened.

An old man entered, walking with a slight limp and

leaning on a hickory cane with a silver cobra's head for a handle. Bertrand looked up and sighed, then said with resignation, "Hello, Arctus."

The old man smiled and replied, "My dear Michel, how have you been?"

If you could imagine a snapping turtle out of its shell, you'd not be far off the mark in describing Arctus Krieger—both in appearance and temperament. Physically he was of medium height, but stooped, his head almost hairless except for a band of whitish, grayish hair on the back and sides of his cranium. His round face was punctuated by a boxer's nose that looked as though it had been broken with regularity, but it hadn't—it was just a twist of nature. His skin had an almost translucent quality to it and seemed to flake, possibly from some disease, and his eyes—well, to put it charitably, they scared the hell out of Bertrand, for they were dark, beady and bloodless, the eyes of a predator with an intensity that was a window to the icy will lurking beneath the surface.

By contrast, Bertrand seemed to possess the fragility of a praying mantis, for his limbs were slender and his touch was deft, as though everything he handled were a thin-shelled egg. His head was a bit large relative to the rest of his body, and his penetrating blue eyes seemed amplified by his wavy white hair.

"May I sit down?" inquired Krieger solicitously. "The leg, you know."

Bertrand motioned to the chair beside the small desk and Krieger sat down, leaning forward to rest his hands and chin on the flared hood of the cobra handle. He silently stared at Bertrand for the longest time, those predator eyes searching for answers, until finally he said, "Michel . . . you of all people. After I thought we'd reached an understanding. You came into the project against your will, of course—a number of our people have—but I thought you had come to embrace Sirius and all it could mean for us.''

Bertrand sighed again. "You are playing with fire, Arctus. With them and with the legitimate government. A single misstep and it will all come crashing down on you—on us all.''

"Misstep?" Krieger sounded incredulous. "I haven't made a misstep in over a quarter of a century, Michel. Why do you think I created the Network? To keep everything bottled up nice and secure. My arm is longer than you could possibly imagine, Michel. I mean, I found you, didn't I?''

Angry, Bertrand rose. "But you risk exposure at every turn! They monitor all of our transmissions and you *know* what they'll do if any of this gets out! It's too horrible to contemplate.''

The predator eyes burned with a fury as he snapped, "*Nothing* is going to get out, Michel! That is, as long as my Nobel Prize winners quit trying to play boy scout. I control you, I control the situation and most importantly, I control *them* because I represent the best means of achieving their goal. We provide them what they require and they meet our demands. It's as simple as that. They abhor the thought of exposure even more than we do—and your 'friend' is a living testament to that abhorrence." For a moment Krieger shuddered, for even he was unnerved at the thought.

"But you *must* bring the legitimate government into the project, Arctus. The Plan is too complex to execute without their cooperation. If you . . .''

Krieger raised a hand to cut him off. "This 'legitimate' government you so proudly hail is nothing but a gaggle of insufferable politicians who can't see past their own elections, Michel. Can you imagine Sirius in their hands? It's absurd. The situation is much better under our control—which brings me to my next point, and you must listen carefully. I am willing to overlook your little escapade and bring you back into Sirius if you will accept the situation as it is and provide a full debriefing under polygraph on your absence. We are kindred spirits in so many ways, you and I, and it would be tragic if Sirius lost you. I mean, look at how far we have come since you joined the project, and you've encountered wonders you could not even imagine.''

In response, the Frenchman remained silent, causing Krieger to sigh as he said, ''Come along. Get your coat. Let's see if we can rekindle your passion for all that Sirius can bring to us.''

Time flowed like the river, and along the way the tunnel widened and narrowed, inhaling and exhaling like a bellows stoking a flame. Frank and Miranda watched as the pigments of stone melded from ocher into olive, and then from olive into a sepia brown as the lantern on the bowsprit played with the subterranean hues. At times the passage became so narrow they had to hunker down in the raft, grazing the droplets of water that clung to the ceiling like sweat on an athlete's forehead. Then, just as suddenly, a new grotto would open before them, but none as majestic as the first. Once they had to portage around a sandbar, but other than that, the trip was remarkably smooth and constant. Hannon figured they were making maybe four miles per hour, and four long hours had passed, so that made sixteen miles via this

unorthodox method of navigation. The thrill and astonishment of the initial experience was behind him now,
and he wondered what lay ahead. He also worried about
Herky's sanity as he grew cramped in the raft and felt
the need to give fealty to his bladder. He figured Miranda probably felt the same, but of course women didn't
talk that way. They couched it in starkly feminine terms
of going to the powder room.

"I need to take a leak," said Miranda. "Pretty soon."

"Yeah, me, too. I wonder how much—yo-ho, another
grotto ahead. Maybe we can pull over and—"

"This be it," came the creaky door of Herky's voice
as he made for shore. "Pull us in, Jesse."

Feeling arthritic, Frank eased himself over the gun-
wale in ankle-deep water and pulled the raft up on the
beach, finding that their landfall was made of yellow
sand, unlike the gravel beach of their departure. It was
a smaller grotto than the first, with a ceiling only about
ten feet high but like the other one it, too, had a shaky
ladder leading up to a black hole in the ceiling. Herky
put the lantern on the beach and whipped out his flashlight.

"Oh, boy," muttered Frank under his breath. "Here
we go again."

Without a word, Herky started up the ladder, and it
struck Hannon how strong this geriatric prospector must
be, but then he figured sixty years of this kind of life
would harden anybody. Once Herky disappeared into the
ceiling, Miranda followed; then, when she was gone,
Frank grumbled and brought up the rear. After a short
climb he heard the sound of boards bumping together,
but his apprehension was soon put to rest as he came
out of the silo and into—what? Hannon climbed out of

the hole and saw that the old-timer's flashlight was illuminating the interior of a wooden shack that was about the size of a glorified outhouse. A circular plywood disc that had covered the opening was laid to one side. Herky worked another rusty lock caught in a latticework of cobwebs; then he doused the flashlight and opened the door.

They stepped out into a desert night that was illuminated by stars and a three-quarter moon, and the terrain that greeted them was unchanged from the landscape they'd left two hours previously, except there was no road. The arid land of scrub and sagebrush was woven into an undulating terrain of low hills, although taller mountains could be seen in the distance. The small shack from which they'd just emerged was at the base of a hill that rose steeply for two hundred feet behind them. Hannon and Miranda looked around, calibrating their bearings as their breath turned to vapor in the frost of a desert night.

"Herky," said Miranda softly, "how did you ever find that underground river?"

Herky groped in his pocket for a slug of chewing tobacco. Then he ripped off a bite with his teeth and chawed while he spoke. "I was lookin' fer a place tuh build our cabin, Sarah. Found a little spring right over thar. This here was a well I dug. Thought it'd be nice tuh have all the water we wanted. Was gonna buy a tub outta the Sears and Roebuck catalog and all. I dig down ten feet and fall onto that riverbank down there. Woulda died there iffin' I dint have a rope tied up here so's I could climb outta the well. Then you and Jesse left."

For some reason, Hannon felt a pang of tremendous guilt.

Herky spat and continued. "You and Jesse left, so's I started explorin'. Nobody knows 'bout the river, 'cept me. I go up it, down it. Then when the guvment started to close this here land off in fifty-four, I dug me the other shaft where we come in at, only the part I dug was from the inside out. I dint like the guvment tellin' me whar I can and cain't go, so I come back here when I want. That's when I seen 'em."

Hannon leaned closer. "Seen what, Herky?"

"Them flyin' saucers, Jesse."

Miranda touched his arm. "Where, Herky? Where did you see them?"

Herky jerked his thumb behind them. "Papoose Lake. Over the hill yonder." He held out the tobacco. "Want some, Sarah? You use to like it."

Miranda passed on the offer, and the three of them hiked up the steep hillside, and when they finally crested the ridgeline they looked out to see nothing. The backside of the hill had a much gentler slope than the incline they'd just climbed, and it continued down towards the dry bed of Papoose Lake where the terrain on the far side uplifted into a range of low mountains. Hannon absorbed the desolate view and sighed, convinced they were chasing a very wild goose. "I don't see anything," he said flatly.

Miranda didn't answer, but reached into her backpack and pulled out a pair of binoculars. She scanned the landscape around the lake bed and saw nothing out of the ordinary, and the desolate view made her begin to share Frank's pessimism. "I don't see anything either. No buildings, no hangars. Nothing like we saw at Area Fifty-one." But then she flipped a switch on the Russian-made device and the binoculars turned into night-vision goggles. Again, she scanned the terrain, but this time she noticed something that seemed unnatural.

It was a line.

A straight line.

She handed the binoculars to Frank, who aimed them in the direction of her pointed finger. "There's a straight line that goes from the far side of the lake bed to the mountainside on the right."

"Hmm. Yeah, yeah, I see it."

"What is it? A road?"

Hannon studied it carefully. It was long, but seemed to come abruptly to an end in the middle of the lake bed, and it was precisely straight. "That's not a road," he replied. "That's a runway." Further inspection revealed more. "That runway leads onto an apron—a kind of taxiway—that abuts that mountain on the right there . . . and I'd guess it's about a half to three quarters of a mile from here. It's not easy to make out because of the angle from our position, but I think it's definitely a runway." Hannon took down the binoculars/night-vision goggles and inspected them. "Say, where did you get these?"

"Carl Lacey lent them to me."

"Did he? Well, so far this trip has been very interesting, but where does it get us? I mean, an airstrip in the desert. That's no big deal. Must be dozens of them. That's hardly anything to . . ."

"Wait a minute. . . . Look at *that*!"

Hannon snapped the goggles back onto his eyes, training them on the apron where it abutted against the mountain. The infrared image glared with a harsh brightness that made him squint, so he switched the binoculars back to optical. "What the . . . ? Well, I'll be damned."

Where the slope of the mountain joined the apron, a network of klieg lights secreted against the terrain came on, illuminating the tarmac.

Miranda didn't say anything as she began rummaging around in her backpack again. Then she pulled out a video camera, flicked it on and went to maximum zoom.

"Are you recording?" asked Hannon, somewhat skeptical. "There's not much light down there."

"Damn straight I'm recording. This is a new Panasonic digital machine with a forty-to-one zoom, and it generates a studio-quality picture. Cost me a fortune." She could see the apron clearly as she panned the lens over the scene, but after the initial surprise began to wane, she said, "The tarmac is lighted, but I don't see anything else."

Herky chewed his tobacco.

"I don't either," said Frank as he canvassed the scene with the binoculars. "Why would a bunch of lights come on for no reason—whoa, look at that. Do you see it?"

"Yeah, yeah, I see it."

A rectangular panel of the mountainside, at the point where it joined the tarmac, slowly rotated up like a garage door rising, revealing an ill-defined but lighted interior.

"Must be some kind of camouflaged hangar," whispered Frank. "Can you make out what's on the inside?"

"Umm, no. I've got it on max zoom, but from this angle I can't make anything out."

Herky spat, then said with a fatigued voice, "Jes you wait, Sarah. They be comin'."

"You've done great so far, Herky," conceded Frank. "I hope you're right about—"

"Uh, oh, uh, oh, uh, oh," chanted Miranda's contralto voice. "Do you see what I see?"

"What the . . . ? Yes! *Yes,* I do see!"

From the interior of the hangar about a half-dozen men clad in coveralls walked out onto the tarmac. They were followed by a small tractor-like vehicle, the kind you often see at airports pushing planes away from the gate. It was towing a large pallet, and as it slowly rolled out, an object resting on top of the pallet was revealed which, for lack of a better description, looked like two saucers welded together, rim to rim, with a hemisphere of a golf ball on top.

"Get this on tape! Are you getting this on tape!?"

"I getting it! I'm getting it!" shouted Miranda.

"Not so loud," admonished Hannon. "Sound carries in the desert. Especially at night."

Foot by foot the saucer rolled out onto the lighted tarmac, the support crew obviously confident they were cloaked from prying eyes as they walked around the dark metallic object. A panel on the underside of the craft was opened to the ground, providing a ramp into its interior. From inside the hangar emerged two figures wearing flight suits and crash helmets, and they walked toward the disc with a distinctive gait. One by one they climbed up the ramp and into the craft; then the ramp folded up behind them. Frank and Miranda remained speechless in a stunned silence as a ring of navigation lights came on along the rim of the saucer and on top of the golf ball; then two of the ground crew plugged their headset umbilicals into some receptacles on the underside of the saucer—again, just like the ground crewmen on a commercial airliner.

"The ones who climbed on board—they must be test pilots of some kind," whispered Hannon.

"Test pilots?"

Frank nodded. "If you're in the Air Force long enough you get to where you can recognize that swagger anywhere."

"But . . . but test pilots?" Miranda asked rhetorically, her eye still glued to the viewer. "Does that mean this, this thing—whatever it is—is one of *ours*?"

Frank's mind raced. "Hmm. Those ground crewmen have headsets they plugged into the bottom of the craft. That means they're talking to the pilots on the inside. I daresay any spaceship from the stars wouldn't have that feature. So, yes, I guess you would have to say it was one of ours and—" He heard Miranda gasp, causing him to turn. "What is it?"

She was shaking as she squinted at the image on the viewer. "That-that's him. At least I think it's him. I-I can't be sure at this distance, but he looks like the one."

"Him? Him who? What are you talking about?"

She refocused her lens on him. "The man in my dream. When Joey was killed there was a man on the other side of the street, reading a newspaper as Joey was crossing over to me. I didn't get a good look at him then, but his face keeps coming back in the recurrent nightmares I've had since Joey's murder. It gets more vivid with each dream, and he's the one."

Hannon trained his binoculars on the man in question, who was wearing a down parka, and as he strained his eyes, four more figures walked into his field of vision. The first one had broad shoulders, and even at this distance you could see he possessed the bearing of a bank president. A second figure followed, but he was slimmer and wore a fashionable sheepskin coat, and despite the distance, Frank could peg him with a glance, causing his instincts to surge like a bull charging a red cape. "Tin Man," he whispered. "There's no mistake. That's Colonel Lawton Tyndale for sure."

"The man you worked for? The one who sold out on that dope deal?"

"One and the same. And that's Major General Owen Shrake right beside him."

"The NORAD Chief-of-Staff?"

"None other. What are those sons of bitches doing?"

"*Frank!* Look at that!"

Hannon didn't notice it because his enmity was focused on Tin Man, but the ground crew had unplugged their umbilicals and moved back from the saucer. There was no noise, only silence, as the bottom of the craft began to glow with a blue light—then, ever so slowly, the object broke contact with the pallet and began to lift off. It was as though an invisible cable was hoisting the craft into the air as it hovered for a few moments, then slowly continued its ascent before heading out across the lake bed and into the night sky. Hannon followed it with his field glasses, and noticed that the stars immediately surrounding the saucer's image had a distorted, wavy effect—like when you looked at something down a blacktop road on a hot summer's day. The saucer continued on—its velocity not great, but its trajectory steady—as it ascended up and across the desert. Miranda and Hannon kept their lenses on it until it grew quite small against the canopy of stars. Then the navigation lights finally winked out.

•   •   •

On the tarmac, Major General Owen Shrake and Colonel Lawton Tyndale absently found themselves taking small steps backwards in order to maintain their distance from the man with the cane. He was a stooped old soul, standing bareheaded in the cold, but he imparted a sense of raw power like electrical arcs from a severed power line. He pointed to the sky with his cane as he commented to the frail-looking gentleman at his elbow. "There it goes, Michel! Damned impressive, isn't it!?" He might have been on the fifty-yard line watching a game-winning play, but in the face of his excitement the Nobel laureate remained silent, eliciting a *tut-tut* response from the old man with the cane. "Now, now, Michel, you should be rightfully proud. You had a pivotal role in this, after all. Now again I make the offer. I'm willing to forgive your past sins and bring you back into the project if you'll just tell me all the details of your, ah, unexcused absence."

But the Frenchman remained silent and stared at the ground, which elicited a sound from Krieger like an exasperated parent. "How tragic, Michel. How tragic. And I thought you had the intellectual power to embrace Sirius and all it's future. Well, I'm afraid we'll have to find out what you've been up to—one way or another."

Michel Bertrand's eyes flared as two of the guards came forward and escorted him back into the hangar as the prototype swooped back over the dry bed of Papoose Lake, then slowly came to a halt above the tarmac. It hovered, then bit by bit, the pilots reduced the antigravitational power and it descended to the concrete apron. There was a bit of a wobble as it settled down. Then the blue light was extinguished.

As Bertrand was escorted into the hangar by the two

guards he cut a frail figure beside them, yet he knew his intellectual powers reached a rarefied level the muscle-bound oafs could not hope to comprehend. As they approached a stairwell that led to the subterranean level, Bertrand paused for a moment and looked across the hangar to an elevator terminus that rose up out of the concrete floor. The elevator door was guarded by two more security men, which put another barrier between him and the secrets locked below. He was one of a handful of people who knew what lay beyond that door, and in that knowledge was something that defied the imagination—something as fearsome as it was fascinating. Yet it was closed to him now.

Had his gamble failed? Was he and the rest of humankind lost? Only time would tell.

"Move along, Professor," ordered one of the guards, and the Frenchman complied, descending obediently to his cell.

As Bertrand disappeared down the stairs, Tyndale and Shrake shuffled back and forth on the tarmac, partly from the cold, partly from nerves. Then Number One came up behind them and murmured, "We are instructed to go inside." Both men swallowed as they looked at each other, then complied with the order. It was the first time since his orientation eight years ago that Tyndale had been to the S-4 site at Papoose Lake, and he had forgotten about the oppressive security that was everywhere.

Tin Man had signed up with Sirius because he knew there were two kinds of people in this world—the controllers and the controlled. He thought that being part of Sirius would mean he'd be one of the elite, the controllers, but now it struck him that he never felt more controlled in his life.

They entered the hangar that was secreted into the side of Papoose Mountain; then Number One told them to halt as the old man with the cane—the one Tin Man knew only as "Krieger"—went past them and pulled a lever. Immediately the camouflaged door rotated down, sealing them inside. They were alone on the empty concrete apron except for the elevator terminus against the far wall and the two Cammo Dude guards stationed at either side. Krieger pointed at the elevator with the cane and asked with a virulent smugness, "You boys know where that leads?"

There was no response.

"Eh? Cat got your tongue? Hmm. So maybe you don't know, but you suspect, surely."

Tyndale could only speculate on the frightening unknowns locked below. Yet despite those unknowns, the one Tin Man feared most was the old man with the bloodless eyes.

Krieger motioned to one of the elevator guards, who could've passed for one of those gorillas in the mist. He came forward and stood beside Krieger as the old man switched hands with his cane and reached inside his coat pocket to extract a large cigar—a casual act that made Number One, Shrake and Tyndale more uncomfortable with each passing moment. Methodically, Krieger went through the smoker's liturgy of clipping the tip and firing it up, then he puffed large clouds of smoke into the air like a steam engine pulling out of the station. When he finally pulled it from his lips, he studied it reverently for a few moments before saying, "Cuban. Still the best tobacco on the planet, bar none. Something about the mixture of sun, climate and soil, I suppose." Then he held it up, saying almost in apology, "My only sin of the flesh, you might say. In all other respects, my body has always been a vessel for my mind." He took several succulent puffs before continuing. "Twenty-eight years. My, my, where has the time gone, I ask you. Twenty-eight years I have been in charge of this project, and over that time there has been no aspect of this enterprise that has escaped my personal attention. No detail has been too minute, no issue too inconsequential, and of all that I have dealt with as head of Sirius, no issue has ever been more important than the matter of *security*!"

The last word came across them like a lash, causing Tyndale, Shrake and Number One to collectively take a step backward.

Krieger's manner was no longer that of the avuncular neighbor showing off his Chris Craft. Now he'd become the predator, rising to the surface to crush its prey within a pair of steely jaws. "Twenty-eight years I have labored every waking moment to get to this point, knowing at every turn some dunderhead could ruin it all by doing something incredibly stupid. That is why I created the Sirius Network, so I could negate any threat that appeared on the horizon before it became a danger. So here we find ourselves, only months, if not weeks away from commencement of the plan, a plan I helped them fashion. A plan that would bring you wealth and position beyond your dreams of avarice. But now I am informed that a minor problem, which had supposedly been taken care of, has now become a potential threat." The predator eyes homed in on Tin Man and Shrake, causing a small rain shower of sweat to drip from their palms.

"We have confirmed that an Air Force lieutenant colonel by the name of Hannon has been on the kiva and has had direct contact with a woman, a journalist named Park. Is that not correct, Number One?" Krieger's eyes remained fixed on Tin Man, as if the old man were an impatient undertaker.

Number One swallowed. "That is correct, sir."

"And we were led to believe that this man Hannon was not a problem. That the situation at Cheyenne Mountain was 'wrapped up and put on ice,' as Colonel Tyndale here so aptly put it. Is that not correct, Number One?"

Tin Man quivered under Krieger's gaze, and felt as if he'd just stepped onto the gallows as the old man reached into another pocket to extract a device that looked similar to a cellular phone. He keystroked in some instructions and the LCD display read, "SEARCHING . . . SEARCHING . . . LOCK ON . . . ARMED."

"A journalist is something of a wild card, isn't it? We probably should have taken her out along with that pathetic fellow Dreason, but I decided against it because when a member of the press gets killed it draws too much attention from their peers. I felt it was better to simply keep her isolated from the people who could tell her something. Now this man Hannon has penetrated our defenses and made contact with her—just when we were told everything was 'on ice.' " His eyes remained fixed on Tin Man as he flipped up the safety cover and rested his thumb on the red detonation button. "This kind of shoddy security is *unacceptable*! And there is no room in the Sirius Group for those who countenance such failure." His voice turned soft. "So you leave me no choice, dear boy, but to carry out the sentence.''

Tin Man took a step backward, slowly shaking his head while he whispered a plea of, ''No . . . please, no.''

''Oh, yes,'' whispered Krieger, and his thumb pressed the red button.

The detonation reverberated through the hangar like a war drum as Tin Man's eyes closed, his heart stopped and his bladder voided. Then he felt something brush against his leg and, amazingly, he opened his eyes to find himself still breathing and alive. On the floor beside him lay Number One—the left side of him gouged out in a red gooey mash, his eyes frozen in a stark death mask. Not feeling the wetness in his crotch, Tyndale looked open-mouthed at Krieger, then to Shrake, then to himself, and found he was splattered with the victim's blood.

Krieger puffed on the cigar as he replaced the radio device in his coat pocket. ''You see, Lawton, I hold the people who report directly to me directly responsible. There was a failure of security, and that responsibility can only lie with the former Number One of security.'' He took another leisurely puff, then continued. ''As of this moment, Lawton, you are the new Number One of security for Sirius Group. I understand that you know this man Hannon better than anyone. You now have the entire resources of the Network at your disposal to run him and the woman reporter to ground, and remove them as a threat to our project. If you fail, then you shall meet the fate of your predecessor here.'' He let his cigar fall to the concrete floor, then ground it out with his good foot. ''Owen, why don't you just run along home to Cheyenne Mountain and make sure there are no more surprises for us there. Think you can do that? And Lawton, have this mess tidied up, will you? It could be a distraction for some of the softer scientific types who work around here.'' He tapped the floor with his cane. ''Now if you will excuse me, I have to walk my dog.''

After the test vehicle had completed a second, shorter hop and was rolled back inside, the lights illuminating the tarmac were extinguished as the hangar door rotated back down to its camouflaged position. Again, the landscape became a benign desert hillside—a home to nothing but sagebrush and the small critters who eked out their existence in the unforgiving terrain.

The three intruders remained in place on the hillside for a time, not speaking as they absorbed all that had happened.

''I don't believe this,'' Miranda said quietly. ''I've just seen it and I don't believe it.''

''I know what you mean,'' replied Frank, scanning the vista with his night-vision lenses. ''And I think we've pushed our luck far enough. I think it's time we got the hell outta here.''

''I'm with you,'' she said, while shutting down her video camera and shoving it into her backpack.

''One last look before we—wait a minute.''

''What is it?'' she demanded.

He peered intently into the night, then handed her the night-vision binoculars and pointed. ''Look out there—in the brush near the hangar door—and tell me what you see.''

She put the lenses to her eyes and scanned the terrain. ''Why it . . . it's that man with the cane, the one we saw with Tyndale and the others. The one who was obviously in charge. It looks like—yes, it looks like there's a dog alongside of him. A Doberman, I think.''

''Weird time for an evening constitutional. Well, we didn't come all this way to see somebody walk a dog. Let's move, Herky. We're going home.''

The old prospector yawned, then said, ''Don't ferget my beer.''

The Doberman ran crazily through the brush, a banshee off the leash as he burned off the pent up energy of the day. His master followed at a glacial pace, rocking back and forth like a lazy metronome as he moved his weight from good leg to cane and back again. He gazed up at the moon, a pool of light painting the arid landscape with its brush strokes of white flame. For eons it had been unreachable by humankind, but now it was a mere stone's throw away—and the stars that surrounded it were closer than any earthling could imagine. Krieger felt like a racehorse at the gate—so many years of preparation and now there was a race to be run, and won, and the effect on the mind was nothing short of narcotic.

''*Daman,* Sringar!'' he called, and at once the canine came to heel at his side, panting with a whiny urgency as a desert hare scampered from bush to bush in the distance. Krieger pointed the cobra-headed cane in the direction of the critter and commanded, ''*Karna,* Sringar. *Umarna!*''

The animal seemed electrified as he launched himself toward his prey, and only seconds elapsed before a small geyser of dust rose above the bush. Then a silence fell and the Doberman came trotting back, the hare locked in his jaws. He dropped it proudly at his master's feet, where the old man caressed its neck, cooing his congratulations. "You are the only one I trust, my treasure. The only one I can trust. So eat heartily. *Katwa!*"

And the Doberman devoured the rabbit with the savagery of a jackal.

EIGHT

⟨≋≋≋⟩

Miranda Park rose out of the marble pool at Caesar's Palace like a dolphin breaching the surface, and after the unremitting stress of the past days the waters had a curative effect which made her feel quasi-human again. She pulled herself out of the heated pool to join Hannon at a table where he was wrapped in a terry-cloth robe, enjoying his coffee from a room service brunch. The full effect of her lanyard-like body emerging from the pool was striking, and the purple bikini they'd purchased in the Caesar's Palace mall certainly did her justice. As she toweled herself off, he inquired, "Feel better?"

She smiled back. "Much. Nothing like a swim to refresh you. Why don't you give it a try?"

Frank sipped his coffee. "Maybe later. I have this lily-white skin that never tans. If I were to go out in the water with my bulk I might be mistaken for a Beluga whale and harpooned by some Japanese tourists. I understand they're partial to whale meat."

A laugh crossed her lips as she slipped into her robe

and took a seat across from him. They were at an isolated table, away from the rest of the people who were spending their Christmas holiday at Caesar's. Only minutes ago a leggy blonde had trolled by him, a bikini with a smile, all hookered up with rouge and lipstick. She was something of a rarity in the public areas of the higher-end resorts these days as Vegas labored (without success) to burnish its image for the family trade. The Caesar's shopping mall, a staggering affair of ersatz opulence, had the bizarre feel of a Disneyland with slot machines—a resort that had become schizophrenic, unable to decide what it wanted to be.

Frank surveyed the pool from behind his Foster Grants. Maybe they were pushing the envelope being out in the open like this, but he remembered the old adage— the best place to hide from the cops was in a police station because they'd never look for you there. Anyway, the open pool eased the tension, and he felt they were reasonably shielded by the ever-churning sea of humanity that coursed through the hotel. He was just glad he'd pulled out ten grand in cash from his account before leaving Colorado Springs, allowing them to avoid the electronic trail of credit cards. It had cost them a hefty room deposit, but by using cash they'd managed to register at Caesar's under the name of Mr. & Mrs. Fred Johnson from Cedar Rapids, Iowa.

He put down his copy of the Las Vegas *Review-Journal* and conceded, "Well, looks like you hit paydirt with old Herky. Guess I owe you an apology. Since you're on a roll, where would you say we go from here? Off to some newspaper or TV station to get your tape published?"

As she sipped the coffee her demeanor, which had

been so upbeat just moments ago, now turned a gray shade of somber as she said, "It's not that easy."

That made Frank a bit squirmy. "What do you mean it's not that easy? You're a reporter, you must know people. We have the tape, the FAA printout, the pictures I took, our testimony. What else do we need?"

She set down her coffee cup and looked out on the pool. There were some children playing on the steps across the way, splashing each other and laughing on this, an unseasonably warm winter's day. "There's a saying in journalism," she explained, "that no editor ever got fired for spiking a story."

"Spiking a story?"

She nodded. "That means putting something controversial on the slush spike and not publishing it. In short, nobody likes to go out on a limb, including newspaper editors. Or maybe I should say, especially newspaper editors, because there is always the danger you could be wrong. You could leave yourself open to a libel suit— or worse, to professional ridicule."

"But we have photographs, the printout, the video," protested Hannon. "Surely that's enough for an editor somewhere."

Miranda shook her head. "These are the days of DreamQuest and Industrial Light and Magic, Frank. Anything can be fabricated on tape. But beyond that, you're missing the point."

"So educate me."

She looked at him intently, then reached across and took his hands in hers to emphasize her words. "I've been thinking about this carefully, Frank. Very carefully. I'm afraid that early on I was overly optimistic. First of all, you have to realize the magnitude of this story. This is a story that will absolutely alter the fabric of our world. Think of how Columbus altered the lives of the Indians when he landed in the New World. That's what this is, except the impact will be greater than anything Columbus wrought. You see those kids over there? Do you think their parents want them to grow up in a profoundly different world with some . . . some unknown force hanging over their heads? No way. They want to see them grow up normally, have backyard barbeques, go on vacations to Vegas, see them go off to college, have grandkids. If you tell them the government is building flying saucers and doing God knows what with human bone marrow, the information will derail their internal compass. They simply will not want to hear it.''

Hannon was starting to feel an incoming tide of exasperation, although Miranda's touch was distracting. ''But surely some newspaper somewhere will—''

''You don't understand, Frank. It can't be just *some* paper. Tabloids run flying saucer stories all the time and nobody cares. It has to be a paper that Congress and the legitimate part of the government simply can't ignore. It has to be the *New York Times*, the *Washington Post*, or the *Los Angeles Times*, and the story would have to have their complete backing, page one and editorial page. If we got that, then the rest of the legitimate media might jump on board and force a Congressional investigation, and with a Congressional investigation we can get protection for ourselves and put the screws to the conspirators who are running this thing and killing people to keep it quiet.'' She squeezed his hands, then let go.

He pondered what she said, not liking it, then drew a breath. ''This is out of my experience. I wouldn't know where to start. Do you know anyone at any of those papers?''

Now it was her turn to inhale long and hard. "Yes, I know someone, but I won't kid you, Frank—the odds of prevailing on this thing are slim. You see, people in power—even newspaper people—don't like to make waves. They like the status quo, they like being in power, and we would be asking them to run a story that would fundamentally alter the power structure in this country—indeed, in this world—by confronting them with a huge unknown. You tell me who has the *chutzpah* to put a match to their own house in the name of truth.'' She looked away, not wanting to meet his gaze.

He contemplated his coffee cup for a while, then bit his lip. "So who should we take it to?''

She shook out her auburn locks before replying, "I have a close friend at the *Post,* and she's in a position of responsibility. That's probably our best bet. We can go to Washington and . . . uh, oh, now what? You've got that look again.''

Hannon wasn't hearing her. Instead, every dram of his attention was absorbed by the newspaper laid open in front of him, by an item under the heading of "Regional News.'' A two-paragraph story read:

BLUFF, UTAH—A convenience store owner and his granddaughter were found shot to death in their store Monday morning in this small crossroads town.

The victims were identified as retired Professor Morgan Raines, 69, and his granddaughter, Sheila, 17, who were discovered by a fuel truck delivery man. The Utah State Police have launched a manhunt to find those responsible for the killings that have shattered the tranquility of this small community. . . .

Hannon looked up at Miranda, knowing their brief hiatus from the new reality was over. "We'd better get out of sight," he said tightly.

Back in their room, Miranda sat curled up on the bed, biting her fist with the newspaper open in front of her, while Hannon paced the carpet, almost blind with a searing rage. "Just who the hell do these goddamn people think they are!? That kid was only seventeen years old, for Christ sake! She waited on me when I was there. Damn it, how the hell did they know I was there?"

Miranda came off the bed and joined him as they cruised aimlessly around the room, sailboats without centerboards.

"An old man and a kid who wouldn't hurt anybody, and they were murdered just because they crossed tracks with me? Okay, dammit, if that's how they want to play it, I'll do it their way. I'll start with that son of a bitch, Tin Man. I'll shoot his toes off one at a time until he tells me who is pulling the strings on this. Then I'll go after them, one at a time. I don't care if—"

The way they began kissing was rather bizarre, in that they were two frightened people pacing in a confined space, contemplating the specter of their own deaths, when all of a sudden they came together in an embrace that seemed choreographed—a tango of attraction and arousal in which they began searching each other's mouths as they pawed off one another's bath robes and tumbled onto the bed. They yanked and pulled their swimsuits off, and she wrapped her arms around his neck to pull his lips against hers, hard, while her legs parted to accept him into her silky wetness. His hardness surged into her, and surged again, generating a maelstrom of emotions for him—from fear to joy, from lust to love—as they brought each other to the threshold of their pent-up desires, then ravenously rushed across.

The stars were out now, offering a natural counterpoint to the gaudy neon of the Vegas Strip as they lay on the bed, both spent from having ravaged each other three times since their morning coupling. Frank was surprised that he still had it in him, but she'd made his journey effortless.

For her, she had found Frank's body a little husky to be sure, but somehow his extra body mass imparted twin feelings of safety and a good ol' boy lustiness—kind of like a teddy bear with a penis.

They had lain in silence for a long time—she on his chest as he stroked her hair—neither of them wanting to spoil the moment by talking about the future. So it was with reluctance that he shattered their interlude by saying, "I'm going after Tin Man first. I'll corner him alone and make him talk. Find out what the bastard knows."

"Then what?" she asked, kissing his chest, noticing that his skin really was starkly white.

He sighed, then ran his hand down along her back, feeling the definition of her muscles as he caressed the buttocks that were round and firm as apples. "All I can think to do is inflict as much damage on this damned conspiracy as I can."

"But that increases your chances of getting caught.

Wouldn't it be better to go ahead and run the trap on my end? It's a long, long shot, but maybe we can get our story published. If it doesn't work, then we can go back to your final option."

Frank sighed, not enjoying this kind of conversation, especially at this kind of moment. "I suppose you're right, Miranda. God knows, I'm no Nobel Prize winner. I'm just a retired military guy and I think in a military way. This thing is so far beyond me that—"

She jackknifed up in the bed like a switchblade springing open, then froze in place and stared at the wall like a zombie. Hannon was startled, not knowing what had provoked her reflex. "Now you're the one who looks as though somebody walked over her grave. What gives?"

She turned and stared at him, or rather through him. "What did you say?"

Dumfounded, he replied, "I said you look as though you—"

"No, no, not that," she corrected him sharply. "Before."

"Uh, well, I just said I'm no Nobel Prize winner and—"

"*Miranda!*" she cried to herself, clasping her head between her hands. "You stupid, stupid fool! It was right there in front of you, all the time, and you didn't see it!" And she fell over on the sheet beside him, rocking her head back and forth. "Uhhhhhh! I can be such a cretin sometimes!"

Hannon was undone, demanding. "What are you saying? Stupid about what?"

She came up on her hands and knees and looked at him, her face smiling as her crème de menthe eyes filled with tears that showed stress, fear and at last, a glimmer of hope. "Don't you understand, Frank? The Secretary of Defense doesn't know!"

"The Secretary of Defense doesn't know? Know about what?"

"About everything! The secret base, the conspiracy, the murders, the landing zone at the Kiva Tower! He doesn't know!"

"Doesn't know? How could he not know? There's no way this could be kept from a Defense Secretary—"

"Frank, listen to me." She spoke with the urgency of someone who'd just latched onto a lifeline and wasn't about to let go. "Listen, listen, listen—what was the date of the exchange on the Kiva Tower?"

"Why, it was the morning of December tenth."

"Exactly. On December tenth Secretary of Defense Treavor Dane was winding up a European trip for NATO. He was on a tour that included Bosnia, Paris and Berlin; then his last stop was in Stockholm on December *tenth* to accept the Nobel Prize posthumously for Michel Bertrand, his old professor at Princeton."

"Nobel Prize?"

"Yes. The medal ceremony is held on December tenth of each year. The prize in physics was announced last October, but Bertrand was killed in a private plane crash shortly thereafter. He and the Defense Secretary were close friends—had known each other since Dane was an undergraduate at Princeton—and Dane accepted the award posthumously on Bertrand's behalf. He got all teary on the podium during the acceptance speech."

"How the hell do you know all that?"

"I'm a science writer, remember? I always follow the Nobel awards closely."

Hannon thought about her supposition, then said, "So he was out of the country. What does that prove?"

"What does that prove!?" She was incredulous. "Think about it. If you were the Secretary of Defense and an exchange was taking place between humans and creatures from another world on American soil, wouldn't you remain in the country to orchestrate the contact—in a command post in the Pentagon, or even Cheyenne Mountain, for God's sake!? You'd want to monitor events minute by minute, second by second. You would want to be where you were on top of things, not out of the country having tea and crumpets with the King of Sweden. And since Dane *was* out of the country, that means he was out of the loop, that he was—*is*—ignorant of everything that's going on in Nevada . . . the conspiracy, the executions, everything."

Hannon remained silent for a long time as he processed Miranda's theory. Finally he shook his head and said, "No . . . no, it's too crazy. Remember that flying saucer we saw? That was one of ours, not theirs, with our pilots. Let's say it was a prototype that was fabricated with materials that were developed over a period of time—maybe years—with technology from God knows where. A project of that magnitude would require millions, if not billions. You'd have to have an army of people involved—from the Defense Department, the CIA, NASA, and on and on. You'd need contractors out the kazoo. It would be too big to keep from the SecDef. He'd have to know. Now, I grant you that the scumbag who is running this thing probably has set it up so the President and the Cabinet can deny responsibility, and maybe he doesn't know about the murders, but as for the project as a whole, Dane would have to be aware of it.''

She stood up and put her hands on her hips, nakedly facing him in defiance as the reflected neon played on the ripples and curves of her muscular form. ''And I'm telling you that you are dead wrong, Franklin Hannon. The Secretary of Defense does *not* know about any of this. And if he doesn't know, then that means the President, the Congress, everyone in the government is in the dark. And on top of that, Treavor Dane is probably going after the Presidential nomination. No politician worth his salt would allow an exchange with another world to take place without controlling his side of the ledger. You can take that to the bank. I'm sure of it.''

If it hadn't been for her nakedly defiant posture he would have dismissed the idea out of hand, but her insistence—and her body—couldn't be ignored. ''Okay, okay, let's say you're right. What do we do? Go up to the Pentagon and knock on the door, saying, 'Excuse us, but we're a couple of fugitives running for our lives and we would like to chat with the Secretary about an invisible government that's killing people around the country'?''

She came back down on the bed, her mind racing, then she smirked. ''I think I know a way we can get to him. It'll be risky, but I think I know a way.''

Hannon remained reluctant. ''Okay, now let's just suppose that your theory about Dane being ignorant is wrong and he knows about it. If we try to get access to him we'll just be walking into a death trap. That would really be our final option.''

She leaned forward and touched his chest. ''But if I'm

right, he'd be in a position to give us protection and go after this conspiracy.''

"That's a big if, Miranda," he retorted sharply. "If you think I'm going to go rushing off for the Potomac just on your supposition—"

But her steely fingers, honed on the unforgiving parapets of El Capitan, squeezed his shoulder so hard that he almost winced as her eyes bored into him. "I am telling you, Frank—the Secretary of Defense does *not* know.''

NINE

The moon peeked through the denuded branches of the birch trees, reflecting off the snow-covered grounds with a Yuletide luminescence. The recent snowfall had not yet been swept from the concrete walking path, so with every step Secretary of Defense Treavor Dane broke a new trail as he mushed through the secluded forest on his family retreat near Gettysburg.

He was an athletic man at six-foot-one, having played guard for the Princeton Tigers basketball team. At forty-two, his body was still lean and hard, and his features projected an image of youth and vitality that seemed genetically engineered for photo opportunities. Dane had come from a family moneyed from the textile trade, and his political ascension had always invited the inevitable comparison to the Kennedy clan—a comparison which Dane did nothing to deflect.

Treavor Dane was known for his informality, accessibility and political luck, but for the last two days he'd felt anything but lucky as he sequestered himself at his family's ancestral retreat under the guise of a virus. At this moment he was nervous, testy and emotionally brittle as he walked out from under the canopy of birch trees. But then, being nervous and emotionally brittle at the Dane country estate was nothing new for Treavor. He walked past the woodshed that held so many bitter memories, like an evil ghost that wouldn't depart. He often thought of burning the rickety thing down, but that would be a sign of defeat, wouldn't it? His backside still bore the scars where the lashes had been administered behind that very woodshed—by a raging father consumed by alcohol and the impotence that springs from inherited wealth. Yet despite the whippings, he had never broken . . . in an overt sense.

As a young man, his matriculation into Princeton had been like an escape from a hellish prison, for at Princeton he'd found the father figure he'd never known and discovered the magical approbation that politics could bring. But now he felt those two elements of his life were in jeopardy as he pulled a sheaf of fax paper from his coat pocket. Under the moonlight he brought the glossy parchment closer to his face so he could once again read the handwritten lines under the moonlight.

It was an epistle.

An incomplete epistle from a dead Nobel laureate.

Frank and Miranda parked their Mustang in the short-term lot of the new Denver airport as dusk was approaching. They had gone over and over their plan during the long desolate drive through Nevada and Utah, but once they hit Colorado neither one had spoken much. Frank turned the engine off and looked at his scraggly beard in the rearview mirror. "It's a long way from Caesar's Palace, I must say."

"Be that as it may," replied Miranda. "They're still looking for us big time."

"No doubt."

"Then should we maybe try and drive to Washington?"

Frank mulled over the option, then shook his head. "No. The bell captain in Vegas is sure to have reported the car stolen by now. If we're pulled over, one check into the NCIC computer and we're toast. Better to go the rest of the way by air."

"Okay. Then let's move. Sooner the better."

Frank left the keys in the ignition and they grabbed their suitcases from the trunk. On the way into the terminal they tossed them into a dumpster, knowing that luggage from this point was superfluous. Upon entering the building they went immediately to the United counter, and with Frank's dwindling cash reserves bought two tickets to Baltimore-Washington International Airport, because Hannon figured surveillance there would be less than at Dulles or National. As they headed for the security area, Miranda scanned the cavernous building, and absently thought the new structure resembled a circus tent with a linoleum floor. That architectural footnote was on her mind when Frank roughly yanked her in a different direction. Keeping her head down, she whispered, "What is it?"

"Damn—there's a guy at the security gate. I've met him before. Oh, hell, what's his name? Masters? . . . No . . . *Mc*Masters. That's it. Met him once when I was golfing with Pinky Pinkston, my FBI friend in the Springs. He came down and played a round with us one Saturday about six months ago. Works in the FBI Denver office.''

"Did he see you?''

"I don't think so.''

They took refuge behind a pillar where silently they thought about the hurdle that had been cast in their path. Frank was reevaluating the cross-country-driving option when Miranda asked, "This McMasters—is he married?''

"Married? I-I suppose so. Can't really say—no, wait. I remember now. Yes, he is married and they have a son. I remember because he told me their names and they rhymed—oh, damn, what was it? Something like Minny and Timmy, or Ginny and Jim—yeah, that was it. Ginny and Jimmy. I remember now. He really got off saying their names together. Weird guy.''

Miranda nodded. "Okay. You wait here and keep an eye on him. I'm going up to the Admiral's Club and find a private phone.''

Special Agent Ted McMasters didn't feel terribly "special'' at the moment. In fact, he was bored out of his mind and more than a little stumped. The word had come down from On High to stake out the airport for Frank Hannon—Frank Hannon, of all people, Pinkston's golfing buddy. What the alert was for, they didn't say—just take him into custody and be discreet. Assistant Director to be notified immediately. As the river of people streamed through the security gates, his eyes glazed over with the realization that he still had two hours to go before he was relieved. Then he heard the paging loudspeaker squawk, "Mr. McMasters of the FBI, Mr. McMasters of the FBI, please go to a white courtesy telephone. You have an urgent message.''

Suddenly he felt as though he were *buffo* under a spotlight. He couldn't understand why the office would break cover with a page instead of calling his cellular phone. Feeling embarrassed, he hustled over to a white receiver and picked it up with a terse, "This is Mc-Masters."

"Oh," came the operator's voice. "Hold on for a moment, sir. I'm connecting you now."

After a few clicks another female voice came on, and the sound of this one was, well, strained—as though she were trying to convey something, but was being held back by an unseen force. "Uh, Mr. McMasters, this is Nurse Hamilton at County General Emergency."

A spike of adrenaline surged into McMasters's bloodstream. "Yes?"

A strained pause. "Mr. McMasters, I-I'm sorry to be the one to have to tell you this—well, actually, we're limited to the information we can give out over the phone . . ."

A wave of impotence hit him like a breaker. That's how it happened, didn't it? An anonymous call from a faceless bureaucrat out of the blue, telling you your life has just been shattered like a crystal goblet tossed in the fireplace. He'd been a messenger like that himself a dozen times, and seen the people fall to the floor in a wail of grief when they received the news. "What is it!?" he demanded.

"Well, sir, it-it's about your wife and child. There's been an accident."

"Accident!? What kind of accident!? Ginny!?"

"Yes, and Jimmy." Her voice caught a little. "I'm sorry, sir. We can't give out information like this over the phone. Would you please just come to the ER as soon as you can. While there's still time.''

Frank peered around the pillar and saw McMasters turn pale and sprint toward the exit, leaving the receiver dangling like a bungy jumper at the end of a cord.

Two minutes later Miranda was by his side, saying, ''Agent McMasters will be indisposed for a while. Let's get airborne.''

Night had fallen over the compound at Papoose Lake, but Tyndale was oblivious to the time of day. In a few minutes he would have to brief Krieger on his dearth of luck in tracking down Frank, and he knew Krieger would not be pleased. Putting some final touches on his notes, he once again felt a drop of perspiration trickle past that damned scar under his armpit.

Then the telephone rang.

He grabbed the receiver and said, ''Number One.''

''This is Number Seventeen.''

Tyndale knew immediately that it was an assistant director of the FBI, one of two in the J. Edgar Hoover Building who were under his control. ''What is it?''

There was a trace of embarrassment in the voice. ''I've had a report our marks may have been at the Denver airport.''

''*May* have been?'' questioned Tyndale. ''Explain.''

A throat cleared. ''We had a man at the Denver airport. Name of McMasters. Not terribly bright, I'm afraid. Apparently our two fugitives fed him a line of bullshit over the phone. Made him believe his wife and child were in a Denver emergency room near death's door. He dropped everything and hauled ass into town without confirming. Upon arrival at the hospital he demanded to see his dying loved ones. The ER people looked at him like he was a lunatic. Needless to say, wife and child were at home watching the tube.''

Tyndale winced. ''And when was this?''

''Over an hour ago. When his backup arrived he went through the security videotape and found two possibles.''

Tin Man seethed, but at least there was still a chance. ''Listen carefully. This is what you do. Get a flight schedule of every plane that left the Denver airport since this McMasters dropped the ball. Ascertain their destinations and get your people to the gate of every flight before they touch down. Maybe we can still catch them.''

The FBI man balked. ''You can't be serious, Number One! There must be a hundred planes an hour flying out of that new airport, going across all of North America. Puddle-jumper commuter flights, too. We've got the major airports covered already—O'Hare, L-A-X, Sea-Tac, Atlanta, Dallas-Fort Worth—and we can notify our people there to check incoming Denver flights, but our marks could be coming down in Memphis or Kansas City or Cheyenne, Wyoming, for Chrissake. There's no way we could cover them all. And it's nine P.M. here— too late in the day to try a short-fused operation like this.''

''All airports, all destinations,'' replied Tin Man flatly. ''Now.''

There was a frustrated sigh on the end of the line. ''Look, if I appropriate too much manpower for a dragnet like this it will raise questions. Thus far I've been able to keep things discreet. I say we don't rock the boat on this.''

"Very well. I will inform Mr. Krieger that you have been uncooperative.''

A strained voice replied, "All right, all right. You win.''

Tin Man smiled to himself as he replied, "I usually do.''

The 757 pulled up to the jetway and Frank felt the rpms on his pulse ratchet up again. The stress was taking its toll on his middle-aged body and he sensed he was nearing the end of his tether.

"Okay," said Frank. "Tell me again how you know this woman.''

Miranda sighed before replying. "Brenna Weston and I went to graduate school at Columbia together. The two of us shared an apartment and we became tight, like surrogate sisters. We had classes together, covered stories together, traded clothes, boyfriends and all that. After graduation she went to the *Washington Post* and has worked her way up to assistant managing editor.''

Frank nodded, his mind preoccupied. Would they be facing a gauntlet once they were off the plane? He didn't know, so he allowed everyone else to get off before taking Miranda's backpack down from the overhead bin. He looked at his watch, then said, "Looks like we're a little early. Well, for better or worse, here we go. If we run into any artillery, you take your friend and make a run for it, and I'll try and draw them away,''

She glanced at the Browning High-Power in his waist band under his jacket and asked, "How the hell did you get that through airport security?''

"Professional secret. Now let's go."

She nodded without comment and they walked down the aisle, looking past the flight attendant with the lacquered smile who wished them farewell. With trepidation he reached the jetway entrance and peered out—just as Miranda shot past him while making a noise between a giggle and a scream. In an eye blink she was in the embrace of another woman in the terminal, rocking back and forth as they both babbled simultaneously. Frank figured it was one of those estrogen moments that should be left to burn itself out, so he took the opportunity to scan the terminal for bandits. Seeing nothing but a trickle of passengers heading for the baggage-claim carousel at this late hour, he exhaled with relief as Miranda and the woman disengaged from each other.

Brenna Weston, the assistant managing editor for the *Washington Post,* had obviously just come from a social function of some kind, for she was wearing a knee-length black velvet dress with a strand of pearls at the neck. Her hair was long, straight and blond, hitting about the middle of her back, but instead of contact lenses she wore a pair of designer frames on her striking features—probably as a way to signal she was some sort of intellectual. Miranda took his hand and brought him closer, saying, "Brenna, I want you to meet Frank Hannon. He's a close friend. A very close friend." As Brenna Weston lightly took his hand, Frank could sense that she was not impressed. Maybe if he'd shaved during the last week he'd have come across better.

"Do you have any luggage?" she enquired.

Miranda hefted the backpack. "Just this."

"Well, it's almost midnight and I suppose you two are tired. Where are you staying?"

Miranda took her by the arm and led her off, saying, "We aren't staying anywhere, Brenna. We're in transit and you're our driver."

They exited the terminal and crossed to the short-term parking garage, where they climbed into Brenna Weston's Saab. As they were paying the toll an FBI sedan pulled up to the terminal curbside and two agents hustled inside at the double time.

Frank and Miranda leaned back in the cushy leather seats of the Saab, unaware they'd just been saved by a tailwind.

The rolling, snow-covered terrain seemed incredibly tranquil under the moonlight, yet it was here that an ocean of blood had been spilled during a fulcrum point of history—where Union forces, and with it the Constitution, had prevailed over the Confederacy to cement a nation for posterity. Hannon wondered if this very night the Constitution faced a greater peril than when the armies of the Blue and the Gray clashed on this very farmland of southern Pennsylvania.

Brenna Weston pulled to the side of the country road and doused her headlights, caught in a state of disbelief at what she was doing. She pointed out the window to a manor house that stood like an obelisk on a distant hilltop, surrounded by forest. Inside lights burned, but other than that, no sign of life could be seen. "That's Trevor Dane's ancestral home," said Weston. "Been in the family for generations, I'm told. Uses it as a getaway from Washington. Now then, Miranda, would you please tell me what the hell this is all about? Why was it so critical to track down the *immediate* whereabouts of the Secretary of Defense? Why have I taken you and your friend here on a midnight tour of a Civil War battlefield? Why do the two of you look as though you've been through hell and come out the other side? Why have—"

Miranda hefted her backpack onto her shoulder as she opened the door, saying, "Maybe later, Brenna."

"Maybe later!? Miranda! What are you doing!?"

"This is where you get off, Miss Weston," replied Frank, opening the rear door. "Believe me when I say you're better off not knowing any more."

Brenna Weston was about to protest again—but the two doors slammed and she was left behind to gape as the pair trudged across the frozen ditch and gingerly made their way through the barbed-wire fence.

For a moment Weston thought about following, but quickly realized she wouldn't get far in the snow wearing a cocktail dress and high-heel pumps.

Lawton Tyndale wanted to rip the phone out by its coaxial roots, having become convinced the FBI was nothing but a congregation of bottom fish unable to pull their heads out of the mud. He'd received nothing but whines about imposing an after-hours dragnet, and then, after all the bellyaching, they'd come up empty-handed. Now he had to go into Krieger and face the music for their fuck-up, which made him antsy. He had to produce Hannon for Krieger—*had* to—or nothing but oblivion waited for him.

He assembled his materials and walked down the corridor to enter Krieger's underground anteroom, where two of the Cammo Dude gorillas eyed him suspiciously. One of them muttered something into the phone, then said, "You may enter."

Tyndale entered a chamber that was antiseptic as a dental office, with all pictures, mementos and photographs purged from the walls and credenza. Stacks of papers peppered a metal desk like sandbags, and in the center of the room was a formica conference table about the size of a small landing strip. Upon entry the Doberman sprang to his feet, a viper on legs, salivating with hope that Tin Man would cross some invisible boundary near his master.

"Down, Sringar. *Urdhvadhar!*" It was a curt command and the dog responded, as if spanked, resuming his prone position with a whimper.

Krieger did not acknowledge Tyndale's presence, for his attention was absorbed by the newspaper open on his desk, and it seemed like a small eon passed before he looked up and said, "What? Oh, yes, Lawton! Come here, come here! Look!"

Tyndale was expecting a welcome hewn from desert stone, so he was understandably baffled by Krieger's mood, which was slightly on the north side of euphoric.

Krieger spun the paper round and stabbed at the page with the dagger of his finger. "It's started, Lawton! Can you believe it? It's actually started! All these years of work, and now to see it actually taking root. It's just incredible! Read man, read! It's tomorrow's early edition of the *Washington Post*. I have it E-mailed to me every night."

Tyndale said nothing as he read the small story on the international page with the headline:

Outbreak Puzzles Health Officials in Borneo

Members of the World Health Organization have expressed concern over a growing viral infection in

the remote regions of Borneo that has surfaced over
the last few days. The nature of the infection appears to deplete the ability of bone marrow to generate red and white blood cells, the result being
acute anemia to the victim, coupled with a shrink-
ing ability to ward off infection.

WHO officials are working with the Indonesian
government to quarantine members of the native
tribal population where the virus was detected only
days ago. . . .

"They must have been satisfied with the delivery,"
bubbled Krieger. "No—more than satisfied—ecstatic.
They've gone to work already and it's happening sooner
rather than later, Lawton, before our very eyes. It's incredible, isn't it? We are on the threshold of our
dreams!" Suddenly, Krieger realized he'd opened his
kimono a bit too far and the euphoria disappeared, replaced by his standard chain-mail countenance. "Now
then, what do you have for me, Lawton? Have you run
this Hannon to ground yet?"

"No, Mr. Krieger."

Tyndale knew exactly how to play it now. His superior was genuinely euphoric, his dreams were coming to
fruition, and Tin Man knew he must wrap his bad news
in bureaucratic paper, making it appear as though the
FBI had blundered in Denver and Lawton Tyndale was
the knight on a white steed who alone could save the
day from oblivion—the only man capable of bringing
Frank Hannon to heel.

"Denver?" asked Krieger rhetorically. "Why Denver?"

"They knew they'd been spotted in Las Vegas. Turning up in Denver could mean that they are travelling east.''

Krieger's mind raced. "We have no way of knowing what Hannon and that woman reporter know—or what they could do with the information they have." The snapping turtle turned more menacing than ever as he pulled Tin Man's face closer to his own. "It's time you knew what is at stake, Lawton. You are Number One of security now and you've been operating in the dark. It must be brought home to you that this is not just some stupid little manhunt. Come along.''

They left the office, and Krieger led him through the warren of corridors to the stairwell that opened to the hangar above. With his shattered knee, Krieger rode a chairlift to the top as Tyndale followed; then the old man struggled off the stool and hobbled towards the terminus of the elevator, where the two guards flanking the door came to attention.

Tyndale glanced at the black saucer lying dormant on its pallet; then he stared at the elevator and his pulse began pounding, not knowing what to expect. Krieger halted and punched in a number on the cipher pad, caus-ing the doors to open; then they stepped inside, where Krieger entered another code on another cipher pad. The doors closed and the lift began its descent. Tyndale no-ticed there were three levels—U, M and L, which he presumed was the lower level.

"If you prove yourself worthy, Lawton, you shall be my understudy," said Krieger solemnly. "Should any-thing happen to me, the project will pass to you, my Number One of security. Therefore you must know everything there is to know about Sirius."

"I appreciate your confidence, sir."

The bloodless eyes stared him down. "No one has my confidence."

The elevator halted.

Krieger looked up at the small lens on the ceiling and said, "It is Krieger and Number One of security. You will grant access."

The doors parted and they entered a low-ceilinged antechamber that held two desks and two more Cammo Dudes, and on the far wall was a polished steel door that looked as though it had been transplanted from the Federal Reserve vault.

Krieger did not speak to the guards as he stepped to yet another keypad and punched in another stream of cipher codes. The massive door opened to reveal an elevated pathway inside an octagonal-shaped tunnel—a tunnel that was inlaid with metallic tiles and illuminated by indirect lights concealed under the walkway. Krieger stepped onto the elevated path and Tyndale followed, becoming aware of a dull electric hum. A hundred feet later they came to a metallic door that had no knob, but to the side of the door there was a black panel that resembled a slate of onyx. Krieger reached out, placed his hand flat against the slate and pressed gently. A laser beam scanned his handprint and a red LED readout flashed up on the slate: "ACCESS—KRIEGER—CONFIRM." To that, the old man chanted, "Access, Krieger, Sirius-one-seven-nine-Omega-seven-Romeo."

There was the sound of a *chung,* and as the heavy metal door swung slowly open, Krieger stepped back and whispered to Tin Man in a cold voice, "Prepare to meet thy fate, Lawton."

With fearful eyes, Tin Man looked within the sanctum—and froze with terror.

The Secretary of Defense entered the baronial library of his country manor and stoked the fire with a poker. It was past midnight and he was wearing a cardigan and slacks, unable to sleep or concentrate on anything but the fax that brought a growing sense of dread with each succeeding read.

To the public at large, Treavor Dane seemed to have the golden touch. Born the heir to a textile fortune, he'd received an Ivy League education before serving a stint in the Peace Corps and the State Department. From there he'd entered politics as a Congressman from Pennsylvania, then on to the Senate where his popularity seemed to grow with each succeeding sound bite. Dane had received a high-profile appointment as Defense Secretary by a President who saw in him the means to shore up his sagging polls, but then on risky missions to Bosnia and Taiwan, Dane had seen his own currency grow— grow to the point that he and his own party realized he was eclipsing a sitting President. So quietly, with his own money (of which there was plenty), he'd begun polling to explore his own Presidential possibilities.

But the disparity between the public and private personas of Treavor Dane was more than a gap—it was a chasm, manifested by the photograph on the mantle—a remembrance of a wife who'd taken her own life, unable to reconcile the dark contradiction she had married. After her death, Dane had used his powerful office, personal fortune and rakish looks to cut a swath through the skirts of Washington—but each conquest had left him more empty than before, until he had nothing but politics and the memory of an old professor to sustain him. Now even those anchors of his life had been turned

PAYNE HARRISON

on their heads with the arrival of a barely legible script through his private fax machine, right over there on his credenza. In frustration he threw another log on the fire and went to the wet bar to pour himself a brandy. He was filling the snifter and contemplating his quandary when a voice behind him said, "Good evening, Mr. Secretary."

The Courvosier sloshed over his hand and onto the floor as he whipped around to see a rather swarthy-looking man standing just inside the door wearing jeans, snow-covered boots and a heavy down jacket. He stepped inside and a woman, similarly attired, entered behind him.

"Who the hell are you!?" barked the Cabinet officer, trying to veil the fact he was frightened.

"I apologize for the intrusion, Mr. Secretary," countered Hannon, "but the situation being what it is, we had to contact you secretly."

Dane started moving towards his desk, and Hannon figured correctly there was some sort of panic button concealed under the desk overhang. He pulled out the Browning High-Power and leveled it at the man who was technically his boss. "Sorry about this, too, Mr. Secretary, but I can't let you call in the Marines. Fortunately I have some experience in covert entry and we were able to slip by them, but they're still there."

Now Dane was really scared. "So just who the hell are you?"

The other man sighed. "My name is Frank Hannon, Mr. Secretary, and up until a week ago I was an intelligence staff officer with the North American Aerospace Defense Command at Peterson Air Force Base in Colorado Springs. To explain why Miranda Park—that's the

214

lady's name—and I are here, I think it best that I begin by putting a question to you up front.''

Cautiously, Dane said, ''Go ahead.''

Frank swallowed, took a deep breath and asked, ''Mr. Secretary, could you tell me if you have any knowledge of a black project headquartered on the Nellis flight range in Nevada at a place called Papoose Lake?''

The bottle of cognac slipped from the Secretary's hand and shattered on the hardwood floor in a foamy explosion.

The doctor had an obesity problem, and Tyndale detested fat men, seeing their girth as a weakness of character. The physician had no discernible neck, and his face looked as though it had been inflated with an air hose, making his eyes tiny slits that peered out from flabby lids. He took out a penlight and explored the patient's pupils, then looked up at Tin Man and shook his head, saying, ''No luck, I'm afraid. Only incoherent babbling.''

''I thought these days there were designer drugs that could make a prisoner sing like a mezzo soprano.''

The leviathan shrugged. ''Sometimes they work, sometimes they don't. He's on blood pressure medication as well, so that may garble the effect.''

Tin Man was fresh out of patience and understanding. ''Then we'll do it the hard way. Bring him out of it.''

Instead of protesting that his patient was too weak to move and needed rest for recovery, the sumo medic knew only too well that his own fate might be tied to Tyndale's ability to break the Nobel laureate. So the heavy-lidded eyes looked up and said to the male nurse, ''Get me some benzedrine from the pharmacy, would you?''

TEN

❦

When the cognac bottle had splattered at the feet of Treavor Dane, Hannon figured he and Miranda had stepped onto a coffin train—that their supposition of his ignorance was, in a literal sense, dead wrong. But Dane had not called for the Marines. Instead, his collegiate features had appeared genuinely shaken at the question, and he'd asked Hannon to continue, which he and Miranda had done.

Now it was three hours later, and Dane seemed transfixed by Miranda's videotape, for he kept going backwards and forwards over the Papoose Lake footage. Finally he stopped and pointed at the waiflike figure on the screen, saying softly, "That's Michel. I'm almost sure of it."

"Michel?" asked Hannon.

"Bertrand," replied Dane.

"Bertrand!?" Miranda's voice had the timbre of a squeegee. "But he's been dead for months! Killed in a plane crash over Lake Superior."

Dane nodded in agreement, then walked to his credenza, saying, "With no trace of the aircraft ever found. I delivered a tearful euology to my old professor before the Swedish Royal Academy only days ago. Then when I returned home"—he held up a sheaf of fax paper—"I found this waiting for me."

"What is it?" asked Hannon.

Dane handed it over, saying, "I think you and Miss Park should read it, Colonel. In view of where you just came from, I think the document speaks for itself."

Dazed and confused, Frank accepted the papers and found they were filled with writing in an irregular, scratchy hand—on stationery with the letterhead of the Green Mountain Inn in New Hampshire. With a sense of fear and fascination, Frank held the paper under the light and began to read the testament of a scholar returned from the dead.

My dear Treavor—

How long has it been? Time seems so short, so compressed, since you were that strapping adolescent in my class—questioning and challenging the basic premises of physics that such an eminent professor as myself was offering to a group of collegiate sophomores. Years later it was with a sense of pride, but not surprise, that I followed your rise to the Senate and then the Cabinet, for I could sense the coals of ambition burning within you even during your days as a student.

Treavor—where do I begin? How do I tell you? How do I convey that which even I can scarcely believe myself—I who have seen it, touched it, even

smelt it, for more than a decade. Even now, in ret-
rospect, it is hard to absorb all that has happened,
but I must persevere for it is vital beyond measure
that you hear my testimony—and to that end, this
old man can only begin at the beginning.

For me, it all commenced eleven years ago. A
man appeared in my office at the Institute for Advanced Research at Princeton. He seemed très sa-
gace, very shrewd, and claimed he was with Los
Alamos Laboratory. As you know, my scientific specialty is gravity waves, and as he peppered me with
a host of questions it became apparent he was incredibly well versed in the field. That surprised me,
because the community of physicists in the disci-
pline of gravity waves is quite small and we all
know each other well, yet I did not know this man.
But when I began to probe his credentials he
abruptly terminated our conversation and left.

That night I returned home and was, quite simply, kidnapped. Before I could turn on the lights of
my living room my arms were pinned and a needle
inserted. I blacked out and some time later—I know
not when—I woke up in a clinical setting. There
was no doctor or nurse, just an older man sitting
at my bedside, smiling wickedly and holding a co-
bra-handled cane. He greets me, says his name is
Krieger, and apologizes for the surgery.

Surgery?

My left side is tender. I painfully raise my arm
and see an incision has been made under my armpit. I demand to know what is happening, but this
man Krieger—whom I would come to know well—
only smiles and replies, ''Whether you like it or not,

you're part of the Sirius Group now. We require
your expertise and the incision holds an implant to
insure your cooperation." Needless to say, I am
stunned, astounded. I start to protest again, but he
orders me to get dressed.

In shock, I comply. He then leads me through a
maze of underground corridors. I have no idea
where I am, and it is only later I learn we are at
a place in the Nevadan desert called Papoose Lake.

Frank and his chair parted company for a moment as
the words "Papoose Lake" crossed his vision, but then
he continued reading, the testament exerting its own rap-
ture on the senses.

Krieger then takes me to an elevator entrance and
we go down. The door opens and I step into an
area that is like a large aircraft hangar, only un-
derground, brightly lit, and that is where I lay eyes
on it for the first time.

My dear Treavor, words fail me now as I attempt
to convey to you the profound and overwhelming
shock that seized me when I first saw it with my
own eyes—for in that single moment the entire bed-
rock of my life, my work, my soul, was capsized;
yet upon seeing it I knew in mon cœur exactly what
it was, and the impact of that vision has forever
shattered me.

It was a vessel, mon ami. A vessel not of this
earth.

ELEVEN

———⊷⧓⊶———

The glowing embers in the hearth warmed the chamber, but an icicle cold, invulnerable to the fire's glow, began to encircle Frank Hannon's soul as he absorbed the testament of Michel Bertrand. That sense of validation, of learning that his and Miranda's quest had a grounding in reality, provided him with a passing sense of relief, but that relief was soon evicted by an eerie foreboding as the physicist's words silently screamed at him from the pages.

It all began on May 20th, 1954, when a military radar operator saw an extraordinary blip on his screen over Arizona airspace. It was traveling at incredible speeds, then it stopped abruptly, then began speeding again, then stop, then speed, stop, speed, stop, and so on. Fighter planes were scrambled and acquired it visually, then a game of cat and mouse ensued before it came down on a remote ranch outside of Kingman, Arizona. A military team

*responded swiftly, and upon arrival they received
the shock of ten lifetimes, for they found . . .*

Hannon came to the end of the last page and looked
up, questioning, "Where's the rest of it?"

Dane looked a bit sheepish. "It came through my personal fax machine just as it ran out of paper, and we
had a power outage during my absence that wiped out
the electronic buffer. So all I have from Michel is what
is in your hands."

Miranda finished the last page and stared at the Secretary. "Have you ever received any briefings, any information at all about Papoose Lake?"

Dane shook his head. "I've known about Area 51, of
course. That has been the test facility for a number of
covert projects, from the U-2 to the stealth fighter. I've
visited there on three occasions myself. But I've never
seen or heard anything about this Papoose Lake. I had
no idea what venue Michel's letter was referring to until
I heard your testimony and saw your tape."

The pall of silence fell over them until Miranda said,
"You've got to take control of the situation. You must
physically seize this Papoose Lake base and put the peo
ple who are running it in irons. You must—"

"I can't," replied Dane softly.

Miranda sat up. "What do you mean, you *can't*?
You're the Secretary of Defense, for God's sake! Go to
the President, call a press conference, but take control
of this thing!"

Dane shook his head. "You don't understand. It's not
that I don't have the will. It's just that, well, I fear I
might be a prisoner."

"A prisoner?" asked Hannon.

Dane nodded. "Yes. In Michel's letter he referred to a surgical procedure—an implant under his left arm. Undoubtedly the same kind of implant that killed your friend Dreason."

"So?" asked Miranda.

"A few weeks ago the chief of my personal security detail—a Marine gunnery sergeant named Hampton—was in the Pentagon handball tournament. Hampton is as tough as they come and he lost in the quarterfinals. After the match I stopped by the locker room to offer my condolences and happened to catch him coming out of the shower. I distinctly remember seeing a crescent-shaped scar under his left armpit."

Frank whistled.

"In view of that, there is no way to tell how insidious their reach is throughout the government," said Dane. "If I try to make a move against them they could easily arrange my demise, because I have no way of knowing whom I could trust—in the Pentagon, the intelligence community, law enforcement. Who knows how pervasive their reach is?" Dane slapped his legs in frustration and rose, plaintively saying, "The country is at risk from an unknown presence from an unknown world, and there is an insidious satellite government controlling things, controlling *me*! They've recaptured Michel and maybe killed him by now. In the face of all this, I am the Secretary of Defense of the United States and I can do *nothing*!"

"You could call a press conference," suggested Miranda meekly.

"And be branded a lunatic before a cry went up for my resignation? I'm afraid that's not an option."

A silence returned before Frank said, "Then it comes

down to having the means—the people—you can trust to take action.''

Dane stared into the fire. ''That is correct, Colonel. Whoever is running this Sirius operation has struck upon the perfect strategy to co-opt any threat to their safety. Everywhere I turn in the Pentagon I see the face of a potential assassin. There is simply no one I can trust. . . .'' He paused, and it was then that Frank noticed a twinkle in the Secretary's eye, and perhaps even the hint of a smile as he turned and looked at them, saying, ''That is, except for the two of you.''

TWELVE

---⊛⊛⊛---

Fort Bragg is a sprawling military complex outside Fayetteville, North Carolina. It is home to the 82nd Airborne Division, the headquarters of the U.S. Special Operations Command and—if you can get anyone to tell you—the Army's Delta Force.

It was a cold and blustery night as Major Andrew Shiloh "Shy" Potter walked out of the U.S. Special Operations Command (SOCOM) headquarters building wearing jeans and a heavy jacket on this, the last Saturday night before Christmas. Potter worked on the J-3 operations staff of SOCOM headquarters, and had just returned from a joint deployment to Egypt with the Army's Delta Force and the Navy's SEAL Team Six. They'd performed a simulated embassy rescue under "full mission profile" conditions, which meant everything but the bullets were real and sleep was a concept only found in mythology. But now they were back home, with Christmas and a warm bed in the offing. The thirty-eight-year-old bachelor had just turned in his leave ticket for the Yuletide season, too tired to spit after spending the last three days and nights finishing off the deployment's after-action report. Now he was headed down to Georgia to spend Christmas with his aging parents before hooking it down to Puerto Rico for a little R&R on the beach with a sweet young thang he'd met in Hawaii during his last furlough.

Potter had just climbed into his Ford Explorer and started the engine when a voice behind him said, "Evening, Shy."

That nearly sent Potter through the Explorer's sun roof as he whipped around. *"What the—!? Who—!?"*

"C'mon, Shy. It hasn't been that long since Baghdad."

Potter flicked on the cabin light, then stammered, "F-Frank? Frank *Hannon*? What are you do—"

"Rest easy, Shy. I'm here on business. Our kind of business. Find us a quiet tavern somewhere. We've got a lot to talk about."

The watering hole was called the Tarheel Grill and it was a fair distance away from the drinking emporiums frequented by the airborne and special ops troopers who might recognize Potter. A schoolmarm of a waitress had come and gone, depositing their orders of bourbon and branch water with an air of disapproval worthy of Carrie Nation. Hannon figured she was in the wrong line of work as he took a sip, then focused his attention on Major Shiloh Potter.

He was shorter than Hannon, but with a muscled compactness that rivaled an artillery shell. His eyes were gold-flecked brown, and told you straightaway he would

225

not suffer fools, and his spike-cut red hair looked as if it had been combed with a rake. His career track had precious little luster to it due to his politically incorrect tendency to tell superior officers to fuck off when he thought they were wrong—and that happened more often than you might think.

Potter raised his glass and said, "To the Bunker Busters."

Hannon clinked his and replied, "To the Bunker Busters."

Potter tossed his back, and as the sour-mash elixir burned down to his stomach he muttered, "We damn near nailed that bastard Saddam. Another twenty-four hours and we'd a had him for sure."

Hannon shrugged. *"C'est la guerre."*

After Saddam Hussein had annexed Kuwait and American troops and planes started pouring into Saudi Arabia, Frank Hannon had found himself sharing a desk in the air intelligence division outside Riyadh with a newly minted Air Force major named Shiloh Potter. In the initial phase of Desert Shield their mutual job involved target selection—i.e., choosing targets for the armada of warplanes that would be unleashed in Desert Storm. Hannon and Potter were thirty days deep into their Desert Shield assignments, pouring over reconnaissance photos, when they were abruptly pulled off and shipped to Wright-Patterson Air Force Base in Ohio, where in a closed hangar they were shown a dozen barrels of 8-inch artillery cannons lying on the concrete floor.

A briefing followed, where it was revealed to them they were going after the biggest target of all—none other than Saddam Hussein himself.

Paranoid and vindictive, Hussein trusted no one and shifted his personal headquarters constantly to keep himself safe from the conspirators he saw lurking in every corner. To that end, he built and maintained a number of underground bunkers in and around Baghdad that were impervious to air attacks with their armor-plated concrete ceilings. Or so he thought. After the invasion, the Air Force set to the problem of nailing Hussein in his own lair, and the concept of the "Bunker Buster" was born.

Simply put, all you need to penetrate a steel-reinforced concrete bunker under fifty feet of earth is a projectile strong enough, fast enough, heavy enough and with enough explosive power to obliterate the interior of the bunker. The Air Force found the answer by tapping the field artillery assets of the Army in the form of the 8-inch howitzer. Once a naked 8-inch cannon barrel was packed with high-yield explosives and fitted with a Paveway laser-seeker nose cone and directional fins, a Bunker Buster bomb was created. The employment of this engine of war was thus: The bomb would be strapped to an F-15E Eagle strike fighter, and the pilot would put the aircraft into a high-speed dive as the bombardier lased the target bunker; then the bomb would be released and plummet to the ground at five hundred miles per hour. The kinetic energy of the fast-moving howitzer was so powerful that it cratered the ground like a meteorite striking the earth, and once the bunker's roof was breached, the three thousand pounds of explosive would detonate.

That left one problem: In order for it to work, the bomb had to land *precisely* on top of the bunker's roof. Anything less than pure precision would only result in an expensive hole in the ground. Aerial reconnaissance did an effective job of finding the air vents that poked to the surface above the bunkers, but their exact location under the earth—relative to the vents—remained a mystery.

Enter Hannon and Potter. The day after the air war of Desert Storm began, the two men were inserted outside Baghdad with a special ops team; and as the night sky lit up with antiaircraft fire, Hannon and Potter went to their designated points inside Baghdad and set up their man-portable seismographs. Eerily, the bombing would halt for, say, a half hour each night except for a single bomb dropped from an F-117 stealth fighter on Hannon's command. The ensuing shock waves from the detonation were recorded on the seismographs; then the data were brought back to Riyadh for analysis by a group of eminent geophysicists. The scientists were able to plot the precise bunker locations by triangulating the anomalies in the seismic waves caused by the large underground structures.

As the war headed for a surprisingly swift conclusion, the Bunker Busters began a race against time. Night after night Hannon and Potter would clandestinely gather the seismic data; then it would be brought back to Riyadh for analysis. Once it was plotted, the F-15E flight crew would begin their mission planning, then take off after darkness fell.

One by one the bunkers were imploded—nine in all—but Saddam Hussein remained elusive as the final "Buster" mission was flown in the waning minutes of the Gulf War.

Although he retained his bloody hold on Iraq, Saddam was profoundly shaken by the systematic destruction of his bunker network, because without his underground lairs he'd been flushed to the surface, and have exposed to the vagaries of the coalition's air power.

C'est la guerre.

Carrie Nation had come and gone with a third round, and after a hiatus of remembrance, Potter asked, "So what's going down, Frankie?"

Hannon struck up a Marlboro, saying, "What's the heaviest op you ever went on, Shy?"

Potter was more than a little surprised by the question. "Well, humpin' a seismograph through a bombed-out Baghdad was pretty heavy, as I recall—but then there was the time we went in and shortstopped some dudes in Iran just before they took delivery of a nuke from some KGB entrepreneurs. But I can't talk about that."

At another time, at another place, Hannon might have been impressed. But not here, and not now. He took out an envelope from his jacket pocket and slid it across the table, saying, "Think about the heaviest thing you ever did and multiply it by fifty times—then maybe, just maybe, you'll start to have an inkling of why I'm here."

Potter felt his breath seize up as he took the envelope. Then slowly he extracted the handwritten epistle and read it with stunned amazement.

DEPARTMENT OF DEFENSE

TO: Major Shiloh Potter, USAF

Dear Major Potter,

This letter is a direct order from your Secretary of Defense, whose orders you are sworn to obey.

*You are to place yourself under the direct per-
sonal command of Lt. Col. Franklin Hannon, whom
you know personally and who has given you this
letter. His orders are to be carried out with all
dispatch—without question and in total secrecy.*

*Colonel Hannon will provide you with a briefing
on the particulars of your critical mission, plus any
support you may require to carry it out.*

> *Treavor Dane*
> *Secretary of Defense*

Potter looked up at Hannon, the sparkle in his gold-
flecked eyes having been extinguished. "If anyone else
but you had given me this I'd have said it was a crock.
What the hell is going down, Frank?"

Hannon pulled on his Marlboro. "I need you to assemble a small team—the best of the best—from Delta,
SEALS or Force Recon Marines. Four plus you should
do it for the pathfinder team, plus air. We'll need people
you know, people you trust. All of it off the books, because we can't trust anyone in the normal chain of command. If you get any questions from your recruits, just
show them that letter. That should convert the faint of
heart."

"So what's the deal?" enquired Potter.

Hannon exhaled a stream of smoke, then replied,
"We're going on an op."

"An op? Where? Russia? Iran? . . . *Iraq?*"

Hannon shook his head.

"Where then?"

Hannon looked around to double-check they weren't
being overheard; then he stubbed out his cigarette and
said, "Nevada."

• • •

The feeling was unlike anything he'd ever known. He'd had a kidney stone long ago, and that had been painful, but this—it was beyond his comprehension or experience. It was like the hottest thing your skin had ever touched was a warm tub, and then you were immersed in a tank of boiling water that scalded the flesh off the bone.

Michel . . . Michel, can you hear me?

The ropes were tight, holding him upright as his head fell forward so he wouldn't choke on his own vomit. At first he'd felt indignant as they'd pinned his arms and ankles to the chair and stripped him of his shirt, and the little metal clips they'd fastened to his Achilles tendons were considered an irritation. But then—

Now tell us, Michel. Tell us so we can take you out of here. Tell us so we can give you a warm bath, a nice comfortable bed and something for the pain. This is all so unnecessary.

It was as though the voice was coming from the other side of a door—muffled and barely discernible. His senses were so overwhelmed by pain and the stench of his own excrement and vomit that his auditory powers could barely function. Yet through it all he had a sense of irony. He'd never considered himself a brave man, and he didn't think he was being brave now. It was only his sense of self-preservation that kept him from answering, for he knew his silence was his only means to staying alive. But in the face of a pain so wicked, was it worth staying alive anymore?

You were at the Green Mountain Inn in New Hampshire when we found you, Michel. Did you tell anyone about Sirius before we got to you? Tell us the truth, Michel. Did you tell anyone about Sirius?

Bertrand mumbled something that he thought sounded like "No," but apparently his interrogator was unhappy with the response and the switch was thrown once again.

The current surged through the alligator clips, causing an aria of pain to ricochet through the chamber as the old man convulsed like a mackerel out of water. Then the switch came off and the Nobel laureate sagged as he uttered something before a final breath went out of him.

They waited for some minutes, but Bertrand stayed there like a marionette with its strings severed. The obese doctor went forward and pulled the head back to pry an eyelid open, then inspected the open pupil with a penlight. Slowly he lowered Michel Bertrand's head back on his chest and pronounced, "The prisoner is in a coma."

Tin Man kicked the interrogator's chair. "I told you not to lose him, you idiot!"

The interrogator—a muscled sort of the Oriental persuasion—shrugged as he said, "I had it on the pussy setting. He was an old man who you'd already drugged. We worked him over for a long time and he couldn't absorb any more."

Tin Man was angry, and more scared than ever. Frank and the woman reporter were still at large, and Bertrand had turned into more of a thorny problem than he'd figured. Had the Nobel physicist compromised Sirius in some way? Now there was no way of knowing. "Did he say anything before he went comatose? Anything at all?" demanded Tin Man.

The interrogator shrugged. "Nothing but incoherent mumbling."

"Indeed? Well, why don't you send the tapes to my office and I'll see if that's the case. Think you can do that without fucking it up?"

Grudgingly, the interrogator nodded.

Tin Man turned on his heel and left in a huff, saying, "And you came so highly recommended."

THIRTEEN

———❧———

Ernest Medford was a hardscrabble sheep rancher who'd scraped out a living in the unforgiving wastelands of central Nevada, leasing large parcels of public land that required upwards of fifty acres to support a single head of sheep. To keep track of his widely scattered herd on the open range, Ernest Medford had climbed out of the saddle years ago and into the left seat of a used Cessna. He kept his aging aircraft parked in a hangar about a half mile from the ranch house, beside a dirt road that doubled as a landing strip. While the Cessna had become an integral part of his business, times were hard—and needed maintenance on the old airplane had fallen behind. He needed a new plane badly, but the money just wasn't there, even for a down payment. That is, until yesterday. From out of the blue some young whippersnapper with flaming red hair had appeared at his doorstep, saying he wanted to lease the hangar for a month. He'd handed the old rancher an envelope of $10,000 cash saying he wanted the Cessna out of the hangar, no questions, and privacy with a capital P. The whipper-snapper had said, "Take it or leave it," right then and there—adding that as far as he was concerned, the IRS didn't need to know anything about their transaction.

Ernest Medford took the money, figuring they were probably druggers—but druggers had used his property before and not paid for it. Should he call the sheriff? He'd called the sheriff more than once about rustled sheep, and all he ever got was the runaround and property tax bills from the county he could barely pay. So Ernest Medford took the money, then flew his Cessna up to the Tonopah airport to trade it in on a model with fewer hours.

He'd made a good deal, but the new plane wouldn't be ready for another week, so he'd hitched a flight back to the ranch and just landed. It was near midnight as he walked under the cold, starry sky towards the ranch house. With his breath turning to vapor as he mounted the front porch steps, he looked back at the hangar in the distance, his curiosity aroused by the *whop-whop-whop* of rotor blades cutting through the air.

Shiloh Potter had been fast asleep, catching up on sack time after the long trip to Alaska and back, when a hand gently shook his shoulder, saying, "Major?"

He came awake and raised himself off the bedroll. "What is it?"

"I think the chopper is here, sir."

Potter heard the dull *whop whop* sound, causing him to quickly pull on his boots and field jacket and exit the hangar. He looked skyward and watched the Blackhawk utility copter descend toward the ground, kicking up dust as it hovered over the small asphalt apron before touching down. The pilot immediately feathered the turbine and extinguished the navigation lights, then pulled off his night-vision goggles. Potter ordered the rusty sliding doors of the hangar pushed open as the pilot popped open the hatch and climbed out, saying, "Think this will do?"

Curly Sikes was a wiry sort, and a member of the 160th Task Force, which provided the air elements to the U.S. Special Operations Command. Based at Fort Campbell, Kentucky, he was a member of the "Nightstalkers" helicopter group, a pilot schooled in the dangerous art of nap-of-the-earth flying . . . in darkness.

Potter did a once-over of the helicopter and nodded approvingly as he noted the OCEAN HAWK logo painted on the side. "Where'd you find this?"

Sikes peeled off his helmet, revealing a scalp of wiry blond tendrils that had earned him the sobriquet of "Curly."

"Picked it up from an offshore outfit on the brink of foreclosure. Dropped the fifty grand in cash on their desk and said I wanted to borrow the bird for a week. I knew the manager from Fort Rucker. He pocketed the *dinero* and said he'd keep quiet. I'm sure that he's sure I'm running drugs."

"So is the rancher. Secure the blade and let's get it inside."

Within a minute the ad hoc team put their shoulders to it and rolled the Blackhawk into the hangar, the tail rotor just clearing the door. Once everything was buttoned up, Potter flicked on the light.

"Derryberry here yet?" asked Sikes, wondering where his copilot was.

"Supposed to get in later tonight. Get some grub, check your gear and then catch some sack time if you can. By the way, Merry Christmas."

"When do we go?"

"Tomorrow night."

"Roger that, Major. But when do we get this brief you've been promising."

"As soon as Derryberry and our briefer get here."

"Right." Sikes sauntered over to take one of the cold sandwiches off the table and a mug of hot chocolate from a hot plate. Along one wall of the hangar were two long folding tables with military equipment arranged on top of them in neat little piles—plus a small Christmas tree that had appeared from nowhere, decorated with aluminum foil from spent sticks of chewing gum. (Special ops troops were known for their resourcefulness.)

Scattered out on the hangar floor were four men in their late twenties to early thirties, all of them senior non-coms. Two were from the Army's Delta Force, one was a Navy SEAL and one was a Force Recon Marine—all veterans of the Gulf War. They were sitting on their respective bedrolls, methodically checking and rechecking the equipment splayed around them on the floor—things such as parasails, night-vision goggles, radio headsets and Heckler & Koch assault weapons. A couple of electric space heaters warmed the air, and laid out on the floor in the corner was something that looked not unlike Count Dracula's cape.

All the men were unmarried, and had been tapped by Potter four days before Christmas Eve for the op. Other men would've howled at having their holiday crashed, but these men were different. They were accustomed to the unexpected and trained to absorb long periods of boredom followed by stark moments of terror. They'd chosen a life devoid of banker's hours and family holidays for a career few could understand or appreciate, for they faced unrelenting training in climates that were hot or cold, muggy or wet, with little to show for it but scars and muscle tissue that was only slightly softer than wrought iron. The payoff for this backbreaking lifestyle? Well, the payoff for these kind of men was something intangible, something you couldn't put on a financial statement—but it was real and definitely present. The payoff was being part of a team of people upon whom you could *rely*. A wife might betray you, a business partner might cheat you, a parent might disown you, but the men in the hangar—although some were new to each other—knew they could rely on the others to take a bullet for them should it ever come to that. In shorthand: There were no slackers here.

While all were trained in the panoply of skills required for their profession, each man had his own particular specialty. Jenkins and Gau were both staff sergeants in the Army's Delta Force—one was a world-class skydiver while the other was a communications specialist who spoke four languages fluently. The Navy SEAL, named Strauss, was a "shooter" trained in counterterrorist assaults. He was also a championship chess player. And the Force Recon Marine, whose name was Hauer—well, he was the sniper, and those sort of people tended to do one thing and do it very well.

Potter was congratulating himself as he studied a U.S. Geological Survey map of Nevada. To braid together an "off the books" op from scratch during the Yuletide season was quite an accomplishment under any circumstances, but a Cabinet officer's line of credit certainly helped. The equipment hadn't been a problem as the troopers were using their personal parasails, firearms and such. A suitable chopper had been the biggest hurdle.

Potter heard the sound of a vehicle pulling up to the hangar, so he went out to investigate. It was a white Jeep Grand Cherokee, the kind that Hannon had told him were used by the Cammo Dude security troops at Area 51. Upon seeing it, Potter was about to go to battle stations when Frank Hannon, a hayseed good old boy named Clarence Derryberry, and a woman climbed out. Potter released the balloon of his lungs and asked, "You steal these wheels from one of those Dudes?"

"Naw. Drove it off the lot of a Jeep dealership in Las Vegas two days ago after I got back from Alaska. Told the salesman I got lucky at the tables." Hannon jerked his thumb. "Picked up your Chief Derryberry here at the McCarran Airport. Does that put us at full strength?"

"Full strength plus a lady. And we got the air inside."

Without another word, Clarence Derryberry entered the hangar. In the small universe of the 160th Task Force, the Army warrant officer had a reputation as one who could thread a needle with a Blackhawk while flying backwards and blindfolded.

"Got the VCR set up?" asked Hannon.

"Inside," replied Potter. "Do we get the brief now? I mean, you've told me the where— Nellis, for Chrissake—but are you going to give us the why of it?"

"Yeah, Shy, you get the why of it now. That was my deal with the SecDef, that everybody on the op was in the loop. Our friends in Alaska have gotten the brief. Now it's your turn."

"Okay. So who's the lady?"

"Her name is Miranda, and she's tougher than any of

the Gila monsters you've got in there. Let's go.''

Once inside, Hannon gathered the small group around the table holding the television and the VCR. Then he took a breath and began. ''Gentlemen, I am Lieutenant Colonel Frank Hannon, until recently a NORAD staff officer at Cheyenne Mountain. I believe Major Potter has shared a letter with you, and I can assure you that we are, indeed, operating under the direct personal orders of the Secretary of Defense of the United States. The footage you are about to see was taken by Miranda Park ten nights ago inside the Nellis boundary at a place called Papoose Lake. You'll find it on your maps at grid coordinates S-4.''

And he hit the play button.

FOURTEEN

—⧉—

The clerk was always so chipper, which Tin Man found annoying, and when this business with Frank was over he'd get rid of him.

The clerk held up the reel of audio tape and said, "This just came back from the audio enhancement people, sir. Want me to load it up for you?"

Tyndale motioned to the reel-to-reel rig on his conference table and the clerk loaded it onto the spool.

"Close the door on your way out," ordered Tin Man, and the clerk complied. Tyndale sighed and rose from his chair, pissed that the interrogator had been correct. Bertrand's responses under duress had been incoherent babbling, and as a last gasp attempt to mine any hard information out of the tape, Tin Man had sent the tape through audio enhancement. Wearily, he clamped the headphones on and hit the play button, knowing the time he had left to serve up Frank Hannon was rapidly evaporating.

•   •   •

There was a hushed atmosphere in the hangar as the commandos lay on their bedrolls, trying without success to get some sleep. There was always a pregame silence before an op, but added to that was the gravity of what was at stake and the unearthly nature of what they were facing. Even the Marine was unsettled.

Potter walked Frank and Miranda to the white Grand Cherokee. Hannon looked up at the clear sunny sky, then checked his watch and said, "We'll converge at grid S-4 in about six hours."

Potter shook his head. "Downtown Baghdad never looked so good to me."

"Me neither."

"Let's move it," said Miranda.

"Yes, ma'am."

And they climbed into the Cherokee, Miranda at the wheel. She fired up the engine, then put her hand over his, saying, "Whatever happens, Colonel Frank Hannon, let me just say I'm proud to have been in your outfit."

Frank looked at her with overpowering feelings of—what?—admiration, awe, desire, tenderness, respect, longing. She was one in a million, this lady, and for her future—if any of them had a future—she deserved better than some worn-out piece of shoe leather like Frank Hannon. Yet he found the idea of living without her more frightening than what loomed ahead of them this very night. He took her face in his hands and gave her a long, deep, wet one, not wanting to stop—like that first kiss in junior high. But finally their lips parted and he said, "Put the spurs to it, lady."

She dropped the Jeep into gear and replied, "You can be so romantic, Frank."

* * *

"Wainwright Tower, this is MATS one-zero-seven, requesting clearance for takeoff."

"Roger, MATS one-zero-seven. You are cleared on runway one-left. Happy holidays."

The first of three C-130 Hercules transports turned into the wind at Wainwright Field in Fairbanks, Alaska, its four engines spooling up to full power under the awesome grandeur of the aurora borealis, which was already dancing in the twilight of the high-latitude sky. As the transport lumbered down the runway, the pilot pulled back on the control column, bringing the hefty-looking craft into the air.

Once all three aircraft joined up in formation at cruise altitude, the lead pilot took up a vector for the southeast and settled in for the long flight.

"There, there, Professor, take a little broth, will you?" The obese doctor held the Nobel laureate's head up and he drank hungrily, evoking a response from the doctor. "Very good. Your recovery has been surprising. You know, for a while I thought we'd lost you. I'll let you rest a while, then I'll come back and check on you." He went to the door, then turned around, saying, "I do hope you'll be cooperative this time. I don't think you can withstand another go-round."

And he was gone.

Michel Bertrand remained motionless on the dispensary bed, finding that he agreed with the "doctor's" assessment. He couldn't withstand another session with those hellish little clips fastened to his ankles. Slowly, he tried to rise, but the pain put him back on the mattress. In his youth he'd been a wiry sort, a gymnast and mountain climber, but now liver spots covered the hands that had once possessed such strength. He felt as worthless as a galleon on the shoals, having come to despise the aged body that carried his brilliant mind.

Slowly, he tried again, forcing himself up as he moved his legs over the edge of the bed. Gingerly, he placed his foot on the linoleum floor and stood, then ventured a few steps. As the soreness of his limbs immobilized him, he wondered if the situation was totally lost. Had his gamble failed? Would there be no redemption? Time was so short, and all he had to hope for was salvation by Treavor, his strapping young surrogate. And the remembrance made him wonder—how could someone like Treavor be so strong and so pathetic in the same moment? How could someone transmit such openness yet possess such secrets? How could the fate of the world hang in the balance on the will of a dark soul? The professor shook his head, then looked into the mirror to see a ravaged face staring back at him, causing him to remember Charles de Gaulle's biting observation: *Old age is like a shipwreck.*

Wearing headlamps, Frank and Miranda eased down the rickety ladder to return to the subterranean grotto. It seemed more haunting than before, and once they'd touched bottom, Frank was glad they'd brought a new Coleman lantern along. The feeling of awe filled Miranda again, but she knew they shouldn't dawdle. Otherwise the heebie-jeebies would set in. "C'mon," she said. "Let's get moving."

"I'm with you," replied Frank.

They fired up the lantern and put it on the bowsprit of the raft; then Miranda retrieved their backpack of equipment and put it in the bow before stepping in to allow Frank to push them off.

"I hope Herky doesn't mind us borrowing this," she mused.

"I'll see that he gets another keg."

"What would you say? Batman? Count Dracula?" Strauss, the leonine Navy SEAL, spread his arms with the rubberized cape behind him like the membrane of a bat's wing.

Jenkins, who was a sinewy sort, looked up from the packed parasail resting on the floor between his legs and pursed his lips. "I'd say Dracula. Definitely has a Transylvanian look to it."

"Aw, you doan know shit, Jenk," countered Gau. "You never did. It's definitely Batman. Put on the hood, Strauss."

The SEAL complied, but unlike Batman's cowl, this hood had no eye slits or pointy ears. It was a hood, period.

Strauss didn't like the claustrophobic effect of the rubber around his face, and was glad to peel it off and drop the cape, which was designed specifically for the black art of kidnapping. When the grab was made, Strauss was charged with the job of "hooding" the mark and wrapping him with the cloak, and in the same moment this would blind and bind the mark so he couldn't fight back. Strauss had done his Batman-Dracula imitation with the intent of breaking up the tension in the hangar and cementing his relationship with the guys from Delta. He'd worked with Delta people before and didn't succumb—at least, not too much—to the disease of interservice rivalry. He was going down on a very hot zone with these people and they were going to need each other, so there was no room for holier-than-thou-bullshit.

Jenkins was methodically checking the parasail rigs of each member of the team. They'd be going out at about 14,000 to 14,500 feet—the max altitude for the Blackhawk—over terrain that had a ground elevation of 4,000 feet. He set the CO_2 firing cartridges for each rig at 10,000 feet, so in the event of a rip-cord and reserve-chute failure, the preset altimeter would trigger the cartridge to fire and sever the binding lanyard, releasing the chute automatically. Jenkins had 1,568 jumps to his credit, and in the macho world of skydiving he'd encountered plenty of jumpers who simply refused to use the auto-release system, seeing it as an insult to their manhood. A couple of those had punched holes in the ground and were dead now, and Jenkins knew it didn't have to be that way. So he rechecked the triggers with meticulous care.

Gau was into electronics. He retested the batteries on the voice-activated headsets that each team member would wear on the op, knowing that the best equipment in the world was worthless if there wasn't any juice. Gau also double-checked the radio the major would use to talk with that Colonel Hannon on the ground, and the thought made him shudder. That Hannon was some kinda bad-ass, and Gau thought he'd seen every different flavor of bad-ass the military had to offer. Which reminded him of something. Looking around, he said to his comrade, "Say, Jenk. What happened to the jar-head?"

Jenkins laid a parasail down and replied, "Our Marine took a walk."

Mitchell Hauer, the Force Recon Marine sniper, lay on his shooting mat under the stars in the desert wasteland. He'd slipped away to unwind from the tension of the hangar and take a final bore sight on his M88 .50-caliber rifle. The barrel rested on a bipod and the wedge-shaped silencer-flash suppressor was screwed into the muzzle. The sniper's black face was caked over with camouflage chalk, for it was an irony that soldiers of African extraction faced a problem with night combat. The epidermis of their dark skin reflected moonlight as well as, if not better than, their Caucasian counterparts and they required camouflage chalk for concealment.

He peered through the 12x infrared sniper's scope and placed the crosshairs on a small cairn of stones he estimated at 260 meters away. He zapped the stones with the laser range finder and the number came back "253.7 M." Not bad for a gut estimate, he thought as he punched the number into the pocket range computer laid open beside him.

Next, he took a Kentucky windage and estimated the crosswind at about seven miles per hour, and the temperature at, say, 26 degrees Fahrenheit. He glanced at the digital readout from his pocket anemometer thermometer perched on a rock near his right shoulder. The three tiny air cups were spinning around on their axes just above the digital readout that said "7.4 mph," and below that was the temperature that read "24° F." *Damn! I'm sooo fine,* he thought as he punched in the numbers on the computer. He noted the windage and elevation readout of the computer's illuminated LCD screen, then made the requisite clicks to the crosshairs on his scope.

He took a .50-caliber round with a full metal jacket and dropped it into the breech, then shoved the bolt home and closed it. He placed the intersect of the crosshairs on the top stone, which was about the size of a grapefruit; then he began his breathing-control routine whereby he used his conscious mind to lower his heart rate—a trick he'd learned from some Nordic biathlon shooters at the Marine sniper school. By slowing his breathing and heart rate, he slowly transformed himself from a wobbly human into a steady shooting platform. When he felt it was right he took a final slow breath, then eased out half of it and held it. Then ever so slowly he squeezed the trigger.

Although silenced, the .50-caliber rifle responded like the kick of a mule as the round sailed out of the barrel with a muzzle velocity of 2,350 feet per second.

Hauer recovered in time to reframe the cairn in the scope just before the top stone exploded from the wallop of kinetic energy arriving in the form of a 500-grain bullet. *Damn! I'm better than fine,* he told himself in congratulation. But then he downplayed his own accomplishment and muttered, ''Enough of this high-tech horseshit.''

He scanned the moonscape with the night sniperscope and found an old pickup, say, two hundred meters distant, wasting away in the unforgiving elements of the desert. It had apparently broken down untold years ago and wasn't worth repairing or even hauling away. It was nothing but a rusting hulk, but Hauer noticed that the left headlamp was still intact. Nodding to himself, he ejected the spent casing and rammed home another round, then clicked the crosshairs to their neutral wind and elevation settings. He snapped the bipod back into its traveling position against the barrel and got to his feet. Purposely keeping his face turned away from the pickup, he wandered aimlessly around the sagebrush with his rifle cradled in his arms . . . until—on his own mark—he spun, threw himself to the ground, and in a heartbeat sighted the pickup and squeezed off the round, using instinct more than vision to frame the shot.

An instant later the headlamp of the ancient pickup shattered like a wine glass tossed in a fireplace.

Lawton Tyndale pushed the headphones against his ears and tweaked the volume until it was almost painful, but he purged the pain from his senses in order to hear Michel Bertrand's final utterance before he went comatose. Then he played it back again and again, and although it was faint as a mosquito's buzz, it was nevertheless there. It sounded like a term that had become part of the modern-day lexicon. The Nobel laureate had said the word "fax" with his final half-breath.

Tin Man pulled off the headphones and said to himself, "Fax?" What could that mean? Bertrand had been bombarded with questions as to whether or not Sirius had been compromised. In that final moment had he broken? Tried to get his confession out, but entered a coma as the beginning of the confession passed his lips? If so, what could "fax" mean? Tin Man pulled open Bertrand's security file, although he'd almost memorized the contents. The physicist had been nailed at the Green Mountain Inn in New Hampshire. It was an isolated facility on a country road. Had he sent a fax to someone from there? Tin Man's mind raced; then he went to his phone and punched in directory assistance. Twenty rings later he was on the phone with the disgruntled manager of the inn who'd already retired for the night.

"Good evening . . . Sorry to disturb . . . Yes, yes, I understand it's quite late, but you see my company's New Year's getaway—we were going to a resort in Vermont—well, damned if the place didn't have a fire. . . . Yes, the whole thing went up in smoke. . . . Well, since I'm on such a short fuse, I wanted to fax you the particulars on our needs. We'll pay premium rates. Don't want to disappoint the crew, you know. Could I have your fax number? . . . Thank you so much. I'll get this out to you first thing in the morning. Happy New Year."

Tin Man slammed down the phone, then picked up the receiver and redialed.

Frank and Miranda rode the slow current in silence, watching the hues of the limestone walls change their coloring like a painter's palette. The portage over the sandbar came and went without incident; then they climbed aboard the raft again to continue their journey toward the exit point.

The ringing woke the Cossack from a hangover in the making, and had it not been the encrypted phone beside his bed he would have cursed like a wakened grizzly. But he held his tongue and lifted the receiver, saying only, "This is Number Eight of Washington."

"This is Number One at S-4."

The Cossack's hazy brain came instantly awake. "Yes, Number One."

"I need a dump on a fax number. It's from the place where you apprehended Bertrand. Write this down."

The Cossack clumsily complied, then asked, "How soon do you need this?"

"Last year."

*   *   *

Curly Sikes reached up and pushed the throttles forward to the max position and locked them down tight, unleashing a stampede of horsepower that surged through the Blackhawk like an electric current. Sikes ran through a final preflight check, then nodded to his copilot, Derryberry, and toggled his intercom button. "Close us up, Major."

"Roger that, Mister Sikes." And Potter slid the side door shut.

"We're outta here," said Sikes as he reached down and pulled up on his collective control, increasing the pitch on the blades so they took bigger and bigger bites out of the air to lift the machine off the ground. Sikes hovered away from the rusty hangar, then flipped down his night-vision goggles as the chopper ascended into the desert night.

At Baltimore-Washington Airport a leased Gulfstream aircraft—the ultimate in private jets—taxied to the end of the runway and received clearance for takeoff. The aircraft had been leased for a week for $70,000 in cash by two pilots from the 160th Task Force, posing as corporate aviators. The lease of the aircraft was secured by the impeccable credit rating of a pharmaceutical company in Florida that did not exist.

The pilot shoved the throttles forward and the Rolls Royce Spey engines responded, as if spurred, sending the aircraft airborne. The landing gear was retracted and the Gulfstream banked to take up a vector for the south west, a Cabinet officer and future Presidential contender in its hold.

*   *   *

In the C-130 cockpit the pilot spoke into his headset. "We're feet-dry, General. Just crossing Monterey Bay, in fact. That puts us about two hours out from the LZ."

"Very well."

"And General?"

"Yes?"

"You did say there wouldn't be any SAMs. Is that correct?"

"I've been told they will be taken care of on the ground."

"I hope so."

"No shit."

Major General Roger Brown was commanding officer of the 6th Infantry Division (Light), the parenthetical word indicating it was a unit of foot soldiers whose main mode of transportation in the new world order of high-tech warfare was their feet. Brown was a brawny man, having played defensive tackle at the University of Washington before embracing a career in the Army, and his troops often called him "Brown Bear" whenever he cut a swath through his Alaska garrison on an inspection tour. His personal trademark was a British military mustache that had been a dark sorrel color in his youth but had turned gray over the years—and lately it had started to fade to white, for he was still reeling from the events of the last week.

Before Christmas an Air Force major with flame-red hair and a lieutenant colonel who could've passed for a Mafia enforcer had rung the doorbell of his quarters at ten in the evening, bearing a personal letter from the Secretary of Defense, ordering him to assemble two air-borne companies of his division. Once the troops were assembled he was to load them onto transports and execute an airdrop to seize an objective *inside* Nellis Air Force Base. The whole thing seemed utterly preposterous and Brown said as much, but the red-haired major told him to call the Dane farm near Gettysburg if he wanted confirmation from the Secretary himself. So Brown picked up the phone, and to his utter amazement he got Treavor Dane on the line, who verbally gave him confirmation in that unmistakable baritone Brown had heard on the evening news so many times. After he hung up, Brown became convinced it must be some kind of new readiness exercise, but the enforcer, seeming to read his thoughts, said, "This ain't no fucking drill, General. And you'd better be prepared for a hot landing zone."

So Brown had complied, discreetly rounding up as many of his airborne troops as possible with the onset of Christmas. But what had really puzzled him was that the Secretary had ordered him to insert a detail of his plainclothes MPs onto Nellis proper just before the drop and covertly take the post commander into custody, which they were now poised to do.

Then, on Christmas Eve Day, the enforcer had reappeared and given his task force the full briefing, and now he understood.

"Romeo-six-eight-Tango, Nellis Control."

Curly Sikes keyed his radio microphone. "Roger, Nellis Control, this is Romeo-six-eight Tango."

"Be advised, Romeo-six-eight-Tango, you are approaching restricted airspace. Please refer to your flight map and come to course zero one-zero."

"Roger, Nellis Tower. Will comply. Just taking a joy ride to see all the pretty flares your jet jockeys light up at night."

"Afraid you'll be disappointed, Romeo-six-eight-Tango. Everybody's gone home for the holidays."

"Didn't think of that, Nellis. Guess we'll just fly around and see if we run into any UFOs."

Chuckle. "Roger that, Romeo-six-eight-Tango. Just stay out of the restricted airspace."

"Oh, absolutely, Nellis. Romeo-six-eight-Tango, out." Curly Sikes killed the flight-com frequency as he moved his cyclic control to the new vector. Then he keyed his intercom. "You copy all that, Major?"

"Got it, Curly." Potter checked his watch, then flashed his penlight on the map board strapped to his thigh. He examined the readout from the Global Positioning Satellite receiver in his hand, then scribbled a small X at their location on the map and made a mental note of their altitude at 14,326 feet. "What's the wind situation, Curly?"

"Weather brief says upper levels at fifteen to twenty knots out of the northeast. Almost optimal for us."

The Blackhawk was cruising along the eastern border of Nellis AFB, about twenty-seven miles from the commandos' landing zone at grid S-4. To reach their touchdown point they would have to be creative with their use of the wind stream, but at this moment it looked doable to Potter—*if* they were more in line with the air currents. Potter did some plotting on the map, then said, "Take us about three clicks due north along the border, Curly. We'll punch out there."

"Roger that, Major."

Frank and Miranda crested the hill and once again beheld the desolation of Papoose Lake. There was no moon, and the brilliance of the stars on this crystalline desert night was nothing short of cosmic—a veritable carpet of diamonds on a sky of black velvet. They unloaded their backpacks and laid out their equipment on a pair of ponchos in weather that was subfreezing. Frank was grateful for their down parkas and the parka pants that Miranda had purchased for them at a sporting goods store in Las Vegas.

He peered through the night-vision binoculars, and the light from the starfield was so brilliant that he had to turn down the sensitivity of the infrared instrument. That done, he scanned the barren lake, which showed not a sign of life. "Don't see a thing," he muttered.

"Neither do I," echoed Miranda as she checked her watch. "Sun's been down for hours. When did we see our mark before?"

"Around midnight. That gives us plenty of time, but we better get the cavalry down on the ground." Frank extracted a whip antenna from a canvas case and let it *sproing* to its full seven-foot length; then he screwed it onto the single sideband transceiver and flicked on the power. He double-checked the frequency, then keyed the mike, saying, "Tunnel Rat to Viking, Tunnel Rat to Viking. Do you copy? Over."

"Tunnel Rat, this is Viking," said Potter. "I copy you. Over."

Frank Hannon's staticky voice came through his earphone. "Tunnel Rats are in place, Viking. It's show time."

"Copy, Rat. We're on the way." Potter pulled the latch and slid the door of the Blackhawk open, and was greeted by a blast of frigid air. Under his Gortex desert assault fatigues he wore two layers of thermasilk long underwear and a down vest, and he was grateful for the Balaclava hood that covered his face, head and ears. He made sure his radio headset and the cranial harness for his night-vision goggles were secure. Then he turned and barked, "Final check!"

His team of four commandos examined each other's parasail harness; then Jenkins gave Potter's rig a final once over before cuffing him on the shoulder.

Potter took a final read on his GPS receiver, then shouted over the rotor blades, "Okay, gentlemen, it's time to rock and roll!" And in quick succession they leapt into the black void of a night parachute jump. Almost immediately Potter yanked his rip cord and felt the parasail break his fall as it opened with a *whump!* Behind him there was a staccato sound of *whump-whump-whump-whump* as the rest of his team deployed their parasails in a HAHO maneuver, meaning "High Altitude-High Opening." By deploying their rigs at such a high altitude, the commandos could ride the air currents for up to forty miles before having to touch down.

Potter flipped down his night-vision goggles, then pulled his lanyards to swing himself around for a better look, and was relieved to see four parasails over his shoulder. He took an azimuth toward Papoose Mountain with his wrist compass, then inquired via his voice-activated stem microphone, "Does everybody copy me?"

"Delta One, copy," replied Jenkins.

"Delta Two here," said Gau.

"Batman copies," said Strauss.

"Marine copies," replied Hauer.

"Okay," said Potter, "let's make us a convoy. Delta

One, you take the point. Follow an azimuth of two-two-eight degrees.''

Jenkins, the world-class skydiver, took his position at the head of a stair-step formation of parasails as they crossed the boundary of Nellis AFB on air currents that pushed them along at seventeen knots.

Potter flipped up his goggles and surveyed the extraordinary blanket of stars, then tried to raise Frank on his voice-activated radio without success. That didn't surprise him because the tactical headsets were FM line-of-sight radios with limited range, so they would have to clear the crest of Papoose Mountain before they could be heard.

A parachute jump was always so incredibly quiet, and one at night seemed doubly so. Nothing but the whisper of the wind as you glided through the starlit sky, rocking under the canopy like a baby in a cradle. Indeed, it was not unheard of for HAHO jumpers to fall asleep during a long descent, but somehow Potter didn't feel that would be a problem this evening.

The world was full of pussies. That was what the Cossack thought. The Sirius man inside the phone company had bleated like a pregnant sheep when roused from his bed to access the phone records in the dead of night. Now a copy of the billing records from the Green Mountain Inn was flowing into his computer via his fax modem. When the dump was complete he would hit his printout button to get a list of the numbers called from the inn for the week prior to Bertrand's apprehension.

Each phone number would also have the destination number's billing name and address—another aspect of Sirius security few people knew about.

The sagebrush zipped beneath the belly of the Black-hawk like a desert conveyor, slapping against the tires with an uncomfortable frequency, while in the right seat Curly Sikes kept his eyes frozen on the undulating terrain as he moved the cyclic control with the deftness of a surgeon. In the left seat Clarence Derryberry, the hay-seed cowboy, matched the terrain to the contours of the map strapped to his thigh, occasionally barking things like "Left," "Right," or "Waypoint at two o'clock."

This was nap-of-the-earth flying by some of the leading practitioners of that very dark art, and it kept the chopper beneath the formidable air-defense radars of Nellis Air Force Base. After making the parachute drop they had taken the Blackhawk out of Nellis air-control range, then brought it down on the deck and turned around to penetrate the border. They had scooted along the ground, guiding the Blackhawk around the base of Bridger Mountain toward the southern approach of Papoose Lake. According to the map, there was a flat geologic depression nestled into the side of the mountain where they could be hidden from view, about six miles distant from Frank and Miranda's viewpoint.

Derryberry examined the topographic map carefully, then keyed his intercom. "Should be just ahead to starboard."

Curly Sikes saw the depression in the ground and pulled back slightly on the cyclic to bleed off the helicopter's speed. He peered down with his goggles, and the bottom of the depression appeared flat enough and the sides wide enough as he put the rotary-wing craft into a hover. "Here we go," he said to Derryberry, and slowly lowered the collective to reduce the pitch of the rotor blades cutting the air. Foot by foot the craft descended into the depression, until the wheels finally settled into the sand. What geologic forces had scooped out this depression remained unknown to Sikes and Derryberry, but it was adequate to provide them with concealment. Sikes clicked his mike switch twice to let Hannon know he was in place, and he received three clicks in response. Then he powered down the engine and settled in for the wait. As the rotor blade revolutions slowed to a near stop, Derryberry observed offhandedly, "The desert outside Baghdad had a different texture to it."

Sikes nodded. "Didn't it, though?"

Jenkins, the Delta Force skydiver, watched the garish klieg lamps of Area 51 as they passed beneath his feet; and from this altitude they seemed like halogen fireflies that transformed Groom Lake into an oasis of light on this cold desert night. He could make out the network of hangars, roads and antennae that comprised the hypersecret base, but quickly his attention turned elsewhere. They were traveling on a southwesterly course, approaching the windward side of Papoose Mountain, and on the far side of that mountain lay their objective. But now they had a problem that caused Jenkins to frantically search the windward side of the oncoming mountain with his night-vision equipment. The team had fallen below the wind current that had easily carried them toward their landing zone, and if they didn't get a boost soon their descent angle would put them down on the wrong side of the mountain. That would mean they'd have to hump over the top on foot—in hostile territory at night—and undoubtedly miss their window of opportunity. In view of that, Jenkins felt their best shot was to try for an "elevator," and he found what he was searching for in the form of a wedge-shaped gulch cut into the side of the mountain.

"Viking, this is Delta One."

"Talk to me," said Potter.

"Have the team string out and follow my lead," advised Jenkins. "I'm gonna try to grab an elevator above that gulch down there."

"Viking copies, Delta One. We're behind you."

"Roger that."

Jenkins tugged on his lanyards to align his parasail so he was flying straight toward the cliff face where the gulch came to an abrupt halt. The rest of the team staggered in behind him, ready to pull away if it didn't work. What Jenkins hoped to find was some ground wind that paralleled the upper-level air flow. If the ground currents were there, then the V-shaped gulch would focus the power of the wind and it would surge straight up like an incoming breaker smashing against the rocks. With trepidation, Jenkins watched the oncoming cliff face approach with terrifying speed . . . until, like a giant's hand plucking him away, the updraft caught his canopy and yanked him skyward with the speed of an express elevator. He tugged on his lanyards to put himself into a spiral that would keep him in the epicenter of the updraft as he traveled higher, higher and higher still—until finally he had the altitude to clear the crest of Papoose Mountain and aim for their landing zone on the leeward side.

Miranda gasped.

"What is it?" demanded Frank.

"I see them!" Her night-vision binoculars caught the first canopy as it popped into view above the silhouette of the mountain. Then came the second, third, fourth and finally the fifth one, winging above the ridgeline like bats shooting out of a belfry. "Damn, that's incredible!"

"Indeed it is." Frank keyed his FM transceiver. "Viking, this is Tunnel Rat. We've got you in sight."

"*Whoooeeee!* Okay, yeah, Rat—we be here," replied Potter. "That was some kinda ride."

"I'm sure. You see the lake bed and the landing strip below you?"

"Lemme see. . . . Yeah. Got it."

"The runway terminates at the base of the mountain, and that's where the camouflaged hangar is. Try to put it down on the slope of the mountain about a quarter of a mile above the hangars."

"Just like we planned," said Potter.

"Just like we planned," echoed Frank, a smile etched on his face.

"Piece of cake."

Miranda was mesmerized by the parasails weaving against the starlit sky, and for a moment she forgot why she was there. "I never saw anything like this before. It is *soooo* cool."

"And with silk canopies they're invisible to radar. But let's just hope the bad guys don't have any intruder detectors on that hillside."

Hannon's entire plan was based on a "decapitation" premise—that is, to cut the head off the snake before it could bite him. Based on the way he'd orchestrated the scene during the saucer test flight, and the way Tin Man had kowtowed to him, it was Hannon's guess that the Doberman's master was the kingpin of the Sirius operation. Therefore, it was Hannon's intent to take him out of the picture and decapitate the Sirius command structure before the cavalry arrived. If they could kidnap the kingpin and suppress the antiair defenses, then they just might have half a chance of pulling this jerry-rigged operation off.

Frank pressed the binoculars tight against his eyes and watched a canopy deflate. "First one is down."

Potter yanked hard on his lanyards for the landing flare, and came down on the slope for a stand-up touchdown. The others soon followed, all quietly except for an *"Ooof!"* from Gau when his foot snagged a rock that sent him to the ground with a belly flop.

Potter released his harness and it fell to the ground; then he immediately unstrapped his silenced Heckler & Koch machine pistol and crouched behind some desert sage. He locked and loaded a clip into the chamber, then did an imitation of a rock formation for five minutes. The rest of his team followed suit, getting their bearings and taking stock of the terrain. The mountain sloped down in front of them a few hundred meters before dropping off sharply to the tarmac, and Potter figured they were above the location of the hangar doors. When satisfied they'd arrived undetected, Potter whispered into his mike, "You hurt, Delta Two?"

"Only my pride and my ass, sir," replied Gau.

Potter took out his night-vision binoculars and scanned the terrain, then said, "Okay, stack and cover the canopies. I'll keep a look-see."

Without a word, as though they were extensions of Potter's mind, the team gathered the canopies together and stacked them in a pile as Gau unrolled a lightweight desert camouflage tarp. They covered the spent chutes, then weighted the tarp with stones and resumed their positions.

Potter swept the landscape, then focused on the hilltop in the distance where he presumed Frank and Miranda were set up. He inspected the wide-open country between them and said into his microphone stem, "Viking to Tunnel Rat. You were right to have us come in the way we did. To get to the grab point from your location would have meant a long exposed crawl."

"Roger that. Now then, move your grab team laterally along the slope towards me about two hundred meters so you're out from behind the hangar complex, then down towards the lake bed at the base of the mountain. That's where we saw him. There might be a footpath along there. He was alone. . . ."

"With a cane," said Potter.

"You got it," replied Frank.

"Okay, people," ordered Potter. "Grab team, move out. Batman, you got your cape?"

"On my back, Viking," replied Strauss.

"Then you take the point. Delta One, you follow."

"Roger," replied Jenkins, and he began his low crawl.

Potter put his night-vision binoculars on maximum zoom and began scanning the terrain on the far side of the hangar complex. Slowly, working in grid blocks, he searched the far ridgeline methodically. Twice he missed it because of the camouflage, but then he realized it was giving off a slightly hotter signature than the surrounding rocks and soil.

"I think I've got it," he said into his stem microphone.

"Whereabouts?" asked Gau.

"In the saddle of the ridgeline across the way. It's a little hotter than the surrounding turf."

"Yeah," replied Gau. "I think I got it."

"Then on your way. Looks like the distance is a click. That's a long crawl. Got your satchel?"

"Two small ones on my back. I'm gone."

Potter surveyed the lay of the land again, and below him saw a kind of promontory sticking out of the hillside like a pointing finger. He started to radio his sniper, but smiled as he watched the Marine already crawling toward it.

"Ho-hum," sighed Potter. "Just another day at the office."

The three Vietnamese janitors lay on the floor of the Chevy van, trussed up and drugged, while three Delta Force "shooters" pulled on their soiled overalls with *Vegas Cleaning* stitched on the back. The lead shooter listened intently to a mobile radio, identical to the one Frank Hannon was speaking into almost a hundred miles away.

"Ground Hog, this is Tunnel Rat."

The leader keyed the mike. "This is Ground Hog."

"They're on the ground. We're good for go."

"Will comply. Ground Hog, out."

He closed the van door and the trio calmly walked to the air-traffic control tower of Nellis Air Force Base and punched the intercom button beside the steel door.

"Yeah?"

"Cleaning crew," replied the lead.

"Oh, yeah. The escort will be right down."

The three shooters waited like statues, each one fingering the silenced Beretta 9mm pistol in his baggy pocket. Then the door opened and the cherub face of a tech sergeant greeted them, saying, "See your IDs?"

They all produced ID cards, certifying they were approved contractors to work on the base. The tech sergeant nodded, then asked, "Where you want to start? Upstairs or downstairs?"

"Downstairs," replied the leader. "But I have to tell you, our regular crew was in a bad accident this afternoon. We're pinch-hitting. Can you show us where the broom closet is located?"

"I didn't think I'd seen you guys before. This way." He led them down the stairs to a closet, where they collected their plastic trash cans, brooms and mops. Then they traveled to another steel door, where their escort rang an intecom button and explained the cleaning crew had arrived. The door swung open and the tech sergeant said, "Just have them buzz me when you're finished."

"Right," said the lead shooter, and they stepped inside the heart of the beast. Although the airport tower is the most visible aspect of an air traffic enterprise, its epicenter is often below ground in the control center where radar operators monitor planes in the air and direct pilots via radio. It was a venue that resembled the bridge of a starship with its glowing screens and multicolored computer lights, but because it was the Yuletide season there was only a skeleton crew of a half-dozen controllers monitoring non-existent military traffic over Nellis. Yet were there to be any intrusion into the controlled airspace of S-4 and Area 51, two F-15 Eagle fighters were on standby in a hangar nearby, ready to take flight and intercept should they be scrambled by the radar controllers.

Moving slowly, the shooter cleaning crew began their labors, emptying the wastebaskets and sweeping the floor as they kept their ears cocked for what was to come.

The Doberman appeared at the doorway of Lawton Tyndale's office, emitting a low growl as his upper lip curled up to expose the slippery white fangs. Tin Man despised the beast because it was a harbinger of an appearance by its master, and the master was true to form.

"The man Hannon." The statement was flat as Krieger held up one of his massive cigars. "I take it you have not found him or the Park woman. Is that correct?"

Tin Man was becoming more irritated with each appearance by Krieger. After the Denver airport fiasco, the old man and his damned Doberman had returned to his door once every twenty-four hours, then every twelve hours, and now every six hours. Always, the question was the same, as was the answer. "Still no sign of them, Mr. Krieger. I am in contact hourly with our area security chiefs and our key people within the Bureau, Treasury and Langley, but still no sign. They must be laying low somewhere."

Krieger studied the end of his hand-rolled Cuban cigar, then sighed as he flicked the ash on Tin Man's floor. "Lawton, Lawton, Lawton—what am I to do with you? Any chimpanzee can 'be in touch with our people' to see if they've surfaced. I made you Number One of security because I felt you alone could provide that insight, that flash of brilliance which could run Hannon to ground. But now you, of all people—you, the one who knew Hannon personally—tell me you have come up empty-handed?''

"I've done everything possible to track—"

"Find him!" The old man's voice came across Tin Man's desk like a scythe. "Find Hannon and the woman by this time tomorrow night or I will know I have made a terrible mistake in your appointment. Do I make myself *clear*?"

The volume of the Doberman's growl increased to a frenzied pitch and the pads of the animal's feet danced in place, as though the floor were afire.

With a dry voice, Tin Man said, "You may rely on me, sir."

"I hope so, Lawton. . . . For your sake." He tapped his cobra-headed cane on the floor. "Come along, Sringar. 'Tis time for our walk."

Gau approached the little pyramid carefully, alert for any sensor alarm that might sound, but there was only the desert and the cold. It had been a long belly-crawl, but now he could see plainly in the moonlight that the little pyramid structure had four metallic disks on its face pointed into the night sky, and he was certain that on the flip side there were four more just like these. This was the phased-array radar screen of a Patriot missile battery, and as deadly as the Patriot was, it was blind if the radar wasn't functioning properly. Gau searched around for the actual missiles, but could not discern their whereabouts—no doubt they were camouflaged somewhere nearby.

He pulled one of the canvas satchels off his back and rolled it over to inspect a small black box that was about the size of a pack of cigarettes. He flipped a switch and

a tiny red light came on. Then he extended the little
box's aerial. He gingerly placed the satchel beside the
radar pyramid before turning around and crawling away.
Just to be safe, he wasn't going to transmit on his voice
frequency until he was at least a hundred meters distant.

"I can't see them," whispered Miranda.

"Me neither," replied Frank. "But I think they must
have arrived at their stations by now."

"Umm. Those guys are apparently very good at what
they do."

"That's what Uncle Sugar pays them for—but, yes,
they are damn good." Hannon keyed his mike. "Viking,
we lost you. Are you in position?"

A whisper came back. "In position. Let us know if
you see the mark before we do."

"Roger."

It was at that moment Frank's other radio squawked,
"Tunnel Rat, this is Husky. Do you copy?"

"I copy you, Husky."

A staticky voice came through, saying, "We are approaching restricted airspace on approach to IP. Fuel is
low. Will have to divert if we do not receive clearance."

Despite the cold, Frank felt himself sweat. It was decision time—stand down or go forward into an unknown
with consequences he couldn't imagine. He swallowed
hard and keyed the mike. "You are good for go, Husky.
I say again, you are good for go."

"This is MATS flight niner-four-Juliet on military flight
plan from Fort Ord to Davis-Mothan. Request clearance
through Nellis sector."

The bored controller looked at the three blips approaching the airspace that was verboten, so he responded with, "MATS niner-four-Juliet, be advised, you are approaching restricted airspace. Come to course one-eight-zero for thirty miles and then I will vector you east again." There was silence on the radio as the three blips remained on course for a crossing into the forbidden zone around S-4 and Area 51, so the controller figured his instructions were not heard. He rekeyed the mike and said, "MATS niner-four-Juliet, please respond. Come to course one-eight-zero immediately."

Nothing.

The controller was raising his hand to call for his supervisor when he felt something very cold and metallic at the base of his neck, and heard a voice that could only be described as icy. "Radio the MATS flight that they have clearance, and that their new call sign is Husky."

The young controller swallowed, then asked, "Who ... who are you?"

"Your new boss," replied the shooter. "Have a look around if you don't believe me."

Slowly the controller turned and saw the other two cleaning men with pistols drawn, covering his colleagues, who had their hands raised in the air like a congregation shouting, "Hallelujah!"

"Transmit now," replied the shooter, "or I'll find someone who will."

Again, the young man swallowed and said into his stem mike, "MATS niner-four-Juliet. Be advised, you are cleared for restricted airspace and, uh, your new call sign is 'Husky.'"

"... and, uh, your new call sign is 'Husky.'"

Major General Roger Brown felt a surge of adrenaline

through his body as he turned to his sergeant major and said, ''Pass the word. We're good for go.''

The sergeant major—the kind of unforgiving lifer who shaved with a blowtorch—turned and began barking orders to his troops, while in the cockpit the pilot pushed the control column of the Hercules forward to begin its descent toward the Initial Point of the drop run.

Potter flipped down his goggles and surveyed the scene carefully. About seventy meters below him was a cobblestone sidewalk that hugged the base of the mountain before it meandered through the sagebrush, not unlike that yellow brick road from the land of Oz. It took him a while to figure it out, but then it made sense to him. If this dude was so powerful and required a cane, then walking around the soft earth of the desert would be problematic for him. He'd undoubtedly had this path built to support his cane when he leaned on it—so that meant he'd come along here for sure. Potter had placed Jenkins the Delta Force skydiver and Strauss the Navy SEAL in the bush on either side of the path, waiting for their mark to appear so they could roll him up.

''Viking, this is Tunnel Rat.''

''Go, Rat,'' replied Potter.

''The cavalry is on final approach.''

''Then our mark better show up soon or . . . hey, do you see that?''

Curly Sikes and Clarence Derryberry were belted in the cockpit of the Blackhawk, silently watching the stars through the canopy as they waited for the radio to speak to them. After the rush of the parachute drop and flying nap-of-the-earth to get the chopper to its staging position, both Sikes and Derryberry were experiencing that "dishrag" feeling when the radio squawked with, "Tunnel Rat to Bright Star."

Sikes felt as if he'd been whiplashed. "Bright Star here."

"The mark is in sight and the cavalry's coming. Move it."

Derryberry's hand beat his to the start switch, and immediately the Blackhawk's turbine began to whine.

Outside the hangar door, Arctus Krieger paused under the stars, reflecting on their unfathomable distances and hidden mysteries. How many times had he taken this walk? To vent the tensions of the day and ponder his role in the destiny of this planet and—who knows?— perhaps others to come. Once he'd been elevated to their table, who could say what would be within his grasp? Something beyond his imagination, surely. And everyone thought he was a tired old man. Well, that was true enough—for the moment at least. But soon he could anticipate the doubling of his lifespan—*if* everything remained intact until "The Plan" came to fruition.

He bent down and rubbed the Doberman's ears. "Come along, Sringar. Let us see what delicacies you can scare up for yourself tonight." And he waved his cane, severing some invisible tether that unleashed the animal on a breakneck run.

"Keep a head on the dawg, Marine," whispered Potter. "He looks like something of a wild card."

"Roger, Viking," replied Hauer. The sniper was thirty yards above, behind and to the right of Potter, lying prone on the small promontory that gave him an ideal shooting platform. He trained his infrared scope on the sprinting Doberman as it knifed through the sagebrush like a running buzzsaw; then he caressed the trigger as if in anticipation.

Potter watched Krieger's metronome gait as he slowly made his way down the cobblestone path. He was, perhaps, eighty meters to the takedown point, so Potter whispered into his microphone, "Okay, boys, make like statues. The mark is on the way."

Lawton Tyndale zipped up his fly, then went to the washbasin to cleanse his hands. An encounter with Krieger always left him with an urge to urinate, and the last encounter had done nothing to strengthen his bladder. Twenty-four hours, he told himself. He had to nail Frank within twenty-four hours or he was dead, just like his predecessor. He'd tried every gambit he could think of to run his old comrade to ground, but every trap had come up empty. What could he have missed? The fear that Krieger inspired in Tin Man was rancid enough, but a cancerous thought was growing within him that maybe, just maybe, Frank Hannon might have outsmarted him—and that was too galling to stomach.

He pushed through the latrine door to find his clerk running down the hall, sticking his head in a series of empty offices. "What is it, Flanders?"

The uniformed clerk wheeled around. "Colonel! You have a call from Washington! It's about the man Bertrand!"

Tin Man felt a rush, the likes of which he hadn't experienced for years, and it sent him pell-mell down the hall to his office where he grabbed the secure line. "This is Number One!"

"This is Number Eight of Washington," replied the Cossack.

"What do you have?"

"I went through the phone records of the Green Mountain Inn. They have a separate fax line. . . ."

"And?"

"One of the numbers called was in Gettysburg, Pennsylvania."

"Gettysburg?"

"Yes, and the name on the billing record was none other than Treavor Dane."

"Treavor Dane?"

"The Secretary of Defense, no less! And it was a long transmission, sent only minutes before we nailed Bertrand outside of the inn."

Tin Man's mind raced. "You're saying Bertrand sent a fax to Treavor Dane and we didn't know about it? How could that happen? We have three people on Dane's immediate staff. There's no way he could receive a fax and act on it without our knowing."

"You'd better hope not."

Tin Man felt his bladder go weak again. Then he turned to his clerk at the doorway. "Send a guard out to get Krieger! *Now!*"

And the clerk vanished.

"Stand up!" barked the sergeant major, who was also the jumpmaster. The paratroops in the belly of the aircraft responded with wobbly legs, for many of their limbs were half asleep from sitting so long in a cramped position. But as they shook out the stiffness the adrenaline began to surge when the sergeant major barked, *"Hook up!"* Each paratrooper snapped his rip cord hook

onto the static line and then checked the parachute rig of the man in front of him as the sergeant major opened the hatch in the bay of the aircraft.

An icy howling wind greeted them.

Miranda could hear the faint *whop-whop-whop* of rotor blades approaching from behind and she turned to scan the terrain with her binoculars. She saw it in the distance, sending up vortices of dust in its wake as it skimmed along the desert floor.

"Flyboys are on the way," she whispered.

"Perfect," replied Frank. "The trap's about to be sprung."

"Uh-oh."

"What is it?" asked Frank nervously.

Miranda squinted through her binoculars. "Somebody just stepped out of that hangar door."

The Doberman was en route back to his master after making a long running loop through the desert when he crossed the cobblestone path and came to a sudden halt. Every fiber of the beast was bundled energy as he sniffed the air and deciphered a new smell on the desert breeze, and the pull on his olfactory nerves was almost narcotic as he trotted down the path in search of the source of the foreign odor.

Arctus Krieger had been lost in thought, breathing the crisp curative vapors of the night desert air when he saw his loyal treasure go off the path, perhaps thirty yards ahead of him. Such a magnificent beast he was. Then the old man heard something—that faint chopping sound. Yes, of course. Must be a helicopter. Flown by one of those peasants over at Groom Lake, no doubt. Strange that one would be airborne at this time of night, at this time of year when operations were all but shut down at Groom and Nellis. Then the chopping sound, which had been so faint at first, seemed to be growing louder. Had some dunderhead strayed over into their restricted airspace again? He often wondered how those flyers found the brainpower to get their machines airborne.

Then he heard the yelp.

He searched the desert. "Sringar!? Sringar, *Daman!*" Was the animal hurt? The Doberman's obedience to Krieger's commands had always been absolute, and his absence made the old man worry, so he hobbled forward on his cane. That was when he heard a voice behind him shout, *"Mr. Krieger! Mr. Krieger!"* And he turned to see one of the security guards coming up the path at double time. It was then that Arctus Krieger realized that something was amiss, that in the great order of things something was out of kilter. The helicopter noise, Sringar's disappearance, the guard running towards him—it all added up to an equation that was not of his making.

"Aw, shit," muttered Potter. "What the fuck is happening now? First the dog, now this. Marine, take a bead on that Cammo Dude coming up the path."

"Roger that," said Hauer.

"Where'd the dawg go?" asked Potter into his mike stem.

"Dead," whispered Strauss. "He was about to have Jenk for dinner."

Quickly, Potter assessed the situation. Krieger was still fifteen yards from the takedown point. The guard was almost on him. The airborne troops were on the way. It was now or never. "Marine, you got the Cammo Dude?"

"Got him," came the whispered reply.

"Drop him."

Krieger awaited the arrival of the thick-necked guard with impatience. What news was this oaf bringing to him? And *where* was his dog?

The guard was puffing, about twenty feet away as he said, "Mr. Krieger, Mr. Krieger . . . Number One wants you back at the—"

The Cammo Dude's head exploded in a grisly fulmination of bone, brains and gristle as the .50-caliber slug lifted his nearly decapitated body off the path.

Krieger backpedaled in shock, his mouth forming the word *"Sringar!"*

"Take him down!"

Potter's shouted command reverberated in the SEAL's ear, causing Strauss to spring to his feet and run towards Krieger with the capture hood open. Jenkins was on his heels.

Krieger heard them, and through the consuming shock of seeing the guard's head disintegrate, his primal instincts came to the fore. Grasping his hickory cane, he twisted the cobra head and a razor-sharp poniard sprang from the tip. He brought the blade up behind him like an oar just as Strauss was raising the capture hood. The blade impaled the sprinting SEAL through the midriff, but the momentum of the stabbed body was like that of a blitzing linebacker as he crashed into his mark. They fell to the sand, the dead commando coming down with such force it snapped off the head of the cane.

Miranda ducked as the Blackhawk swooped over them close enough to touch. Then she watched as the craft screamed across the lake bed toward the takedown point.

Frank yelled, "Go get 'em!"

And Miranda yelled something, too, but she couldn't remember what it was.

Krieger picked up the cobra head and made a pathetic swipe at Jenkins before the younger and stronger man pounced on him with the cape and hooded his cranium. Then he rolled the old man over and yanked the lanyard tight until Krieger was trussed up like a pig in a poke.

Jenkins looked down at Strauss, lying lifeless in a pool of his own blood, then shook his head and muttered into his mike stem, "The son of a bitch got our SEAL! The old fart had some kinda damn sword cane."

"I saw," replied Potter. "Cavalry is on the way."

Seized by anger, Jenkins administered a swift kick to the trussed-up bundle on the ground, saying, "You're lucky we got orders to take you alive, you piece of shit."

In the cape, his arms pinned, Krieger let out a cry of pain as he felt the business end of Jenkins's boot. Then he struggled, millimeter by millimeter, to reach something around his neck. It was a tiny device with a button on it.

A panic button.

He pressed it about the time Jenkins saw the first flare.

Curly Sikes kept the Blackhawk level as it skimmed over the runway, while in the left seat Clarence Derryberry popped the magnesium flares and tossed them out the open window to mark the drop zone. The last one had hit the runway as Curly Sikes pulled back on the cyclic to avoid ramming the slope of Papoose Mountain—just as a string of Cammo Dudes came piling out of the hangar to the sound of an alarm klaxon. That was when Curly saw multiple flashes blazing from the figures on the ground—only a moment before his helicopter shuddered in midair.

"Be advised, Husky, the landing zone is hot! I say again, the landing zone is hot! Get on the ground as soon as you can!"

The lead pilot didn't take time to answer as he heaved back on the control column to bring the lumbering Herc out of its descent and into alignment with the string of torches on the ground. The airborne beast responded and flared into a level run at five hundred feet as the pilot throttled down and flicked the toggle switch on the jump light.

In the bay of the aircraft, the sergeant major saw the red light go to green, causing him to yell, *"GO! GO! GO!"*

The young paratroopers piled out the doorway and into the black void, sandwiching their general, who was in the middle of the first stick. When Roger Brown felt the yank of his chute opening, the first thing he saw was the fireball of the Blackhawk as it imploded on the side of Papoose Mountain, causing him to mutter, *"Shhhiiiitttt!"*

For Tin Man, it was the most overwhelming moment of his life, for he'd just emerged from the hangar to the staccato sounds of small-arms fire when the helicopter erupted on the mountainside above him. The force of the explosion knocked him to the tarmac. Then, as he tried to stand, he noticed the Cammo Dude on his right, then the one on his left, spout bursts of crimson from their backs before they fell back to the ground. He dove behind one of the bodies for cover, then looked up to see the horror of horrors— three C-130s dropping their little mushrooms against the starlit sky.

"Dane," he hissed through his teeth. "Bertrand got to Treavor Dane!" He whipped his handheld radio to his lips and keyed the mike. *"Security!* We have an intrusion by hostile aircraft! Authorize air defense to fire!"

Gau was mesmerized by the unfolding battle, and as soldiers sometimes do in the heat of an engagement, he forgot for a moment why he was there. Then a whine pierced the air, which caused him to whip around and witness a pair of camouflaged clamshell doors opening behind him. Then his eyes grew wide as the boxlike container of the Patriot missile launcher rose out of the ground like some desert serpent raising its head to strike. That shook Gau out of his trance, and he pressed the detonator button on the transmitter just as the Patriot missile roared out the bunker, so close he was singed by the exhaust plume.

Staff Sergeant Ward Chaffee was the last man out on his stick when he saw a small torchlike object heading straight toward him. He knew exactly what it was when his canopy deployed and brought him up short like that proverbial duck sitting in harm's way. But then the missile streaked away in a lazy uncontrolled spiral—like some Fourth of July pyrotechnic—before it arced backward and impacted against the mountain. The lanky Chaffee exhaled in relief, but didn't have time to relax as the flares on the ground started coming up fast. With the drop almost completed, he thought the pyrotechnics were over for the evening.

But he was wrong.

Dazed and confused, Gau wondered if an eardrum was broken as he staggered to his feet to the firecracker sounds of weapons firing. He regained enough equilibrium to see the smoldering hulk of the Patriot radar station that his satchel charge had destroyed, and like Chaffee, Gau also thought he was home free; but he was equally wrong, for with his good ear he heard another whine. He spun around and realized it was coming from over the ridge, so he clambered up the side and peered down to see a second missile launcher emerging from a bunker—but these were not of the Patriot species that operated on radar. Instead, these were Chaparral air-defense missiles, which relied on a heat-seeking guidance system in their nose cones. In a sprint, Gau yanked the second satchel charge off his shoulder as the four rapier-like missiles began rotating toward the heat signature of the Herc's hot turboprop engines. Gau armed the detonator on the run, then flung the satchel into the bunker and dove away as the first missile roared off.

Chaffee was almost on the ground when he saw the second torch streak into the sky. But this one did not go off into an errant spiral. Instead, it made a beeline for the portside engine of the C-130 he'd just leapt from.

The wing disintegrated in a blinding flash; then the flaming hulk cartwheeled toward the earth in what seemed like slow motion. The spectacle bordered on the hypnotic, causing Chaffee to nearly forget he was about to touch down—but at the last moment he had the presence of mind to put his ankles together and roll as he hit the sand beside the runway. He struggled to his feet and released his harness as the *boom-boom* of double explosions echoed in the distance from the Chaparral launcher going up and the C-130 impacting on the ground.

Quickly, Chaffee got his bearings, sizing up the objective, his distance from the shooting and the paratroopers assembling around him. He crouched down and pulled his M-16 around to lock and load a clip, then searched the sand for the equipment cache that was supposed to have come down with him. He found it hiding behind some sagebrush, and quickly broke the capsule-like container open, just as his captain yelled, "Mortar!"

Chaffee was in a weapons platoon, in charge of the 50mm mortar section. Two of his crew materialized at his side, and without a word they quickly set up the tube as Chaffee raised his binoculars and took a Kentucky windage. Chaffee figured he'd start by ranging in on the burning hulk of the helicopter on the mountainside to insure the mortar rounds were kept off his own troops. Then he'd walk the rounds down the slope toward the tarmac where the bulk of the hostile fire was coming from. "Range! Four hundred meters!" barked Chaffee. "Take a bead on that burning chopper!"

"Range four hundred!" echoed the mortarman as he clicked the elevation knob.

"Hang!" order Chaffee.

"Hang!" echoed the mortarman as he held the little projectile above the muzzle.

"Fire!"

The mortarman dropped the projectile tail first down the tube, then leaned away and covered his ears as the round blasted out of the muzzle with a *WHUMP!* on its high-arc trajectory.

Chaffee winced at the sound, then began searching for a different equipment capsule.

Tin Man was starting to feel his confidence return. Apparently Frank hadn't anticipated the size of the force secreted in this underground base. Initially, the invaders had enjoyed the element of surprise, but as the alarm spread, a stream of Cammo Dudes had poured out of the hangar from their underground billets—upwards of a hundred. Tin Man knew his security force had been recruited from special forces and police SWAT team veterans—many of them drummed out of prior jobs because of their attitude problems. So these were men who knew how to use weapons, and after the initial shock they responded to the incoming threat by taking the higher ground and picking off the paratroopers as they tried to move toward and secure the hangar complex. Obviously, things weren't going as smoothly as Frank had planned, because the paratroopers' advance had been stymied and they were simply exchanging small-arms fire at a distance now. The Cammo Dudes had already silenced the sniper, and Tyndale felt if no further paratroops came down from the sky, he just might contain it by holding the invaders in place until their ammo ran out—then he could set about the business of retrieving Krieger and taking the head off Secretary Dane.

Just how Dane had engineered this strike without the Network learning of it made Tin Man uncomfortable and angry. When things were secured he would order a full investigation of—

WHAM!

The first mortar round fell on the mountainside behind him, causing Tin Man to spin round and look up. There was a pause that was deafening in its silence before a string of eruptions began walking down the mountain-side towards him and his cordon of guards with a re-lentless *WHAM! WHAM! WHAM!* Then a second mortar began ranging on the Cammo Dudes spread out on the ridge to his right, but on the slope above him a pair of machine guns opened up in defiance and began raking the attackers.

First the alarm klaxon, and then the explosions. Medical instruments shook on the shelves. The cacophony of sound brought a rush of adrenaline to Michel Bertrand unlike anything he'd ever known, causing him to cry in exhultation, "Treavor, my child! You have come for me!"

Puffs of ricochet dust were whipping the desert around General Brown as he talked rapidly through his field radio. He'd been told there would be resistance—but they were encountering company-sized resistance from people who knew how to shoot. The mortars were having an effect, but there was the danger the other side might call in some air support. He needed something to break the battle wide open, so he keyed his mike and shouted, "I want the TOW on the hangar door! NOW!"

·   ·   ·

With the mortar situation under control, Chaffee had gone looking and found the equipment capsule holding the TOW missile. He broke it open and hefted the heavy bastard onto its tripod, then yanked off the covers at either end of the pipe as his captain shouted, "TOW on the hangar door!" Chaffee remembered the videotape he'd seen and figured he had a pretty good idea where the camouflaged hangar should be. He looked through the infrared range finder and licked his lips, then grabbed the controller knob, armed the missle and hit the red button as an errant bullet sliced through the fabric of his sleeve.

In a snapshot, Tin Man had gone from confidence to feeling naked as the explosions made their way towards him. He panicked and rose to flee back into the hangar, leaping through the hatchway as a mortar round impacted with a *WHAM!* where he'd just been, the concussion blast knocking him to the concrete floor. Under the hangar klieg lights was the black saucer-shaped craft; the stairwell leading down to the billets, offices and laboratories; and against the far wall—well, there was the elevator entrance with two nervous Cammo Dudes standing with their side arms drawn, not quite knowing what to do.

Tin Man was the kind of creature who had a sixth and seventh sense as to how to twist any situation to his own advantage—and he had no loyalty except to himself. Another man might have cratered at that point, but being what he was, Lawton Tyndale saw his plight through a different lens—even with mortar rounds dropping around him—and knew what he had to do.

He waved his own side arm and shouted, "We've got

them on the run! We need every man we can muster to seize control! Out there fast!''

The confidence he transmitted was remarkable, for it steeled the pair of Dudes as they ran toward the open hatchway in the hangar door. They hadn't taken two steps outside before they were cut down by a mortar round, but not giving it another thought, Tin Man ran to the elevator and punched in the cipher coding beside the intercom phone. Then an interminable wait followed as the elevator began its ascent.

The Tube-launched, Optically tracked, Wire-guided antitank missile roared above the heads of the troops like an angry hornet, streaking toward the hangar door as the wire unreeled in its wake. Chaffee felt nervous sweat on his brow despite the cold as bullets ricocheted around him and, amazingly, he realized his mortar crew was out of ammo. He concentrated on placing the crosshairs on the hangar door as the electronic impulses traveled up the wire and into the missile's guidance system to put it in the center of the range finder's crosshairs.

The elevator arrived and Tin Man leapt inside. Rapidly he punched in the memorized numbers for the lower level and the doors closed to begin the descent. The mid-level light had just flashed on when the elevator bucked violently, throwing him to the floor.

Roger Brown watched the eruption of yellow and orange flame that sent out a *BAA-WHUMP!* of a concussion wave that pancaked everyone and everything on the tarmac, and blasted a massive gap in the hangar door.

And with the conflagration, all resistance crumbled

and the Cammo Dudes began hightailing it over the countryside. Brown barked into his radio, ''They're on the run! Alpha Company, move out to pursuit! Bravo Company, move in and secure the hangar!''

And he rose to follow but was brought up short, his mike cord acting like a tether, for the young man who carried his field radio lay dead beside him.

Although shaken, the elevator continued its descent until it reached the lower level and halted with the doors closed. Tin Man looked up into the camera lens and said, ''It's Number One! We are on full force alert! Open up immediately!''

The doors parted and he stepped into the antechamber with the two guards holding drawn weapons. ''What's happening!?'' demanded the larger one. ''We heard the alert but we're blind down here!''

Tin Man placed a comforting hand on his shoulder and smiled that smile. ''We're under attack but we're getting things under control. We need every available man topside to mop up. Come with me.''

''But our orders are to stay here under all circum—''

''Move it, mister! Or I'll inform Krieger you chickened out under fire!''

The Dudes exchanged glances, then the large one said, ''Nobody calls me chicken.''

Tin Man slapped him on the back. ''That's the spirit! It's almost over now anyway.'' Then he shoved his 9mm into the Dude's ribs and pulled the trigger, and dropped the second one before he could react. That done, he reached inside the elevator and punched the button for the top level before stepping back to remain behind.

Once the lift was on its way he turned and stared at

the vaultlike door at the rear of the antechamber, knowing what was locked within—and with that knowledge his confidence returned.

Hannon stared at the body of the Navy SEAL lying in a pool of his own blood. Then he motioned to Jenkins and said, "Get him upright."

Jenkins allowed himself the pleasure of another small kick to the hooded prisoner which elicited an *"Ooofh!"* Then he yanked Krieger into a sitting position.

Potter was nearby jabbering on his radio, and behind him was Miranda, panning the scene with her camcorder.

Potter jabbered into his radio, then said to Hannon, "The area appears secure. There are some hostiles still on the run in the countryside, but we'll have choppers in here at daybreak to mop them up. The airborne commander is in the hangar."

"What's the casualty count?" asked Hannon.

"Rough count at eleven killed, twenty-three wounded—not counting the C-130 that went down. That general is pissed. Resistance was heavier than we figured."

The larger radio with the whip antenna squawked, and Frank put the handset to his lips and keyed the mike, saying, "This is Tunnel Rat."

"This is Bluebird. I have the chief on board. Is the area secure?"

"Roger. Bring him in."

"Will comply. Pop some more flares."

"We're ahead of you," replied Hannon, and he nodded to Potter, who jabbered into his radio again.

Then Frank looked down and motioned to Jenkins. "Okay, let's see who we've got here."

Roughly, Jenkins unwrapped the hood and pulled it off to reveal an old man with a look that was—how did Frank recall it later?—a look that was bewildered yet menacing. Arctus Krieger surveyed the scene around him, pausing to examine the smoldering helicopter and the soldiers loitering around the tarmac. Then he sighed and said, "This is terribly inconvenient."

FIFTEEN

⸻ ∞ ⸻

The Gulfstream V jet took a long slow bank over the lake bed before coming onto final approach with its navigation lights on. Through the windshield the pilot saw a string of torches flare to life along either side of the runway, providing him with an adequate frame of reference for landing. Slowly the Gulfstream approached; then it smoothly touched down and engaged its thrust reversers before taxiing up to Major General Roger Brown's position on the tarmac outside the hangar. As the aircraft turned to park, Brown saw the words *United States of America* painted on the sleek blue and white fuselage. The Rolls Royce Spey engines were feathered; then the hatch opened and two Marine guards deplaned with their M16s at the ready. They were followed by two men in civilian clothes, and then . . . in a reflexive motion, Brown brought his heels together as he came to attention.

Secretary of Defense Treavor Dane descended the steps wearing a wolfskin parka (a gift from the Russian

Defense Minister). He extended his hand and said, "General Brown, I presume?"

In shock, Brown took the proffered hand. He was never told the Secretary himself would be coming. "Uh, yessir. I mean, yes, Mr. Secretary."

Dane nodded, then looked at the hangar complex with the large doors that were a burning hulk. Brown could sense the Secretary was intimidated by the carnage as he inquired, "Is the area, ah, secured, General?"

"Yes, sir. But I have to tell you, Mr. Secretary, we sustained some heavy casualties. There was more resistance here than we were led to believe. I think that . . ."

"All in good time, General. At this point we need to commence an investigation of . . ."

"You wished to see me, Mr. Secretary?"

It was an old man's voice, but with a crusty authority, and Dane and Brown turned to see a stooped figure flanked by Shiloh Potter and Frank Hannon. Behind him was Jenkins and Miranda Park.

"Who is he?" demanded Dane.

Frank replied, "The guy who was in charge."

To that, Krieger smiled and replied, "I am in charge, young man. More than you could ever know."

Dane stared at him for some time, then said, "Colonel Hannon, Major Potter, take this man into custody. We'll interrogate him later. For now I want to have a look inside that—"

Krieger cut him off by saying, "If you will allow me, Mr. Secretary, perhaps I could guide you."

Dane hesitated, and Krieger sensed his misgivings. "Surely you are not afraid of a simple old man, Treavor. Come along—I can save you some time, and with me as your guide you'll be less likely to damage something."

Dane was about to agree when another voice—soft with a French lilt to it—said, "Do not trust him, Treavor."

Dane spun round to see Bertrand, haphazardly dressed in slacks and topcoat, supported between two young soldiers.

"*Michel!*" Dane's voice was almost a bleat as he rushed to embrace the old professor, and Frank noticed Krieger glare at them.

Bertrand disengaged from the embrace and said, "I see you received my message."

"Only part of it," replied Dane. "But with the help of these two people I was able to figure out the rest."

"Which two people?"

Dane pointed. "Frank Hannon, a lieutenant colonel in the Air Force, and Miranda Park, a reporter."

Bertrand's eyes flared at the words "a reporter," but then he caught himself and said, "Miranda Park? You are a science writer if my memory serves me."

Miranda nodded. "It does serve you, Dr. Bertrand. I'm grateful you didn't go down over Lake Superior."

"A subterfuge, but a necessary one, I'm afraid."

Dane interceded, "Michel, what is happening here? How did it happen? What . . . ?"

Bertrand raised a hand to silence him, saying, "Ah, my Treavor. Always so impatient. Come with me and let us go inside." He stared at Krieger, who glared back, prompting the professor to say, "Confine this man, Treavor, he is quite dangerous—and if you employ means to restrain him that are cruel and unusual, so much the better."

The snapping turtle responded, "You need me! I have the codes!"

"Codes?" asked Frank. "What codes?"

"In good time, Colonel," responded Bertrand. "In good time. Let us get out of the cold."

They passed by the bodies lined up on the tarmac—those of the Cammo Dudes and the young men of the 6th Infantry Division. Potter pointed at one of the figures and said, "Hauer, our sniper. Saved my ass before they got him."

Bertrand looked at the bodies and shook his head, saying, "What a horrific scene. I owe them a great debt. We all do."

He led the newcomers through the charred remains of the door and into the hangar proper, which they entered with a profound sense of awe and trepidation. As they approached the black saucer-shaped object, they found it was singed by the TOW blast but otherwise unscathed. Bertrand pointed and said, "Our first operational prototype—forty years in the making and extremely crude by their standards, of course, but it's genuinely ours. I must confess that reverse engineering is an exasperating process."

"Reverse engineering?" asked Frank.

"Yes, Colonel. Suppose you handed Galileo a cellular phone and told him to build it from scratch. Think of what a daunting task that would be. That is what we faced here, but we have made great strides."

"But if this is the result of reverse engineering," observed Miranda, "you had to have something to reverse-engineer from."

"Precisely, dear lady. Come along."

Bertrand leaned on Dane's arm as he led them to the

elevator and entered a cipher code on a small keypad beside the door. There was a delay, then the elevator doors parted.

General Brown started to enter, but Dane brought him up short, saying, "Colonel Hannon, Miss Park and Professor Bertrand for now, General. I'm sure we'll be all right."

Gruffly, Brown said, "At your orders, Mr. Secretary. But I think we should secure the lower levels first."

"I'll take that chance for now, General." Dane nodded at his mentor.

Bertrand pushed in the cipher code to take them to the mid-level. As they descended, Frank eyed the old man carefully—and that was when something odd struck him. The Frenchman's attitude, his posture, his body language transmitted something that was totally foreign to the personality of a freed prisoner. As though his liberation was secondary to—what?

The doors parted, and as Bertrand led the way out Frank's heart started thumping like a rabbit's foot. The old man stepped out onto a catwalk that was suspended along the wall of a large underground hangar, and Frank felt Miranda's hand clutch his tightly as they held back, allowing Bertrand to proceed ahead of them. The professor stepped forward and placed his hands on the guard rail, then paused and peered down, seeming to draw strength from the vision below him like a sovereign surveying his realm. Frank took a deep breath . . . then stepped forward to gaze down and behold the unearthly vessel that had fallen from the sky.

The effect on the senses was nothing less than stupefying, for it was crescent shaped and huge, resembling a bat wing, and it was about half-again as large as the

B-2 stealth bomber in terms of its span from tip to tip—
that is, if both of its "wing" tips had been intact, but
they weren't—one was missing, as if chopped off by a
giant cleaver. An umbilical hose dropped down from the
catwalk system and disappeared inside a hole on the dor-
sal side of the craft near the missing tip, and a few an-
tiskid work mats were laid out on the top side to keep
technicians from slipping off, although there was nary a
sign of the worker bees in the deserted hangar. Frank
and Miranda both swallowed hard as they grappled with
the vision before them, but through the shock they
forced themselves to examine the craft carefully. The
vessel's skin had the appearance of polished aluminum
in that it was a light gray, and in the center of the leading
edge were two rectangular panels that resembled wind-
shields but were not transparent. Other than those panels,
the umbilical opening, and the broken tip, the skin of
the craft was absolutely seamless, with no rivets or fas-
teners of any kind to be seen. It appeared as though it
had been cast as a single piece of metal, but in fact it
had been built in components, and those components
were joined in a process that could only be described as
"atomic" welding—a fastening process that joined the
borders of the components at the molecular level, re-
sulting in a seamless junction.

Bertrand waved his hand and said in his soft French
accent, "This is from the Sierra Madre crash in 1982.
Our crown jewel, you might say. Although it's bigger
than a stealth bomber, it only weighs a tenth of that
aircraft. Amazing, is it not? Our recovery team executed
a magnificent retrieval job, but once we had it in our
possession we had to build this facility to accommodate
it." Bertrand paused and took a few moments to gather

his strength, then explained, "This came to us at exactly the right moment. My predecessors on the project had pushed the envelope as far as they could with the remains of the other crashes. This vessel gave us a renewed lease—so our efforts were redoubled. More people were brought in, myself among them, and we pressed on. You saw the results of our efforts topside just a few minutes ago. Now then—let me give you a closer look." He led them to an open cage-like elevator in which they descended to the floor, and when Bertrand stepped onto the hangar tarmac, it was with reluctance that the visitors followed.

The craft rested on tricycle landing skids that extended from the undercarriage on thin telescoping rods, and in the center of the belly was a ramp that led up into the interior. "Mind your heads," he admonished them. "They are, shall we say, diminutive creatures." And he clutched Dane's arm for support.

Hannon had to crouch down as he entered what could only be described as the bridge of the vessel. The bulkheads had the same polished aluminum look as the exterior, but in the center was a column that was filled, or rather suspended with, a liquid crystalline substance of some kind; and at the base of the column were symbols that resembled hieroglyphics you might find at Giza along the Nile.

Bertrand pointed at the bulkhead. "It appears to be aluminum, but actually it's a matrix of magnesium orthosilicate formed into tiny spheres that can't be seen with the naked eye, and with a bonding that is beyond our experience. The material is light as a feather, but you can't penetrate it with a rifle bullet. Now, then, come with me."

He moved up to an elevated platform that held the control panel with eight small chairs facing it. Part of the panel had been removed, exposing a network of material that resembled a jellyfish turned over on its back. The segment of the panel that was intact was smooth except for some raised hieroglyphic symbols on its surface. Bertrand sat down in one of the tiny chairs and motioned for the others to follow suit.

The other men and Miranda scrunched up and sat down at the control stations. They could see through the windshield panels, and Frank mused they were like one-way mirrors, except they were fabricated from a highly advanced substance that wasn't exactly a metal, a liquid or a plastic, but a little of all three.

Bertrand punched a symbol on the panel and said, "Now then, Miss Park, being a science writer I would surmise you know something about astronomy." Immediately the see-through windshield was filled with the image of a stellar nebula. "Do you know what that is, Miss Park?"

Miranda was nervous to the point of distraction, but nevertheless she tried to focus on the image. After a few anxious moments she replied, "It's a nebula of some sort."

Bertrand smiled. "Very good, young lady. Do you know which one?"

Miranda felt as if she was failing a final exam as she shook her head, saying, "No . . . no, I don't."

Bertrand acted like a patient teacher as he said, "This is one of the better-known astronomical phenomena, Miss Park. This is the Crab Nebula. Every amateur astronomer knows it well."

Miranda focused on the image again, then stammered,

"But . . . but this, this isn't the Crab Nebula. A nebula to be sure, but not the Crab Nebula."

"Oh, yes, it is, dear lady. The difference is that now *you are seeing it from the other side.*"

Miranda couldn't disguise her openmouthed wonderment. "But the Crab Nebula—that's three hundred light years away!"

Bertrand smiled paternally. "Three hundred thirty, actually. But I think you're beginning to understand." He punched more of the hieroglyphics and more astronomical images flashed up on the screen as he provided a narration. "A binary star system near the Pleiades— again from the other side. . . . A neutron star from up close. . . . A star's corona being siphoned off by a black hole. . . . A comet close enough to touch. . . . The Horsehead Nebula from a different angle, and, oh, here's something closer to home, Jupiter's red spot. . . . Just a small sampling of the imagery captured in their logs and navigational data banks."

Suddenly the imagery disappeared and was replaced with the see-through panel as Bertrand said, "Below-decks are the quarters and propulsion systems, although they aren't propulsion systems in the conventional sense of the word."

"So how do they travel such incredible interstellar distances?" asked Miranda, lusting to know.

For a moment, Bertrand seemed energized. "That is why I was brought into the project. To attempt to replicate their gravity amplification systems."

"Gravity amplification systems?" mumbled Frank. "You lost me."

Bertrand nodded. "They utilize a power source— an element not found on earth—that when bombarded with neutrons generates discrete quatities of antimatter. This is combined with matter in a reactor chamber belowdeck that is the size of a soccer ball, and it results in anni-hilation.''

Miranda's mind raced. Then she said, ''That would generate enormous energy.''

''Precisely. And they channel this energy into a battery of gravity amplifiers that compress the space-time continuum to bring two linear points together. Think of it this way, Colonel—a tablecloth on a long table is the space-time continuum in its natural configuration. Place a fork at either end of the table. Now then, stand at one end and pull up the tablecloth until it looks like the compressed bellows of an accordion. The fork at the far end travels up to you, and in a linear sense the distance is reduced to a mere fraction of what it was. This is how they travel interstellar distances, by using artificial gravity to compress the space-time continuum.''

Miranda was, quite simply, speechless.

''I am very weary,'' announced Bertrand. ''I think you have seen enough for now.'' And he led them back down the ramp. He pointed at the underside of the ''wings'' and said, ''The hangar bays are there. That is where they house small reconnaissance vessels. The prototype you saw on the tarmac was modeled after one of them. They generate smaller amounts of power for antigravitational flight. Only the mothership can execute the interstellar voyages. . . . Excuse me. I must sit down.'' And he rested on a large spool of cable.

''The man with the cane,'' said a bewildered Frank. ''The one you told us not to trust. Who the hell is he and what *is* this all about?''

Bertrand smiled faintly at the question. ''His name is

Arctus Krieger. A brilliant man. He received his Ph.D. from CalTech when he was twenty-one, then went into the CIA for assignment to India. Later went into the CIA's technical directorate and rose to the post of deputy director when Richard Nixon recruited him to run a project that was code-named Sirius.''

"*Nixon?*" Frank was incredulous.

"This project?" Dane was confused. "Krieger was appointed by a President?"

"*Oui.*"

Dane was fuming. "Then how could all this be here without my knowledge?"

Bertrand sighed, knowing that rest would not be forthcoming. "To answer your question, Treavor, I'm afraid it's a long story."

SIXTEEN

───◆◆◆───

The old man casually folded his arms as his small audience listened with rapt attention.

"It all began on May 20th, 1954. One of their reconnaissance vessels deliberately fell to earth in the wastelands outside of Kingman, Arizona. They wanted to see how we would respond. Four live creatures were aboard—two injured and two unharmed—and they were taken into quarantine at Los Alamos while their vessel was transported to the Nevada test facility for analysis.

"Eisenhower faced an unprecedented situation, so he set up a satellite government to manage this newfound 'relationship,' and he placed Richard Nixon in charge. This satellite government would report directly to the President and interface with the conventional government only for support purposes. Something akin to formal diplomatic relations were born and we began receiving drips and drabs of their technology to begin our reverse-engineering efforts."

"What did they receive in return?" asked Miranda.

"Nothing at first. It was only much later that it became clear what they were after."

"And what were they after?" asked Frank.

Bertrand shrugged and said, "What we are all after, Colonel. Survival."

Dane was incredulous as he echoed the word. *"Survival?"*

Bertrand seemed not to hear him as he continued. "After Krieger's appointment in 1969, the 'visitors' became very concerned about Nixon because he started to lose his mind over Watergate. They feared he might expose the project and place their survival in jeopardy, for the public might demand we respond to their presence with nuclear weapons, and who knew where that could lead? To calm their fears, after Nixon resigned, Krieger offered to take the project out of the hands of politicians altogether and keep it totally covert, using funding channels already set up in the black budget. The 'visitors' agreed, and the project has been Krieger's ever since, and in so doing I believe he surprised them at the force with which he took control of the relationship and dictated the agenda. He demanded more and better technology from them"—he pointed at the mothership—"which you see here. He totally controlled this facility, threatening them with exposure if they did not meet his demands."

"And what were those demands?" asked Frank.

To the question, Bertrand shook his head and offered a wry smile, then said, "To understand the answer, young man, you would have to peer into the mind of Arctus Krieger. You see, he never found anyone he considered his equal, except perhaps myself; and we had an unusual relationship, one that bordered on the bizarre. I was his prisoner, yet he relied upon me, and shared his darkest secret.''

''And what was that?'' asked Hannon.

''Beyond anything he wanted to sit at their table. To be the one from our species worthy to be their equal. To be the one who, albeit covertly, would have dominion over this world. . . . and who knows, once they extended his lifespan with their medical science, perhaps other worlds as well. To achieve that he was willing to provide them with anything.''

There was a pause, then Miranda gasped as she exclaimed, ''Bone marrow! Human bone marrow! That is what they are receiving in return!''

Bertrand's countenance betrayed his surprise. ''I must confess you astonish me, my dear. Just how did you know that?''

''We found a container on the Kiva Tower,'' replied Frank.

''Did you? What an unfortunate oversight.''

''What do you mean by 'unfortunate,' Michel?'' asked Dane.

Bertrand eyed his protegé carefully, then said, ''Come along. It has been a tiring night and I am utterly spent. Help me to the elevator, will you, Treavor?''

Dane complied and they entered the cage lift. As they rose to the catwalk Miranda pressed, ''Why do they want human bone marrow? For what purpose? I don't understand how . . .'' She froze for a moment, then almost shrieked, *''The virus!''*

''Virus? What virus?'' demanded Dane.

''In Borneo! The one that is attacking bone marrow.''

Bertrand's face turned ashen but he remained silent.

And that was when the intercom phone beside the elevator rang.

Tentatively, Hannon reached out and picked it up, cautiously saying, "Yes?"

It felt like the business end of a set of brass knuckles when he heard that familiar voice say, "Hello, Frank. I can see you through the security camera."

Hannon looked at the receiver as though it were a viper. Then he growled, "It's over, Tin Man! Your ass is mine now!"

"We'll see, Frank. We'll see. As usual, you're in over your head. Now then, let me speak to Treavor Dane, will you?"

"I'll see you in hell, Tin Man—"

"Put the honorable Secretary of Defense on the phone, Frank."

Hannon grimaced, then shoved the receiver towards Dane. "A Colonel Lawton Tyndale wants to speak with you, Mr. Secretary, but beware. He's one of them."

Miranda saw Bertrand's face contort, almost like a wince. "Tyndale? He was at my interrogation."

"Interrogation?" asked Miranda. "What went on here?"

But the Frenchman remained silent.

Gingerly, the Secretary took the phone and said, "This is Treavor Dane."

It seemed he was on the phone for eons, saying things like, "Yes.... Uh-huh.... I see.... Uh huh.... Understood." Towards the end of the conversation he stared at Bertrand for the longest time, then said, "I think we have seen enough. Let's return to the surface."

They stepped back into the elevator, and it was then that Miranda noticed they were on the mid-level, causing her to ask, "What is on the lower level?"

Bertrand punched in the cipher code for topside and said, "We've seen quite enough for one night, my dear. Besides, I do not have the access codes for entry to that level."

Miranda shot back, "The codes? Were those the codes Krieger was talking about?"

"I am very weary, young lady. I must rest. Ah, here we are."

The elevator doors opened and they were greeted by a nervous General Brown, and it was at that moment Frank sensed a change in the Defense Secretary's posture as he ordered, "General Brown, see to it that Dr. Bertrand receives medical care."

Brown called for a medic as the sound of rotor blades cut through the air. "Are those the helicopters?" asked Dane.

"Yes, sir," replied Brown.

"Colonel Hannon, Miss Park, General Brown, will you accompany me, please." Dane led them out to the tarmac, where two Blackhawk helicopters were coming down for a landing as the first rays of dawn began to appear over the desert horizon.

Dane pulled the wolfskin coat tighter around his shoulders and shouted over the sound of the rotor blades, "A frosty morning, isn't it? Colonel Hannon, Miss Park, I am in your debt. I think it is time to bring your adventure to a conclusion. I will have you flown out of here and transported to wherever you want to go. The Bahamas for you, isn't it, Colonel? And back to San Francisco for you, Miss Park? I'm sure it will be good to get some normalcy back in your lives."

"Now wait just a damn minute!" Miranda was seeth-

ing. "We've put our butts on the line to help you take control of this place! If you think you can brush us off now you are mistaken, *Mr. Secretary*!"

Dane sighed. "I'm afraid you must leave the situation in my hands, Miss Park."

"Your hands!? You've got to go public with this, this whatever you want to call it—a bunch of 'visitors' doing God knows what with human bone marrow! You've got to get to the bottom of it!"

Miranda's fury delivered a blow to the Cabinet officer's authority, causing him to pause before replying, "And I shall get to the bottom of it, Miss Park. I thought that went without saying. I'll need some time to get a better handle on the situation, and I have to inform the President first, of course; but in view of your contribution I would say you are entitled to the first exclusive on the story when the Administration is ready to go public. Does that sound reasonable?"

That took the wind out of Miranda's sail. "Your word on it?" she asked.

"Of course," replied the youthful Secretary, with a sincerity that was remarkable.

"When?" inquired Frank.

"Oh, a month or two, I should think. General Brown?"

"Yes, sir."

"Would you be kind enough to insure Colonel Han non and Miss Park get to wherever they want to go?"

"If those are your orders, Mr. Secretary."

"They are."

Brown motioned toward the nearest Blackhawk. "Then come with me, please."

305

Dane nodded to them, saying, "Colonel Hannon, Miss Park. My compliments. Good-bye."

Emotionally exhausted, no longer capable of defiance, Frank and Miranda allowed Brown to lead them to the chopper and the three of them climbed in. The crew chief slid the door shut, and in a moment the helicopter had spooled up to full power and was lifting off. Brown looked out the plexiglass window to see the Secretary of Defense conferring with Shiloh Potter, causing him to tap the plexiglass as he said, "You know, you're probably looking at the next President. He's the darling of the Cabinet and the party and probably has a clear shot to the nomination if he wants it."

"He wants it," replied Miranda, as she tucked her backpack under her arm, feeling the camcorder beneath the canvas.

SEVENTEEN

———⟨∞⟩———

AIR FORCE TRANSPORT CRASHES
All Hands Lost

WASHINGTON—The Pentagon announced today that a C-130 Hercules transport plane went down over Nellis Air Force Base during a routine training exercise. The cause is under investigation.

The crash is unusual in that it is the second one in as many months involving the Hercules aircraft— the previous one occurring in Greenland—and Air Force officials have ordered a system-wide review of safety maintenance procedures. .

Miranda put the Nassau *Times* newspaper down with a sense of disgust and revulsion she'd never known. The Caribbean scene of blue water and white sand outside the hotel restaurant did nothing to assuage her fury. "I don't like this, Frank."

Hannon leaned back and sipped on his Mai Tai, then

said, "It's out of our hands now, Miranda. The ball belongs to Treavor Dane now. It's his call. Let's just try and put it behind us and get the beach house built. We'll hire a boat tomorrow and head out for the cay. It'll help take your mind off things."

She rubbed her arms and said, "I hope so." Then she picked up the newspaper again and turned to the next page, where she saw a small story that was headlined:

VIRUS IN BORNEO CONTINUES TO PUZZLE HEALTH OFFICIALS

* * *

"This is Navy-three-eight-Quebec to White Cloud control. Navy-three-eight-Quebec to White Cloud. Do you copy, over?"

In reply, a fuzzy but discernible voice came through the pilot's headphones. "White Cloud copies Navy-three-eight-Quebec, over."

"Any vessels in our area?"

"Nearest vessel is forty-seven miles to your northeast."

"Roger that, White Cloud. Thanks."

Curly Sikes punched the button on his Global Positioning Satellite receiver, his fingers and hand still wrapped in burn dressings. He'd just made it out of the Blackhawk before it erupted into flames on the slope of Papoose Mountain, and knew he really shouldn't be on flight status; but he wanted to be on this mission because his copilot Clarence Derryberry had died a horrible death when their aircraft went down . . . and there was the issue of payback.

The door of the Navy helicopter slid open, allowing

Major Shiloh Potter to look down five thousand feet to the slate-cold surface of the Eastern Pacific. It was a clear night, with moonlight reflecting off the waves with a funereal luminescence.

The helicopter was 127 nautical miles off the California coast, and at least 47 miles—according to the White Cloud radar controllers—from the nearest surface vessel. With his face betraying conflicting feelings of fatigue and satisfaction, Potter reached back into the cabin and roughly hauled his bound and gagged prisoner by the scruff of the neck to the ledge. Krieger looked down into the awaiting abyss and his teary eyes flared with terror. There was not a hint of defiance in his countenance anymore, for that had been siphoned away by the electric burn marks that now riddled his aging body, put there during the long and relentless interrogation. Potter was satisfied that every dram of information Krieger had ever known about Sirius was now on tape, meaning that the old man's usefulness was over. He held his prisoner over the edge for a few seconds more—a vendetta for his men who had died in the assault on Sirius base—then he shoved the old man into the void.

The bound body plummeted toward the surface in a mile-long free fall, and what thoughts raced through Krieger's terror-stricken psyche remained unknown. When it finally impacted on the water at 120 miles an hour, the frail body disintegrated into pieces and slowly disappeared under the waves to serve as nutrients for the ravenous aquatic life that lurked below.

Then, as a final requiem to the soul of Arctus Krieger, Shiloh Potter picked up the silver cobra head from the old man's broken cane and flung it over the side.

His fellow traveler and interrogator leaned over to

take a final look into the void, then said, "Let's return to S-4."

Potter nodded and said, "Roger that, Colonel Tyndale."

The last C-130 went wheels-up off the runway and banked away into the night sky on a northern vector for the long return flight to Alaska, leaving Major General Roger Brown behind with a skeleton crew of troops to guard the hangar complex at Papoose Lake. The Cammo Dudes had all been rounded up and loaded onto a C-141 Starlifter transport that had appeared out of nowhere with a contingent of MPs. Where they had flown to, Brown had no idea, and he was contemplating that open question when his aide ran up to him at double time.

"Yes, Captain?"

The huffing and puffing aide replied, "Commo says the SecDef is on his way back. Landing in minutes."

Brown nodded and said to the sound of approaching rotor blades, "A rendezvous, no doubt."

The Navy helicopter popped over the ridgeline and came towards them as the Gulfstream jet reappeared for landing. The two aircraft touched down almost simultaneously, and as the Gulfstream taxied to a parking position, the door to the helicopter slid open, allowing Lawton Tyndale to emerge wearing his field jacket.

The Gulfstream halted, the hatchway came down and a tired Treavor Dane deplaned. There were no greetings between the Secretary of Defense and Brown. Just an exchange of nods before Dane looked at Tin Man and asked, "Do we have everything we need?"

"Yes, Mr. Secretary," replied Tyndale.

"Where is Dr. Bertrand?"

"Inside," said Brown.

"Then let's get on with it."

They went inside the hangar and found Michel Bertrand waiting beside the elevator. Dane searched the face of his mentor and asked, almost in the voice of a child, "Are you sure this is the best course?"

"I am certain, Treavor," replied the Frenchman. Then he stared at Tin Man with contempt and asked, "Do we have the access codes?"

A nod. "I have them, sir."

"In view of what you did to me I had no doubt you could extract them from our dearly departed Arctus Krieger. Come along. General Brown, you remain here by the phone. You may be needed."

Brown dug in his heels. "If I may, Dr. Bertrand, Mr. Secretary, I and my men have gone through a bizarre experience. Many of our number have been killed, and yet I do not know what is underground here. All I have seen below is the vault door and the bodies you had my men clean out."

The Secretary of Defense replied, "I am afraid that's the way it has to be, General. You have your orders."

Brown grumbled, then said, "Yes, sir."

Dane, Bertrand and Tin Man stepped onto the lift and the doors closed. Tyndale entered the codes and the car descended to the bottom level. They rode in silence. Then the doors parted and they stepped into the antechamber to the smell of a disinfectant that made the nose wrinkle. Dane nodded at Tyndale and said, "Proceed, Colonel."

Without a word Tyndale stepped forward, and while reading from a card he punched in another stream of cipher codes on a keypad. The massive door opened to reveal the elevated pathway inside the octagonal-shaped tunnel. With his heart beating rapidly, Dane asked, "Did

311

you obtain the particulars from the man Krieger?''

"Yes, Mr. Secretary," replied Tyndale assuringly. "I have it."

"Then let's move forward." As the trio started walking down the pathway Dane became aware of a dull electric hum. Then they came to the door with a black panel beside it that resembled a slate of onyx. Carefully, Tyndale inspected the door and the security panel.

"Use caution, Colonel," urged Bertrand. "I have been down here on many occasions. Any flaw in procedure will result in automatic security measures."

"I am Number One of security, Professor," replied Tin Man. "You need not worry." He reached into his pocket and extracted a pair of white cotton gloves and a roll of clear thin plastic that was about a foot square. He unrolled the plastic and placed his gloved hand over the handprint ingrained upon it; then, with a precise movement, he placed the plastic against the black panel and pressed gently. A laser beam scanned the handprint on the plastic sheet and a red LED readout flashed above his hand: "ACCESS—KRIEGER—CONFIRM." To that, Tyndale held up a cassette tape recorder and hit the PLAY button. A voice that was strained and raspy—but still definitely Krieger's—said, "Access, Krieger, Sirius-one-seven-nine-Omega-seven-Romeo."

There was the sound of a *chung* and the heavy metal door slowly swung open under its own power as the electronic hum disappeared. Tyndale stepped back to reveal a small anteroom, then a glass door that led into a chamber that could only be called a habitat.

Bertrand raised his hand, saying, "Remain here, Colonel. Come along, Treavor."

Dane swallowed, then stepped forward and peered inside. Through the glass was a chamber, about twenty feet in diameter, with a dirt floor and a stone bench. The circular wall was sandy-colored and constructed of adobe, while on the ground of the kiva was a ring of stones.

Sitting on the bench was a slight figure, its back to Dane, with long gray hair coming down to its shoulders, which were covered with a blanket woven in a distinctive pattern unique to the Anasazi.

At their approach the figure rose and turned, causing Treavor Dane to gasp for breath.

Three hours had elapsed before the phone beside the elevator rang and Brown snatched it, saying, "This is General Brown." He listened intently, then turned around and inspected the black saucer prototype that rested on the aluminum pallet behind him. "Yes, I believe so. . . . Very well, Colonel." He hung up and turned to his aide, saying, "Get me a dozen men, Captain."

The captain saluted and ran off. Moments later twelve tentative young men were cloistered around the black saucer as Brown ordered, "We've got to move this out to the tarmac. Put your shoulders to it and roll it outside." With trepidation the young men bent down and grasped the edges of the pallet—interestingly, none would touch the vessel itself—and began guiding the disc around the charred debris to the tarmac outside. To their amazement, it was incredibly light, and three of their number could have easily accomplished the task.

Once out on the tarmac, the aide ventured to ask, "General, sir—what, exactly, *is* this thing?"

Brown shrugged. "I was told it is an experimental

aircraft of some kind. But that is not our concern. We have our orders. You are to pass the word that all personnel are to move into the billets belowdeck out of view of this hangar and the runway.''

''Sir?''

''You heard me, Captain. Move it.''

''Yessir.'' And he was off, leaving his general to pace along the tarmac. The predawn sky was turning into the blue indigo of twilight when the aide reappeared with the news that all hands were assembled below. Brown nodded and said, ''Go and join them, Captain. I will be with you shortly.''

As the captain hustled off, Brown strode to the intercom phone beside the elevator, picked it up and hit the buzzer. It was answered immediately with: ''This is Treavor Dane.''

''All my men, except for myself, are assembled in the billets belowdeck, Mr. Secretary.''

''Very well, General.''

Brown noticed that Dane's voice was strung tight as a guitar string, and he remembered that in combat the first piece of normalcy to go was a soldier's natural speech.

''These are my orders, General,'' said the Secretary of Defense. ''You are to join your men in the billets below and remain there until I personally come to retrieve you. You and your men are to make no attempt to look out toward the tarmac until I notify you otherwise.''

Brown didn't like the sound of that. ''Now listen, Mr. Secretary. My people have gone a long way on trust to carry out your orders. We've had men killed. I think they deserve an explanation as to what this entire business is all abou—"

Suddenly, Dane's voice flared with, "You will do as I order, General, or you will be relieved! Is that *clear*!?"

Brown rankled, but knew he had no choice. The not-so-fine print in the Constitution made it clear who his boss was. "Very well, Mr. Secretary. Give me five minutes."

And he hung up the phone.

Once below in the billets, Brown informed his troops they were to stay in place until notified, to which they responded with a chorus of grumbles. Brown grumbled, too, but he had his orders—directly from the Secretary of Defense. But these young men were his responsibility and this operation was the most bizarre thing he'd ever experienced. He'd taken casualties on the word of a politician. He wasn't about to jeopardize their lives any further just on Dane's word, so carefully he eased up the steps to the stairwell opening in the hangar floor. Micron by micron he raised his eye up to floor level until he could see the vacated hangar and the terminus of the elevator. His pulse had begun racing, as though he were illicitly spying on a girls' locker room, when the doors of the elevator parted. Out stepped an ashen-faced Lawton Tyndale and the Secretary of Defense, followed by Bertrand and then . . . Brown's lungs seized up and his throat turned Sahara dry as he beheld the unimaginable, the unthinkable, the unknown —and he pulled his head back down.

Flanked by Michel Bertrand, the creature walked towards the black saucer on the tarmac. He was a shade under five feet tall, with a slender body that evoked the fragility of a butterfly. His arms were longer in relation to his torso than his purely human hosts, and he possessed three long, delicate fingers with an opposable thumb, each one having vampirelike fingernails. His head was lightbulb shaped and covered with the long gray hair of his human ancestry, but his face betrayed a different genetic strain, for it was punctuated with a pair of wraparound-sunglasses eyes, no discernible nose except for a couple of small holes, and a lipless slit for a mouth. The skin color was gray, but with a human elasticity and texture. As they exited the hangar this creature—who had been part ambassador, part prisoner, and belonging to two worlds, yet neither—raised his unearthly eyes and gazed up at the stars. A frosty wind blew, causing him to cling tightly to the blanket wrapped around him as they walked toward the black saucer prototype.

With a familiarity that came from his role as technical advisor to the Sirius Group, the creature reached out and pressed a panel on the underside of the craft with one of his three long, delicate fingers, and immediately the hatch lowered to a ramp. Without hesitation he walked up, then paused and turned, staring at Bertrand with those insectlike eyes for the longest time before giving him a slight nod of the head to seal the covenant.

The Frenchman nodded in return. Then the visitor entered the craft and closed the hatch. The three humans stepped back, perhaps thirty yards, and shortly thereafter the underside of the saucer began giving off its blue glow before it slowly lifted off the pallet and rose into the indigo sky, leaving the arid moonscape of Papoose Lake behind.

''That will be all for now, Number One,'' said Bertrand softly.

"Yes, sir," replied Tin Man, and he left to return to the hangar.

Bertrand breathed deeply, the soreness of his wounds still weighing heavily upon him as he sighed, "You must understand, Treavor, when a species achieves technological advancement they begin to expand their life spans through medical science. But by doing so, the genetic pool of the species becomes weakened because those who would've been culled out through natural selection live on to have offspring, who continue to further weaken the gene pool. Ultimately, a crossover point is reached where the genetic strain becomes so weak it cannot be salvaged by medical science and the life span of the species begins to shrink. That is what happened to the visitors, so they began to search their part of the galaxy for a more robust genetic strain that would be compatible with their own." The Frenchman looked up at the stars and pondered their unfathomable mysteries. Then he continued. "They found our planet almost a millennium ago when we were little more than primitive tribes, yet in us they struck the mother lode because the human genetic strain was a compatible source of DNA to resuscitate their species. So having found an adaptable supply, that left the problems of extraction."

"Extraction?"

In remembrance, Bertrand could only shake his head. "They made a decision, these beings. It was a bad decision, but what would you have done in their place? They physically kidnapped an entire people—a tribe in the American Southwest—and forcibly bred their own genetic strain to those of the Native Americans. This created a heartier race that they used as something akin to a laboratory farm—extracting bone marrow from them as it was needed. But the impact of this small initial supply began to wane as each succeeding generation of the half-breeds became weaker through inbreeding. And there were social problems—these half-breeds were neither fish nor fowl—a race of outcasts who were outliving their usefulness. The one who just departed, our technical advisor, was one of these.''

Dane was overwhelmed. ''So what does this mean?''

Bertrand stared at the ground and replied, ''Since their inbreeding program failed, they realized they had to have a fresh, ongoing, massive source of human genetic material to graft onto each new generation of their own kind. To obtain that genetic strain they will employ any means, and I mean *any* means.'' Bertrand pointed toward the sky. ''And he was sent to us as an ambassador, as living proof of the lengths they will go to.

''What Krieger offered them was a covert means to obtain the bone marrow, but Krieger was blind to the issue of exposure from the legitimate government. If enough Senators and Congressmen start probing the black budget, there is no way to tell where it could lead.''

''But what would happen if this Sirius Project did see the light of day?''

The Frenchman shuddered. ''Don't you understand anything I have told you, Treavor? If they cannot obtain the marrow through covert means, they will obtain it through enslavement—by methods we could not begin to counter. The earth would become little more than a giant Petri dish, and don't pretend for a moment they could not or would not do it. The only reason they agreed to the covert method is their fear we might start shooting with nuclear weapons before they could intercede, and therefore jeopardize their supply. But any threat of exposure will compel them to override that fear and act swiftly, and I do mean *swiftly*."

Dane shifted back and forth in the cold, trying to absorb all that he had heard and witnessed as Bertrand continued. "You see, Treavor, I agreed completely with Krieger's premise—provide them what they require covertly and receive some of their dazzling technology in return. Where we disagreed was the issue of the legitimate government interceding. I felt it best that Sirius regain its legitimacy but not surrender its secrecy, but Krieger would have none of it. Then, with your appointment to the Pentagon, I saw an extraordinary opportunity—to depose Krieger and bring Sirius under control of the legitimate government again—a government that was headed by someone with whom I had influence."

To that, Treavor Dane almost gagged as he choked out the words. "Michel . . . you . . . you mean you did all this— "

"To get rid of Krieger and take over Sirius? Of course, Treavor. This project is a physicist's dream come true. Just think of it! In the decades to come I shall travel to the stars. And you, my treasure, made it all possible."

"But, Michel, I can't—"

The Frenchman's hand came across Dane's face like a lash, causing the younger man to stagger back in shocked silence.

"There now, Treavor. Listen carefully. You will go on to become President and I will take charge here. The virus will spread on a worldwide basis requiring massive bone marrow treatments—treatments that your government will provide. You will be hailed by all as the great healer. The visitors will receive what they require and provide us with better technology, and everything will be in its proper place.''

Suddenly Dane gasped. ''But the woman. The reporter. She knows too much.''

To that Bertrand threw back his head and laughed. ''Flying saucers? Visitors from outer space? Secret bases in the desert? Why do you think I showed her the vessel? Because the truth is stranger than any fiction I could invent. No one will believe her, so she represents no threat. She will be laughed out of any newspaper in the country. You see, Treavor, the genuine threat of exposure came from the legitimate government, and I am happy to say that is now under our control, isn't it, my treasure?''

Leaning against the hangar door, Lawton Tyndale lit up a cigarette as he watched the frail little Frenchman slap the robust Defense Secretary. The kind of sicko mind games that had gone on between them years ago made no difference to Tin Man. All he knew or cared about was that his position as Number One was now reestablished after a few precarious days. Bertrand, the very man he'd had on the rack, had recognized his abilities and put him to work on Krieger. It took a really cold bastard to act so dispassionately, but Tin Man had to admire that pragmatism. It was just like the U.S. government using all those Nazi scientists to build rockets after the war, wasn't it?

And when Bertrand had given him the chance to prove himself, he had not faltered. He'd just turned up the juice until Krieger begged to give him the access codes. And if Tin Man hadn't done it, then Bertrand would have found someone else, for it soon became apparent to him that the little Frenchman was ten times tougher than Krieger had ever hoped to be. Tough enough to be pragmatic.

Ah, yes, simple pragmatism. It was a concept Tyndale vigorously embraced—and something Frank just never understood.

EIGHTEEN

———— ∞∞∞ ————

The school of blue-green parrot fish cruised over the sandy bottom as though they were linked together with some invisible tether. When Frank Hannon drifted on the surface in his snorkeling regalia, he usually found the images from Neptune's realm to be nothing short of hypnotic. But since he and Miranda had arrived in Ambergris Cay, they'd both been preoccupied with the events that had brought them together, and even the tonic of the blue Bahamian waters and white sand were unable to salve the festering sore in their souls. Each day they checked the CNN satellite feed, but nowhere was there a hint of any news emerging from the Pentagon or the White House on the events of Papoose Lake. As days flowed into weeks, and weeks into months, "the announcement" they'd been waiting for had been conspicuous by its absence.

Through it all, a routine had evolved whereby Frank and Miranda worked on their new bungalow in the morning, then had lunch and a siesta before a bit of snorkeling or sailing as the sun dipped toward the horizon.

Frank now cruised above the bottom with spear in hand, looking for a pair of black beads protruding above the sand, and it wasn't long before his vigilance was rewarded. He dove and brought the spear down hard, but the flounder was too fast for him and scurried away. Frank followed, kicking his flippers and watching until the flounder finally halted and reburied himself in nature's camouflage. This time Frank approached from behind to take him from his blind side, and this time the strategy worked. He thrust the spear into the creature's back, then raised it above the surface as it flopped on the end of the barbed point. Miranda was twenty yards away and had seen it all. She waved in acknowledgment and started back to shore, with Frank kicking his flippers to join her.

The embers of the beach campfire glowed their last, the plastic plates held the denuded remnants of the flounder, and the stars were out on a moonless Bahamian night. Miranda lay in the crook of Frank's arm on the giant beach towel, he wearing a T-shirt and she a cotton wrap around her bikini.

"Think the plywood will get here tomorrow?" she asked, not really interested. "It would be nice to get the bathroom finished out."

He shrugged. "Who knows. A Bahamian clock seems to have a different speed than Greenwich Mean Time."

Under any other circumstances the venue, the evening and the company would have been sublime, but the events of Papoose Lake hung over them like a cloud. They were like a couple dealing with some terminal illness, and they filled the void between them with small talk. But the waiting had taken a toll on Miranda, causing her to sit up and draw her knees under her chin.

"What is it?" Frank asked.

"What do you think?"

He sighed, like a weary husband who'd had the same argument with his spouse too many times. "We did all we could, Miranda. Dane holds all the cards now, and it's up to him. He is the Secretary of Defense, after all. The only thing we can do now is wait."

Miranda bristled. "Well, I'm sick of waiting. We've been waiting for six months and not a peep out of the White House or the Pentagon. It's like it never happened and I'm about to go nuts. Being chased was better than this."

Frank shrugged. "So what do we do? Send Dane a wire? Request an interview?"

"I've already done that."

Frank sat up. "You did? When?"

"Three weeks ago when we went to Nassau. No reply."

"Then there's nothing further to be done, except wait."

To that she reached for the shortwave radio, and flipped it on. After a few moments of static a voice came on with the BBC World Service. The announcer with the British accent said:

Now to scientific news. Victims in Borneo of a bone marrow disease caused by a viral infection have received encouraging news from American medical officials. It appears a curative treatment has been developed by the United States Army Medical Lab-

*oratory whereby patients undergo a minor proce-
dure that extracts bone marrow from their hip for
bonding with an antiviral agent. The marrow is
then reintroduced to the hip, where it combats the
virus while stimulating the patient's own immune
system.*

*To insure speedy delivery of the treatment to a
rapidly growing disease that has now appeared in
Hong Kong, Malaysia and Australia, a U.S. military medical team had been dispatched to Borneo
to offer assistance.*

*In other news from America, the political for-
tunes of Secretary of Defense Treavor Dane appear
to be gaining momentum as he increases his visits
to New Hampshire for the primary to be held there
seven months from now. . . .*

Miranda flicked off the radio and stared him down
with those crème de menthe eyes, saying, "Like I told
you, Frank, I'm *sick* of waiting."

NINETEEN

⊷⊶⊷

Brenna Weston came out of the Washington Metro station and strode down the street. It was one of those hot, muggy D.C. summers and she was anxious to get inside to the air-conditioned environment of the *Washington Post* offices. Congress was out of session and much of the District had fled the city for a summer hiatus, so Weston's work as assistant managing editor responsible for Capitol Hill had slim pickens. Her reporters were putting together a couple of profile pieces on some Senators who had Presidential ambitions, but they were the longest of long shots and everybody knew it. In a nutshell she was experiencing editor's withdrawal—the need for a story to assuage her town-crier instincts. The last time she'd experienced such a withdrawal was back in December when she'd dropped off Miranda and her swarthy-looking boyfriend outside Treavor Dane's estate. She'd searched high and low for Miranda ever since, but came up empty-handed. She'd even tried to set up an interview with Dane, but the Pentagon reporters of the *Post* kept getting in her way—issues of turf. So the story had died. She sighed and entered the doors to the paper.

Across the street, Frank and Miranda watched Brenna Weston enter the front door of the *Post*. Frank looked at Miranda and said, "You sure you want to do this?"

"I'm sure."

He turned away. "You said yourself the odds of them printing it are slim."

She tapped her purse which held the videotapes. "They broke Watergate. Maybe they'll have the balls to break this, too."

Frank sighed. "I never did figure out how you ran that camcorder of yours when we were inside that . . . that vessel."

"Professional secret."

"Think it will convince them?"

"There's only one way to find out."

"Okay, let's kick ass, then." And he opened the door.

TWENTY

––––⦚⦚⦚––––

The desert sky was filled with stars as Michel Bertrand stood alone on the tarmac, and as always he pondered their mysteries. He had taken such an incredible gamble to reach this moment and now was to receive his just rewards. While some men might covet wealth, power or sex, Bertrand lusted after the means to regain his lost intellectual potency, for it was said that a theoretical physicist's prime productive age was twenty-seven. While Bertrand had no expectation that the visitors could turn the clock back that far, he knew they could and would rejuvenate his aged wreck of a body with their extraordinary medical science and he would have years, if not decades, to embrace all that they could teach him. And all it would cost was a little bone marrow. Tragically, some people would die in the process, but that was necessary to induce the masses to subject themselves to the "treatment." And at the end of the day wasn't that a better option than enslavement of the entire planet? Bertrand thought it ironic that the human tendency toward self-destruction was the only thing that kept the visitors at bay.

Lawton Tyndale strode up and said, "Communications says they should arrive any moment, Professor."

"Very well, Number One. And remember, before you leave for Washington, make sure Major Potter is fully briefed on all your duties."

"Certainly, Professor."

"And you may not recognize me when I return, so don't be surprised."

"As you say, sir . . . and Professor?"

"Yes, Number One?"

Tin Man cleared his throat. "Well, Professor, I just hope there are no hard feelings about, well, about what I had to do to you. It was my job, after all."

Bertrand gave him a thin smile. "I have nothing but hard feelings for you, Number One. However, you seem to have certain talents that are helpful to me. That is why I selected you as the man to keep an eye on Treavor for me. He can be such a child, and children are sometimes unpredictable. That is why I need you to monitor him, and what better way to do that than as a flag-ranked officer in the Pentagon—would you not agree, Number One?"

"I agree completely, Professor."

"Then we understand each other. Ah, here they are now. That will be all, Number One."

Tyndale looked up at the approaching lights, then turned around and headed back into the hangar.

The four lights descended, then executed their pinwheel maneuver before one of their number peeled off and came down not a hundred feet from Bertrand. Like the human prototype it, too, was saucer shaped, but with a luminosity that was, well, unearthly. It gently settled onto the tarmac and deployed a ramp, beckoning Bertrand to enter.

Flushed with anticipation, he stepped forward and walked up the ramp to what he knew would be a glorious future.

Once on board, the ramp retracted and the saucer joined the others. Then in formation they took a vector toward the constellation of the Dog Star—a star also known as Sirius.

EPILOGUE

———— ∞∞∞ ————

Treavor Dane huffed and puffed over the hills surrounding his Gettysburg estate like a relentless juggernaut in the predawn hour. His mind was filled with the upcoming primary season and the near-sexual delight he would take in trouncing the opposition. Michel was right, of course. Michel was always right. He would become President. No one could match him. In a little more than a year he'd be in the White House, and it was a heady thought. The press was already lapping up the story about how the Defense Department, *his* Defense Department, had come upon a cure for the bone marrow virus.

He jogged past the stable and then slowed to a trot as he neared the back door of the kitchen. Pulling the screen open, he glanced at the distant woodshed, then reached up and touched his cheek in remembrance.

He entered the breakfast room and took the offered towel from his manservant. He tried to get in his morning run no less than five days a week, before sunup, before the phones started ringing with the business of the Pentagon and the upcoming campaign. It was a rare moment of solitude, one that he savored as he wiped his brow with the towel and sat down to breakfast. He was just gulping down his orange juice when the phone rang, causing him to glance at the clock with irritation. Who would be calling him at 5:19 A.M.? There wasn't a war on, and there hadn't been any hint of conflict when he went to bed. He was wondering what it possibly could be when a Marine guard poked his head in and said, "It's the White House Press Office, sir. The gentleman on the phone said it was urgent."

Lawton Tyndale exited the taxicab and paid off the driver, having dispensed with his limousine earlier in the evening. He checked his Rolex and saw that it was past 5 A.M. as he entered the front door of his trendy new townhouse in Georgetown. It was the end of a long night that had started in the Chinese embassy, where he'd met the wife of the Bolivian ambassador—a ravishing nymphette with silky olive skin and raven hair who was her husband's junior by twenty-three years. That her physical needs were not being met was obvious as she accosted him in the cloakroom, and it was all he could do to deflect her advances to arrange a discreet tryst at the Ritz-Carlton. Once they were ensconced in a suite, her nymphomania seemed inflamed when she learned he was the new deputy chief of the Defense Intelligence Agency, and it was then that Tin Man realized what Henry Kissinger had said was true—power *is* the ultimate aphrodisiac.

He closed the door to his townhouse and went to his bedroom, where he disrobed for the second time that evening, placing his soiled clothes in the hamper for his cleaning lady to process. From his armoire he selected a pair of silk pajamas made in Thailand, then put on a matching silk robe before entering the bathroom to brush his teeth. His oral hygiene completed, he looked in the mirror and noted with satisfaction that he cut a rakish figure even in bedclothes, and he couldn't help but smile in self-appraisal, for at last he was a truly contented man. His new two-star appointment as deputy chief of the DIA was the perfect perch from which to monitor the man-child of Treavor Dane. And when Dane moved on to the White House, Tin Man would surely follow.

Tin Man had never ceased congratulating himself on the bold action he'd taken at Papoose Lake to seize the initiative. It was a stroke of genius beyond measure, and now he was enjoying the results of his bold vision— state dinners, limousines, private jets, a staff to cater to every whim, women at every turn, and he was the linchpin to the mother of all covert projects. Yes, life was good.

It was 5:30 A.M. when he doffed his robe to slide between the silk sheets of the mahogany four-poster. Tomorrow was a workday, but since Tin Man was his own boss, he pretty much called the shots as to when he'd come and go in the office, so he was looking forward to sleeping in. Visions of the Bolivian nymphette were dancing in his head as he was drifting off just before the doorbell rang.

The doorbell? At this hour?

In the same moment he was pissed and alarmed. Who would ring the doorbell of the deputy DIA chief at this time of night? He fleetingly thought about hitting the panic button on his bedside table that would summon the D.C. police, plus a special detail of MP watch officers, but he quickly dismissed that idea. Instead, he pulled open the drawer of his nightstand and removed a Sig-Sauer automatic. Given the sensitive nature of his new position, it paid to be cautious. He got out of bed and quickly put on his robe as the doorbell repeated its insistent refrain; then he went downstairs, gun at the ready, and put his eye to the peephole, which evoked a response of ''What the . . . ?''

Frank Hannon's face greeted him through the fish-eye lens, causing Tyndale's mind to race. Why was Frank here? Had his anger reached a breaking point and now he wanted to assault, perhaps kill, Tyndale for getting the better of him? Tyndale was thinking about calling for backup when he noticed something about Frank that made him hold off. Under the porch light he could see that Frank was, well, smiling; and for some reason Lawton Tyndale found that smile more unsettling than any unsheathed weapon. He swallowed, put the gun in his pocket and opened the door.

''Mornin', Tin Man. Looks like a lovely day in the offing. Probably gonna be a warm one, though.''

Tyndale didn't like the cocky manner. ''What are you doing here, Frank?''

Hannon kept on smiling. ''I just wanted to tell you. I got a new job in my retirement.''

''New job?''

''Yeah, a new job. Paper boy.'' And he shoved a rolled-up newspaper into Tin Man's solar plexus. ''That's the late edition of today's *Washington Post*. A little something for you to read over your orange juice. Have a nice day, Tin Man.'' And with that, he turned on his heel and strode down the sidewalk.

With a sense of perplexity and growing anxiety, Tin Man watched the receding figure of Frank Hannon, then ever so slowly he unfolded the newspaper.

And read the half-page headline with horror.

AUTHOR'S NOTE

In 1989, a man named Bob Lazar went on a television news program in Las Vegas and caused a local sensation with his account of a fantastic story. He claimed that he was a physicist who'd worked for a brief time on a hypersecret government project to "reverse engineer" the technology of alien spacecraft.

Lazar said that the project was not located at Groom Dry Lake—where there had been rumors about such things for years—but at a facility designated "S-4" at Papoose Dry Lake some seven miles and a mountain away from Area 51. He claimed to have seen *nine* different saucerlike craft in a network of camouflaged hangars at the S-4 site where he worked with a group that was attempting to replicate the gravity amplification system of the alien vessels. He also testified that he witnessed a brief test flight of a small "sport model" craft while he was engaged on the project.

Lazar said his TV appearance was motivated initially from a fallout with his superiors over security matters, and later because he feared for his life and felt the information should be in the public domain. His story received pervasive local coverage in Las Vegas and gained some currency with the tabloids, but for the most part it was ignored by the mainstream media.

After Lazar's TV appearance he began to encounter severe credibility problems, in that he claimed he had degrees from Cal Tech and M.I.T. (he didn't), and some time later he pled guilty to a charge of pandering for an illegal brothel in Las Vegas. In a court of law he would be destroyed on cross examination.

But as devastating as Lazar's credibility problems were, there was another dynamic that intriguingly cut the other way, in that while he was evasive about his educational credentials, Lazar's story of what he saw, and did not see, at S-4 remained remarkably precise and consistent over time—as did his testimony on the technical aspects of the gravity amplification system he claimed to have worked on.

In recent years, the community of observers who followed the Lazar story basically broke into two groups—believers or debunkers—and that is where the matter rested.

Until April of 1995.

Glenn Campbell (not to be confused with the singer) has been the lead activist engaged in the effort to open up Area 51 to public scrutiny and fiscal accountability. To that end he has published the *Area 51 Viewer's Guide* and operated the Area 51 Research Center in Rachel, Nevada. As a sidebar to his role as public activist, Campbell became a self-described "collector" of UFO stories and folklore, but in that role he was always careful to remain neutral and above the fray on the UFO debate. ("They're here" *vs.* "They're not here.") Simply put, as a result of his passive, strictly neutral and nonjudgmental posture on the UFO issue, Campbell became a one-man clearinghouse of information through the newsletter and web page he publishes.

Then in April of '95, Glenn Campbell encountered a story so extraordinary that, if true, could eclipse even Lazar's claims.

The source: a man who says he is a retired seventy-year-old mechanical engineer. His claim: that he worked on the alien reverse engineering project for *thirty* years. His role: to build simulators for human pilots based on the alien craft.

The events of the Kingman, Arizona, "crash" as recounted in *Forbidden Summit* are taken in large measure from the retired engineer's testimony. But as compelling as his story is, what may be even more telling is that the engineer claims he has passed this information to Campbell *with the approval of his superior.* What this could mean is that we have entered a transitional period—slowly moving from a governmental posture of denial and cover-up to one of public education in order to prepare the body politic for what is to come.

As the late Carl Sagan once said about the UFO issue, "Extraordinary claims require extraordinary proof." True enough, but to bring Sagans's premise to fruition an extraordinary investigation is needed to gain access to the "extraordinary proof" if it, in fact, exists.

Therefore, unless and until a blue ribbon Congressional or Presidential investigation is impanelled with free rein to grant immunity and supoena witnesses and documents, and to provide protection for witnesses, we

may never know the truth about the monumental events
that may be transpiring—even as you read these words—
at a place in the Nevada desert known simply as S-4.

—Payne Harrison